## The Girl from Junchow

"An engrossing adventure that sweeps readers in lush waves of drama and romance."
—*Library Journal*

"Furnivall deftly evokes the details of a bygone era."
—*Publishers Weekly*

## The Red Scarf

"This romantic confection can make a reader shiver with dread for the horrors visited on the two heroines imprisoned in a labor camp and quiver with anticipation for their happy endings. Furnivall shows she has the narrative skills to deliver a sweeping historical epic."
—*Library Journal*

"Furnivall again pinpoints a little-known historical setting and brings it vividly to life through the emotions and insights of her characters. Beautifully detailed descriptions of the land and the compelling characters who move through a surprisingly upbeat plot make this one of the year's best reads."
—*Booklist*

# The Russian Concubine

"I read it in one sitting! Not only a gripping love story, but a novel that captures the sights, smells, hopes, and desires of Russia at the dawn of the twentieth century, and pre-Revolutionary China, so skillfully that readers will feel they are there."　　　—Kate Mosse

"The kaleidoscopic intensity of British writer Kate Furnivall's debut novel, *The Russian Concubine*, compellingly transports us back to 1928 and across the globe to the city of Junchow in northern China . . . Lydia is an endearing character, a young woman with pluck and determination . . . With artistry, Furnivall weaves a main plot that hinges on Lydia's love affair with Chang An Lo, a Chinese youth who is a dedicated Communist at a time when Chiang Kai-shek's Nationalists are gaining ground . . . Furnivall's novel is an admirable work of historical fiction."　　　—*Minneapolis Star Tribune*

"Furnivall vividly evokes Lydia's character and personal struggles against a backdrop of depravity and corruption."　　　—*Publishers Weekly*

"The wonderfully drawn and all-too-human characters struggle to survive in a world of danger and bewildering change . . . caught between cultures, ideologies—and the growing realization that only the frail reed of love is strong enough to withstand the destroying winds of time."　　　—Diana Gabaldon

"This stunning debut brings the atmosphere of 1920s China vividly to life. . . . Furnivall draws an excellent portrait of this distant time and place."　　　—*Historical Novels Review*

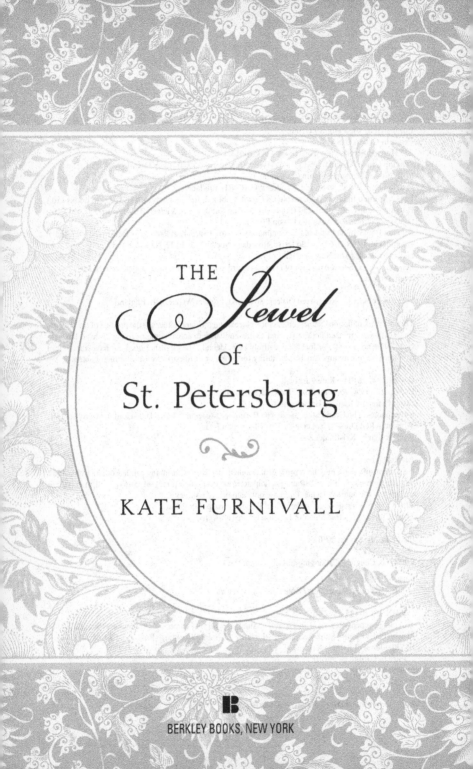

# THE *Jewel*
## of
## St. Petersburg

### KATE FURNIVALL

BERKLEY BOOKS, NEW YORK

**THE BERKLEY PUBLISHING GROUP**
**Published by the Penguin Group**
**Penguin Group (USA) Inc.**
**375 Hudson Street, New York, New York 10014, USA**
Penguin Group (Canada), 90 Eglinton Avenue East, Suite 700, Toronto, Ontario M4P 2Y3, Canada
(a division of Pearson Penguin Canada Inc.)
Penguin Books Ltd., 80 Strand, London WC2R 0RL, England
Penguin Group Ireland, 25 St. Stephen's Green, Dublin 2, Ireland (a division of Penguin Books Ltd.)
Penguin Group (Australia), 250 Camberwell Road, Camberwell, Victoria 3124, Australia
(a division of Pearson Australia Group Pty. Ltd.)
Penguin Books India Pvt. Ltd., 11 Community Centre, Panchsheel Park, New Delhi—110 017, India
Penguin Group (NZ), 67 Apollo Drive, Rosedale, North Shore 0632, New Zealand
(a division of Pearson New Zealand Ltd.)
Penguin Books (South Africa) (Pty.) Ltd., 24 Sturdee Avenue, Rosebank, Johannesburg 2196,
South Africa

Penguin Books Ltd., Registered Offices: 80 Strand, London WC2R 0RL, England

This is a work of fiction. Names, characters, places, and incidents either are the product of the author's imagination or are used fictitiously, and any resemblance to actual persons, living or dead, business establishments, events, or locales is entirely coincidental. The publisher does not have any control over and does not assume any responsibility for author or third-party websites or their content.

Copyright © 2010 by Kate Furnivall
Excerpt from *The Russian Concubine* © Kate Furnivall
Cover design by Richard Hasselberger
Cover photos: The Grand Staircase at The Hermitage Museum © Larry Dale Gordon / Getty Images;
Woman in Red Dress © Yolande DeKort / Trevillion Images
Book design by Kristin del Rosario

First Edition: August 2010

Library of Congress Cataloging-in-Publication Data

Furnivall, Kate.
  The jewel of St. Petersburg / Kate Furnivall.—1st ed.
    p.  cm.
  ISBN 978-0-425-23423-5
  1. Young women—Russia (Federation)—Saint Petersburg—Fiction.  2. Aristocracy (Social class)—
Russia (Federation)—Saint Petersburg—Fiction.  3. Saint Petersburg (Russia)—Fiction.  I. Title.
II. Title: Jewel of Saint Petersburg.
  PR6116.U76J48    2010
  823'.92—dc22

                                                                                    2010012308

PRINTED IN THE UNITED STATES OF AMERICA

10  9  8  7  6  5  4  3  2  1

*To Carole and Wendy*
*with love*

# *Acknowledgments*

I am deeply grateful to Jackie Cantor for her patience and humor while bringing this book through its birth pangs, and to all her team at Berkley, especially Pam Barricklow, a true miracle worker. Many thanks also to Amy Schneider for her impressive skill in polishing the manuscript.

Brilliant thanks to my agent, Teresa Chris, for her constant guidance, as perceptive as ever, and to Patty Moobrugger for her support.

My gratitude also to Elena Shifrina for her enthusiastic assistance with research and the Russian language, and to Susan Clark for her musical advice. I am indebted to Marian Churchward for transforming my scrawl into a readable manuscript and for sharing my chocolate biscuits.

Huge thanks to my husband, Norman, for his encouragement and understanding, and especially for his cool ideas.

# One

TESOVO, RUSSIA
JUNE 1910

VALENTINA IVANOVA DID NOT INTEND TO DIE. NOT HERE. Not now. Not like this. With dirty feet and tangled hair and her life barely started. She looked down at her fingers in the fuzzy green gloom of the forest and was surprised to see them so steady. Inside she was shaking.

She always paid attention to fingers rather than faces because they told so much more. People remembered to guard their faces. They forgot their hands. Her own were small, though strong and supple from all the hours of piano playing, but what use was that now? For the first time she understood what real danger does to the human mind, as flat white fear froze the coils of her brain.

She could run. Or she could hide. Or she could stay where she was, molded to the trunk of a silver birch, and let them find her.

Dark figures were flitting silently from tree to tree, swallowed by the sullen vastness of the forest around her. She couldn't see them now, couldn't hear them, yet she knew they were there. They seemed to vanish like beetles into the bark, invisible and untraceable, but each time she flicked her head suddenly to one side or the other, she caught their movement at the corner of her eye. A trail of air, thin and secretive. A shift of light. A break in the twilight of the forest floor.

Who were these people? They carried rifles, but they didn't look like hunters. What hunters wore black hoods? What hunters had face masks with narrow slits for eyes and a jagged hole for a mouth?

She shivered. She wasn't willing to die.

Her feet were bare. She'd kicked off her shoes after the long gallop up the slope through the fields. The sky was still dark when she'd crept out of bed. She'd ignored the hairpins and the buckles, the gloves and the hat, all the paraphernalia that her mother insisted a young lady must wear at all times outdoors. At seventeen, she was old enough now to make her own choices. So she'd pulled a light sleeveless dress over her head, sneaked out of the house, saddled up Dasha and come up here to her favorite spot on her father's country estate. She'd plunged into the dark somber fringe of the forest from where she loved to watch the dawn rise over Tesovo.

Her bare toes relished the black earth, moist as treacle. The wind had whipped her long dark hair in a fan across her cheeks and twined it around her neck. There was a freedom up here that loosened something inside her, something that had been wound too tight. It was always the same when the family left St. Petersburg and arrived in Tesovo for the drowsy months of summer and the long white nights when the sun scarcely bothered to drop below the horizon.

That was until she saw the rifles.

Men in hoods. All in black and moving with stealth through the shadowy world of the forest. Sweat pooled in the hollow of her back as she dodged behind a tree. She heard a murmur of blurred voices, nothing more, and for a while she waited, willing them to leave. But only when the crimson dawn drew a line like a trail of blood between the trees did the men suddenly spread out, vanishing completely, and Valentina felt her heart thump in panic.

A whisper? Was that a whisper behind her?

She spun around. Peered into the shadows but could see no one.

A moment later a shape flicked. Dark and quick, off to one side. Another directly ahead. They were circling her. How many? She sank down into the dense mist that rose from the ground and, crouching low, she started to run through the thick undergrowth. Thin gray ropes of mist coiled around her ankles and fronds reached for her face, but she didn't stop until she almost crashed into a pair of legs crossing an animal trail in front of her. She froze. In her leafy cavern under the ferns on the forest floor she didn't breathe. The legs paused, her terrified gaze fixed on a cloth patch that was badly sewn on the knee of the trousers, but then they moved on. She jinked to her left and scuttled farther. If she could find the edge of the forest where her horse was tethered, she could . . .

The blow came from nowhere. Knocked her flat on her back. She lay sprawled on the damp earth but struck out at the hand that seized her shoulder, sinking teeth into its wrist. Bone jarred on her teeth but she bit harder and tasted blood. The hand abruptly released its grip with a curse and she bounded to her feet, but a heavy swinging slap cracked against her jaw and sent her crashing into a tree, cheek first.

"She's over here!" a deep voice yelled.

Valentina tried to run. Her head was spinning but she saw the second slap coming and dropped to one knee. She heard her attacker's hand snap as it smacked into the trunk instead and a bellow of rage. Her feet were up and running, but the earth wouldn't keep still. It was swaying under her, merging with the gray mist and flaring into flames each time she crossed a streak of sunlight.

"Stop her!"

"Shit! *Dermo!* Put a bullet in her."

*A bullet?*

The sound of a bullet rattling into the breech of a rifle ripped into her mind. She jerked behind a tree and saw her hands quivering uncontrollably on the peeling bark.

"Wait!" she called out.

Silence. The noise of bodies crashing through the forest ceased.

"Wait!" she called again.

"Get out here where we can see you."

"No bullets?"

A voice laughed at her, an angry sound. "No bullets."

They hadn't fired at her yet. Maybe they couldn't risk the noise of shots. In the countryside sound travels far. She tried to swallow, but her throat was raw. These men weren't playing games. Whatever it was they were doing, she had disturbed them at it and they weren't going to let her just walk away. She had to talk to them.

"Hurry up! *Bistro!*" the angry voice shouted.

Valentina's heart stopped in her chest as she stepped clear of the tree.

❧

THERE WERE FIVE OF THEM. FIVE MEN, FIVE RIFLES. ONLY one, the tallest figure, had his rifle slung loosely over his shoulder as if he didn't expect to use it. The black masked faces stared blankly back at her, and her skin crawled at the sight of them.

They didn't put a bullet in her. That was a start.

"It's just a girl," one scoffed.

"Quick as a bloody rabbit, though."

Three of them moved nearer. She tensed, up on her toes, ready to run.

"Don't look so fierce, girl, we're just . . ."

"Get away from me."

"No need to be unfriendly."

"You're trespassing on my father's land," she said. Her voice didn't sound like hers.

"The land of Russia," one of the hoods growled, "belongs to the people of Russia. You stole it from us."

*Chyort!* Revolutionaries. The word swelled in her head, crushing all other thoughts. Stories circulated throughout the salons of St. Petersburg about men like this, about how they intended to seize control of Russia and kill off all the ruling classes. She would be just the beginning.

"What are you doing here?" she demanded.

A loose lecherous chuckle came from the one closest to her. "Enjoying the view."

She felt her cheeks flush. Her thin muslin dress was plastered to her body where sweat and sodden foliage had streaked the material. Defensively she looped her arms in front of her but shook her hair back from her face in a gesture of defiance. The three loomed closer, and one moved behind her to cut off her retreat. Caging her. She breathed warily. She couldn't see their faces behind their black hoods, but she could tell by the speed of their rangy limbs and the eagerness in their voices that they were young. The other two men seemed slightly older, more solidly built, and kept themselves farther away across the break in the trees, murmuring to each other in low tones. She couldn't tell from their masks whether they watched her, but the taller of them was clearly the one in authority.

Why were they here in Tesovo? What were they planning? She

had to get away, had to warn her father. But two of the young men started shouldering each other, jostling like jackals for the spoils.

"Who are you?" she asked, to shift their thoughts from herself.

"We are the true voice of Russia."

"If that's so, your voices should be heard in the Duma, our parliament, not by me in a forest clearing. What use is that?"

"I can think of one use," the stockiest of the three responded. He touched her breast with the tip of his rifle.

She knocked it fiercely to one side. "You may claim the land," she hissed, "but don't think you can claim me."

His two companions burst out into coarse laughter, but he yanked his belt from his waist and wound one end around his fist, swinging the buckle threateningly. "Bitch! *Suka!*"

Valentina's heart slid into her throat. She could smell his anger on him, sour in the fresh morning air.

"Please." She addressed the tall man among the trees. There was a stillness about him that frightened her even more than the unfocused energy of his men. "Please," she said, "control them."

The man stared back at her from within the dark folds of his hood, slowly shook his head, and walked away into the forest. For a moment she panicked and her hands clenched together to stop them shaking. Yet it seemed that he'd left instructions because the man to whom he'd been talking pointed abruptly to the one standing behind her.

"You," he said. "Deal with her. The rest of you, follow me."

*Deal with her.*

They were well trained, she'd give them that. The angry one with his belt in his fist strutted away at once with no comment, the other alongside him. Behind her the solitary figure shifted his rifle purposefully and shuffled his homemade boots in the damp earth.

"Sit," he ordered.

She thought about it.

"Sit," he said again, "or I will make you."

She sat.

❧

AN HOUR PASSED, MAYBE MORE. VALENTINA LOST TRACK OF time. Her limbs ached and her head cramped. Each time she attempted to move or to speak, her guard made a sound of disgust behind her and jammed the metal tip of his rifle into whichever part of her anatomy took his fancy: her ribs, her shoulder, an arm. Worst was the nape of her neck.

But he didn't shoot her. She clung to that faint thread of hope.

What were the others doing? The question ricocheted around inside her skull, splitting her thoughts into a thousand answers.

They could be thieves. She hoped so fiercely that they were here to rob her father's house that she almost convinced herself it was true. Here to steal the antique paintings, the gold statues, the Oriental carvings, her mother's jewels. It had been tried before, so why not again? But what thieves would wait till daylight? What thieves were stupid enough to rob a house when the servants were up and about?

She pulled her knees to her chest. Sank her chin on them and in return received a prod in the spine from the rifle, but behind her heels she'd dragged a stone to within reach. She wrapped her arms around her shins and shivered in the breeze that was thinning the mist. Not that it was cold, but she was frightened. Frightened for her parents and for her sister, Katya, who would be rising from their beds about now, totally unaware of the black hoods that stalked Tesovo. Katya was only thirteen, a blond bubble of energy who would come bounding into Valentina's room to entreat her for a swim in the creek after breakfast on their first morning at Tesovo. Mama liked to keep to her room first thing in the morning, but Papa was a stickler for punctuality at breakfast. He would be ruffling his whiskers and glaring at his pocket watch because his elder daughter was late.

*Papa, be careful.*

"Are you Bolsheviks?" she asked suddenly, tensing herself for the blow.

It came. On the neck. She heard something crunch.

"Are you?" she asked again. She wished she could turn and look into his hooded face.

"Shut your mouth."

The second blow was harder, but at least he had spoken. It was the first time she'd heard his voice since he'd ordered her to sit. She wasn't certain how far behind her he was crouched, silent as a spider, except that it was obviously less than a rifle length away. She'd been submissive so long, he must have dropped his guard by now, surely. If she was wrong . . . She didn't care to think about that. She needed to lure him within reach.

"You know who my father is?"

The rifle slammed into the side of her jaw, jerking her head almost off her neck. "Of course I bloody know. You think we're stupid peasants or something?"

"He is General Nicholai Ivanov, a trusted minister in Tsar Nicholas's government. He could help you and your friends to—"

This time he thrust the tip of his rifle against the back of her head, forcing it forward till her forehead was jammed against her knees.

"Your kind is finished," he hissed at her, and she could feel his breath hot on the bruised skin of her neck. "We'll trample you bastards into the earth that you stole from us. We're sick of being kicked and starved while you stuff your greedy faces with caviar. Your father is a fucking tyrant and he's going to pay for—"

Her hand closed on the stone hidden under her skirt. With a violent twist she spun around and slammed it into the front of the hood. Something broke. He screamed. High-pitched, the way a fox screams. But she was too quick, gone before he could pull the trigger. Racing, ducking, dodging under branches and plunging into the darkest shadows while his cry fluttered behind her. She could hear him charging through the foliage and two shots rang out, but both whistled past harmlessly, raking the leaves and snapping off twigs as she stretched the distance between them.

She slid down a slope on her heels, desperate to find the river. It was her route out of the forest. She swerved and switched direction till she was certain she had lost her pursuer, and then she stopped and listened. At first she could hear nothing except her pulse in her ears, but gradually another sound trickled through: the faint but unmistakable ripple of water over rocks. Relief hit her and to her dismay she felt her knees buckle under her. She was stunned to find herself sitting upright on the damp earth, fretful and weak as a kitten. She forced herself shakily back onto her feet. She had to warn her father.

After that she moved at a steadier pace. It didn't take long to locate the river and set off along the narrow track that ran along its bank. Disjointed thoughts crashed around inside her head. If these hooded men *were* revolutionaries, what plans did they have? Were they just hiding out in Tesovo's forest, or had they come here for a specific purpose? Who was their target? That last one wasn't hard. It had to be Papa.

She clamped her lips together until they were bloodless in an effort to silence the shout of rage that roared inside her, and her feet speeded up again, weaving a jerky path through the overhanging branches.

A sound jolted her and she recognized it at once: the noise of a horse's hooves splashing through water. Someone was coming upriver. It was shallow here, a silvery burble over a bed of stones, the morning sunlight flouncing off the eddies and swirling back up into the trees. She crouched, curled in a ball behind a bush, the skin stretched tight across her cheeks as if it had somehow shrunk in the last few hours.

~~

L iev Popkov!"
    The big man on the ugly flat-footed horse swung round at the sound of her voice. "Miss Valentina!" He was leading her horse, Dasha, behind.

The expression on his face under his black corkscrew curls surprised her. It was one of shock. Did she look that bad? Normally Liev Popkov was a young man of few words and even fewer expressions of emotion. He was several years older than herself, the son of her father's Cossack stable master, and he seemed to have time and interest only for four-footed companions. He leapt out of the saddle and stomped in his long boots through the shallows. He towered over her as he seized her arm. It surprised her that he would touch her. He was only an outdoor servant, but she was far too grateful to him for bringing her a horse to object.

"I heard shots," he growled.

"There are men in the forest with rifles." Her words came out in gasps. "Quickly, we have to warn my father."

He didn't ask questions. He wasn't that kind of person. His gaze scoured the forest, and when satisfied, he swept her up onto the back of her horse.

"What made you come up here?" she asked as he untied Dasha's reins.

His massive shoulders shrugged, muscles stretching the greasy leather tunic. "Miss Katya came looking for you. I saw your horse was gone"—he rolled a hand fondly over the animal's rump—"so I rode up. Found her tethered." As he handed her the reins, his black eyes fixed on hers. "You well enough to ride?"

"Of course."

"You don't look good."

She touched her cheek, felt blood and saw scarlet slither down her fingers. "I can ride."

"Go slow. Your feet look bad."

She gathered the reins in her hands and twitched Dasha's head around. "Thank you, Liev. *Spasibo*." With a brisk touch of her heels she set the horse into a canter, and together they raced off down the river, water scything like a rainbow around her.

She rode hard through the forest, with Liev Popkov and his big-boned animal tight on her trail. At one point a tree was down across their path, but she wasted no time finding a way around it. She heard an annoyed shout behind her but she didn't stop, just put Dasha to it and lifted her into the jump. The horse soared over it, pleased with herself, and swerved to avoid the roots that writhed up from the black earth to trip the unwary.

They burst out of the forest fringe into the open, into the quiet sunlit somnolence of the landscape, a quilt of greens and golds, of fields, orchards, and pastureland that was spread out lazily before her. It made her want to cry with relief. Nothing had changed. Every-thing was safe. At the top of the slope she reined in her horse to give her a moment to breathe. She'd tumbled out of the forest nightmare back into the real world where the air was scented with ripening apples and the Ivanov mansion sat half a mile away at the heart of the estate, fat and contented as a honey-colored cat in front of a stove. It quickened something inside her and, like Dasha, she breathed more freely. She shortened the reins, eager to ride on.

"That jump was dangerous. You take risks."

She glanced to her right. The young Cossack and his horse were silhouetted against the sun, solid as a rock.

"It was the quickest way," she pointed out.

"You're already hurt."

"I managed."

He shook his head. "Have you ever been whipped?" he demanded.

"What?"

"That jump was difficult. If you had fallen off, your father would have had me whipped with the knout."

Valentina's mouth dropped open. A knout was a rawhide whip, often with metal barbs attached, and although its use had been abolished in Russia, it still prevailed to enforce discipline. One hung coiled like a sleeping snake on the wall of her father's workroom. For a moment they stared at each other, and the sunlight suddenly seemed lost to her. What must it be like to live each day in fear of a whip? Liev's features were heavy and solemn, already set in grooves despite his young age, as if there had been little in his life to smile about. She felt ashamed and embarrassed.

"I'm sorry," she said.

He grunted.

She was the first to look away. She stroked Dasha's feathery ears, then clicked her tongue to set her off at a gallop down the grassy slope. The air buffeted Valentina's lungs and dragged at long strands of her hair, and one stirrup threatened to snap loose from her bare foot. She leaned forward, flat along Dasha's back, urging her to a faster pace.

The roar of an explosion shattered the silence when they were only halfway down the slope. One end of the house shuddered and seemed to leap up into the air, before it disintegrated inside a gray cloud of smoke. Valentina screamed.

## Two

Nyet! No! The word filled Valentina's mind, echoing inside it till there was no room for other words. Nyet! No room for words like *blood* and *pain*. No room for death.

Their horses skidded to a halt on the gravel in front of the house and Valentina threw herself out of the saddle. There was noise everywhere. People frantic, servants running, shouting, crying. Panic leaping from face to face; the air was thick and heavy with it. There was the stink of smoke, shattered glass underfoot. Riderless horses hurtled into view from the stables, skittering in terror. She heard the word *bomb* repeated again and again.

"Papa!" she screamed.

Her father's study was at that end where the smoke was pouring out, swallowing the house in greedy gulps. Each morning when at Tesovo, her father would go into his study to write his ministerial letters immediately after finishing his newspaper over breakfast. Her heart lurched as she started to fly toward the crumpled wing of the building, but after only two steps she was jerked to a stop. A fist like an anchor chain had seized her wrist.

"Liev," she screamed, "let go of me!"

"*Nyet.*"

"I have to see if Papa is—"

"*Nyet*. It's not safe."

His filthy fingernails dug deep into her white skin while in his other hand lay the reins of the two horses. Dasha was prancing wildly, nostrils flared, but the ugly one just stood flat-footed, its curious brown eyes fixed on Popkov.

She stopped struggling and drew herself up to her full height. "I order you to release me, Liev Popkov."

He looked down at her imperious figure. "Or what? You'll have me whipped?"

At that moment Valentina caught sight of her father's back—she recognized his navy frock coat—stumbling into the dense pall of rubble dust.

"Papa!" she yelled again.

But before she could make Popkov release her, the blackened form of a man emerged from the smoke, choking for air. In his arms lay what looked like a broken figure. He was cradling it, his head bent over the boneless body, its sooty legs dangling limp and unheeding. The man was bellowing something, but for some reason Valentina's ears weren't working. She couldn't make out what he was saying. The man drew closer and with a shock she realized it was her father, but her father with a cocoon of black dust encasing his skin, his whiskers, his clothes.

"Papa!" she screamed.

This time the Cossack let her go. As she scrabbled to her father's side, her eyes took in one of the figure's feet. It was wearing a single red shoe, one she herself had helped her sister choose in the shop on Nevsky. The rest was blackened like Papa: her legs, her dress, her face, even her hair, except for one stray strand on the side of her head that was still blond. But streaked with scarlet.

"Katya . . ."

Valentina tried to shout the name, to make her sister open her blue eyes, to sit up and laugh at the game she was playing. But the word had no life. It died on her lips.

"Katya . . ."

Her father was bellowing at the servants. "Ride for the doctor! For God's sake, bring him here at once. I don't care what he's . . ."

His voice thickened and seemed to splinter. Valentina stood at his side, her face frozen, but when she reached out to touch the broken doll, her father swung his arms away.

"Don't touch her."

"But I—"

"Don't touch her. You did this to her."

"No, Papa, I rode up to—"

"You should have taken her with you. She was looking for you, waiting for you. It's because of you she's hurt. You—"

"No," Valentina whispered.

"Yes. I was still in the breakfast room, but she was fretting because you'd gone off riding without her. She must have wandered into my study where . . ." His mouth collapsed into a low cry. "I'll have the murdering savages shot, I swear to God I will."

"Katya . . ."

The blond-black head moved. The red shoe started to judder and shake, and a strange unearthly sound rose in a thin thread from the lacerated throat. Grasping his child tighter to his chest, crooning her name, her father hurried to the wide steps up to the front door, Valentina at his heels. As he stepped over the threshold he snapped his head around to look at her. What she saw in his eyes made her halt.

"Get out, Valentina. Get out of here. As horses mean so much more to you than your sister, go and help catch them."

His eyes almost closed and for a moment he swayed unsteadily. With his foot he kicked the door shut in her face.

❧

VALENTINA STOOD THERE AND ROCKED BACK ON HER HEELS, staring at the door. At the iron studs in it, at the place where she and Katya had nicked its surface with a stone to show how deep the snow had risen last Christmas.

"Katya," she moaned.

Where was Mama? Gathering hot water and bandages?

An earsplitting squeal behind her made her swing around. Horses were charging about the drive in panic, tossing their heads, kicking their heels. Who had let them out? Flecks of foam littered their mouths and flanks. What had happened in the stables? Had the revolutionaries been there too? The grooms and stable boys were pursuing the frightened animals, coaxing and calling, but there was no sign of the stable master, Simeon Popkov, a powerful man who knew how to take control and steady nerves. He was nowhere to be seen.

Where was he? And where was Liev?

She abandoned the steps and flew around the side of the house toward the stables. Had he already caught the men who had done this terrible thing to Katya? Surely Papa would forgive her selfishness if she brought him one of the revolutionaries responsible.

"Simeon!" she shouted as she raced into the stable yard.

Abruptly she stopped, lungs pumping. The yard was quiet and oddly empty. Only Dasha and the ugly mount that was Liev's were tethered to an iron ring in the wall. They were jumpy, edging in circles, bumping into each other. At the far end of the yard beyond the stalls stood the shack that was the stable master's office, its door hanging open. In the dim interior she could make out a broad male figure, his back toward her. He was kneeling on the ground, his black head bowed.

"Simeon," she called out. She could hear the fear in her voice.

But even as the word left her mouth she realized her mistake. It wasn't the stable master; it was his son, Liev, huddled over something on the floor. She burst into the shack.

"Liev, where is . . . ?"

His father, Simeon Popkov, was there in front of her. The stable master was lying stretched out on his back on the ground, limbs askew, black eyes open. His throat had been cut to the bone. She'd never have believed there could be so much blood. Crimson seemed to flood her world. It had taken over his tunic, soaked his hair, laid claim to the floor. Specks of scarlet floated in the air, and the smell of it made her choke.

Her mind grew hazy. She blinked, as if her eyelids could sweep away what lay before her, blinked again and this time focused on the Cossack's son. Tears were coursing down his cheeks and his hand was holding his father's, wrapping the strong fingers in a grip that would cheat death if it could. She put a hand on the young man's back, feeling the tremors under his shirt.

"Liev," she whispered gently. She touched his hair, the black wiry curls, wanting to draw out the splinters of pain but not knowing how. "I'm so sorry. He was a good man. Why would they harm him as well?"

Liev raised his head and gazed bleakly at the splashes of crimson on the wooden walls. Words roared out of him. "My father was nothing to them. Nothing! They did it just to prove they could, to show their power. And to give warning to those who work for other families of your class."

She stood there for a long moment, her chest too tight to breathe, seeing in her head the broken figure of Katya, reliving the expression in her father's eyes. Listening to the pain in the guttural moans that shuddered out of the Cossack's throat. Her hand lay on his shoulder in an attempt to offer comfort, though she knew that comfort was the last thing either of them wanted. A thrashing tide of anger was rising within her.

"Liev," she declared, "they will pay for this."

He lifted his dark eyes to hers. "I'll not rest," he growled, "and I'll not forget. Not till they're dead."

Her gaze slid to the dead body of Simeon, who had been the first to lift her up onto a horse's back when she was scarcely three years old and the first to pick her up from the dirt each time she fell off. He would dust her down, tease her with his huge laugh, and throw her straight back on again.

"I'll not forget," she echoed. "Nor forgive."

ॐ

THE HOUSE LAY SILENT, THE ROOMS DARKENED. EVERYONE moved on tiptoe and spoke in low whispers, the way they would around the dead. Valentina wanted to throw open the curtains and shout, *She's still alive!* But she kept quiet, ignoring the ache that crippled her chest, and sat close beside her mother on the chaise longue in the drawing room.

They were past words. Locked inside themselves, waiting for the doctor's heavy tread to descend the stairs. The room was hot, the sun straining to creep between the curtains, but Valentina remained cold deep in the center of her bones. Her eyes followed her mother's delicate fingers, watched them crouch in the lap of her lavender morning gown, hooked around each other, twisting and digging, tugging at the lace cuff on her sleeve, while the rest of her slight figure sat quiet. It upset Valentina more than the expression of despair on her mother's face or the two fierce bursts of color on the white skin of her cheeks. Elizaveta Ivanova was a person who believed in restraint at all times. To see her hands so out of control made the world feel unsafe.

"How much longer?" Valentina murmured.

"The doctor has been up there too long. It's a bad sign."

"No, it means he's still helping her. He hasn't given up." She tried to smile. "You know how stubborn Katya is."

Elizaveta Ivanova gave one dry harsh sob, then silenced herself. She had been brought up as part of that breed of women who regarded a wife's role in life as being a decorative and largely voiceless adornment to her husband, to look attractive and well mannered on his arm at all times, and to produce children for him, one of whom was expected to be a boy to continue the bloodline. In this latter area she had failed. She had given birth to two healthy girls but seemed unable to forgive herself the lack of a son, viewing it as a punishment from God for some unknown mortal sin. Now this curse on her younger daughter.

Despite her mother's daily routine of social engagements, Valentina sometimes thought her lonely. She slipped an arm around her in a rare gesture of physical contact between them and was astonished by the warmth of her body. Her own skin was chill as marble. Even now her mother's luxuriant golden hair was elegantly dressed on top of her head and she sat rigidly upright inside her armor of French silk and lace, of amethyst brooch and whalebone stays. It occurred to Valentina for the first time that maybe her mother already knew how dangerous a place the world was, and that was why she never relaxed. Security police were scouring the fields and forest, but so far had found no men with rifles.

"Mama," she whispered softly, "if the revolutionaries hadn't kept me in the forest, I'd have been back here long before Katya woke, she'd have been with me down at the creek instead of wandering into Papa's . . ."

Elizaveta Ivanova turned her head to inspect her daughter, her nostrils flared, her eyes almost colorless as if their usual deep blue pigment had been washed away by hidden tears. "You are not to blame, Valentina." She held her daughter's hand in hers.

"Papa thinks I am."

"Your father is angry. He needs someone to blame."

"He could blame the hooded men in the forest."

"Ah." Elizaveta Ivanova released a long sad sigh. "That would be too easy. Be patient with him, my dear. He has more on his mind than you know."

Valentina shuddered. Nothing, she was certain, would be easy from now on.

෨

THE BEDROOM WAS STIFLING. WHAT WERE THEY TRYING to do to her sister? Suffocate her? A fire burned in the grate although it was a hot summer's day, the curtains were drawn shut, and a dim light cast shadows that to Valentina felt like secretive figures hiding in the gloom. She had been allowed five minutes, that was all, and only because she had pleaded so hard. Immediately she knelt beside the bed, rested her arms on the embroidered silk counterpane, and balanced her chin on her hand, so that her eyes were level with her sister's.

"Katya," she whispered. "Katya, I'm sorry."

The face on the pillow tugged at her heart. It was Katya as she would be in fifty years' time, her skin and her hair gray and lifeless, her lips thin, drawn into a tight line of pain. Valentina gently kissed her cheek and smelled the dirt on her. Once when she was young, one of the gardeners had dug out a rats' nest from under a shed, and she and Katya had watched wide-eyed when the small furry bodies squealed as they fought to escape. They had given off a rank musky odor that had stuck in Valentina's nostrils. That was what Katya's skin smelled of now.

She didn't know if Katya was awake. Conscious or unconscious. They said the doctor had given her something. What did that mean? Morphine? How could her precious blond sister who was always bursting with laughter and energy be hiding under this little old lady's skin? Tentatively Valentina touched the dusty arm that lay outside the cover, and it felt like a stranger's, gritty and rough. Where were the satin-smooth limbs that loved to swim in the creek and pull down branches from the willows to build silvery dens to hide in?

A large tear splashed down onto her sister's arm and startled Valentina. She didn't know she was crying. She rested her cheek against her sister's hot arm, and it felt like a furnace under her skin.

"I, Valentina Ivanova, caused this," she murmured under her breath, so that her ears as well as her mind would bear witness to the words. She scraped away her tears and said loudly, "Katya, it's me, Valentina."

No response.

She kissed her sister's filthy hair. "Can you hear me?"

No response.

"Please, Katya."

A gray-gold eyelash fluttered.

"Katya!"

A slit of blue showed in one eye.

Valentina leaned closer. "Hello, *privet*, my sweet."

The slit widened a fraction. Katya's lips moved, but no sound emerged.

Valentina placed her ear to her sister's lips and felt a faint whisper of breath. "What is it? Are you in pain? The doctor has . . ."

"I'm frightened."

Valentina's throat closed. She kissed the soft cheek. "Don't be frightened, Katya. I'm here. I'll look after you and keep you safe. For the rest of our lives." She squeezed her sister's small hand and saw a slight movement at the side of her tight bruised mouth. A smile.

"Promise me," Katya breathed.

"I promise. On my life."

Slowly Katya's eyes fell shut and the narrow slit of blue vanished. But the edge of the smile stayed, and Valentina cradled her limp hand until they came and made her leave.

# Three

GIRLS, *MESDEMOISELLES*, TODAY IS A GREAT HONOR FOR OUR school. A day to remember. I expect the best from each of you. Today you must shine brighter than . . ."

The headmistress stopped in mid flight. Her neatly drawn eyebrows rose in disgust. The girls held their breath, waiting to see on which wretched creature her wrath would fall. In her somber dress with its high neck and cameo brooch, Madame Petrova was marching up and down in front of the benches in the grand hall of the Ekaterininsky Institute, eyeing each pupil with the unbending scrutiny of a general reviewing his troops.

"Nadia," she said crisply.

Valentina's heart sank for her friend, who had dropped ink on her clean pinafore.

"Sit up straight, girl. Just because you are in the back row doesn't mean you can slouch. Do you want the broom handle tied to your back?"

"No, Madame." Nadia straightened her shoulders but kept her hands discreetly over her soiled pinafore.

"Aleksandra, remove that curl from your cheek."

She glided farther along the ranks.

"Emilya, put your feet together, you are not a horse. Valentina, stop fiddling at once!"

Valentina flushed and stared down at her fingers. They were drumming on her knees, desperate to keep warm. She couldn't play with cold fingers. But she folded them obediently on her lap. Her heart was hammering. It was always like this before a performance, but she had practiced the Nocturne till it accompanied her through her night dreams, the way the sound of screaming horses still did. She hadn't ridden a horse since the day of the explosion and had no intention of ever doing so again, but still the sound of them wouldn't leave her, however hard she thundered across the piano keys.

"Valentina."

"Yes, Madame."

"Remember who you are performing for today. The tsar himself."

"Yes, Madame."

This time she would play Chopin's Nocturne in E Flat better than ever before.

❧

JENS FRIIS GLANCED AT THE DOMED CLOCK ON THE WALL. The afternoon was crawling past as though it had frostbite in its toes, and he was tempted to yawn.

He stretched out his legs and shifted position with irritation. He was tired of the interminable poems and songs, as well as uncomfortable on an absurd chair that was not built for someone like himself with limbs like a giraffe's. Worse, he was annoyed with Countess Serova for dragging him to this schoolgirl frivolity when he was short of time. He needed to study the blueprints of the new construction that had only come in this morning and, damn it, it was cold here in this hall. How on earth did the poor wretches stand it? On the benches arranged along the wall, the rows of pupils sat stiff and upright in their dark frocks with white capes and pinafores, like delicate snow carvings.

His gaze moved dutifully to the *institutka* who was singing. Pleasant enough voice, nothing special, but the song was dull, one of those tedious German *lieder* he loathed, the ones that go on forever. He glanced at the door and wondered what the chances were of escape.

"Jens," Countess Natalia Serova whispered next to him. "Behave."

"I fear such elitist delights are above my churlish brain."

She gave him a glare from steady blue eyes, then turned away. He could smell her perfume. Most likely from Paris, like her hat, a frivolous confection of silk and feathers that made him smile. Her long fitted coat in the palest of greens showed off her girlish figure though he guessed she must be about thirty, and emeralds glittered at her ears and throat. She had exquisite taste, no doubt about that. As the son of a Danish printer, Jens had grown up in Copenhagen with the stink of ink forever in his nostrils, but now at twenty-seven years old he was learning to appreciate the finer fragrances on parade in St. Petersburg.

"You are very provoking. Listen to Maria," she murmured under her breath.

Ah, so this songbird was Maria, the countess's niece. Vaguely he recalled her from the time the countess had dragged him to a concert here two years ago, when Jens had the honor of meeting Tsar Nicholas for the first time. Countess Natalia Serova had introduced him, he must not forget that. He owed her much, even if her husband did make good use in return of Jens's skills as an engineer to do work on their estate.

This time Tsar Nicholas was sitting bolt upright in a high-backed chair in the center of the hall, and it was impossible to tell whether he was bored or amused. The muscles of his face were so rigidly well trained. He was a small man and hid his weak chin behind a prominent chestnut beard, in the same way that he hid his slight frame inside a series of bulky military uniforms designed to impress. Today he was resplendent in a peacock blue jacket weighed down by an abundance of medals and gold braid.

Jens was not the only one who believed that Tsar Nicholas Alexandrovich Romanov was the wrong man in the wrong job, unlike his big brash bullying father, Tsar Alexander III, a man who had stood six feet six inches in his bare feet and thought nothing of behaving like the iron fist of God. But now, more than ever before, Russia was in danger of slitting its own throat, in desperate need of a leader of wisdom and strength.

"Bravo," the tsar called out. "Well done, Mademoiselle Maria."

Applause burst out around the hall. The niece had finished, thank God. Jens breathed a sigh of relief because now he could leave and get back to work. But a grand piano that dominated the far end of the room suddenly stirred into life and music started to flow throughout the high-ceilinged room. Jens groaned inwardly. It was something by Chopin, one of his least favorite composers, always so plaintive, so full of despair, whining in your ear like a cat in heat.

He glanced at the pianist and saw that she was a slight young creature with a mane of dense dark hair pulled back from her face by a black hairband. About sixteen, he'd guess, maybe seventeen. She wore the Ekaterininsky Institute uniform and should have looked as shapeless and anonymous as all the other girls. But she didn't. There was something about her that caused his eyes to linger, something in the way her hands moved with hypnotic grace. As if they were part of the music itself.

She had small strong fingers that flowed over the keys, connecting to something he couldn't see, something that was part of her private world. The music soared, rising in a minor chord and flooding his senses with its beauty, then without warning, when he was totally unprepared, ripped his heart out. He closed his eyes, aware of the music alive inside him. Of its notes touching places within him, secret corners. With an effort of will he forced open his eyes and studied the girl who could transform music into such a weapon.

Her body didn't sway dramatically on the stool. Just her hands. And her head. They moved as if they belonged to the music, rather than to her body. Her skin was palest ivory and her face almost expressionless except for her eyes. They were huge and dark, full of an emotion that to Jens looked closer to fury than rapture. Where had a girl so young found such powerful feelings? As if she drew them in with each breath.

Finally the music sighed to an end, and the girl hung her head. Her dark hair curtained her face from view, and she placed her hands quietly in her lap. Only one telltale tremor shook her spine, and then silence filled the hall. Jens looked at the tsar. Tears were rolling unchecked down Nicholas's face. Slowly he raised his imperial hands and began to clap, and immediately applause echoed around the hall. Jens looked again at the young pianist. She hadn't moved but her head was turned to one side and her luminous dark eyes were directed straight at him. If it weren't too absurd to be true, he'd have sworn she was angry with him.

"Mademoiselle Valentina," the tsar said, his voice thick with tears, "thank you. *Merci bien.* That was a magnificent performance. Unforgettable. You must come and play for my wife and my dear daughters when they are next at the Winter Palace."

The girl rose from the stool and dropped a deep curtsy. "It would be a great honor," she said.

"*Pozdravlyayu.* Congratulations, my dear girl. You will be a great pianist."

For the first time she smiled, "*Spasibo*, Your Majesty. You are too kind."

There was something about the way she murmured it that startled Jens. He almost laughed out loud, but the tsar seemed not to notice the faint rustle of mockery in her words.

"So," Jens's companion whispered. "At least you enjoyed the Chopin, if not the singing."

Jens turned to Countess Serova. "I did."

"Friis, good heavens, man, what are you doing here?"

It was Tsar Nicholas. He was strutting over to his entourage to stretch his legs before the next performance. Everyone rose to their feet. He was considerably shorter than Jens and had a habit of rocking up and down on his toes. The women ruffled their finery in greeting and the men ducked their heads in acknowledgment of his attention.

"Friis," Tsar Nicholas continued, "you're not here to flirt with the girls, I hope."

"No, Your Majesty, I am not. I'm here as a guest of Countess Serova."

"Shouldn't you be hard at work? That's what I expect of you, you know. Not to parade in front of Petersburg's elite young ladies."

Jens bowed, a crisp click of his heels and a dip of his head. "Then I shall take my leave."

Nicholas's manner became serious. "You are needed elsewhere, Friis. I can't afford to waste a good man on"—he waved a jeweled hand at the school hall—"on this frippery."

Jens bowed again and turned to leave. As he did so, he cast one more glance around, seeking out the pianist. She was still watching him. He smiled but she didn't respond, so he tipped his head to her and walked out of the room. As the door closed behind him he felt as if something of himself still lay on the hall's polished floorboards. Something he valued.

❦

J ENS!"

He stopped midstride. "Ah, Countess. As you see, I am in a hurry."

"Wait," she called. Her footsteps echoed along the school's empty yellow corridor, hurrying to catch up with him. "Jens, I'm sorry. I didn't intend that rebuke from the tsar to happen."

"Didn't you?"

"No. Forgive me."

"Countess Serova," he said, lifting her gloved hand and pressing it to his lips, "there is nothing to forgive." But his voice was brittle with irony.

She exhaled sharply. "Don't be so arrogant, Jens," she said. "Not with me."

She stretched up and placed a kiss full on his mouth. Her lips were soft. Tempting. But Jens stepped away. She gave him a reproachful gaze and walked back the way she had come.

Damn the woman. Damn her.

❦

J ENS WRAPPED HIS HEAVY RIDING CAPE TIGHTLY AROUND HIS shoulders. The dismal gray mist clung to his clothes and hair and even to his eyelashes. On horseback he drifted like a ghost through the city, over bridges that were illuminated by streetlamps day and night now it was winter. Carriages rattled past unseen in the fog and cars blared their klaxons at each other, while pedestrians kept a firm hold on their purses and wallets. It was a day for pickpockets and thieves.

The temperatures were harsh this year, harsher than usual in St. Petersburg. The Moika Canal had frozen over and the Neva River disappeared in a deathly pall that swallowed the city. It was a winter of bitter strikes in the factories and of shortages in the food shops. Unrest slid and slithered through the streets, workers gathered on corners and smoked their cheap *makhorka* cigarettes with resentful fury. Jens heeled his horse into a canter and swung away from the wide boulevards, leaving behind the fashionable Nevsky Prospekt with its sables and its silks.

The streets grew narrower, the houses meaner till dirt and despair hung in the damp air. A pack of three feral dogs snapped at the horse and received the tip of Hero's metal shoe in exchange. Jens gazed along the street at the pinched faces and the blackened buildings. The cold was so intense it had cracked windows.

This was why he was here. Places like this. Streets that stank. No water to wash. Just wells that turned sour and backed up in the rain, and pumps that iced over. This was why he was here in Petersburg.

❧

I T WAS FOUR O'CLOCK IN THE MORNING WHEN VALENTINA tapped the door with her fingertips.

"*Vkhodite*, come in, my dear." The voice was soft and welcoming.

She turned the handle and entered Nurse Sonya's private quarters, where shadows had settled on the carpet like tired dogs in the dim light.

"*Dobroye utro*, good morning," Valentina said in greeting.

The nurse was in her fifties, seated in a rocking chair and tapping the floor with her foot in a steady rhythm to keep it in motion. Her large form was engulfed in a battered old housecoat and a Bible lay open on her lap, her finger trailing over each line she read.

"How is she tonight?" Valentina asked at once.

"She's sleeping."

Sleeping? Or just pretending? Valentina knew that Nurse Sonya was not good at knowing the difference. Katya had endured three operations in the last six months to try to repair her shattered spine, and since the last one her mobility had definitely improved, but still she was unable to walk. Not that she ever complained. No, Katya wouldn't. But purple hollows gathered under her eyes and a sallow bruised look to her face betrayed when the pain was bad.

"What have you given her?" Valentina asked quietly.

"A little laudanum, the usual dosage."

"I thought you were cutting back on it."

"I tried, *malishka*, little one. But she needs it."

Valentina made no comment. *What do I know about laudanum? Just what I see in Katya's eyes.*

The nurse stilled the rocking chair and studied Valentina's face with a look of gentle concern. "Guilt is a terrible thing, my dear." She shook her head, and her hand trailed across the wafer-thin page open on her lap. "God forgives us."

Valentina walked over to the window, pulled the heavy curtain to one side, and stared out into the night. Lights flickered as sleighs and carriages with bright torches continued to charge through the city that prided itself on its reputation for never sleeping, on its reputation for wild living and even wilder dying. St. Petersburg was a city of extremes. All or nothing. No one in St. Petersburg seemed to have any time for anything but their next drink, their next dissolute party, their next insane throw of the dice. She stared out at it all and craved something more for her life.

"No," she murmured to the nurse, "it's not God's forgiveness I want."

༄

IT WAS STILL DARK. THE KIND OF DARKNESS THAT IS THICK and heavy, the kind that clogs the mind. The first muted sounds of the house coming to life drifted upstairs as servants laid fires and polished floors. Valentina was perched cross-legged on the end of Katya's bed, a towel spread out over her lap.

"I hear Papa has bought a new car while I was at school," Valentina said.

"Yes. It's a Turicum. From Switzerland."

"Isn't that fearfully expensive?"

"I expect so. But Tsar Nicholas has just bought himself a new Delaunay-Belleville. You know what it's like at court; they've made a big fuss of it and all rush to copy him."

"Who is driving it?"

"Papa has hired a chauffeur. His name is Viktor Arkin."

"What's he like?"

"Very smart in his uniform. Rather quiet but I suppose good looking in a serious sort of way."

"You always did like a man in uniform."

Katya laughed delightedly, and Valentina felt pleased. Some days it took more than that to make her sister smile. But she noticed that Katya's eyes were blurry this morning, as though the fog had slunk up the Neva River and slid into her head overnight. One of her feet was propped on the towel and Valentina's hands were massaging its delicate skin, manipulating the joints, bringing a semblance of life into the paralyzed limb. A fine sheen of lavender oil eased the repetitive movement and scented the air, disguising the odor of a sickroom.

Katya snuggled into her pillows, her hair a haze of pale gold around her head. "Tell me again about the tsar." She watched Valentina's busy hands. "What was he like?"

"I've told you already. He was handsome and charming and complimented me on my playing."

Katya narrowed her blue eyes, as if she were peering at something very small. "Don't think I can't see through your lies, Valentina. What happened yesterday? Why didn't you like His Imperial Majesty?"

"Of course I liked him. Everyone likes the tsar."

"I shall call for Nurse Sonya to throw you out of here if you don't . . ."

Valentina laughed and paused in working oil into the pale toenails. Her sister's foot lay on her palm as dead as a doll's. "All right, all right, I admit it. You know me too well. You're correct, Katya, I didn't like Tsar Nicholas yesterday. But only because he strutted into the room as if he owned the whole world, not just the Romanovs' half of it. Gaudy as a peacock. A small man in big shoes."

Katya suddenly banged her hand on her forehead with mock annoyance. "Of course, I remember now. He told you he wanted you to play the piano for his wife and children when he heard you play before at the school two years ago. Didn't he?"

"Yes. And I was stupid enough to believe him then. I practiced and practiced and practiced, waiting for the summons. But it never came." She moved Katya's foot down onto the sheet. "I have far more sense this time." She smiled at her young sister. "You can't trust a tsar. Lies come too easily to his royal tongue."

Katya's eyes opened wide. "Was he there again?"

"Who?"

"I remember that you told me there was a man with Tsar Nicholas when you played for him before."

"No, I said no such thing."

"Yes, you did."

Valentina picked up the other foot, placing it on the towel. She dipped her fingers in the warm oil and started to massage the dry skin on the heel. "What on earth are you talking about?" She kept her eyes on Katya's toes as she gently eased them apart, one by one.

"There was a man. With the tsar two years ago when he visited your school," Katya insisted. "I remember, you said he was . . ."

"Don't be silly."

"You told me he looked like a Viking warrior."

"That's absurd."

"With fiery hair and green eyes."

"You're imagining things."

"No, you told me. He stood by the door, and you said . . ."

Valentina laughed and tweaked a toe. "I said a lot of silly things when I was fifteen."

But Katya's gaze was fixed on her sister. "You told me you had fallen in love with him."

Valentina's fingers pummeled the scrap of flesh behind the ankle bone. "If I said such a thing, it was just schoolgirl nonsense. I didn't even speak to him. I scarcely recall now what he looked like." But the blood had risen to her cheeks.

"You told me," Katya said softly, "that you intended to marry this tall Viking warrior."

"Then I was a fool," Valentina insisted. "I don't ever intend to marry."

# Four

K ATYA WAS RIGHT. ABOUT THE VIKING. VALENTINA HAD
tried to laugh about it but couldn't. She was angry at him now.
He didn't remember her, it was obvious, but that didn't matter. Why
should she expect him to, after the way she'd played when she was
fifteen?

No, that wasn't what irked her. It was the way that he'd walked
out yesterday. As soon as she'd finished playing, he had left with an
eagerness that was insulting: he'd jumped to his feet and, after a few
words with the tsar, had loped for the door as though he couldn't
get out fast enough. Was he so disappointed that he couldn't bear to
stay? But she had been so proud of her performance this time. His
indifference to it was like a bee sting in her flesh.

She sat down hungrily at the piano in her parents' music room
and as always stroked its surface. It was a beautiful glossy black Erard
grand, which she loved. She let her fingers touch the keys and immediately the tension swerved out of her body, like a train jumping the
tracks. As instant as that. It was always the same. Her fingers caressed
the ivory and started to flow steadily up and down its length, moving
at different speeds, rising and falling, warming the muscles, stretching the tendons. The rich exuberant sound that rose from the body
of the Erard soothed her, calmed some of her excitement. Because

she *was* excited, but for all the wrong reasons. She wanted to see the Viking again.

Katya was right about that.

Valentina had been stunned when he'd walked into the hall just behind the tsar yesterday, tall and upright in his frock coat. She hadn't expected him. He was the tallest man in the room by far, lean and broad shouldered with an air of invincibility about him. Two years ago at the Ekaterininsky Institute concert he had strolled in among a party of the tsar's courtiers and dazzled her fifteen-year-old eyes with his energy and his fiery red hair. His vivid green eyes had swept the room with a look of amusement, as though the whole situation were too absurd to take seriously.

On that occasion she'd watched him, all through the singing and the dancing, wanting to catch his eye, but she'd seen that he was bored by the performances and had eyes for no one except the beautiful woman by his side, dressed in green silk and fine emeralds. When her own turn came to play, Valentina had been determined not to bore him, but his presence had made her nervous and she hadn't played well. At the end he'd applauded politely, smiling at his companion as if at a secret joke. Valentina had been furious with herself. But you couldn't love someone you've never even spoken to, someone you've just seen across a room. It was impossible.

Her fingers abandoned the exercises and launched into Mozart's Sonata in C Major, a piece she always relished, but abruptly she lifted her hands from the keys. There were times, odd, uncomfortable moments when she was playing and the music was really seizing hold of her, that she would break off like this. Aware that her mother considered her passion for the piano to be excessive and therefore unbecoming in a young woman. She knew her mother could never understand why she had no interest in going shopping with her, choosing dresses, all the things young ladies were meant to do, instead of sitting at home on a piano stool hour after hour. Worse, Valentina sometimes feared that her mother felt that if she wasn't going to behave like a proper girl, she might as well have been the longed-for boy.

She wished Katya had been there to hear her yesterday. With a sudden movement she rose, drew a chair from beside the wall, and placed it next to her piano stool. The chair was padded in a creamy brocade and had slender fluted mahogany arms. She sat again on her stool, then rested first one hand on the chair and then the other. Without using her legs at all she tried to swing herself off the stool toward the chair seat, but missed it completely. Her arms became entangled and the chair edge stabbed her shoulder blade as she tumbled like a rag doll to the floor. She glared at her legs as if the fault were theirs.

"*Chyort!*"

It took five awkward attempts, but finally she succeeded. Her heart was racing and her arms shook with the effort.

"*Chyort!*" she swore again. Then she stood up and ran up the stairs to her room.

~

IN FRONT OF HER AT HER DESK VALENTINA HELD A LIST, NEATLY written out on a sheet of ivory-tinted paper. It was a list she had drawn up four months ago and which she kept locked in the drawer of her table away from prying eyes. Maids peeked into everything. But the paper was already dog-eared at the edges because she liked to handle it, to remind herself. Her eyes traveled down each point methodically.

*1. Contact every spine specialist in Europe.*

With painstaking care she'd scoured medical journals in the library for articles on spinal damage, and she'd written to doctors as far away as Berlin, Rome, Oslo, even London. Few had bothered to reply.

*2. Make Katya happy.*

She smiled at that one. Such a simple aim. Four months ago, making Katya happy after her operations had seemed the easiest of all on her list: she would read to her, play cards with her, whisper secrets, and pass on the latest tittle-tattle from school or from the servants' hall downstairs. She brought her ribbons and jigsaws, as well as the latest books from Belizard's bookstore. From the parks or the riverbank she collected magpie feathers and the first coppery maple leaves of autumn. She smuggled in chocolate from Wolf & Beranger's or risked the sticky confections from the bazaar at Gostiny Dvor.

But now she understood that making Katya happy meant far more than that. It meant creating a whole new future for her. Those words in the silence of her head felt huge.

So what next?

*3. Find employment.*

She ran a finger over the word *employment* and her stomach lurched. For years she'd had a dream. Ever since she was a gawky gap-toothed child she had planned it, while others giggled in corners and played with toys. To be a concert pianist. That was her aim. To tour the greatest concert halls and palaces of Europe, performing before heads of state in Rome and Paris, London and Vienna. But it was gone. Blown apart by the bomb. It couldn't happen now. It would mean years of dedicated work at the St. Petersburg Conservatoire, and she no longer had that luxury. She had to care for Katya. She stared at her fingers, at their strong tendons and well-rounded pads, and she felt disloyal to them. Disloyal to herself. She had to forget the dream.

But how? How could she tear it out of her head when she could still see herself at the keys, pouring her heart into the music, then rising from the piano, her audience on their feet? She would wear a scarlet Parisian gown, a single strand of pearls in her hair, and she would play the finest concerts in Europe. She could actually see herself. Feel her heart thudding.

"Forget the dream." She said it aloud.

The paper in her hand shook. Find employment. Yes, she had made her decision about that.

She must talk to Papa. She knew that wives and daughters of distinguished families didn't go out to work and that Papa would be ashamed if she did so. He would regard it as demeaning to the Ivanov name. But she would explain to him, persuade him to agree.

*4. Make Papa forgive me.*

*One day, Papa. One day.*

What saddened her most was that she and her father had always had a quiet understanding, and now that was gone. He had never been an attentive parent and constantly put his work before everything, but he and she had always had a special bond between them. Katya was the one he petted, indulged, and smiled at most, and Valentina understood why: she was the image of her mother when she was young—blond, blue-eyed, and with a gentle smile. Whereas Valentina was like her father: dark-haired, brown-eyed, and possessed of a single-mindedness that matched his own.

Over the years he had made no secret of the fact that he often found his elder daughter maddening, but even when he was reprimanding her for some misdeed, there was a gleam of pride in his eye, a hint of respect in his voice. The way he might feel about the son he never had. But since the bomb he had withdrawn from her, and she felt the loss keenly. *He needs someone to blame*, her mother had said, but it didn't seem right that it was her.

*One day, Papa, one day, you will forgive me.*

*5. Obey Mama.*

She was still working on that one.

*6. Play the piano better every day.*

What was the point now?

*7. Play for the tsar.*

She laughed at herself and drew a line through it.

*8. Marry the Viking.*

The words were already crossed out with fierce black strokes of ink. A silly girl's fancy. She shrugged it off, ignoring the heat that rose up her neck.

*9. Buy a gun.*

She stared at that one and felt her pulse quicken. She'd not yet worked out a way to do it. The revolutionaries had come once. They could come again, the way bad dreams came back when you thought they were gone. But next time she would be ready for them. *Number 9.* She underlined it in black ink. *Buy a gun.* She sat with her eyes fastened on the list and thought out each point in detail. Finally she picked up her fountain pen and wrote one more:

*10. Find a Bolshevik.*

Find *the* Bolshevik. That was what she really meant. The promises of the police and of her father to make the bombers pay for their crime had proved as meaningless as the lies of the tsar himself. The men in hoods had vanished into thin air. Oh yes, pockets of known Bolsheviks had been rounded up and questioned, but no one knew anything of the ghosts who walked in the forest.

*Find a Bolshevik.*

❧

DOBROYE UTRO, GOOD MORNING, MINISTER."

"*Dobriy den*, good afternoon, Minister."

"*Dobriy vecher*, good evening, Minister."

Those were words that Viktor Arkin liked least. Instead of "Good morning, comrade."

"Yes, master. *Da, barin.*"

"No, master. *Nyet, barin.*"

Those were words that grated in his gut.

Every day Arkin drove Minister General Nicholai Ivanov in the Turicum along the Embankment in St. Petersburg to the Ministry of Finance, and each day he listened to the words that were spilled in the back of the car. The minister had a loose tongue. Often he would talk too openly with colleagues as Arkin drove them across the city to meetings. Once Minister Ivanov had even been fool enough to leave his attaché case lying on the seat in the car after too many brandies at the Donon. Arkin had read its contents meticulously and made notes for an hour before he returned it to the minister.

Worst were the evenings. Waiting outside restaurants like a dog in the cold. Outside nightclubs. Outside brothels. Outside the mistress's apartment on Izmailovsky Prospekt. But some days Madam Ivanova requested the car instead of the carriage, and on those days Arkin smiled.

༄

A RKIN WATCHED ELIZAVETA IVANOVA WALK DOWN THE front steps of the house and considered how women of this class moved differently, held themselves differently. You could wrap them in rags and still you would know who they were, what they were. Beautiful, elegant, fragrant parasites.

She approached across the gravel, picking her way with delicate care over the thin layer of snow that had fallen since the drive was last brushed an hour ago. He stood beside the car in his maroon uniform and peaked cap with its gold band and waited for her instructions.

"Arkin, I want you to drive both my daughters into town today. To Gordino's restaurant on Morskaya." Her blue eyes studied him assessingly, and he knew she was wondering whether she could trust him.

Both daughters. That was rare. The crippled one didn't go out much even though he had removed the front passenger seat of the car to allow for her wheelchair to be stored there. It must be the influence of her dark-haired sister. The one who looked at him with eyes that were not easily fooled by a chauffeur's uniform and a submissive lowering of his gaze.

*Into town today*, she'd said. For one fraction of a second he almost let the wrong words slip out. *Today is not the day for your daughters to be in town. Keep your daughters at home.* But instead he nodded politely and opened the car door.

༄

Aᴿᴷɪɴ ʟɪꜱᴛᴇɴᴇᴅ ᴛᴏ ᴇᴠᴇʀʏ ᴡᴏʀᴅ. Hᴇ ᴀʟᴡᴀʏꜱ ᴅɪᴅ. Tʜᴀᴛ was his job.

The Turicum was a magnificent monster of a vehicle. Imported from Geneva, all deep blue leather and fearsome brass fittings that he polished each day within an inch of their life. He sat up front in the driver's seat, swathed in his maroon coat, and today the air had the bite of a tiger. To keep it at bay the daughters were bundled up with a weighty bearskin rug over their knees and fur hoods over their ears.

*It will be cold for the marchers today. No bearskins. No fur hoods. Just the heat of anger in their bellies.*

As he drove through the city, the streets of St. Petersburg slid past with their tall pastel buildings and people scurrying about their business, unwilling to linger in the freezing wind. It gave him satisfaction to see the cars and carriages jostling axles, the horse-drawn *drozhky* lumbering along, heedless of the klaxons that demanded room to pass. The more traffic, the better. The more chaos there would be.

He listened to their girlish chatter. Worthless words. An expression of delight as Madame Duclet's fashionable dress shop came into view on Morskaya, a murmur of approval as they passed the renowned Zhirov establishment with its windows full of exotic china from the Orient and silverware from England. When he glanced around he saw Katya's hands nestled in the warmth of the rug, but her eyes watched the outside world the way he would watch a circus.

"Today," Valentina announced, "we shall do exactly as we please."

"Yes," Katya laughed, "we shall."

Seldom had Arkin seen the younger one allowed out without her mother or Nurse Sonya as chaperone. Today she seemed to smell freedom. But suddenly he had to brake hard. The road was blocked by a line of policemen, dark and menacing. He brought the car to a halt, but the carriage in front swayed dangerously as the horse slammed against its shafts, unnerved by a noise from up ahead. It sounded like distant thunder. Except it wasn't. He sensed his passengers listening to the sound carefully. It was more like the drag of waves on a pebble beach, harsh and grating. Coming closer.

All movement down Morskaya had ceased and pedestrians were backtracking along the pavement, casting nervous glances over their shoulders. Drivers found no room to maneuver around the police cordon but were wedged within the stationary traffic as tempers were roused and arguments flared.

"What is it, Arkin?" Valentina asked. She leaned forward, close to his shoulder, in an attempt to see what lay ahead. "What is causing the delay?"

"It's the strikers," he answered, careful not to alarm her. "They're marching up Morskaya."

"Strikers? They're the ones causing such trouble in the factories, aren't they? I've read about them in the papers."

He made no comment.

"Prime Minister Stolypin has denounced them," she added. "For trying to destroy Russia's economy. They've managed to shut down our mines and stop our trains running."

He still made no comment.

"I can't see them," Katya complained. "The police are in the way."

"Look, there are the tops of their placards," Valentina pointed out. He could hear the unease in her voice.

*Wait. Just wait. You will see more than you want.*

Ahead lay the backs of policemen, a solid wall of them from one side of the street to the other.

"Do you think there will be trouble?" Valentina was so close behind him he could feel her breath warm on his collar. He pictured her hands, white and nervous, and the hairs rising on the back of her neck. "Why are these men on strike, Arkin?"

*Didn't she know? How could she not know?*

"They are demanding a fair wage, Miss Valentina. The police are advancing on them now."

Slowly, relentlessly. Advancing on them. He could make out batons in their hands. Or were they guns? The chanting of the marchers drew closer, and instantly a sense of real danger sparked in the street. It crackled in the air and people started to run, slipping on ice, skidding on snow. Arkin felt his pulse kick into life.

"Arkin." It was Miss Valentina's voice. "Get us out of here. Do whatever you have to, but get us away from here."

"I can't. We're trapped in traffic."

"Arkin," Valentina ordered, "please drive us out. Now."

He felt the muscle tighten at the corner of his jaw, and his maroon gloves curled around the rim of the steering wheel. "I cannot drive the car anywhere at the moment," he said evenly, looking straight ahead through the windshield. "We are stuck."

"Arkin, listen to me. I have seen what Bolsheviks can do. I'm not going to sit here with my sister like a helpless calf and wait for them to do it again."

He heard it then, the whisper of fear. He swiveled around in his seat and looked her full in the face. For a moment their gaze held, until at last he looked down. "I understand, Miss Valentina."

"Please do something."

"There's no need to be afraid of them," he lied. "The marchers only want better pay and working conditions. No one is going to harm you. Or Miss Katya."

She lifted her hands as if she would shake him. "Then take out the wheelchair," she ordered. "I'll push it up the street myself."

"No need for that."

Abruptly he swung down hard right on the steering. He shouldered the back of the carriage in front with the Turicum's fender, forcing it out at an angle. Ahead of them a horse whinnied, but now the heavy car's wheels were free and Arkin could maneuver it up onto the curb of the pavement and into the open.

"I'll get you out of here."

*Five*

"WHICH ONES SHALL WE CHOOSE?"

"You can have the meringue, it's your favorite."

"What about the chocolate one?"

"No, you can't have that," Katya laughed. "I want it."

With a delighted smile Katya circled her fork over the silver tiers of the cake stand in the middle of the table.

"I shall choose first," she announced.

Valentina wanted to act as if nothing had happened. She wanted her sister to enjoy herself, that was why she'd brought her here—and it had been a long time since she'd seen Katya so bright and animated. But Valentina's cake fork felt like lead in her fingers.

Arkin had been as good as his word. He'd barged the car along the sidewalks, indifferent to the shouts from the pedestrians who scattered at the approach of the big blue motor. He found a route out of there, just as he'd promised. They drove to another restaurant, La Gavotte, with no further comment on what had passed, and Valentina selected a table against the rear wall, near the door to the kitchens. As far from the front of the establishment as it was possible to be.

Around her everything went on as normal, the waitresses bobbing about in black frocks with frilly white aprons and frivolous twists of white lace in their hair. All so courteous. All so polite. No anger here. No shouts. The customers were smiling and smartly dressed, bathed in the healthy glow cast by the pink glass wall lamps, picking at patisseries, sipping hot chocolate. Laughing. Talking.

Valentina was stunned by her own fragility. No one else seemed frightened, and certainly no other customers appeared ready to bring up their lunch over the pristine white tablecloth. Everyone else was breathing normally. Was it she who was foolish, or was it them?

"Valentina."

"Yes?"

"Are you all right?" Katya was peering at her closely.

"Yes."

There was a space between them that felt fragile. Breakable. Valentina refused to touch it.

Katya deliberately changed the subject. "The new car is good, don't you think?"

"Yes."

"And Arkin was excellent."

"He drives well."

Valentina cast a wary glance at the wide arched windows that looked out onto the road through net curtains. Something in her chest gave a slippery shudder.

"Can you hear something?" she asked. "I thought I heard . . ."

Katya's hand wrapped itself around Valentina's and they lay on the cloth together, Katya's fingers like fine strands of delicate porcelain, whereas Valentina's were more robust, a strong pad of muscle on each finger. All those piano scales.

"It's all right to be frightened sometimes," Katya said, "after what you went through in the forest."

Valentina looked back at the net curtains. "You weren't frightened today."

"That's because my life is so dull, I am too stupid to know when I should be afraid and when I should not. You have more sense."

"Katya," Valentina asked softly, "do you think—"

That was the moment when the barrage of bricks hurtled through the windows, when tiny raindrops of glass sliced like diamonds through powdered cheeks. When one arrow-shaped shard lodged in a woman's neck, that was the moment the screaming began.

༄

VALENTINA WAS RUNNING. SLIPPING AND SLIDING ON THE snow but still running. Her legs didn't know how to stop. The wheels of the chair screeched and skidded.

"Valentina, don't!" An icy hand seized hers. "Please stop. Please."

It was Katya. Begging her. With an effort her legs stumbled to a halt, but her fingers still gripped the handles of the wheelchair as though they had become a part of it, stiff and rigid, welded to the metal. The scream of the woman with the glass in her neck echoed in Valentina's mind. She dragged air into her lungs and felt it peel away her flesh, it was so cold.

"Valentina, we'll freeze to death."

Katya had twisted around in her wheelchair, her ungloved hand pulling at Valentina's sleeve. Her blue eyes were panicked.

Valentina looked around, momentarily baffled to find herself in a narrow dirty street where household slops had frozen into treacherous yellow mounds on the pavement. A drainpipe, covered in snow, was lying like a corpse in the gutter and windows were blanked out with cardboard. Paint peeled, walls cracked. A man was watching them, his beard and his dog as ragged as his clothes.

Oh God, what had she done?

The moment the bricks hit the window, she'd had only one thought. To get Katya out of there. *Out. Away. Safe.*

Her hands had seized the wheelchair with her sister in it and had propelled her straight through the door into the restaurant kitchen, then out the back of the building into an untidy courtyard. From there her feet had started running. *Out. Away. Safe.* The words hurtled around in her head. She'd darted down streets she'd never seen before, as if she knew instinctively she would be safer here among the destitute and the forgotten than among her own kind, where bombs and bricks had become the tools of speech.

Katya's cheeks had turned white. She was freezing to death. The north wind had whipped up from the gulf, and neither of them was wearing a coat or gloves or even a scarf. Everything had been abandoned at La Gavotte. She could almost see blood congealing in Katya's veins. She was killing Katya. All over again. She headed straight for the nearest door. It was split down the middle and patched with strips of rough planking, but she banged on it hard. After a long wait it was opened by a child, no higher than her hip.

"May we come in? Please. *Pozhalusta*. We're cold."

The boy didn't react. His face was crusted with scabs, and one filthy finger picked at a ripe spot on his chin.

*"Pozhalusta,"* she said again. "Is your mother here?"

He stepped back and she thought he would swing open the door for the wheelchair to enter, but instead he pushed it shut. She banged the wood so hard that the crack widened.

"Open the door," she shouted. *"Otkroite dver."*

The door eased back just enough for one blue eye to peer up at her. "What do you want?" a girl's voice asked.

"My sister is freezing to death out here. Please let us in."

But she'd learned her lesson and didn't stop there. This time she accompanied her request with a push against the door that took the child by surprise, so that she stumbled backward. Before she could recover, Valentina had the wheelchair and herself inside the dim hallway and the door firmly shut behind them. The musty reek of rat droppings loitered on the stairs.

"Thank you," she said. *"Spasibo."*

In front of her huddled three filthy urchins, two identical boys and a girl with dirty blond hair. The twin boys were nervous, their clothes torn and misshapen, trousers not meeting their ankles. The girl, younger than her brothers, was staring at the wheelchair with wide-eyed curiosity.

"Is your mother in?" Valentina asked.

The girl pointed to a door without shifting her gaze from the spokes of Katya's chair. "Is it a bicycle?" she whispered.

One of the boys clipped her lightly around the ear. "Don't be stupid, Liuba. It's for cripples."

Valentina opened the door the girl had indicated and pushed the chair into a small room that was only fractionally warmer than the air outside. A stained sheet was draped over a section of the window in an attempt to keep out the cold, turning the air gray and streaky. It smelled of damp plaster and unwashed bodies.

"I'm sorry to intrude."

A woman was breast-feeding an infant on the end of a narrow bed. Her body was as scrawny as an old woman's, but her eyes were still bright and young. She was wearing fingerless mittens, a brown scarf knotted around her head. She fastened the front of her dress.

"What do you want?" Her voice was tired.

"My sister and I need help. Please . . ." Valentina hated to ask for something from this woman who so clearly had nothing to give. "My sister is cold. She needs warmth. Some hot food."

"My children need hot food," the woman said sullenly, "but they don't get any."

Valentina took Katya's cold hand in hers and massaged it vigorously. The woman immediately placed the infant on the bed and went over to the small black stove in the corner. She opened its metal door, a tiny wisp of flame within it, barely alive. No wonder it was so cold. Using tongs, the woman removed a heavy stone that lay inside the stove, wrapped it up in a blackened piece of toweling that lay ready for the purpose, and placed it on Katya's lap. Katya's hands burrowed under it.

"Can't you put more wood on the fire?" Valentina suggested.

"No."

"I have money."

The three children edged closer. The girl held out a grubby palm. "We can buy firewood."

Valentina had to trust them. She pulled two white ten-rouble notes from the purse in her pocket, even though she knew it was far too much for firewood. "Bring some food too. Hurry! *Potoropites!*"

All three children vanished.

"Here, take this." The woman held out the blanket from the bed. Valentina looked at it. Probably riddled with lice.

"*Spasibo.*" She wrapped it around her sister's shoulders and tucked it around her limp legs, aware of the woman's watchful scrutiny as she did so, and for the first time in her life it occurred to her to wonder how much the wheelchair was worth. As much as this woman's family earned in a month? In a year? She had no idea. This wretched, damp place was smaller than Valentina's bedroom at home. Part of the ceiling was hanging down and black mold was crawling up one wall. "Thank you for helping us," she said, genuinely grateful. "There was an attack by strikers on the restaurant we were in, and my sister and I escaped, but without our coats."

The woman nodded her head at Katya. "Is she sick?"

"She was in an accident."

The baby on the bed started to whimper and the woman said, "Pick her up."

Valentina looked at the squirming bundle.

"Pick her up." The woman's voice was sharper this time.

"What?"

"You want my help. In exchange I want yours. A moment's peace from the child." She smiled, and there was a flash of youth in it. "Don't worry, I won't steal your sister's chair."

A flush burned its way up Valentina's cheeks as she picked up the baby. It had almost no hair and little twigs for legs.

"Valentina." It was Katya's faint voice. "Let me hold her."

Valentina brought the child close to the wheelchair but didn't hand it over. "It is dirty," she muttered. "You don't want . . ." But she saw the needy look in Katya's eyes. She deposited the child on her sister's lap and was appalled when she leaned down and kissed the bony little head. A smile spread across Katya's face. Wherever she had been, she was coming back.

❧

THE AROMA OF HOT *PIROZHKI* CHANGED EVERYTHING. THE three children seemed to swell out into their skin before they'd even been given one of the meat pies from the greaseproof paper package. They sat on the floor, in front of the blazing logs in the stove, and watched the fire with the kind of fascination that Valentina would give to a performance of the ballet.

"Shouldn't they wash their hands?" Valentina suggested as she placed a pie on each palm. The dirt on their fingers was blacker than the floor.

"The water pump is frozen." The woman shrugged and took a large bite out of a slice of bread spread with black currant conserve. As she chewed on it, Valentina watched the features of her face melt with pleasure and grow astonishingly younger.

"What's your name?" she asked.

"Varenka Sidorova."

"I'm Valentina. My sister's name is Katya."

Katya was sipping hot tea and honey from a tin mug, and there was color in her cheeks now. The infant lay like a kitten on her lap.

"Varenka, what does your husband do?"

The woman's eyes grew cautious. "He works in a factory."

"Is he a Bolshevik?"

She saw the tightening of the skin under the woman's eyes. "What do you know of Bolsheviks?"

"Was he in the march today?"

Varenka started to laugh. The children looked around at her, astonished, as though unused to the sound, but the laughter didn't stop. It went on and on, rolling from her open mouth. Veins in her neck stood out and tears slid down her cheeks, but still the laughter filled the air. She dropped to her knees, and then the laughter stopped as abruptly as it had begun. She yanked off the headscarf, releasing a crop of chestnut curls. Valentina stared. Katya gave a small smothered gasp. One side of the woman's head was hairless, and a wide white scar, glistening as though wet, ran from her temple right across her skull to the back of her head. She regarded the sisters with a mixture of pity and hatred.

"Five years ago in front of the Winter Palace gates," she said in a hard voice, "your soldiers came at me with their sabers when we marched to speak to the tsar. We intended no harm but they mowed us down. Yet I survived. And because of that, you survive today. Because of my help, you survive. But do you deserve to?"

Valentina lifted the baby from Katya's lap and laid it on the bed. "I think it's time we left."

"You!" Still on her knees, the woman was pointing at Valentina. "I promise you that one day soon we will come for you and your kind, and this time you will not survive. You idle rich. You parasites." She spat on the floor. "The workers will demand justice."

Valentina took out her purse and upended it on the table. Roubles clattered everywhere, and the children scurried around like mice, gathering them up. "Take this because you helped me today. I am grateful." She walked over to the kneeling woman and let her fingers touch the shiny scar on her head. Not wet, but smooth and slippery, as colorless as something that lived underground. "I'm sorry, Varenka."

"I don't want your pity."

"Valentina." It was Katya. "She wants us gone."

"Yes, you're right. Before my man gets back." Varenka glared defiantly at Valentina. "My Bolshevik."

A loud bang on the front door startled them. Before they could react it came twice more, like a hammer blow, and they heard the wood splinter. The woman scooped up the baby and clutched it to her breast so hard it started to whimper. Valentina's heart pounded. "Wait here, Katya," she said.

"No, Valentina, don't . . ."

The hammering on the door came again. Without hesitation Valentina opened the door into the dismal hallway and unlocked the shattered front door onto the street. A massive figure blocked out the light.

"What the fuck are you doing in this shit hole, Valentina Ivanova?"

It was Liev Popkov.

# Six

A RKIN WAS A MECHANIC, BUT IN HIS HEART HE REGARDED himself as a skilled surgeon of machines. He took good care of his hands and read constantly about the latest inventions, expanding his knowledge. Thank the Lord he could read. Not that the Lord had anything to do with it. Most peasants couldn't read or write, but his mother was the exception and used to rap his knuckles with her knitting needle to jog his sluggish brain into action.

"Viktor," she used to say when he was at her knee struggling with a jumble of letters, trying to cram them into the shape of words, "a man who can read is a man who can rule the world."

"But I don't want to rule the world."

"Not now. But one day you will. Then you will thank me."

H E SMILED TO HIMSELF AT THE MEMORY. "SPASIBO, THANK you," he murmured. Now he was twenty-three, and he did want to rule the world. His mother had been right.

"Arkin."

He lifted his head. He was crouched on the concrete floor of the garage, rinsing the oil and horse dung off the spokes of the Turicum's wheels, leaving their blue paint gleaming. His cloth splashed grimy suds onto his boots.

"What is it, Popkov?"

The Cossack had entered the garage on silent feet. For a big man he moved noiselessly. Like the wolves in the forest back home.

"What?" Arkin asked again.

"The mistress wants to speak to you in the house."

"About this afternoon?"

"How do I know?"

Living on a farm in the middle of the godforsaken steppes teaches a man patience. In the countryside life is never in a hurry, the rhythms are slow, and Arkin knew well how to wait. He had left his village six years ago when he was seventeen, determined to live and work in St. Petersburg. Here he could feel the heart of Russia beating. Here the ideas of great men like Karl Marx and Lenin grew and spread underground like the roots of a tree. In this city, he was convinced, lay the future of Russia. He turned back to finish off the wheel before rinsing out the cloth and hanging it tidily on a hook. When he looked round, Liev Popkov was still there, as he'd known he would be. The big man was a law unto himself in too many ways for Arkin's liking.

"What the hell were you doing?" Popkov demanded.

Arkin removed his long brown apron and hung it on another hook. "Doing? I was protecting them."

"Letting them run loose? Is that your idea of protecting them?"

"They're not children, Popkov. They're young women. They make their own decisions, right or wrong."

"This city is dangerous."

"Dangerous for them? Or for the workers who die in the factories every day?"

"You're a fool," Popkov snorted.

"No," Arkin said patiently. "I'm just doing my job."

༄

I T WAS THE FIRST TIME ARKIN HAD SET FOOT IN THE HOUSE beyond the servants' kitchen, and it was hard not to stare. Why would anyone want so many things? Pictures taller than himself hanging on the walls. Rubies festooned like drops of blood around a mirror and strips of gold around the plinth of each statue. A footman ushered him into a small sitting room. It struck Arkin as the most feminine room he had ever stood in, all lilacs and creams. Flowers scented the air with exotic fragrances that were new to him.

Elizaveta Ivanova was sitting very upright on an elegant chair, a glass of hot water in one hand. Her lavender gown made her look like one of the flowers herself. He bowed, with his hands at his sides, and waited for her to speak. She took her time. A full minute ticked past.

"Arkin," she said at last, "explain yourself."

"Certainly, madam. I drove the two young ladies to take tea at Gordino's, but we were prevented from approaching it by a crowd of strikers marching up Morskaya."

"Go on."

"We were caught in a line of blocked traffic, but I managed to maneuver out of it and take the young ladies to a different establishment of their choice."

"You should have brought them straight home. The streets were dangerous."

"I did suggest it, madam. But both young ladies were against the idea; they declined to return home."

"Now why doesn't that surprise me?" The words escaped from her, startling them both. "What I don't understand is where were you when they left the tearoom? You have a responsibility, Arkin, when you chauffeur for this family. I thought that was explained to you when . . ." She stopped, holding the glass of water near her mouth but not actually touching it. "They are headstrong," she murmured.

He gave her a faint smile. "You know your daughters, madam."

"Well enough."

"I deeply regret that the marchers forced me to park the Turicum in a side street and when I returned on foot to the tearoom, the place was in a state of panic. Miss Valentina and Miss Katya had gone."

"Did you search for them?"

"Of course, madam."

Did he search? Did he shout their names? Did he race like a fool from street to street and shop to shop? Did he seize people by their lapels and demand whether they had seen a wheelchair? Yes, he ran until his lungs hurt and cursed those young girls till his tongue burned, but still he didn't find them.

Elizaveta Ivanova nodded. "Of course you did. I can see you are a reliable young man."

"I'm sorry, madam. I apologize for giving you cause for concern."

"How did you find them in the end?"

"I came back here and gathered a team of men to search more thoroughly."

She remained silent, forcing him to voice more than he wanted.

"Liev Popkov found them," he admitted with reluctance. "He traced the tracks of the wheelchair in the snow."

Like a bloodhound, the Cossack had been. Scouring the pavement, his face inches from the ground, finding the faintest of treads from a tire even when the surface had been trampled on.

She let the conversation cease. Sipped her water, her throat contracting above the creamy pearl necklace. "Katya is unwell," she said after a silence.

"I'm sorry."

"It wasn't your fault."

The fairness of her comment astounded him. Most employers liked to blame servants for everything. He waited, but no more words followed.

"Would you like to speak to Popkov himself about it?" he asked.

She gave the smallest of shudders. "No," she said. "I wouldn't."

❦

IT WAS THREE O'CLOCK IN THE MORNING. VALENTINA HAD been sitting in the dark for two hours. When she heard Nurse Sonya's heavy tread finally leaving Katya's room, she waited a few minutes, then slipped out into the corridor. Her bare feet were soundless and she turned the doorknob to the sickroom with no more than a faint click. A fire crackled in the grate behind a mesh guard and on the bed a bulky quilt had been pushed aside, so that it lay humped like a range of mountains. The slight figure of her sister lay immobile under a sheet, though her head tossed restlessly on the pillows as if it belonged to someone else.

"Katya," Valentina whispered.

Instantly the blond head lifted off the pillows. "Valentina?"

"How are you?"

"Bored."

Valentina knelt on the end of the bed. "You know what gave you the fever, don't you?"

"What?"

"That kiss on the filthy baby's head."

"It was worth it," Katya smiled.

"You didn't tell Mama or Nurse about it, did you?"

"Of course not. I'm not stupid."

"Think of it as an adventure. But one we won't be repeating. I overreacted, I'm sorry."

"Don't say that. Don't say you won't take me on any more adventures."

"If you really want adventures, Katya, you must get better. I'll give them to you," she promised, "only not quite as dangerous as that one."

"An adventure isn't an adventure if it isn't dangerous. I wouldn't have missed it for the world." She pushed her damp hair from her eyes. "Tell me what the woman's scar felt like when you touched it."

"Like warm glass. Hard and slippery."

"I felt sorry for her."

"I didn't."

"I don't believe you."

"It's true, Katya. I hate them. I don't care whether they call themselves Mensheviks, Bolsheviks, or Social Revolutionaries, they're all the same to me. I hate them because of what they did to you." She moved forward and kissed her sister's hot cheek.

Katya lifted her hand and tenderly stroked her sister's dark hair. "It'll go eventually, the hatred," she said with confidence.

"Did yours?" *Your hatred of what they did to you? Of what I did to you?*

"Yes."

Valentina didn't tell Katya it was too late. That the hatred had already burned its way down into her bones.

❧

SHE KNOCKED ON THE DOOR OF HER FATHER'S STUDY. IT was time to tell him of her decision.

"Come in. *Vkhodite.*"

She pushed open the door. Her father was seated at his broad leather-topped desk and raised his head from the papers he was studying.

"You asked to see me?" he said. He didn't look pleased about the interruption.

"Yes."

He folded his arms. An unlit cigar flicked impatiently between two fingers. He was still a good-looking man, though a little heavy now from too many banquets at the Winter Palace, but she remembered him lean and fit when he served as a general in the Russian army. He wore his hair swept back from his face, with thick eyebrows over shrewd deep-set eyes. Dark as her own. They assessed her now.

"Sit down," he said.

She sat on the chair in front of the desk and tucked her hands neatly in her lap. "Papa, I wish to apologize for taking Katya down to the Rzhevka district yesterday. I was trying to keep her safe from the strikers who—"

"I accept your apology." He brushed a hand over his dark whiskers, as though he could brush away his thoughts. "What you did," he said, "was foolish, but I realize you were trying to protect your sister."

She had expected worse.

"Is that all?" he asked. "I am busy."

"No," she said. "That's not all."

He placed his cigar in an ashtray, then lined it up precisely beside a pen and a red pencil in front of him. His eyes lingered on the cigar as if he preferred to smoke it in peace. Her father had an orderly mind, which was why he worked where he did. Valentina didn't know exactly what he did as a government minister, but she knew it had something to do with finance. She used to imagine him in his office at the Chancellery counting the tsar's money, tall stacks of roubles right up to the ceiling.

Finally he grew tired of her silence and glanced up.

"What else?" he asked with a touch of impatience. "I have work to do."

"Papa, I don't want to return to school when the new term starts."

He stared at her, surprised. No hint of the anger she had expected.

Then he smiled.

"I hope you approve, Papa," she added quickly.

"I do indeed. Your mother and I have discussed the situation and we are convinced that schooling can do nothing more for you. It's time to think about your future."

It was only tiny, that first prickle of unease. She gave it no thought.

"I agree, Papa. I'm so pleased you think so too. That's what I've been planning. I have an idea."

He sat back in his chair and picked up the cigar on his desk with pleasure. He dispensed with its band, clipped one end, and smelled its fragrant leaves before taking his time lighting it. She had the feeling he was already celebrating something.

"So, Valentina," he said, "for once we agree. You are a good daughter now."

Now. Even so. It was a first step.

She tried to hold the moment, to not let it trickle through her fingers. "This idea of yours, have you discussed it with your mother?"

"Not yet, Papa. I wanted to discuss it with you first."

"Foolish girl." He smiled and exhaled a twisting string of smoke in her direction. "What do I care for dresses?"

"Dresses?"

"Yes, the dresses you have an idea about. You must discuss them with your mother. Mothers are the ones who deal with such matters."

She inhaled quickly. Tasted the smoke. "Papa, I didn't mention dresses."

"Well, don't worry, I'm certain your mother will want to talk about them." He nodded indulgently. "I know what ladies are like when it comes to gowns."

He rose from his seat and marched across the room, his body thick-waisted inside his frock coat. He was making a lot of noise, his sleeves rustling, his feet striding over the polished boards, his fingers tapping his shirt front. She knew these signs, recognized them as indications that he was exceedingly pleased. What was happening here? This conversation was not going right.

"I won't need more than a few dresses," she pointed out warily.

"No, my dear. If you're to make a catch you'll need at least thirty or forty gowns, I imagine. But I leave all that to your mother. The important thing is that the decision is made and we have already compiled a list of names for you to consider."

"Papa, what do you mean, *make a catch*?"

He looked at his elder daughter fondly. "Find a husband, of course."

"A husband?" Her hands fell off her lap.

"Yes, of course. Isn't that what we're talking about? Leaving school and finding a husband." He drew on his cigar with obvious pleasure, paced the room, and flicked away stray strands of tobacco from his shirt front. "You'll soon be eighteen, Valentina. Time to behave responsibly. Find a suitable husband this season and get married. Plenty of fine strong officers out there from good families."

"I am not getting married, Papa."

"Let's have no foolishness, Valentina. What are you going on about now?"

"I am not getting married."

"You just said you were ready to set about planning your future."

"Yes, but not as a wife."

"What else is there for you, my dear girl? Your mother and I . . ." He stopped, as if struck by an unwelcome thought. In the middle of the room he seemed to swell inside his clothes, and the veins on his cheeks filled with blood. "What is this idea you have for your own future?"

She stood up to face him. "Papa, that's what I've come to tell you. I want to train to become a professional nurse."

❧

THEY SAT HER DOWN. NOT IN THE STUDY. NOT IN THE drawing room, where serious discussions usually took place. Her parents sat her down in the music room, the room she had poured her hopes into for so many years. They sat her on the piano stool with its tasseled seat that she had frayed and picked at when the music wouldn't come right. Her mother took a seat on the chair by the window. Though her face was under the usual control, her fingers held a handkerchief screwed into a tight ball in one hand. Her mother's silence was almost worse than her father's outburst.

"Valentina," General Ivanov said, "you must rid your head of this unpleasant notion at once. It astonishes me that you give such an idea even a moment's serious thought. Look at the education you've received, the music lessons. Think about all that it cost us."

He was striding back and forth in front of her, the edge of his frock coat flapping with agitation. She wanted to put out a hand to quiet it. To quiet him.

"Please try to understand, Papa. I can speak four languages and I can play the piano and I can walk well. What does that fit me for?"

"It fits you for marriage. That's what all young ladies are groomed for."

"I'm sorry, Papa, I told you. I don't wish to marry."

Her mother's intake of breath was too much. Valentina turned to face the piano, her back to them, and lifted the lid. Her fingers found a soft chord and then stretched to another, and as always the sound of the notes calmed her. The trembling in her chest grew less. She played a snatch of the Chopin piece and saw a flash of the flame-haired Viking lounging in the corner of her mind. Behind her all movement had ceased, and she imagined her parents exchanging glances.

"You play well, Valentina."

"Thank you, Mama."

"Any husband would be proud to have you entertain his guests after dinner with a piece by Beethoven or Tchaikovsky."

Valentina clamped her fingers together to keep them off the keys. "I want to be a nurse." She spoke quietly. Patiently. "I want to look after Katya. Nurse Sonya won't be with us forever."

A sigh drifted across the room, and suddenly her father's tall dark figure was standing right behind her. His hand stroked her hair and settled on her shoulder. She didn't move. He hadn't touched her in the six months since the bomb at Tesovo, and she feared that if she so much as shifted a muscle, he would retreat and not touch her for another six.

"Valentina, listen to me, my dear child. You know I want the best for you. Nursing is a miserable occupation, full of whores and alcoholics. It is not suitable work for a respectable young lady."

"Listen to your father," her mother urged gently.

"They have lice. They have . . . diseases." It was clear from the way he spoke that he didn't mean just smallpox or typhoid.

"But Nurse Sonya isn't a whore or an alcoholic," Valentina pointed out. "She doesn't have a disease. She's a respectable woman."

His hand tightened its grip on her shoulder, and she sensed it wanting to tighten its grip on her mind. "There is another way," he said, "for you to help Katya. A better way to make it up to her."

"How?"

"It's not difficult."

"What is it, Papa? What can I do?"

"Marry well."

She swung back to the piano, disappointment catching at her throat. She didn't want to cross her father.

"You heard me, Valentina." The general's voice was beginning to rise. "Damn it, girl, you must marry well. You must marry now. I insist on it. For the good of the Ivanov name."

# Seven

"EXPLOITATION! DEPRIVATION! STARVATION!"

Mikhail Sergeyev was good. He knew how to work a crowd, how to spark the emotions in men and put fire in their empty bellies. Arkin assessed tonight's crowd with satisfaction. Most were peasants like himself, simple workmen who had flocked from the rural provinces to find employment in the factories of St. Petersburg. Most couldn't read. Few could even write their name. Oddly, that fact saddened Arkin even more than the terrible conditions under which they worked in the factories or in the mills. The knowledge that the minds of the masses were being deliberately stunted by depriving them of education was to him the harshest injustice of all. It was why he believed in Leon Trotsky's theory of permanent revolution. He had gone with Sergeyev to hear Trotsky address a meeting, and they had both been so enthralled by this man of vision with his bush of unruly hair and forever-glinting spectacles that they had walked the streets all night, unable to rest. He had shown them a new world. One in which justice and equality weren't just empty words but were the living, breathing heart of every man's life. From that moment on, they had started to recruit others to the socialist cause.

"Men of Russia"—Sergeyev was passionate in his urging—"we have to fight for our rights ourselves. The iron fist of tsarism

must"—he paused and gazed around the room at his audience—
*"must* be overthrown."

There were shouts of approval.

"They gave us the Duma to shut us up." Sergeyev said the words
mockingly. "Yet Prime Minister Stolypin treats it with scorn. Instead
he puts Stolypin neckties, the hangman's noose, on all who dissent."
Sergeyev yanked up his own tie as if he were being throttled by a
rope, and the crowd roared. Arkin added his voice to theirs.

"Does Stolypin care that there is no bread on the table for your
children?"

"No! *Nyet!* No!"

"Does Stolypin care that you are made to work in conditions that
even a dog would bite off his leg to escape?"

"No! No!"

"Does Stolypin care that—"

"Comrade Sergeyev!" The shout came from a whippet of a man
who was on his feet, a cigarette dangling from the corner of his
mouth.

"Sit down!" a voice yelled.

Sergeyev held out a hand to demand silence. "Speak, comrade.
All have the right to be heard."

"Comrades," the man said, raising his voice, "this talk will lead
us nowhere. We cannot fight the enemy, we must make treaty with
it. The Duma was only a first step. All the time we are working
and arguing for more concessions. Alexander Guchkov, leader of the
Octobrists in the Duma, is working hard to obtain agreement for
better conditions in the mines of—"

"Alexander Guchkov," Sergeyev thundered, "is nothing more
than an instrument of tyranny."

This delighted the crowd. "*Da!* Yes!"

Sergeyev drew himself up to his full height. "The *only* answer is
the seizure of power by the workers. Strength to the unions."

Thunderous applause. Voices clamoring. Hands pushing and
pulling at the intruder in their midst until he swore they would all
be wearing Stolypin's neckties before long and stalked out of the hall
in defeat.

"Power to the workers!" Sergeyev bellowed.

Against the wall, Arkin lit himself a cigarette and nodded. *A
dictatorship of the proletariat,* Leon Trotsky had called it. It would be a

bitter and bloody battle, but it was coming. The only question was when.

❦

THE PRIEST WAS CLEVER. THERE WAS NO QUESTION OF THAT. Father Morozov understood people. He tempted the gnawing bellies into the church hall with a cauldron of hot stew. No meat, of course, just vegetables, but they were pathetically grateful all the same, and it fed more than just their bodies, it fed their anger. That they were reduced to this. It enraged the sense of injustice in them, even before they were funneled into the hall for Sergeyev's speeches. The only trouble with Father Morozov was that he believed in God and in God's love for all mankind, however miserable an example of the human race a person might be. That got in the way sometimes.

The priest was standing like a crow behind his cauldron of steaming stew, ladling it out into enamel mugs, listening to the men's woes, offering a word of advice or a shred of comfort. He never tired. He never changed from the tall patient figure in homespun black with a slight stoop and a thick beard. He was probably no more than forty but he looked much older; his hair had already lost its color. Maybe it was the result of all those years of hearing other people's pain, or maybe it was the loss of his wife.

Arkin stood beside Father Morozov, waiting for a brief gap in the hungry flow of mugs.

"Father, we have the equipment."

"Here?"

"Downstairs. Come down when you've finished."

The priest nodded and smiled fondly at the next man in the queue. Arkin admired his coolness. No one would know he dealt in death.

❦

BOMB MAKING WAS A DELICATE BUSINESS. FATHER MOROzov was the brains, the one with the plans. Mikhail Sergeyev was the provider who acquired the necessary equipment, no questions asked. And Arkin himself supplied the hands. None of the others liked to touch explosives.

The three men worked well together, but today Arkin noticed that his comrade Sergeyev was restless. He was constantly up and down from the table where Arkin was working, irritating him, until Arkin put down the pliers in his hand. The basement room was so cold that their breath curled like smoke each time they spoke, and Arkin worried that the gelignite might congeal if the temperature fell too low. He looked at Sergeyev. His jacket was filthy and full of holes, his scarf so greasy and wound around his neck so many times it looked like a thick serpent that had fallen asleep.

"What is it, comrade?" Arkin asked. "You gave a good speech today. You should be pleased."

Sergeyev fiddled with the cigarette packet in his hands, the *makhorka* tobacco smelling cheap and unpleasant in the enclosed space. Arkin had forbidden him to smoke anywhere near the detonating caps. Two of the caps lay on the table in front of him, and his eyes were drawn to them even as he spoke to Sergeyev. Long thin copper capsules containing a small quantity of mercury fulminate. Highly explosive. Arkin always handled them with respect but liked to lay one across his palm, as harmless looking as Sergeyev's cigarette. So much power in his hand, it made his heart beat faster.

He had been surprised by how simple it was to learn about explosives. In St. Petersburg's library he'd studied Alfred Nobel's ingenious invention, so that he understood better the five rough shaped sticks of gray gelignite clumped together on the table in front of him. Gelignite was an explosive compound of nitroglycerine and nitrocellulose mixed with nitrate of potash and wood meal. Twelve percent more powerful than dynamite. *Dermo!* That was a lot of power. And the compound was unaffected by damp and free from noxious fumes when it was detonated. He wrapped his hand around one of the sticks, felt its cold slick surface on his skin. Mr. Alfred Nobel, he thought, was a man of exceptional character. Who else could inflict so much destruction on the world and still sleep easy in his grave?

"Arkin," Sergeyev said, "I'm sorry, but I must leave now."

Arkin raised an eyebrow. "What's the matter? Not nervous, are you?"

"No. It's my wife. She's due to have our baby soon but is still working in the glue factory. It makes her sick."

"Ah, family."

"Don't say it like that."

Arkin smiled. "Sergeyev, the day will come when families will be a thing of the past." He glanced at the priest. "Religion too. The opiate of the masses, as Karl Marx pointed out. The only priority will be the state. If you have the perfect state system, you will have a contented population. The state *must* come before the family. It will *be* our family."

"I agree with you, of course," Sergeyev said, and shrugged awkwardly. "But not tonight." He stood up and headed for the door. "Don't blow yourselves up," he laughed and left quickly before the others could object.

Arkin and Father Morozov turned back to the table.

"He's a good man," Morozov said.

"He's a rousing speaker and he's committed to the cause," Arkin agreed as he inserted one end of the safety fuse into the open end of the detonating cap. With pliers he crimped the edges carefully around it. Squeeze it too tight and it could explode. "But he has no stomach for killing."

"And you?" the priest asked.

"I'll do whatever I have to."

"Even working for a family you despise? For Minister Ivanov."

"Yes, Father, I work for that parasite and yes, I spy on him. Like you, I do whatever our cause requires of me. Ivanov has thirty servants to pamper just four indolent people. If all the servants throughout Petersburg were released to work at something that was of use, what a different city we would have."

"Have you suggested this to the Ivanovs?" Morozov asked mildly.

The irony amused Arkin. He laughed and wound a strip of wire around the sticks of gelignite with the two detonators clutched in their midst. He measured out the fuse. It consisted of a length of cotton fiber wrapped around a core of fine gunpowder, the whole thing coated in white varnish to protect it from damp. This one was a slow burner, two feet per minute. It gave time for escape. He cut a length of four feet.

His pulse was steady, and that pleased him. Father Morozov said a prayer over the bomb and drew the sign of the cross above it. He always did that.

Before they killed.

❧

JENS PLUNGED DEEPER INTO THE DARKNESS. THE NOISES inside the tunnel were drilling into his head, but still he liked to come down here regularly. He needed to climb down into the sewers to ensure that the work was progressing fast enough, to check for himself that the overseers were keeping the men digging along the lines he had laid down.

The air grew thicker and he had to bend double beneath the low roof. Water dripped onto his shoulders. In his hand a powerful flashlight threw a circle of light onto the curved walls so that he could inspect the brickwork with careful attention, and every few paces he reached out to touch it. His eyes were not enough, he needed his fingers too. A rumble came from up ahead. Under his feet ran the rail for the wheels of the trucks that disposed of the excavated rock and soil, and he felt a vibration skipping through them.

"Truck rolling," he called out.

The three men behind him jumped to the side of the tunnel wall and stood with their backs pressed flat against it. The noise of the truck was deafening as it passed, stacked high with rubble. The two pushers straining to keep it moving were clothed in anonymous overalls and cloth headgear against the ever-present dripping water, faces black with grime. They could have been men, but they weren't. They were women. The men did the digging.

"Line free," he called out.

But he'd spotted a shudder in the movement of the truck. He walked over, kicked at a rail, and felt it shift. He turned to the man behind him. "Get this tightened. I don't want any accidents."

He was sick of the accidents, sick to his stomach. It was the darkness. Workers didn't see things. The shifts were too long, the tools too blunt, the wages too low.

And he was the one they blamed.

❧

BLOOD MADE EVERYTHING SLIPPERY. JENS HELD THE MAN down in the chair with brute force. He blocked out the screams and ignored the curses. He kept one arm locked across the man's chest, pinning him from behind to the seat, the other fist gripping his elbow tight, immobilizing it. The man arched his body in pain and jerked his head back, cracking it against Jens's jaw.

"Hold him," Dr. Fedorin urged.

With one final wrench, which brought forth another gut-churning groan, Fedorin straightened up. His hands were scarlet. Sweat had painted a sheen on his skin and there was a slash of blood across his brow where he'd brushed his hand.

"It's the best I can do, Sergeyev."

Through glazed eyes the man stared down at his shattered right forearm and uttered a moan. The bones were still visible through the mat of blood, but there were no longer jagged edges spiking in all directions. Jens felt Sergeyev's chest start to shake. He released his grip on it.

He rested a hand on the tunnel digger's trembling shoulder. "The doctor has done a fine job."

A fine job? How dare he call such a mangled mess *a fine job*? He knew Fedorin had done all he could, but what in God's name would this man live off now?

"Give him more morphine," Jens said.

"What good is morphine to me?" Sergeyev groaned. "I can't work." Nevertheless he accepted several drops on a spoon when it was offered.

"It'll mend," Dr. Fedorin assured him. "It may not be as straight or strong as it was before, but it'll mend. You're young enough for it to heal fast."

He bathed the damaged limb with boiled water and iodine, then proceeded to stitch the wounds while Jens kept up pressure just inside the man's elbow to reduce the blood loss. When fresh lint, bandages, and splints were all in place and Sergeyev's arm fixed in a sling, Jens drew a bottle of brandy from the drawer of the table that made do as his makeshift desk. He poured three slugs into tin mugs.

"Here. Get this down you."

He thrust one into the good hand of Sergeyev and gave one to the doctor. Dr. Fedorin knocked back half the drink in one swallow and began to scrub his hands in the rest of it over a bowl, shirt sleeves rolled up to his elbows. They were in the wooden hut that served as Jens's office at the entrance to one of the tunnels, but he knew these accidents shouldn't be happening. Somewhere somebody was cutting corners. He poured the digger another brandy and, now that the worst was over, the man's gray pallor started to fade.

"*Spasibo*, *Direktor* Friis." He raised his mug to Jens and Fedorin. "*Spasibo*."

"Sergeyev, here is money for a *drozhky* ride home." Jens handed over a fistful of notes from a drawer. "Take it and feed your family."

The man set down the mug and took the money. His fingers gripped it hard, smearing blood on the notes, but it was an uneasy moment. Jens laid his hand again on the man's shoulder. "You are a good worker, Sergeyev. I'll need you back here when your arm is mended."

The digger studied the roubles in his hand. "You'll keep my job open for me?"

"Yes, I will."

"The foreman won't like that."

"The foreman will do as I say."

The man gave a half-smile. "*Da*. Of course he will."

Jens again felt that uneasiness seep into the hut. "Go home," he said. "Go home and get better."

"It will need a clean dressing," Dr. Fedorin pointed out.

Sergeyev still stared at the money. "I can't pay you, *Doktor*."

Fedorin glanced at Jens. "Your *Direktor* is good enough to cover the costs."

At last the man looked up at Jens. "*Direktor*, tell me, do you intend to pay personally for every man who needs a doctor here in the tunnel? To hold the job open for every digger who is injured? Every factory worker in Petersburg? Even for men like me who will now have a crippled arm?"

Jens took a grip on the man's good arm and hoisted him up out of the chair. "Get out of here, Sergeyev. Go home to your wife."

Clutching his right arm with his left, Sergeyev headed for the door.

"What I do in these tunnels," Jens said sharply, "is my business."

Sergeyev turned abruptly and his eyes fixed first on Jens, then on Fedorin. "Not for much longer," he said softly.

❧

H E COULD HAVE BEEN MORE GRATEFUL, THE BASTARD," the doctor said.

"He was humiliated. He wanted to throw the money back in my teeth. It's work in decent conditions that he wants, not charity."

"Jens, my good friend, sometimes I think you do not even now understand the Russian soul. Your Danish mind is too rational. The Russian soul is not."

Jens smiled at him and raised his glass. "*Za zdorovye!* Good health! To the Russian soul and the Russian mind. May they triumph over the enemies of progress."

"Which are?"

"Complacency and corruption. Stupidity and greed."

"Hah!" Fedorin slapped Jens on the back. "I like that."

"The trouble is that no one is warmer hearted than a Russian, yet no one is crueler. There is no middle path in Russia; it is all or nothing. Look at Tsar Nicholas. He believes he was put on this earth by God himself to rule Russia and is even convinced that God sends him omens to guide him. He has spoken of them to me."

"Don't depress me, my friend."

"He chases after spiritual guides such as Monsieur Philippe of Lyons and St. Serafim of Sarov. And that foul monk, Grigori Rasputin. The tsarina is besotted by him."

"I'm told she believes the illness of her son, Tsarevitch Alexei, is a curse from God and they try to keep it secret."

"How bad is it, this illness?" Jens asked.

Fedorin poured himself another shot of brandy. "The tsar's son is a bleeder. That's why they hide him away at Tsarskoe Selo."

Jens did not let the shock show on his face. "A hemophiliac?"

*"Da."*

"They don't live long, do they?"

"Not usually, no."

"God help Russia."

Fedorin knocked back his brandy. "God help all of us, my friend."

He shook hands and left Jens's office. Jens poured his own brandy over his desk and scrubbed the blood off the wood with it. Whatever Dr. Fedorin said, Jens felt a kinship with the Russian soul, with its black aching moods of despair. He'd come here when only eighteen years old to escape servitude in his father's printing business and had studied engineering in St. Petersburg instead. During the nine years he'd been here, he'd learned to love Russia with a passion. He wasn't ready to see it brought to its knees by greed.

❧

EXPLAIN IT TO ME, WILL YOU, FRIIS?" MINISTER DAVIDOV instructed.

The map of the city was spread out before the group of six men. Jens lit a cigarette and narrowed his eyes through the smoke, taking in the tension in the faces around the table. Andrei Davidov was a man whose voice rarely rose above a murmur. At times people forgot to silence their own tongues and listen to his, but Jens knew such people were fools.

"Minister." Jens leaned forward and picked up a tapered ivory pointer from the table. "Let me show you." He traced the tip of it along one of the lines that zigzagged across the map. "See this blue line; this depicts the sewer tunnels completed. Notice how they cluster around the central area and the palaces."

Davidov nodded. His eyes were hooded but watched the pointer intently.

"This one"—Jens indicated a series of green lines—"represents those under construction."

The minister drew his craggy eyebrows together and flicked the cover of his watch open and shut with a sharp little snip. "Do we need so many?"

"Indeed we do, Minister. Petersburg is expanding every year; the population is increasing as more peasants pour in from the fields to work in our new factories. That is why this one"—he drew the pointer along a thick red line—"shows the planned tunnels that have not yet been started."

There was a heavy silence in the room while Davidov contemplated the map. It was broken only by a snort from Gosolev, who was in the habit of taking snuff. "I am thinking of the cost. Everything," Davidov said, "comes down to cost."

"We need a new water and sewage system in this city, Minister. Sickness and diarrhea are rife in Petersburg's workforce because of the lack of clean water for hygiene. How can we rid the city of its slums without sufficient sewers and water pipes?"

"The cost," the minister murmured once more. "Last year we had to strip funds from the Trans-Siberian Railway to find the million roubles for that damn statue of our emperor's father."

"Minister," Jens said in a voice no louder than Davidov's, "this was once marshland. It floods. We have to pump out the tunnels day and night while we construct them. There have been roof collapses because of"—he narrowed his eyes at Khrastsyn farther down the table—"because of lack of wooden supports and shortages of lamps."

"You shouldn't pamper the poor," Davidov cut in.

"How right you are, Minister," Khrastsyn agreed. "They work better when they are hungry."

Jens looked from one to the other and placed both hands down on the table, as if to crush their words. "The men work best," he pointed out, "when they are not afraid of dying every moment." He drew a deep breath. "The tsar has asked me to report personally to him on the progress this water scheme is making. It is something dear to his heart. Shall I tell him I am prevented from proceeding faster by you, Minister, and by you, Khrastsyn?"

Davidov raised one heavy eyebrow. "Is that true? That His Majesty asked you to report to him?"

"Yes," Jens lied.

"Khrastsyn," the minister ordered, "let us rethink those funds."

Jens lit himself another cigarette, surprised to see his hands so steady. He had just made two powerful enemies.

⌘

THE COUNTESS SMELLED OF ATTAR OF ROSES. SHE LAY stretched out on the bed.

"You are irritable today," Natalia Serova announced.

She took a handful of Jens's red hair between her fingers and twisted it gently, just enough to pull on his scalp. Sometimes he thought she would like to tear him into little pieces so that she could put each piece in her pocket and own him completely.

"I'm not irritable, Natalia. I am impatient."

"Impatient for what?"

"For the changes that must come."

"Oh, Jens, please don't start that again." She leaned down and kissed his brow. "For once in your life, silence that whirring Danish brain of yours."

"Davidov is trying to remove me," he said.

"Oh, for heaven's sake, Jens, can't you just do what the man asks?" She brought her hand down hard on his bare chest and pushed him away roughly. "You know that he has Stolypin on his side, don't you? Don't even think of going up against our prime minister." She rolled her eyes dramatically. "Because you will lose." She moved away across her huge bed and slumped among the pillows. "Please don't tell me you'd be that stupid."

He reached out and stroked her foot. "No," he said, "I'm not that stupid."

"Stolypin is a force of nature. He's a giant and storms over everyone."

"Including Tsar Nicholas himself, who is afraid of him. Just like he was afraid of his own father." Jens sat up. "I am sick of politics. Tell me, how is your son?"

"Alexei is well, thank you."

He had been having his affair with the countess for a full three months before he learned she had a son. She had once confessed to him that her husband, Count Serov, was not the boy's father but refused to tell him who was, except to admit she had a weakness for green-eyed suitors. It would explain why Count Serov paid the boy scant attention. Alexei was six now, and Jens enjoyed taking him riding.

"My niece, Maria, is coming to stay with me for Christmas," she told him as she ran a fingernail down his spine. "You might like to meet her again. Remember the concert?"

Jens recalled the concert with instant clarity. The unforgettable music. The mass of hair at the piano, the huge dark eyes. The anger in them directed straight at him.

# Eight

"NURSE SONYA, WHAT IS IT LIKE?"

"What is what like?"

"Being a nurse. Always helping someone."

The woman inspected her with a kindly gaze. "Why do you ask?"

"Because I've decided to train to be a nurse."

"A nurse? You?" Nurse Sonya burst out laughing, and Valentina felt it like a slap on the face. The older woman noticed her expression and silenced her laugh at once. "Are you serious?"

"Yes, I am."

"Have you told your father and mother?"

"Yes, I have."

There was an abrupt silence. Outside in the garden, huge snow-flakes were drifting down like white apple blossoms.

"Well? What did he say?"

Valentina tried to laugh. "Papa, would prefer that I marry an officer."

"Valentina, you can't be a nurse."

"Why not?"

"Because you're too thin-blooded. You're too fragile. You'd wither and die in the harsh reality of a hospital. They are not pleasant places, I assure you."

"You survived it."

"I was raised on a farm."

There was nothing Valentina could say to that. She inspected her own hands, viewing their palms and their straight fingers. They didn't look fragile to her or thin-blooded. They looked strong.

"Nurse," she said as Sonya was leaving, "will you teach me things? About nursing, I mean."

The nurse shook her head, her eyes soft and sad. "*Nyet*, no, *malishka*. I cannot teach you about nursing. That way we'd both end up being horsewhipped in the snow."

The door shut quietly behind her. Valentina unlocked her drawer and took out her list.

❧

*S*PASIBO, *BARYSHNYA*. THANK YOU, YOUNG MISTRESS." THE kitchen maid bobbed a curtsy.

"Merry Christmas, *Shastlivogo Rozhdestva*, Alisa," Valentina responded.

It was the annual Christmas evening ritual of presenting every servant with a gift from the Ivanov family. There were festive swathes of greenery and a brightly decorated Christmas tree from the fir tree market next to Gostiny Dvor. Valentina stood first in the line, passing out sweets and soap, shaking each hand in turn. Next to her, her mother wore gloves and a fixed smile as she handed out a length of good woolen material to each of the women, and a new razor and a pouch of tobacco for the men. Elizaveta Ivanova insisted that her male employees be clean shaven, even the gardeners. Her father stood with his back to the fire, legs apart, as he toasted his coattails and presented each member of his staff with a small velvet bag of coins. Valentina heard the chink of them as they landed in the outstretched hands and was curious as to how much they contained.

"*Shastlivogo Rozhdestva*. Merry Christmas, Miss Valentina."

"Merry Christmas to you, Arkin."

This was the first time she'd seen the chauffeur out of uniform. He was wearing a neat jacket and clean white shirt. He looked lean and athletic. A determined face. The forthright way his gaze met hers made her wonder what went on behind those cool gray eyes of his. She placed the absurd sweets and soap in his spotless hand.

"*Spasibo,*" he said, but the smile he gave her wasn't quite a chauffeur's.

"Arkin, you drove well the other day. When we were caught in the car on Morskaya. Thank you."

He seemed about to say something but changed his mind and gave her a respectful nod of his head instead.

"Where is Liev Popkov this evening?" she asked. "I don't see him here."

His polite smile hardened. "Popkov is otherwise engaged, I believe. In the stables."

She frowned. "Is a horse sick?"

"You'll have to ask him, Miss Valentina."

"I'm asking you."

His eyes remained on her far too long for politeness. "I don't believe it's a horse that is sick."

"Liev? Is he unwell?"

"Valentina, you are slowing the line, my dear," her mother said firmly. "Come along, Arkin."

Immediately he moved onward to accept his next gift. Something about this chauffeur, something carefully hidden under that polite exterior of his, sent a shiver down Valentina's spine.

❧

L IEV? LIEV?"
      Where the hell was he?

"Liev Popkov!" she shouted again in the stables.

And then she found him. Eyes shut, heavy limbs lifeless. Stretched out on his back on a pile of straw in a vacant stall. Her heart stopped. Not again. First his father, Simeon, and now him. The smell of blood in her nostrils all over again.

She started to scream.

"For fuck's sake, stop that racket, will you? You're scaring the bloody horses."

He had one eye half open, scowling at her while he scratched his armpit.

"You stupid dumb Cossack," she yelled at him, "you frightened the life out of me. I thought you were dead."

His scowl faded. He mumbled something unintelligible and

lifted a vodka bottle to his lips, spilling trails of clear liquid down his throat and over the straw. The bottle was almost empty.

"Liev, you're drunk."

"Of course I'm bloody drunk."

"I thought I smelled blood."

"You always did imagine things."

"I'm not imagining the trouble you'll be in."

He grinned at her then, his mouth a dark cave in the shadows, and upended the bottle to his lips.

"Liev! Don't!" she scolded, but more softly this time.

He tossed the empty bottle toward her at the entrance to the stall, but it fell short. "What are you so frightened of?"

"I don't want you whipped."

"Hah!"

She held out the packet of sweets and soap. It felt absurd. "My father has a proper present for you."

He laughed, a big guttural explosion that burst from his chest. "He's already given it to me."

"The pouch of roubles?"

His eyes narrowed into black slits. "*Nyet*, not the roubles."

"What then? The razor and tobacco?"

In response the big man suddenly sat up, swaying violently, and yanked his black tunic up over his head, revealing a broad chest matted with thick black curls. Valentina couldn't tear her eyes away. She'd never seen a man half naked before, not this close.

"You're drunk," she said again, but the words had lost their sting. "Put your top back on at once before you freeze to death."

She might as well not have spoken. He threw the tunic aside and rolled over on the straw so that he was lying face down.

"Liev!" This time it came out as a faint gasp. She put a hand over her mouth and stared at his back.

The massive muscles were striped. Red tracks ran diagonally across them, so regular they looked as though they'd been painted on. The paint was still wet and glistening. Slowly she walked into the stall, where she dropped to her knees in the straw beside him. The lash cuts were deep in places, raw edges of flayed flesh laid bare. "Why?" she whispered. There was no need to ask *Who?*

Liev rolled away, seized his tunic, and pulled it over his head.

She couldn't understand how he could even move with a back like that.

"Why did he do such a thing?" She felt shame for her father, sour in her stomach.

Popkov ferreted out another bottle from under the straw. This one was full. "Yesterday," he said, "I went to your sister's room when the nurse wasn't there."

"Oh, Liev. I'm so sorry."

He shrugged and poured more of the alcohol down his throat. "I wanted to give her a small gift for Christmas, that's all."

"But it's her bedroom."

"I've been in there many times to lift her in and out of her wheelchair."

"But never without Nurse Sonya present."

He snorted. "*Nyet.* Your father walked in when I was sitting on the end of the bed talking with her. So he whipped me."

Suddenly Valentina was hitting him in a fury. Her fists hammered down on his chest, pummeling its granite muscles.

"You stupid dumb oaf," she shouted, "you brainless Cossack, you're crazy. You deserve to be whipped."

He just laughed, then seized one of her wrists and pressed the neck of the vodka bottle into her hand.

"Here, have some."

She stared at the innocent-looking drink, gave a deep bone-shaking shudder, and raised the bottle to her lips.

❧

VALENTINA FELT VERY WARM. SHE COULD HEAR THE NIGHT wind scratching at the wooden stable walls. Something pleasant was floating around in her head, something with wings like a butterfly or a moth. Her lips no longer seemed to belong to her and kept curling up into vacant smiles. She was seated on the floor, leaning back against the side of the stall with a pile of straw tucked around her legs. How did all that heat get inside her stomach? Whenever she shut her eyes a whirring sound set off inside her skull and she found herself tipping sideways.

"Valentina, you've had enough. Go to bed." Popkov kicked her, but gently. He slid his boot over the straw and prodded her thigh as though she were a pig. "Get out of here," he growled.

"What did you give her?"

"Give who?"

"Tell me."

He paused, staring down at the straw. "A horseshoe. I polished it and"—she could tell he was embarrassed—"and wove ivy and berries through it."

Valentina thought it the most beautiful gift she could imagine. "Nothing for me?" she asked.

He raised his black eyes to hers. "You've got my vodka. What more do you want?"

She laughed then, and felt the world drifting in confusion out of her reach. "Mama and Papa are making me go to a Christmas ball," she said, and closed her eyes. The darkness started to spin alarmingly, so she forced them open again. The wretched creature was watching her with amusement.

"You're drunk," Popkov said.

"Go away," she muttered, the words slow and slurred.

The next moment she was floating in the air, her hands and feet weightless. When she squeezed her eyes open a crack she saw darkness whirling around her like dust.

"Liev, put me down."

But he ignored her.

Dimly she was conscious of being carried into the dark house through the servants' entrance, but her eyes slid shut and opened only when she was plonked on her own bed with no attempt at courtesy.

"Liev," she murmured, struggling to keep the ceiling from somersaulting on top of her, "I don't think—"

"Sleep," he growled.

"*Spasibo*, Liev," she said softly. "Thank you." But he had already left the room.

❧

"PLAY FOR ME."

Katya was in her wheelchair and they were alone in the music room. Valentina's head still throbbed at the base of her skull but at least she could turn it now without it falling off. Vodka, she vowed, would never touch her lips again in this lifetime. She'd cursed Popkov. Cursed his uncorked bottle. Cursed the way he had led out the horses the next day, whistling a jaunty folk song with no hint of a brain pickled in alcohol.

"Please," Katya said, "play something for me."

"I won't be good today," Valentina muttered as she lifted the lid of the piano. Just the sight of the keys, lined up and quietly waiting for her, loosened the tension within her.

Katya laughed. "You're always good, Valentina. Even when you say you're bad, you're good."

Valentina was unaware of what she would play until her fingers found the keys. From under them came the opening bars of Chopin's Nocturne in E Flat, the piece she had played for the Viking. Instantly she forgot there was a world outside. Aching head or no, her music professor would be proud of her as she balanced the melodic line perfectly against the left-hand chords, producing a pure cantabile legato in the right hand, feeling the music flow with each beat of her heart. Through her lungs. Across her shoulders. Down to her wrists and fingers.

"Valentina." It was her mother. When had she walked into the room?

"Valentina," Elizaveta Ivanova said again, "it's time to start getting dressed for the ball tonight. You agreed to go, remember?"

Valentina's hands froze above the keys.

*Number 5* on her list: *Obey Mama.*

Her hands sank down onto the keys in a harsh jarring chord. "Yes, Mama, I agreed."

Carefully she closed the piano lid and walked over to a small silver box on the table beside Katya's chair. She removed a brass key from the box, returned to the piano, and locked it, then walked over to the window. She opened it a crack and tossed the key out into the snow. Without a word, she walked out of the room.

❧

VIKTOR ARKIN'S FACE WAS DISTORTED. ONE EYE SLID away into his hairline while his mouth stretched to the size of a wrench. For a second he stared at his reflection in the curved surface of the Turicum's brass headlight and wondered what else in him might be distorted, somewhere deeper where he couldn't see. It worried him how much he loved this car. It was dangerous. To love something or somebody that much—it created a weak spot inside you. He couldn't afford weak spots. Nevertheless he smiled fondly at the gleaming blue curve of the front fender and ran a cloth along its graceful line.

"A visitor for you."

Arkin looked around at the sound of Liev's voice. The Cossack stood in the doorway. He looked amused. Not a good sign.

"Where?"

"In the yard."

Arkin folded his polishing cloth and placed it on the shelf before moving past the Cossack and out of the garage into the yard where darkness was just beginning to fall, laying shadows like dead creatures on the cobbles. On the right stood the stables and the coach house, in front of him a water pump and trough, but to the left rose an archway over a path that led around to the front of the house. Just beside the archway stood a young woman. She wore a headscarf tied tightly under her chin against the icy wind and a long belted coat that looked as though it had once belonged to a man. Her manner was awkward, a self-conscious dip of her head.

"A friend of yours?" Popkov laughed and gestured to his own stomach, making a wide imaginary bulge over it.

The woman was heavily pregnant. Even under the coat it was obvious.

"Go and polish a hoof or comb a mane or something," Arkin said, and went over to the woman. He greeted her cautiously.

"Can I help you?" he asked.

"I'm here with a message. From Mikhail Sergeyev."

Immediately he took her arm. It was thin and unresisting. He led her into the garage, where, out of the wind, her face relaxed and she gave him a shy smile.

"I'm Mikhail's wife, Larisa."

In that moment, something came undone inside him. All that he'd been keeping so tight and orderly in his head seemed to shift out of place. The way she said it, so simply, so proudly. *I'm Mikhail's wife, Larisa.* Her hand resting on her swollen stomach. He recalled his mother saying the same. *I'm Mikhail Arkin's wife, Roza,* her hand resting on her swollen stomach. Two weeks later she and the unborn child were dead from septicemia because his father had no money for a doctor. It happened on his ninth birthday. With a sense of something close to pain, he found himself wanting a child of his own, wanting a woman with a swollen belly that carried that child, despite all that he'd said to Sergeyev about families being a thing of the past. He smiled at her, shaken.

"Is something wrong?" he asked.

She nodded. Her lips were pale, her eyes dark-ringed and anxious. "It's Mikhail. He was hurt in an accident at work."

"Is it bad?"

"His arm is broken."

He gave her a smile of reassurance. "It will heal quickly," he said. "Mikhail is strong."

But he knew what it meant for them. No work meant no money. For food, for rent, for the baby. He reached into his pocket and pulled out his last three cigarettes and a few coins. It was all he had.

"Here, give this to your husband."

She let him place his offerings in her small hand. "Can you spare it?"

"Get him to Father Morozov's church hall. There's hot food there."

"*Spasibo,*" she whispered. "His boss gave him enough roubles to pay our rent."

"That's unusual. Who is this man?"

"*Direktor* Friis."

"Are you still working in the glue factory?"

She shrugged. "*Da.* Yes."

He felt the fire in his gut kick into life, the one that burned to bring justice to this wretched city. One brass headlight. That's all it would take. He could wrench it off the car and give it to her to sell. Enough to mean life for the new baby, enough to prevent its mother's milk drying up from starvation.

"He's worried," she said nervously, "about . . . the job he has to do with you tonight."

"Tell Mikhail from me not to worry. I'll deal with it. Go home and rest. Eat something."

"*Spasibo.*"

"Good luck with the baby."

She smiled, a gentle hopeful smile. Slowly she set off back across the uneven cobbles with the rolling gait that belongs to a drunken man or a pregnant woman. Arkin watched her until she was out of sight, standing there in the wind. So the time had come. He felt a nerve start up on the edge of his jaw, and no matter how hard he tried to control it, he couldn't. But he was ready for what he would have to do tonight.

# Nine

JENS WAS NOT A DANCING MAN. HE'D COME TO THE DAMN ball to waylay Minister Davidov, for no other reason, but so far there was no sign of him. He lingered briefly in the Anichkov Palace's opulent anterooms but their marble columns and lavish gilt moldings were hardly relaxing, so he took himself off to a salon where a game of cards was in progress.

After an hour he was content to pocket a handful of roubles and promissory notes. He enjoyed gambling. But he was wary of it, too. He'd seen what it could do to a man. He'd sat at a card table with a man who put a revolver to his forehead in the middle of a game and blew his brains out. And once on a station platform he'd embraced an old friend who was being carted off to ten years in Siberia for taking part in a conspiracy. The man had risked everything on an intrigue at court to oust Grand Duke Vladimir from control of the army. He'd gambled and lost.

Yes, Jens liked to gamble, but he picked his moments. Tonight was one of them.

～

FRIIS, I DIDN'T EXPECT TO FIND YOU HERE."
Jens was surprised that Davidov sought him out among the crowd, but it made the first step that much easier.

"Good evening, *dobriy vecher*, Minister."

They greeted each other with a formal incline of the head, not exactly a bow but close. The minister was a saturnine creature with heavy eyebrows, and after the clash the other day in the meeting over the tunnel funding, there was a certain frigidity in his manner. He was wearing an elegant tailcoat with a stiff white waistcoat and collar but had the look of a man with his mind set on things other than enjoying himself. Nevertheless his cheeks were florid instead of their usual ash gray, and Jens wondered how much good French brandy he had already consumed.

"Good evening, madam."

Jens bowed over the hand of Andrei Davidov's wife, a small, fluttery middle-aged woman in a violently purple gown. She smiled a lot, as though to make up for her husband's solemn face.

"What a lovely evening," she beamed. "My goodness, how I love to see you gentlemen looking so grand."

The place was thick with military men in dress uniform. Elaborate braid and colorful shoulder boards strutted the grand rooms as young soldiers vied with each other to attract the flutter of a fan from one of the young ladies. At social events in St. Petersburg the army officers dominated the room, magnificent in their white or blue or scarlet uniforms, the Hussar Guards always the most splendid and the most arrogant. It was the army that had made Russia strong, and they never let St. Petersburg forget it.

The master of ceremonies, in powdered white wig and tight red breeches, struck the marble steps three times with his golden staff to announce yet another new arrival.

"Do you dance?" Madam Davidova asked Jens, her head tilted to the side like a hopeful sparrow.

Jens's stomach sank. He glanced at Davidov.

"Go ahead," the minister urged. "Not a dancer myself."

"I'd be honored, madam," Jens responded with a gallant bow. As he offered his arm to escort her toward the dance floor, he said casually over his shoulder, "Davidov, a word or two later, if you don't mind."

Davidov's eyes narrowed, but his wife chirped, "Of course you will, won't you, Andrei?"

Jens turned to his dance partner with new respect. He smiled. She smiled back.

❧

THEY DANCED A MAZURKA. IT WAS ONE OF THOSE ENERGETIC dances that gave him the shudders, a set of eight couples weaving inexplicably between partners. Finding the right path among the sliding steps was worse than threading his horse through a forest in the dark.

He was concentrating so hard on the fast tempo that he almost missed the pair of deep brown eyes staring at him from across the room. He stumbled. Apologized to his partner. But when he glanced back, the dark eyes had gone, lost amid a swirl of elegant coiffures and a shimmer of silk. He recalled a striking impression of a long pale neck, a delicate line of cheek, and a white dress with high white gloves. The images had vanished in the crowded ballroom, but he'd recognized those eyes. And he intended to find them again.

❧

DON'T WASTE YOUR BREATH, FRIIS."
     "Minister Davidov, I suggest you listen to what I have to say."
"More money. That's what you're after. More funds for the bloody sewers."

Jens found a tight smile. "I'm not here to talk sewers."

"What then?"

"Land."

The minister expanded his narrow chest. "I'm listening."

"The population of Petersburg is increasing at a rapid rate, as we both know. The result is a severe housing shortage. So the cost of a house or apartment in the center of the city is growing exorbitant."

"I am aware of that."

"Yet there are many vacant plots. Scraps of scrubland in the poorer areas and on the outskirts of the city that are available for a few hundred roubles. But no one wants them."

"Because they're in the bloody slums." Davidov snorted out a coil of cigar smoke. "If you want to go off and live packed into a filthy shack with ten other families, feel free. But don't expect the rest of us to follow you." He started to move away.

"Some of those areas won't be slums much longer."

The minister stopped. Turned back. And Jens knew he had him.

"People always want houses. But at the moment the wealthy only want to live where there are shops, restaurants and, more importantly"—he paused, making Davidov wait—"modern hygienic sewers and water supplies."

He watched the minister's eyebrows lift. "Go on."

"Modern bathrooms. Modern kitchens. These are made possible by the tunnels I am building under the city. And it means that a plot of land, worth nothing one day, can be worth a small fortune the next."

Davidov's thin lips stretched into what was meant as a smile. "You're right." He drew on his cigar thoughtfully. "Damn you, you're right."

"Who is the person," Jens asked softly, "who controls which tunnels are excavated into which areas? Who is the person who knows which parcels of land will therefore rise in value?"

Davidov placed sinewy fingers on Jens's wrist, gripping hard.

"You do," the minister said in a hoarse whisper. "You bastard."

❧

JENS FOUND HER.

The chandeliers in the ballroom glittered in the tall mirrors, turning them into golden worlds within worlds. The young girls in their first season in St. Petersburg society wore white. Like lilies. Delicate and untouched. They stood together in small clusters with fragile smiles. Nervously they fingered their long white gloves and gazed with doe eyes at the young bucks who strutted for their benefit. Those whose dance cards were not yet filled with the names of captains and lieutenants stood close to the windows and fanned themselves with a languid motion as though too hot to dance.

Jens lit one of his Turkish cigarettes, leaned an elbow on a bronze statue of a seminaked javelin thrower, and watched the dark-eyed girl. She was dancing. The orchestra went from mazurka to polka to polonaise, and she went from blue uniform to scarlet to green without pause, but he noticed she never danced with the same man twice. She moved well. That was what struck him first. The graceful way she held her shoulders and head, not stiffly erect like some of the girls, but in a smooth flow to the rhythm of the music. Her spine made him think of a lithe young cat, smooth and supple, her feet neat and light.

"I'll introduce you if you'd like. I know her mother."

"Madam Davidova," he said as she popped up at his side, "what a pleasure to see you again."

"You're staring at her." She tapped him sharply with the ivory handle of her fan. "She is too young for you. I hear your taste is for older women."

He gave her a long look, tucked her arm through his own, and led her onto the dance floor for a waltz. "You dance well," he said as they glided around the room.

A flush of pleasure rose from her bosom up to the heavy pearl and amethyst necklace at her throat. Her bird eyes twinkled up at him. "She doesn't look happy."

"I hadn't noticed."

"Liar! Ask her to dance with you."

He found himself liking this woman. And she was right: the girl's face possessed a solemn expression that scarcely varied from partner to partner. She seemed to listen to what they had to say but added little herself. Only now and again did she dart a look up at them with her large brown eyes suddenly animated, as if they had said something that caught her interest. Jens found himself wondering what kind of comment would catch her interest.

"Time to interrupt them, I think," he murmured to Madam Davidova, "if you're sure you don't object."

"Not at all. It's ages since I've had the pleasure of a waltz with a dashing young officer." She fluttered her eyelashes at him in anticipation, making him laugh.

He guided her over to where the girl was moving in the arms of a lieutenant, and Madam Davidova immediately broke into introductions.

"My dear young girl, this is Jens Friis." Madam Davidova turned amused eyes on Jens. "Valentina is the daughter of my dear friend, Elizaveta Ivanova. The two of you have much in common, I believe. You're both enthusiasts of"—she hesitated for no more than a quiver of a second, adding a sparrowlike twitch of her head—"of stargazing."

Jens didn't even blink.

"It's rare," he said with a gallant bow to Valentina, "to meet a fellow enthusiast. May I cut in for a moment or two? To talk stars, you understand."

"Well, no, actually I . . ." The young lieutenant started to refuse, but he was no match for Madam Davidova.

"Delighted to dance with you." She launched herself into his arms with the speed of a military attack.

The lieutenant had no alternative but to relinquish his partner. Jens stepped in and swept Valentina away.

❧

S TARS?" VALENTINA QUERIED.
    "Yes. Orion's Belt. The Great Bear. The North Star."
There was a pause.

"That's it?" she asked.

"You want more? There's the Giant's Hammer and Astralis Gigantis . . . I could go on. Awesome sights, all of them."

"What makes you think I'm interested in stars?"

He flashed her a teasing smile, aware of her gaze on him, one eyebrow raised in a delicate arch. "I wanted to ask you something. How else was I to hack a path through that forest of uniforms around you?"

She gave him a mock frown. "Tell me what it is you want to ask."

He became serious. "Why were you angry with me? At the concert, I mean. Scowling at me as though I had the devil on my shoulder."

She threw her head back in a laugh that was so relaxed and natural in this unnatural world of jewels and corsets and crimped curls that it took him totally by surprise. It was a wonderful sound. Rich and infectious. He spun her in a quick turn across the floor. This close he could see that her eyes were not just brown but gold and brown, as if whoever painted them had dipped the brush in the wrong color pot. His gaze drifted to the creamy smoothness of her throat.

"It was nothing," she smiled. "I was just being a silly schoolgirl."

"And now?"

"Now I'm not angry with you any more. Nor am I a schoolgirl anymore."

"So what are you? One of this season's debutantes, here at court to find a husb—?"

"I'm here because my parents ordered me to be here."

"Ah."

He could feel the sudden heat of her anger, though she hid all trace of it from her face, but her fingers in his betrayed her. He let her dance in peace, no more questions. She seemed to float deep within the music as he guided her away from the throng of swaying couples toward the ballroom door, and as soon as she saw it within reach he heard her take a deep breath. Felt her small ribs expand under his hand on her back and he had a sense of a creature scenting freedom.

"Would you care for me to show you the Astralis Gigantis?" he asked with a straight face. "A star that not many people have ever seen before, I believe."

"I would be fascinated."

He liked the hint of mockery in her voice.

She turned quickly to walk through the double doors to the refreshment room beyond, and as she did so he smelled the fragrance of her hair. The beautiful dark waves he'd seen at the school were pinned up in an elaborate coiffure high on the back of her head, emphasizing her high cheekbones and long neck. As she walked in front of him, a small slight figure in her white silk gown nipped in to her tiny waist, he experienced a strong impulse to extract the large pearl hair comb in her coiffure and release the thick coils. As though it would release *her*. He felt an urge to set free whatever it was she was holding in so tight.

He steered her to one of the tall windows that stretched from floor to ceiling, draped with golden velvet and decorated with silk flowers. Valentina leaned toward it as though the night outside held something she wanted.

"Which one is this Astralis Gigantis of yours?" she asked softly.

"It's up there somewhere, I promise you, just waiting to be found."

"I hope so. I like to think there are more to discover."

"There is always more to discover, Valentina."

She made no comment but swayed to the distant music, her reflection insubstantial among the shadows outside.

"May I have something to drink?" she asked.

So he fought his way to the refreshment room, but by the time he returned with a glass of lime cordial in one hand and a stiff brandy in the other, it was too late. The uniforms had gathered around her. Like bees. He could hear their hungry buzz. He pushed his way through them to where a tall fair-haired captain of the Hussar Guards in a scarlet uniform was holding her dance card between his fingers, talking heatedly. Jens took one look at Valentina's face and placed the drinks on a table, plucked the dance card out of the captain's fingers, tore it in two, and returned it in the man's hand with a curt bow.

"Excuse us," he said, and tucked Valentina's hand under his arm. "We have a star to inspect."

As they walked out of the room, he felt her shaking. For one appalling moment he thought she was crying, but then he glanced at her face and saw the laughter.

# Ten

A SLEIGH RIDE. VALENTINA GASPED, THE AIR WAS SO COLD. The wind tugged at her beaver fur hood and her hands were tucked firmly inside the fur muff on her lap. She liked the cold. It scraped away the stink of cigars from her skin. The Viking had bundled the rug around her, so that only the tip of her nose and her chin gleamed pale in the stretch of moonlight.

The sleigh was fast over the snow, its greased metal runners singing like music, the horse's hooves barely audible. The Viking drove the open sleigh with relish. It should have made her nervous but didn't. Her mother would faint with horror if she found out. Valentina shouldn't be here at all, she knew that, but in her opinion she shouldn't be at the ball either. The sleigh flew through the streets of St. Petersburg, along the granite Embankment, past the bridge where the towers of the Fortress of St. Peter and St. Paul loomed. Mist lay like a winter coat on the river, blurring the reflected lamplight into greasy smears.

He didn't talk. That suited her. She closed her eyes, listening to the hum of the runners. He was taking her away from the city lights so that they could look at the stars. A smile rose to her chilled lips. No one had ever shown her the stars before.

꿍

That's Odysseus. He was a great warrior whom the gods couldn't bear to let die, so they flung him up into the heavens where they could wrestle with him whenever they grew bored."

Valentina pointed to another cluster of stars. There were thousands of them, sharp pinpricks of light in the thick black arc of the sky. "What are they? They're beautiful. They seem so close."

"They're Zeus's handmaidens. Each one was an earthling girl when the all-powerful god fell in love with them. He stole them. Raised them up to be his eternal handmaidens. It's said they all have flowing brown locks and deep brown eyes."

She suddenly realized he'd stopped looking at the night sky and was staring directly at her. "You'd better watch out," he said. "You're just his type."

She laughed. "I wouldn't mind being up there, looking down on all the puny efforts of the tiny creatures on earth. It would be a relief. To be free from all"—she waved her fur muff in the vague direction of the city—"this."

He raised his head and sat up. They had been leaning back in the sleigh as they gazed at the stars.

"Is it so bad?" he asked softly.

She thought about it. About bombs in the hands of revolutionaries. Two government ministers had been murdered by them: Sipyagin at the Mariinsky Palace, and Vyacheslav Plehve had one tossed into his carriage. Even Alexander II, the tsar's grandfather, was killed by one. The magnificent Church of the Savior on Spilled Blood was built on the spot beside the Griboedov Canal where the fatal explosion took place. She thought about her father's face when he said, *You did this to her*, and about the lifetime of dress fittings and tea parties her mother would condemn her to. About the woman with the shiny scar stamped on her skull. About Katya.

"No," she lied, "it's not so bad."

"You play the piano like an angel. Isn't that worth staying down here for?"

"I'd persuade Zeus to let me play it in the heavens too."

"Ah yes. Join in with the music of the spheres. He'd be a fool not to let you."

She couldn't see his face as she leaned back in the sleigh, concentrating on the gleaming diamond chips in the sky above her. The moonlight streamed from behind him, robbing him of any features. Just his hair shone bright where it curled out under his thick fur hat, but it shone purple, not red, in the strange thieving light.

"What is it you do?" she asked. "Other than walk out of concerts and drive sleighs like a madman."

His laugh echoed through the vast silence of the night. They were outside the city, on the edge of the forest where the snow lay like a silver tablecloth spread out for them in the moonlight and the trees huddled behind them like a dark ragged army, whispering together.

"For your information," he said, "I didn't walk out of the concert. The tsar ordered me back to work."

"Oh."

"As for sleighs, yes, I like to drive them fast when I have a good horse between the shafts." He leaned a fraction closer, and she could see his breath trail from his lips in the frosty air.

"What is it you do?" she asked again.

"I'm an engineer."

"An engineer? Does that mean you make things?"

"Yes, you're right. I make things."

She could hear the smile in his voice. He was laughing at her. She sat up straight, forcing him to twist in his seat beside her. Now she could see his face.

"What kind of things?"

"Tunnels."

"Tunnels? What sort of tunnels?"

"For water. For sewage. For drains. But I've also built them through mountains. For trains."

Valentina was speechless. She'd never in her life met anyone who did anything so constructive.

"And for fun I tinker with engines," he added. "I like fiddling with metal."

She stared at his silvery face and saw the way the words slid out over his lips as if they were nothing. *I've also built them through mountains.* Such small words for something so big. She wanted to cry, she envied him so much. Instead she said, "How interesting."

But he must have heard something in her voice. Or seen something in her face. Because he studied her for a long moment, during which the horse lifted its head and pricked its ears toward the black line of the forest as if it had heard something.

"Playing the piano the way you do is a rare talent," Jens said softly. "You are still young, yet you play with your whole heart and soul."

She looked away.

"You must have worked very hard," he said, "to be so good."

"You can't call that work. Not real work. Not like building tunnels."

"Valentina." He touched her arm. His gloved hand was outside the fur rug while hers was underneath, so it hardly counted as a touch. But she was aware of it even so. "Valentina, which do you think gives people more pleasure? A tunnel? Or music? Which lifts the heart and makes it sing? Beethoven or Brunel?"

She laughed and felt a rush of gratitude toward this unruly Viking who had whisked her away to the middle of nowhere to study the stars. "Who is Brunel?"

"An English engineer. Isambard Kingdom Brunel."

It was the way he said it. The respect in his voice.

"Is he good?" she asked.

"He was one of the greats."

She nodded. "I'm jealous."

"I know."

Again he brushed her arm with the touch that was barely a touch. "Women are not given the chance," he acknowledged, "to be useful. But it will change, Valentina, given time."

"I haven't got time," she said fiercely.

Her comment took him by surprise. She could see it in the sudden stiffness of his jaw. But the words wouldn't stay in her mouth. "How would you feel if you had to sip tea and admire dresses and jewelry all day? Your mind would melt, I swear. I want to do something . . . more. I'm not a Russian *matryoshka* doll, I don't want to be just an ornament. I want dirty hands and an exhausted brain and—"

A noise emerged from the forest. The sound of horses, the approach of heavy wheels as something forced its way between the trees. Without a word, Jens picked up the reins and deftly clicked the somnolent horse into motion, so that the sleigh glided out of the moonlight and plunged deep into the shadows.

❧

THE WAGON NUDGED ITS WAY OUT OF THE FOREST. IT WAS lumbering toward the snowbound road like a large hump-backed animal, pulled by two elderly, heavy horses that wheezed as they hauled it into the moonlight. Behind the wagon five men trudged over the ruts and ridges, forcing their shoulders against the tailgate whenever the going grew tough. To Valentina it looked as though they'd been walking for a long time.

The Viking was watching the dark figures intently. In the blackness she couldn't see him, but she could sense the sharp spike of his curiosity. His hand gripped her arm, but she didn't need to be told. *Don't move.* The man at the front, the one leading the horses, was carrying a rifle. He shouted orders to the men behind, but she couldn't make out the words. Jens bent close, his breath intimate on her cold cheek.

"They'll be gone," he whispered, "as soon as they get the cart up on the road."

She nodded and risked taking her eyes off the rifle. The Viking was so close she could feel his pulse racing through him. He was no more than a darker shadow, invisible in the black forest, but she could hear his breath. In and out. Steady as a rock, reassuring her.

"Probably hunters," he murmured.

*Probably not*, she thought but didn't say.

"On their way home," he added.

But both of them knew there was no elk meat in that cart. The moon plucked at the tarpaulin that was covering it, tied down with ropes, and whatever lay underneath looked bulky. The horses strained to haul their load up onto the raised level of the road, and the men pushed from the rear while the one at the front yanked hard on the animals' leading rein. It pained Valentina to see a person handle horses' mouths so harshly, but curses abruptly sliced through the silence.

Jens saw it coming before she did.

"It's tipping over," he warned.

The weight in the wagon had shifted. One of the horses tried to rear out of the shafts, its hooves flashing, but the men fought hard, pushing and pulling till finally they halted the cart's descent and manhandled it up the rocky slope onto the road. With a lurch the wagon settled on the snow-packed ground and the men leaned heavily against its wheels, chests heaving. That was the moment in which

Jens's horse took it into its head to call out a greeting to the exhausted nags. Jens tightened the reins and swore under his breath.

"Valentina," he spoke softly. No sign of panic in his voice. "Say nothing."

The man at the head of the wagon was striding fast toward the forest's edge, searching for the source of the sound. Rifle alert in his hands.

"Over here," Jens called out.

The man veered in their direction. She could hear the crunch of his feet over the snow. It clashed with the thumping of her heart.

"Cover your face with your hood," Jens murmured without turning away from the man.

She pulled the beaver skin low over her face till only a small hole remained. She heard a bullet slam into the breech of the rifle as the footfalls drew closer and stopped. Jens's hand crept under the rug and grasped hers.

"*Dobriy vecher,*" he called out. "Good evening, friend. The lady and I came out for a quiet sleigh ride. We've no interest in your business, whatever it may be."

To her surprise the man's response was a loud laugh as he slapped the shoulder of Jens's horse with amusement. Valentina tried to draw air through her tiny hole, but her lungs had forgotten how.

"Clear out of here," the man said easily. "Take her back to Petersburg before she freezes her sweet little arse off."

Jens withdrew his hand and flicked the reins into action, making the animal leap forward so fast the man had to jerk out of its path.

"*Spokoinoi nochi,*" he called. "Good night, comrade."

The horse picked up its feet, eager to be on the move, and Jens kept the sleigh traveling fast across the snow in the direction of St. Petersburg.

Valentina emerged from her hood. "That man wasn't so dangerous."

The sleigh shook and juddered beneath her, so that she had to cling to its side.

Jens laughed. "I'm glad you think so."

A loud crack reverberated. At first Valentina thought something had broken on the sleigh, one of the runners or a shaft fixing. But Jens swore furiously and whipped the reins along the horse's back to drive it faster. One of his hands seized the back of Valentina's neck.

"Down!" he ordered.

He forced her to the sleigh floor, face down in the dirt. She spat out a mouthful of filthy slush and that was when she heard the second crack. Followed by a third. Rifle shots.

Jens didn't let the horse slacken its pace for two miles.

Finally he prodded her shoulder. "Safe now."

Her limbs uncurled and she slid back onto the seat, aching and embarrassed.

"I was . . ." She stopped. What was the point in trying to explain? She'd seen what horrors men are willing to inflict on each other. A rifle? A bomb? It was all the same.

"Frightened?" He snorted and allowed the horse to slow to a walk. "Damn right, you should be. So was I."

She stared at him. "Were you?"

"Of course. Rifle bullets aren't exactly friendly."

~⁀⌒~

H E SMILED AT HER AND PULLED HIS FUR HAT DOWN OVER his ears. She could feel adrenaline tingling in her fingers. Or was that the cold? "The man wasn't trying to kill us," he said confidently. "The bullets went far too wide of the sleigh."

"So why shoot at all?"

"To scare us off and show what we will get if we're stupid enough to report the incident to the police."

The cold was seeping up her arms, tracking its way to her heart. The shuddering in her chest wouldn't stop.

"Are you all right?"

She nodded jerkily. "I'm not dead. Not yet." She laughed, but it sounded sad.

Abruptly he halted the sleigh. The horse stopped in its tracks but stamped its front hooves, unhappy about doing so. Maybe it too was frightened of the rifle. Jens didn't say anything. On an empty ice road in the dark, far from everything but wolves and rodents, the Viking put his arms around Valentina and pulled her to his chest. All he did was hold her. But the moment her cheek touched the warmth of his heavy overcoat, her body seemed to turn itself inside out. All the wrong parts were on the outside, the fragile parts, the secret corners. She clung there, trembling. She inhaled shakily, and his coat smelled of a masculine world. Of smoke and horses and cards and wide-open spaces. But she could smell his tunnels on him too: dark places, narrow passages, bricks.

For a long moment he didn't speak, just held her head close while he stroked the fur of her hood as though it were her hair and murmured words in a language she didn't understand. When finally she sat up, he peered into her face and what he saw must have reassured him because the green eyes smiled at her. He took up the reins and chirruped the horse into motion.

"Forgive me, Valentina Ivanova. I should never have brought you here."

She shook her head in disagreement but kept her lips closed tight. She feared they would let out the words, the ones crammed inside her mouth like chunks of ice, the ones that confessed she knew the man, the one with the rifle and the false laugh. She'd looked into those sharp eyes before.

It was Arkin. Her father's chauffeur.

❧

THE LIGHTS OF ST. PETERSBURG PEELED PAST THEM AS THE sleigh skimmed along the Embankment, past the palatial façades with their classical columns and golden fountains. The river had the look of a restless soul, black and moody, never still.

"What do you think was under the tarpaulin?" Valentina asked.

"Probably something stolen. Machine parts maybe. Whatever it was, it was heavy."

"Why would they steal machine parts?"

"Thieve from one factory and sell to another. I know in my own work that getting hold of the right equipment can be a lengthy process."

"Do you buy from people who steal?"

He gave her a sharp sideways look. "Is that what you think?"

"I have no idea how business is conducted. I didn't mean to—"

"Would you?"

"What?"

"Would you buy from people who steal? If you were in business."

She thought seriously about the question. Would she?

"Yes," she answered, surprising herself. "Yes, I think I would. If I had to."

He laughed. "Good," he said. "Then we shall get on well."

Didn't he know? They were already getting on well.

# Eleven

OUTSIDE THE ANICHKOV PALACE AGAIN THEY STOOD together in the drive in front of the triple-arched entrance. A thousand lights blazed out in a brash display of gaudy wealth. The palace belonged to the dowager empress, the tsar's mother, who was adept at maintaining a magnificent rival court that eclipsed her daughter-in-law's halfhearted efforts. The guests had grown raucous at this late hour. Some were spilling out into their carriages to move on to other balls that would go on until five o'clock in the morning. There was the clatter of wheels and the jangle of harness. The night was loud and the stars felt worlds away. Neither Valentina nor Jens made any move to re-enter the party.

"Your chaperone will be waiting," Jens said.

"She will."

"Will you be in trouble?"

The way he looked at her made her want to stay here exactly like this, with his tall figure in the gray overcoat so close she could touch it. She pushed back her hood.

"My friend's mother is acting as my chaperone tonight. She's watching over several of us now that the new season is starting. I expect she'll be furious, but"—she slid him a conspiratorial smile—"I shall say I have been improving my knowledge by learning about the stars. Anyway she has probably been so intent on her own enjoyment that she scarcely noticed I was gone."

"The whole room would notice you were gone."

"*Spasibo*. Jens. Thank you for showing me the stars tonight."

He glanced over his shoulder at the palace, seemed about to say something, then inclined his head instead. "It was my pleasure."

So formal? So suddenly correct? His face not the face that had peered so intently into hers beside the forest. Is that what a court party did to a person? Made him someone else?

"I wish you luck with your tunnels," she offered, because she didn't know what else to say.

"Thank you."

"Shall I tell you something?"

"Please do."

His feet didn't move even an inch closer, yet she felt him edge nearer.

"I know as much about tunnels," she said, "as you do about stars."

His long elegant nose gave a snort.

"I may not know the chemistry and biology I need, but I do know my stars," she said.

She wanted him to laugh but he was staring at her instead, a hard questioning stare. "Why on earth would you need to know chemistry and biology?"

"I intend to become a nurse."

He studied her face and she couldn't tell what was going on behind the shadowy green eyes. She saw him breathe heavily.

"My friend is a doctor." He spoke in a careful voice. "He tells me that to be a nurse you need to be tough. To deal with the blood and the wounds. And you need to work hard."

"I work hard."

Slowly he smiled, one edge of his mouth curling higher than the other. "I believe you do."

"I'll not faint at the sight of blood. And I can be tough."

"Maybe you'll have to work at that one."

"Trust me. I can do it." With a lift of her chin, she set off and hurried toward the grand entrance.

"Valentina!"

She turned. Jens still stood there, like the mast of a Viking sailing ship, tall and straight. The night air swirled around him.

"May I call on you?" he asked.

She didn't even make him wait, didn't pretend to think about it. "You may."

"I enjoyed this evening."

"Even the rifle shots?"

"Especially the rifle shots."

She knew exactly what he meant.

❧

T HE ENORMOUS BRAZIERS OUTSIDE THE ANICHKOV PALACE burned with flames that licked at the darkness, painting it a strident orange. Hundreds of coachmen, beards stiff with ice, warmed their hands on the welcome heat throughout the night and abandoned it only reluctantly when summoned back to their carriage by a departing guest.

Arkin watched the sables and the tiaras descend the palace steps. So expensive, so showy, so worthless. Butterflies to be stamped on. What about women like Sergeyev's wife? Heavily pregnant yet still slaving to earn a pittance, barely enough to stay alive. Did these butterflies have no conscience? But it was not the women he was interested in tonight, it was the men. One man in particular.

Prime Minister Stolypin.

Arkin had changed into his chauffeur uniform, even though Minister Ivanov was not attending the ball tonight. The uniform made him invisible among all the other chauffeurs and coachmen, and he needed to be nothing more than one of the shadows of the night lifting off the thick blue ice of the Neva.

The incident earlier this evening in the forest had set him on edge. Was it an omen? That tonight was a night when things would go wrong? It was the first time they had been caught hauling the guns, and he'd had to restrain himself. The open spaces out there always made him jumpy. A quick bullet, two bodies in the snow. It would have guaranteed silence, but the police would inevitably have come sniffing around and found the cart tracks through the trees. No, just a few shots over the head of the pampered pet in the sleigh, that was enough. But even so. He clenched his teeth and told himself he didn't believe in omens.

A murmur flicked like a spark around the groups at the braziers, and Arkin was quick to react. He moved silently toward the palace.

Someone important was leaving the ball, someone who could stir the jaded coachmen to pause as they took a nip of vodka and turn to look. The tall figure of Prime Minister Pyotr Stolypin was descending the steps with three others: two young men in bright uniforms and a pretty young woman with almost white-blond hair and a large laughing mouth. These three were nothing to Arkin. He saw only Stolypin.

Arkin reached for the sack that was hooked onto his belt under his liveried coat. *This is political*, he told himself. *Political. This man is inflicting terror on the people of Russia.* Sixty thousand. *Sixty thousand.* That was the number of political prisoners he'd had executed or sentenced to penal labor in his first three years in office. Thousands more peasants were tried in military field courts when Stolypin decreed that all farm communes must be dismantled. Hundreds of newspapers and trade unions were being closed down by force because their aims did not coincide with Stolypin's.

*I am fighting against revolution.*

The prime minister's words were etched in his brain. No matter how many times Stolypin claimed he was in favor of reform or how many lies slid off his tongue, he believed the only way forward was through vicious repression. Arkin had seen the results of it all around him. Heard the screams at night, seen the heartbreak, felt the scourge on the backs of the workers. Tonight's action would be a service to Russia. If he died himself. . . . He shrugged and stood in silence in the black shadow of a sedan car. He pushed an arm inside the sack and lit the fuse. Instantly his heart rate rocketed. He had two minutes. One hundred twenty seconds. No more.

*This is political.*

But in his head reared an image of his father, a proud barrel-chested farmer arguing with and defying a tall bear of a man who had come to the rural provinces to address a village meeting. That tall man was Stolypin. Another image of crimson streaks slithering down flayed flesh into the dirt, his father's fingers clenched in agony, his back caving in with each lash of the knout. The shame, not for himself but for his father, would never go away.

*This is not personal, this is political.*

Everyone knew Prime Minister Stolypin wore body armor at all times and surrounded himself with security men, because this would not be the first attempt on his life. Arkin could see them gathering like cockroaches around the carriage that had drawn up, a pair of horses breathing heavily into the cold air. Arkin had expected a car, but it made no difference. The young people climbed in as other cars and carriages milled around, drivers and footmen jostling for space.

*Fifteen seconds.*

Lights from the palace threw long shadows, distorting the shape of the carriage, as Arkin edged closer. The prime minister clambered up the steps into its interior, booming his big laugh.

*Thirty seconds.*

The sack hissed in his grip and there was the smell of scorched fibers as the fuse burned down. With Stolypin safely inside the vehicle, the guards relaxed and started to move toward the front. Arkin slipped forward into the deep shadow at the back, threw the sack under the carriage, and stepped away quickly.

*Forty-five seconds.*

He was counting each tick of the clock in his head.

"Hey, you!"

A hand gripped his shoulder and his heart stopped. Sweat gathered at his throat. He turned and saw a giant guardsman towering over him. "What do you want?" Arkin demanded gruffly, surprised to hear his own voice so calm. "I'm in a hurry. My minister has ordered me to fetch his car."

The man registered Arkin's livery. "What's your name?"

"Grigoryev."

"Well, Grigoryev, you tell your minister to wait until . . ."

Arkin stopped listening. Stolypin was stepping out of the carriage. He was shouting something over his shoulder to his companions inside.

"Wait here," the prime minister called, "I must remind Prince Vasily that we are riding together tomorrow."

Arkin watched every movement as if it were slowed a hundred times. The gleaming shoe pressing down on the red carpet into the palace, the gloved hand opening and shutting like a mouth talking, the lift of a shoulder, the twist of the beard as Stolypin hurried away.

*Sixty seconds?*

Oh God, he'd lost count.

He tried to pull away from the guardsman's grip but it remained firm. Quickly he pointed toward the two horses at the front of the carriage, which were tossing their black heads and restlessly stamping the ground. Could they smell the fuse burning?

"You need to help keep those animals quiet or the prime minister's carriage will be off without him. He won't like that."

Instantly the guardsman lost interest in Arkin and headed forward. Other horses were whinnying, struggling to back away into the darkness, and Arkin cast a glance at the shadowy space beneath the carriage, but nothing was visible.

*Ninety seconds? Or was it more?*

He swung away and started to run, counting in his head. Thirty paces. Would it be enough? He dragged icy air into his lungs, cursing as his legs leapt over curbs and dodged wheels, cursing Stolypin, cursing the guardsman.

Cursing his luck.

He threw himself behind a magnificent Rolls-Royce, solid as a rock, just as his mental clock clicked to one hundred twenty. For two seconds he crouched there, heart slamming into his ribs, not thinking. Nerves raw.

The explosion tore a gigantic hole in the night. A bright flash ripped through the darkness and the force of the blast rocked the Rolls-Royce on its wheels, smashing its windows and bending its solid metal panels. Arkin's ears pulsed painfully. Glass rained down on him like ice daggers from the night sky. He forced a breath into his empty lungs and made an effort to stand, but what he saw as he stared at the scene of destruction in front of him made him wish he'd just kept running.

Screams, bodies, and blood filled the gap where the carriage had stood. A slick scarlet stream leaked across the road, while the smell of gelignite and fear hung in the night air sharper than the ice daggers. Figures lay on the ground, but panic sent others fleeing this place of death. Arkin felt sick. Directly in front of him lay the two beautiful horses that had pulled Stolypin's carriage. One was clearly dead, its back twisted at an impossible angle; the other had lost both its rear legs, but it was alive and screaming. Men in uniforms were running around waving guns in their hands, seizing anyone still on his feet. Arkin wanted to melt away into the darkness, away from the carnage, away from the powerful man standing like a vengeful devil at the top of the palace steps, bellowing his fury into the night air. Prime Minister Pyotr Stolypin. He was still alive.

Arkin cursed him under his breath. Then, oblivious to the risk, he drew a gun from under his jacket, hurried over to the horse, and put a bullet in its brain. The animal's brown eyes widened in surprise as it died, forelegs thrashing. Tears rolled down Arkin's cheeks.

～

FAILURE LAY LIKE COLD GRAY ASH IN HIS MIND.
"Well done."
The words meant nothing. Arkin shook his head.
"No."
"Viktor, the tsar will tread more carefully in future. You have frightened him and his government. They will be wary of rejecting our demands for—"
"You aren't thinking straight, Father Morozov. Stolypin is still alive."
"I know." The priest rested a hand on Arkin's shoulder, and his patient gaze sought out Arkin's soul. "Don't deny yourself the satisfaction of striking a blow for the new world we are building. You and I both know we have to tear down the old one first."
"Stolypin will retaliate." Arkin's eyes darkened. "More deaths."
"It is the price we must pay."
"Tell me, Father, how do you think your God deals with that? How do you balance your religious conscience with planting bombs? What excuse do you give in your prayers each night?"
The priest lifted the engraved cross that hung around his neck and placed his lips on its battered surface, then leaned close to Arkin's forehead. His lips were cool, and against his will Arkin felt a shiver of calm slide through the bones of his skull into the burning tangle beneath.
"The war we fight is a just war," Morozov told him firmly. "Never doubt that. It is God's holy battle for the souls of his people of Russia. He is our pillar of fire by night and our pillar of cloud by day. We wear his breastplate of righteousness."
Viktor Arkin turned away. "Father, they will come searching for us." He gestured around the basement room. "You should leave here at once."
"I shall return to my village. It's not far outside the city, so I can come back here quickly if needed. What about you?"
"I'll stay close to my government minister. He will be angry after

this attack on the prime minister, and when he's angry he is indiscreet. He thinks of me as no one, a maroon uniform with nothing inside it, so in the car he says things out loud that would do better to stay in his head."

"As I said, Viktor, God is on our side."

Arkin picked his cap off the table and headed for the door. "You know we shall have to kill all of them in the end," he said quietly. "Even the women and children."

"Death is a beginning; look at it that way. The beginning of eternity for them, the beginning of a just and honorable new world for those who choose to build it here. Paradise on earth."

Arkin saw in his mind a pair of large dark brown eyes and soft full mouth. *Do whatever you have to,* she'd said to him in the car when the marchers were coming close on Morskaya. Calm as a cat in the sunshine. Her little blond sister beside her on the blue seat, eyes huge as a child's in a candy store.

*All of them. Kill all of them.* That day would come. His hand shook as he seized the door handle.

# Twelve

U PSTAIRS THE CORRIDOR WITH ITS HIGH CEILING WAS cold. The wind raced straight through the attic, struggling under the roof tiles in an effort to push inside. Valentina heard the rattle of it and felt its echo inside herself, a wild kind of moaning that seemed to come from the forest. *Then we shall get on well,* he'd said. She smiled. She recalled the way his fingers held the reins, the smell of his coat. His hand on the back of her neck. *May I call on you?*

No light came from under Katya's door; nevertheless she opened it and slipped inside. Making no sound in the darkness, she kicked off her dancing shoes, raised a corner of the quilt, and slid into the well of warmth.

"Katya," she murmured. She wrapped an arm around the still figure and held her sister close, twined their feet together, and laid her cheek beside Katya's shoulder. She lay in the bed for several minutes before her nostrils registered an odor among the sheets, a sickly coppery smell that she knew too well. She sat up quickly.

"Katya."

No answer. That was when she felt the moisture. It was all down her arm.

"Katya!"

She twisted around and frantically found the switch of the bed-side lamp. Her own hand was bright red.

"No! Katya!"

Her sister was lying peacefully on her back. On the far side of her was a pair of long-bladed scissors, and they were sticking upright out of her wrist. Like a knife in butter. Everything was red, the sheets drowning in scarlet, all from such a small jagged hole. Valentina leapt from the bed, seized the belt from Katya's dressing gown on the chair, and bound it tightly around the limp arm, just above the elbow. The flood slowed. She tied a hard knot. The scarlet flow faltered and stammered to a trickle. Katya's face was as white and as lifeless as her pillow, her blond curls the only part of her that seemed to possess any spark. Her eyes were closed.

"Katya." Valentina cradled her in her arms for one brief agonized moment. Her heart hurt in her chest as she pressed her lips to her sister's cold cheek. Then she ran for Nurse Sonya.

❧

VALENTINA WAITED AT THE BOTTOM OF THE STAIRCASE and watched the first spiny fingers of dawn sneak under the shutters. A thumbprint of pink sunlight appeared on the veined marble of the floor. She watched it grow and when it was the size and shape of a child, she heard footsteps descending the stairs. They were slow and ponderous, as though each foot were heavy.

"Dr. Beloi." She looked up into a broad face with a neat little beard on the point of the chin. "How is she?"

The doctor plodded on down. His coat smelled of laudanum and two fingers of his left hand were badly stained with nicotine, but he was one of the finest medical men in St. Petersburg, as well as the costliest. He placed a hand on Valentina's shoulder as if to pin down her impatience.

"She's still alive. Your mother is with her now."

Valentina released a small noise.

"Your sister will come through this . . . aberration. God forgive her." He shook his head and pinched a finger and thumb to the bridge of his nose as though he had a pain there.

"She won't die?"

"No, don't look so frightened. She won't die. Thanks to you. You saved her life."

"She won't die," Valentina murmured again.

"She'll be weak for a while because she's lost so much blood. You should go and change your dress. It's covered in blood."

He patted her shoulder again as if she were a fretful pet and plodded on across the hall. Valentina remained gazing up the stairs. As a footman swung open the front door, the doctor turned back and beckoned her to him.

"Valentina, come here."

She came, reluctant to leave the stairs.

"Tell me, young lady, how did you know how and where to apply a tourniquet?"

"I read things."

"Well, your parents will be thanking God on their knees that you went into your sister's room when you did last night. She'd have been stone cold long before anyone found her this morning."

Valentina just looked up at the galleried landing above. Her fingers couldn't keep still.

"You did a fine job stemming the flow of blood. Worthy of a real nurse, my dear."

His words drew her attention. "Dr. Beloi, how would I go about becoming a real nurse?"

"Good God, girl, don't be absurd."

"Would you give me an introduction to one of the hospitals, so that I can train?"

"Valentina, this is no time to be making jokes."

"I'm not joking."

He sighed and pinched his nose again. "I will do no such thing. Your parents are distressed and have enough problems without you adding to them. It's just a silly notion you've got into your head because of this"—he waved a hand, clutching at straws—"this mistake by your sister."

"You won't help me?"

"Certainly not. Go and comfort your poor mother instead of coming out with such absurdities. Nursing is not for the likes of you."

"Why not?"

"Don't be foolish, girl. You know perfectly well why not."

He pulled on his coat with a dismissive shrug and left the house.

❧

VALENTINA PUT DOWN HER BOOK.
"I think we should forget about Mr. Rochester's misfortunes now and talk about you instead."

She was sitting on the edge of Katya's bed, reading *Jane Eyre* aloud to her sister. It was one of her favorite novels, so packed with bird imagery that she constantly saw Katya fluttering through its pages, her wings damaged, her eyes bright and desperate.

Katya looked at her with muted defiance that brought faint color to her cheeks. "Let's not," she said.

"You're going to have to tell me, my sweet sister."

"I already have."

"No, I mean really tell me."

"What I said is true. I was tired. I'd had enough." She put a hand over her eyes, the fingernails soft and white. Blocking out the world. "Enough of everything."

Gently Valentina removed the hand. "Enough of me?"

The blue eyes blurred with tears. "That's not fair."

"What you did wasn't fair."

"I know."

Valentina shuffled up until she was sitting next to Katya, an arm around her thin frame. She stroked the bandaged arm.

"Tell me about the ball," Katya said.

"It was dull. Too many stiff military types. Too much testosterone."

"What's that?"

"It's what men use instead of perfume."

Katya chuckled. "You know so much."

"No, I've just looked through some medical books." She turned her head and placed a finger under Katya's chin, tipping it to face her. "Katya, is that why you did it? Because of the ball?"

Her sister lowered her eyes, but Valentina continued to wait in silence.

"I knew you'd find yourself a husband there," Katya whispered at last. "That's what they're for."

"Rubbish, you silly thing. It was horribly dreary. I only went because Mama made me, you know that." She entwined both arms around her sister and pulled her close, smelling the eucalyptus embrocation that Nurse Sonya had rubbed on her skin. She kissed her hair.

"I'll not leave you," she promised.

"You didn't meet a husband then?"

"No, of course not. I just danced a bit. Drank lime cordial and looked at the stars."

"The stars?"

"Yes."

"Did you meet anyone special?"

Valentina pictured a pair of intense green eyes probing hers. And hard gray ones behind a rifle barrel.

"No," she smiled. "No one of interest."

❧

VALENTINA AND HER MOTHER SET OFF TOGETHER TO GO to a bookshop. The sky was heavy with snow, the clouds like leaden weights sinking down to crush St. Petersburg. In the car Valentina could not keep her eyes from the back of the chauffeur's head. She wanted to beat her fists on the stiff shoulders of his padded coat and say, *You frightened me. You frightened me so much I made a fool of myself in the sleigh. In front of a pair of green eyes.* She wanted to say, *Tell me what was under the tarpaulin.*

Instead when he politely opened the car door for her to alight, she looked him directly in the face and said, "There will be no moon tonight. Unlike last night."

She saw the sharp eyes grow blunt. Confusion made him blink.

*Nothing more to say about my sweet arse? No rifle now to make you strong?*

She left him standing beside the car and walked with her mother into the warmth of the bookshop on Morskaya. She'd make him wait. Damn him, she'd make him wait until his feet froze in the gutter.

❧

DO YOU HAVE A SECTION ON ENGINEERING?"
She spoke quietly so that her mother at the other end of the shop wouldn't hear. The assistant craned forward to catch her words.

"Indeed we do, miss. Let me show you where—"

"No, just tell me. I can find it."

She headed quickly for the shelf he had indicated. She inspected the titles, but not many were available: one on bridge construction, several on mining, one on the building of the Kremlin in Moscow. None on tunnels.

*Choose. Quickly.*

One on cars. He liked engines; he said he liked fiddling with metal. Her finger lay on its leather spine, ready to extract it from its position, when her eye caught the name on a book below it. *Isambard Kingdom Brunel*. She snatched it off the shelf, hurried to the counter, and paid for it. The assistant wrapped it in brown paper.

"What's that?" Her mother's voice was curious.

"It's a biography of Brunel."

"And who is this Brunel, Valentina?"

"Just an Englishman, Mama," she said casually. "Look, I've bought a book for Katya as well." She held up a copy of the poems of Charles Baudelaire.

"Will she like that?" her mother asked doubtfully.

"Yes."

"You are good to her." Elizaveta Ivanova smiled affectionately. "I want you to know that your father and I are deeply grateful to you for what you did, for saving her life. She is lucky to have you." She touched her daughter's hand, the one holding the book for Katya. "So are we. I mean it, my dear." As if embarrassed by her display of affection, she added more formally, "By the way, Valentina, I forgot to mention. Captain Chernov from the Hussars—I believe you spoke with him at the ball—left his card this morning. He is coming to call on you tomorrow afternoon."

～

A S HE DROVE THEM HOME ARKIN LISTENED TO THE SILENCE in the car. Something had happened in the shop. The spark that had made the girl's dark eyes challenge him earlier had gone. *There will be no moon tonight.* Her words nagged at him. Yet she couldn't know about last night. Damn it, she couldn't.

He needed to speak with Sergeyev. But after the bomb he had to lie quiet. *Quiet.* He sounded his klaxon at a cart blocking his road because noise was the only way he could keep the other sounds out of his head. *Quiet* was something he could only dimly remember. *Quiet* was no more than a word now. Paradise on earth came at a high price and he was willing to pay it, but the nights were hard. His mind was beyond quiet.

Behind him the mother was filling the heavy silences. She pointed out a new dressmaker's establishment and promised to arrange fittings for her daughter, suggesting different styles of gowns. As Arkin listened he realized that he liked the sound of Madam Ivanova's voice. It was brighter than the rest of her. Hearing just her voice as he sat in the driver's seat, he could picture her without the wary look that was always in her eyes. She didn't trust people, and she didn't trust life. Nothing wrong with that. He knew exactly how she felt.

He slowed at a crossroads on Nevsky and heard her daughter say quite distinctly, "Mama, I'm worried about Papa. This bomb attack on Prime Minister Stolypin could be the start of a plan to attack all the tsar's ministers. They could come for Papa again."

"Valentina, we have to leave such things for your father to deal with. Don't interfere. He doesn't like it. He is the one who makes these decisions, not us."

"Do they frighten you, Mama, the revolutionaries?"

"Of course not. They are a disorganized rabble. And anyway, don't forget that we have our army to protect us."

"Men like Captain Chernov?"

"Exactly." There was a long uncomfortable silence before Elizaveta Ivanova added, "Please don't be difficult about this visit by him, Valentina."

Arkin could imagine them behind him. Believing their Captain Chernov could keep them safe.

⁓

ARKIN WOKE IN A SWEAT. SOMEONE WAS SHOUTING, BELlowing in his ear. The bed was tangled and he tried to kick his legs free, but they were trapped. Cobwebs gathered on his face in the pitch blackness, threads like hot wires, scorching his skin. Still that shouting. Wouldn't the bastard ever stop? His head hurt; his heart pounded so hard that his stomach abruptly heaved and he vomited on his sheets.

A different hammering. A fist on a wall.

"Shut the fuck up!" Popkov's voice.

Too late Arkin clamped a hand over his mouth, and the terrible shouting ceased. It had been coming from his own throat. He sat up in the darkness and yanked his legs to the floor, where the touch of the cold boards on his bare feet brought him to his senses. He came back to his cramped little room above the stables and wiped the sweat from his eyes.

What kind of man has nightmares about the horses he killed? What about the people he'd slaughtered? Each night the dream came to him, vivid images of the black horse with its hind legs blown off, twisting itself in half to sink its massive yellow teeth into what was left of its bloody rear end, trying to gouge out the pain. Its screams splitting the night.

Where were the people? Where were *their* screams?

Dear God, what kind of man was he becoming? He stripped off his soiled nightshirt and stood shivering. The dark suited him. He liked the way it blacked out everything. It was only the future that was bright.

## Thirteen

THE COUNTESS'S SON WAS FEARLESS. JENS COULD NOT DENY that. He bobbed over every obstacle Jens set him to. He was not a talkative child, but as he spent his days incarcerated with a dry stick of a tutor, who could blame him for keeping his words locked inside his head? But he would release great whoops of childish joy when his stubby little pony took off in sudden darts of energy, the boy's heels drumming its fat sides. A trickle of sun flashed through the trees, sending arcs of light bounding across the trails.

"Alexei," Jens called over his shoulder, "let's head down to the stream."

"Can I jump it?" the boy yelled.

"You fell off last time."

"It didn't hurt."

His mother had complained that her son's shoulder was black for a fortnight and had forbidden them to jump the stream again till he was older.

He grinned at Jens. "I won't fall."

"Promise?"

"I promise."

"Keep your heels down, boy."

They barged through the undergrowth to where the stream

carved a path through the black earth. The boy's cheeks were red. Jens watched his small hands tighten on the reins; a quick kick and the pony gathered itself for the jump, but at the last moment Alexei yanked hard on the reins, forcing the pony to skid to a halt. The small figure leapt out of the saddle and dropped to his knees in the freezing water.

"Get out," Jens ordered.

But the boy was holding a dog. Or rather, a dog's head. The large brown body lay under the water, but Alexei had lifted its head above the ice to allow the animal to breathe. He was stroking its wet muzzle, pulling weeds from its eyes.

"Alexei, leave it. It's dead."

"No."

"Come out of the water. You'll freeze to death."

"No."

Alexei had never defied him before. Jens swung from his saddle and heaved the lifeless animal out of the water. It was a large hound with rough black fur and white young teeth. It lay limp in his arms, soaking his clothes, and with Alexei still hanging on to one of its dripping ears, they waded back onto dry land.

"I want to bring it home," Alexei said.

"Why?"

The boy clutched the sodden head to his chest. "If I die in a river, I want someone to bury me."

Jens couldn't argue with that. He strapped the dog onto the pony's back with his belt, then lifted Alexei onto Hero and swung up behind. He wrapped the shivering boy in the folds of his coat and rode fast.

"Uncle Jens, did you ever have a dog?"

"Yes. When I was a boy, a strong sled dog. All heart and teeth, he was. Gave me a few scars to remember him by. Every boy should have a dog."

The small head nodded, then swiveled around, and eager eyes gazed up at him.

Jens sighed. "I'll speak to your mother."

# Fourteen

Jens called on Valentina as he'd promised. He stood on the doorstep and felt as awkward as a young dolt from the fields with straw in his hair. It was laughable. He had wined and dined the finest ladies of St. Petersburg's elite without batting an eyelid, except to flirt with them. Yet this tender slip of a girl could make his feet feel too big and his shoulders too broad just by turning her head on that neck of hers and letting her velvet brown eyes study him for a moment too long. There was a music in her movements that made others clumsy, even in the way she had uncoiled from the filthy floor of the sleigh and settled on the seat beside him. As smooth as the breath of a summer breeze on the Neva.

The door was opened by a liveried footman who showed him into the reception hall. Impressive indeed. Jens glanced around at the gilt chandelier and the marble statues that lined the niches in the walls. Russians loved to display their wealth as ostentatiously as peacocks unfurl their gaudy tails.

"Miss Valentina is engaged at present. In the blue salon."

The footman was a wiry fellow with a narrow face and extraordinarily large hands. Jens passed him his card.

"Please inform her that I am here."

The footman vanished. So she was engaged at present. Maybe a friend from school? It was the custom for the ladies of St. Petersburg to drive around to each other's houses in the morning handing out their visiting cards, and then to call on each other in the afternoon for tea, followed by a string of engagements and parties in the evening. It was nothing for a woman to change her dress six or eight times in one day. Jens thought about Valentina's words in the moonlight: *I want . . . more.* He couldn't blame her. But nursing? That was a different matter.

"Miss Valentina will see you now."

He entered the blue salon. Presumably it must have been furnished in blue, but he didn't notice. All he saw was Valentina: her slender form seated on a brocade sofa, hands quiet in her lap, her back straight, too straight. He had the feeling something was making her uncomfortable. Was it his intrusion? Yet she smiled at him, rose to her feet, and held out her hand.

"How kind of you to call."

Her manner was formal, as though she'd never been curled up against his chest on an icy road in the dark.

"I hope I find you well."

"Very well, thank you," she responded. "Though I've felt the cold these last few days."

Her dark eyes held his for a moment longer than necessary, and there was that teasing spark in them before she lowered her lashes and turned away with a rustle of silk.

"Let me introduce you to Captain Stepan Chernov."

Only then did Jens notice the other occupant of the room. A fair-haired captain of the Hussar Guards, a broad handsome face with a confidence that came from having killed people. Jens had seen it before in the military, that belief in their own invincibility after they'd fought in battle and survived. But today there was no stink of blood on him, and he made an impressive figure in his immaculate uniform and highly polished boots. Jens bowed politely and thought about putting him to work in one of his tunnels. Dirty him up a bit.

Valentina smiled at the captain. "This is Jens Friis. He's an engineer. I believe you met each other at the ball the other night."

"Did we?" Captain Chernov asked. "I don't recall."

"Apparently so," Jens replied. "The halls were crowded."

But they both remembered. Jens could see it in the other man's eyes. That moment when Jens had arrived bearing lime cordial and had whisked Valentina away from under the captain's nose. Chernov had not forgotten.

They sat down in high-backed chairs and a maid served them tea in paper-thin porcelain cups with ornate gold rims. Doll's cups. Jens could have crushed his in his hand. Valentina guided the conversation down safe paths; she talked about the latest restaurant on Nevsky, then invited gossip about Prince Felix Yusupov, heir to the richest family in Russia, who had just returned from Oxford University to the Moika Palace. She touched on Kschessinska's latest performance at the ballet. But she was bored. Jens could see it in the stiffness of her shoulders. So he was interested when she turned on Chernov with wide innocent eyes.

"Tell me, Captain, do you hunt?"

A simple question, although Jens heard the undertone in her voice. But the captain was young and had not yet learned to listen to what women say behind their words.

Chernov leaned forward, balancing the ridiculous cup on his knee. "I do." He gave her a broad smile, anticipating her approval. "I was in the tsar's hunting party last year with the American ambassador."

"Wasn't that the hunt when half the forest was slaughtered?" Jens asked mildly.

"Yes." Chernov nodded at Valentina, unaware of what was happening. "Eighty stags and a hundred and forty wild boar. Not a bad day's haul. I have a pair of magnificent antlers on my barracks' wall from one of the animals I downed."

"How clever of you," Valentina said.

The moment stalled. Too late the captain sensed he had been tripped up. Leaving Chernov to wallow in his blood-splattered hole, Jens stretched out his long legs and contented himself with studying the way Valentina's hair tumbled in gleaming ripples around her shoulders. Darker than the night sky. Swept back at the sides by pearl clips, her ears just visible, soft fragile shells.

"Do you hunt, sir?" Chernov asked in an attempt to drag Jens in with him.

"No, I don't, Captain." Jens decided to help his companion dig a little deeper. "But I'd be interested to know what kind of rifle you favor?"

Valentina's dark eyes flicked to Jens and she tilted one eyebrow at him. But before either of them could learn the secrets of the captain's preference, the door opened and Elizaveta Ivanova walked in, elegant in pale blue crepe de Chine. Both men rose to their feet.

"Captain Chernov"—she held out her hand—"my husband is free to see you now. He's in his study. Let me show you the way."

But the captain delayed her. "Before I leave, with your permission, I'd like to invite Valentina to a display of Hussars' swordsmanship next Friday afternoon." He turned to Valentina and bowed with such style, Jens wanted to chop off his knees. "I'd be honored if you would attend the event."

"No, I—"

"Of course she will," her mother enthused. "Your displays are legendary. Fine demonstrations of skill . . . and danger. I'm sure my daughter will be impressed by them."

"No, Mama."

"Madam Ivanova." Jens stepped forward. She was small like her daughter and he towered over her despite the height of her fair hair, braided on top of her head. "Valentina has agreed to a previous engagement for next Friday afternoon."

"Oh? What might that be?"

"I came today to confirm it. An inspection of the tsar's commissioned engineering works. It's an official tour and Tsar Nicholas himself will be there, as well as Minister Davidov and his wife."

He saw Valentina's eyes grow wider. "How wonderful."

Her mother frowned.

The captain scowled at Jens. "Not a suitable amusement for a young lady, surely."

"And watching men pretend to stab each other is?" Valentina asked.

"I'm sure you would not want to disappoint Tsar Nicholas," Jens addressed her mother. "He was enchanted by your daughter when she played the pianoforte for him at the concert. A great credit to you."

He saw her waver.

"With a chaperone, of course," he added.

He heard Valentina draw breath.

"Very well," her mother conceded reluctantly. "She will have to wait till another occasion for a display of swordsmanship. But come now, Captain Chernov, my husband is waiting to speak with you. In the meantime," she said briskly to Jens, "I wish you good afternoon, sir."

She escorted both men from the salon, but as the door was closing behind them a light burst of laughter skipped through the gap.

❧

VALENTINA STOOD ON THE CURB AND EYED ST. ISABELLA'S Hospital with excitement. It was larger than she'd expected and its pale stone was blackened with age, flaking like an old man's skin. Its tall windows were barred with rusty iron strips, but not even that discouraged her. The cold was intense, and she tucked her hands into her muff.

*To be a nurse you need to be tough.*

That was what he had said. She straightened her shoulders, pushed open the door, and walked into a large vestibule that smelled of disinfectant and something else, something unpleasant, something that made her stomach flip over. The interior was large and gloomy with too much brown paint. Corridors led off to places she couldn't even imagine. On one side was an office with a glass hatch that slid from side to side, and behind it a woman sat in residence. Her fingers rippled a coin over her knuckles as Valentina approached.

"*Dobriy den*, good afternoon." Valentina offered a smile but didn't receive one in return. "I am looking for someone to speak to about nurse training."

"You want to hire a trained nurse?"

"No. I want to find out how to become a nurse."

"Well, you need to send the girl in herself. Our *medsestra*, our Sister, will want to speak to her directly."

"It's for myself," Valentina pointed out. "I'm the one."

"You want to become a nurse?"

"Yes."

The woman turned away and busied herself with some paperwork. Valentina assumed she was searching for a form but then noticed the narrow shoulders shaking. She felt her cheeks flush crimson.

"Is there someone I should speak to?"

"Up that corridor there. Third door on the left. Gordanskaya is the name."

"Thank you," she said. "*Spasibo.*"

"Girl, you want some advice?"

"Yes."

"Don't waste your time."

❧

N AME?"
"Valentina Ivanova."

"Age?"

"Eighteen," she lied.

"Do you have your parents' permission to be here?"

"Yes."

"Do you have any nursing experience?"

"Yes."

"What kind?"

"My sister is paralyzed. I help take care of her."

"Have you had a job before?"

"Yes."

"Doing what?"

"I worked in an office."

"Why did you leave?"

"I found it dull."

"So you think nursing won't be dull?"

"It will be more interesting than filling out forms all day."

*Medsestra* Margharita Gordanskaya threw down her pen on the desk, leaned her bulk against the backrest of her chair until the wooden frame creaked, and narrowed her eyes so that her fleshy cheeks threatened to swallow them.

"Get out of here," she said in a crisp voice. It bounced off the walls of the small room.

Valentina stood her ground. "Why? Don't you need more nurses?"

"Of course we do. We're desperate for them. But not like you."

"What's wrong with me?"

"Everything. So go."

"Please tell me why."

The narrow eyes popped open. Brown and humorless. "You're a liar, for a start. The only truth in that pack of rubbish you told me was your name and the bit about your sister."

"I learn fast."

"No."

"Tell me, what's wrong with me?"

The *medsestra* shook her head, making her roll of chins surge alarmingly. "Look at you in your finery. You're a rich young woman with too much time on your hands and nothing to do. You'll tire of nursing in five minutes. Please don't waste my time."

Valentina had worn her plainest dress. Her oldest coat.

"I won't tire of it," she insisted.

"I cannot afford to waste the hard-pressed resources of this hospital on training the likes of you." Gordanskaya rose to her feet. Her starched uniform fought a momentary battle to contain the swing of her impressive bosom and won. "Now, for the last time, young woman, please take your fancy clothes and your fancy ideas out of my office."

Valentina looked down at her sable muff, at the way her fingers were squeezing the life out of it. Without a word, she walked out.

∾

ARKIN LAY FLAT ON HIS STOMACH ON THE WET GROUND, his coat stuck to him, his attention fixed on the empty horizon. He'd brought along three young apprentices from the Raspov foundry, one with a handcart, all of them eager as puppies. He was glad of their company. The job wasn't hard, but it was risky. The train had to slow in exactly the right place to offload its cargo or they would be spotted. He'd chosen a section of rail track that was dead straight so that no one in the front carriages could look behind. Here the pine forest crept close on one side, its dense trunks offering easy cover. The wind swirled through the branches above their heads, gusts dislodging frozen icicles that fell into the snow beneath with a thud that made them all jump.

A puff of smoke billowed on the horizon. Arkin felt his pulse kick. Beside him the youngest of the apprentices raised his head and grinned. Arkin nudged him.

"Keep down, Karl. Be patient."

"If the wrong stoker is on board, he won't be able to stop."

"It's arranged. Trust them."

Karl nodded but with a frown. He was a boy of sixteen with a lion's mane of sandy hair whose father was the engine driver on the train. His enthusiasm for every task was so infectious that Arkin slapped the boy's bony shoulder affectionately. "Don't worry, your father can handle this."

"Of course he can."

The noise of the steam engine pumped through the chill air, raising a string of crows from the trees. Their ragged calls sounded a warning and Arkin's mind was caught by a moment's fear. Not for himself, but for the boy. The birds seemed to cry *Karl, Karl*. No. Omens were for the weak-minded.

The growl of the engine grew louder with the endless grinding of pistons, and suddenly it was in full view, steaming toward them down the track. Arkin turned his head and checked on the other apprentices farther back among the trees with the handcart, two pale young faces in the twilight of the forest. He signaled. *Keep down*. There was a screech of metal and a hiss of brakes that grated on his nerves. He tasted soot in his mouth. Slow and cumbersome, the train drew to a halt and it took only seconds for Arkin to leap from his position, open the heavy sliding door of the last wagon, and seize the small crate that was being pushed toward him.

The boy kept guard. He watched for anybody fool enough to come looking. The crate was manhandled into the cart and immediately the two apprentices started to haul it back to the dark cave of trees. The wagon door slammed shut, and the train started to move. Only at the last moment did the window of the next carriage fly open and a rifle spit out a single bullet before Arkin yanked Karl away from the track. They raced for the trees. Blood dripped like crimson flowers on the snow at their feet.

"Are you hurt?" Arkin shook the boy, worried.

"No, but you are."

Arkin blinked, then felt the sting of pain. He put a hand to his ear and his fingers came away painted scarlet. He laughed and wiped it on his trousers. "It's nothing. A scratch. Now let's see you shift this cart."

They all stole away through the trees with the precious crate, their breath coiling in front of them. Arkin thanked Morozov's God that this time the crows had been wrong.

❧

THE FOG WAS THICK AND WAYWARD. IT TWINED ITS fingers around Arkin's neck and clutched at his face, leaving his skin damp and chill. He urged the ugly brute of a horse under him to a faster pace, but it had a mind of its own and paid no heed. It chose its own pace. Like it chose its own path. The creature belonged to Liev Popkov, so what else did he expect of the damn thing? The village appeared on the side of the road with no warning, gray and ghostly, sliding in and out of sight as the fog curled around the wooden cottages. Arkin could hear the drag of an unseen river somewhere nearby as he rode past a blacksmith's forge where a furnace was belching out scorched air. He called down to the man in the leather apron.

"The priest's house?"

"At the far end." The man drew a cross in the dirt floor with the fiery tip of the metal spike in his hand. "Can't miss it."

Arkin didn't miss it. Above its door loomed a large iron crucifix painted white that seemed to leap out of the fog as if to seize him by the scruff.

"Stop here, you brute," he grunted, tightening the reins, and for once the creature did as it was told. He swung quickly from the saddle, a burlap bag over his shoulder, and rapped on the door.

"*Vkhodite,*" a small voice called out. "Come in."

Arkin opened the door. The smell of lingering damp mingled with scents of cooking and burning pine cones. It reminded him of that feeling he used to have as a child in his own village—that the outdoors was always in danger of slipping indoors if he left a window open. He closed the door behind him now, shutting out the fog.

The place was sparsely furnished: a couple of *poloviki*, handmade rugs, on the floorboards; a few rough chairs; a woven basket that looked like a dog's bed in front of the fire. Disheveled stacks of books in one corner. There was no sign of Morozov. But across the room a young girl of no more than four or five was perched on a wooden stool, frying onions in a skillet on the stove. She shook the pan expertly to prevent burning while she regarded Arkin with large blue eyes that were speculative rather than welcoming. Her hair was striking. It fell in a long straight sheet halfway down her back, so pale it looked almost silver.

"Hello," he said and smiled.

She didn't return the smile. "My father is busy," she said.

She picked up a kitchen knife that was far too big for her small hand and started chopping garlic on a board beside her. It was oddly disturbing to see such a young child performing these tasks with the ease of long habit, but Arkin recalled that Morozov's wife was dead and this tiny mite of a girl had clearly taken on her role.

"May I speak with your father?" he asked. "It's important."

Her attention turned away. He was of less interest than her onions, but she pointed with the knife blade toward a door at the back of the room. He walked over and lifted the latch. Instantly he regretted it. In the middle of the cold bare bedroom a man with head bowed was kneeling on the floor stripped to the waist, flagellating his back with a small whip. Each of its five tongues of rawhide had a tight knot at the end, and each knot was tinged with crimson. The man was Father Morozov.

"Excuse me," Arkin said quickly and withdrew.

In the outer room he sat down on one of the wooden chairs and waited.

"I told you he was busy," the girl said.

"Yes, you were right."

He'd never have believed it of the priest. What the hell was Morozov thinking? Day after day he was fighting to relieve the pain of others, and yet at the same time he deliberately inflicted it on himself. It sickened Arkin. He sat in silence until the bedroom door opened and the priest walked in, fully clothed in his cassock, the usual gentle smile on his face. Arkin looked for the self-satisfaction such penitence must bring but saw none.

"Hello, Viktor, I've been thinking of you. Was the delivery of the grenades a success?" He sat down with no sign of discomfort, physical or mental, though he must have heard Arkin enter his room.

Arkin smiled despite himself. "Yes, that's why I've come. The crate is hidden in Sergeyev's bathhouse at the moment, but it's not safe there. His place is probably being watched. We have to move it quickly."

"The grenades themselves? In good condition?"

In response Arkin reached into his burlap bag and extracted its contents: a short canister with a metal handle attached and a box of ammunition. He passed them across to the priest, who inspected them carefully.

"German military equipment is always the best," he commented.

The crate had been smuggled across borders, adding to the stockpile of arms. When the moment came they would be ready. The armaments were spread around St. Petersburg and moved regularly, some buried in pits deep within the city, which meant if one cache was discovered, the rest were still safe. Precautions were always necessary, infiltrators a constant danger. Arkin constantly had to fight his irritation at the slow pace of the glorious revolution.

Unexpectedly Arkin thought of Valentina Ivanova in the car. *Get us out of here*, that was what she'd said. Imperious, yes, but it was the *us* that stuck in his mind. Not *me*, but *us*. It was Katya, the little cripple, she wanted to save, her loved one. He despised all that the Ivanov family stood for. Exploitative capitalists. But he couldn't help a grudging respect for the older sister. He recognized in her the same single-minded determination that stirred and breathed in himself.

"Trotsky has agreed to come and talk to us," he informed the priest.

"*Otlichno!* Excellent!"

"So we will need the church hall."

"I'll arrange it."

"I must leave now. The minister wants me to drive him to his mistress's party this evening." Outside, the fog had thickened.

"Here." The little child jumped off her stool and thrust at him a hefty slice of black bread covered in fried onions. "My name is Sofia."

"*Spasibo,*" he said, surprised, and took a bite. It tasted hot, full of spices and garlic. "Wonderful, thank you."

"What's wrong with your ear?" she asked solemnly.

The bottom of Arkin's left earlobe had been shot off by the rifle bullet from the train and was covered in a thick black scab.

"Nothing much. Just a scratch. What's a little pain?" His gaze met the priest's, and for that moment they understood each other better.

"My father says pain is how we learn."

"Then the whole of Russia is going to learn, Sofia."

He finished off the bread and onions, swung up into the saddle, and cantered back into the swirling fog. Within seconds he had become invisible, one thought still pulsing in his mind. *The whole of Russia is going to learn.*

# Fifteen

Valentina hurried through Alexander Square, shadows rolling across her face as a fitful wind herded the clouds across the sky.

Nothing was ever easy.

She'd traipsed around three other hospitals and the response was the same. *You're too wealthy. You're too well educated. You're not right.* Yet she could roll bandages with her eyes closed and already knew all the bones in the body, as well as the pressure points and arterial system.

*You need to be tough.* She took Jens's visiting card from her pocket and looked again at the address. She would walk. She asked the way twice but even so, at one point she found she'd taken a wrong turn and wandered into a quiet side street with a white-faced church up ahead. A golden cross on its dome cast a long shadow on the road. A group of men huddled over a brazier at the far end as though waiting for something. As she was passing the church, a young man came out of it in a hurry and hoisted up two sacks from a handcart parked outside.

"Arkin. What on earth are you doing here?"

She might as well have stuck a knife in the chauffeur's ribs. He jerked back and stumbled under the weight he was carrying, dropping one of the sacks. As it hit the ground, the side of it split and two potatoes rolled out.

She stared at the sack. Arkin stared at her.

"Why are you here?" he asked quickly.

"I have taken a wrong turn."

"It seems to me you have no idea where you're going."

He said it not with his chauffeur's face. This one had hard lines and arrogant edges. His words froze in the icy air between them, and she wanted to push them back into his mouth. She crouched suddenly, picked up the two potatoes, and held them out to him.

"Yours, I believe."

"*Spasibo.*"

She waved a hand at the sacks. "What are you doing with these?"

"I'm helping Father Morozov."

She glanced at the church. "Is he the priest here?"

"Yes. He distributes food among the poor."

She could feel his eyes on her, curious. "I'm trying to find my way to the main road. Would I do better to retrace my steps?" she asked.

"That's up to you. You can go on, or you can go back to what is familiar." It seemed that he wasn't talking about the road. Still, he pointed over her shoulder. "The main road is back that way."

"Thank you."

As she started to leave, he lifted up the sacks, one under each arm, and strode back inside the church, unaware that he was leaving a trail of potatoes behind him. She watched him disappear, then picked up each potato and marched into the church. The air was colder, the entrance hall cramped. In front of her stood a set of ancient wooden doors leading into the body of the church, but to her left lay a short passageway that ended in stone stairs going down. A potato lay on the top step.

She descended soundlessly. The stairs wound down into an underground room, dim and cavernous with a vaulted ceiling and the smell of damp stonework so strong it slapped her in the face. Men's voices rose from rows of seats lined up in front of an unoccupied table. The men had their backs to her.

"All they want to do is talk. Talk and more talk. I'm sick of it," someone said.

"I'm with you on that, Oleg. We've had enough of words. It's time for more action."

"Stop complaining." Arkin's voice. "We all want to see more action. He's coming to address us today and then we'll be able to find out what plans he's—" He stopped.

He'd seen her. All eyes followed his gaze, and she heard the rumble of annoyance as they became aware of her presence.

"You forgot the rest of your potatoes." She held out her handful to him.

The men's eyes crawled over her. Scarves were pulled tighter, obscuring faces. She noted that the sacks had been dumped on the table, the split one spilling its lumpy contents like a gutted pig, but under the potatoes lay something that bore no resemblance to a vegetable, something angular swaddled in black cloth. Arkin was approaching her fast.

"My dear girl, let me relieve you of those."

The voice came from behind her. She spun around and found a black figure standing over her on the bottom stair.

"Thank you," she muttered and thrust the potatoes at him.

"This is Father Morozov." Arkin had reached her side. "What on earth are you doing down here? I thought you'd left."

"Brother," the priest said in a warm voice intended to smooth the edges off Arkin's rudeness, "that is no way to welcome our visitor." He inspected her face with thoughtful eyes and fingered his beard as if it were an aid to decision. He was clothed in a rough black cassock and a tall battered black hat, a brass crucifix pinned to his chest just below the straggling ends of his beard. "You are welcome to join us, whoever you are, my dear. We are gathered here to join in prayer for our country in these troubled days and to ask our dear Holy Father for guidance and wisdom."

No sound came from behind but she could sense them watching her. The priest's face was as lined as the skin of an old apple, but she didn't think he was any older than her own father. She smiled at him. Her cheeks felt stiff.

"Thank you, but I must leave now. I just wanted to bring you the potatoes that were dropped outside."

It sounded stupid even to her own ears. So when he stood aside, she scampered up the stairs quickly. The men from the brazier parted to let her through, and she walked at a brisk pace to the end of the road. Aware of their eyes on her, she wondered who was coming to address them today. And what plans he had.

࿇

THE FRONT DOOR BANGED SHUT, ALERTING VALENTINA. A
wave of chill air from outside ruffled the calm on the upstairs
landing, and she ceased pacing. Instead she peered over the balus-
trade and inspected the floor below. Unaware of her above him,
Jens was taking the stairs two at a time, the light from the gas lamp
spiraling down onto his fiery hair. His hand flew up the banister rail,
quick and purposeful. Did he always arrive home from work like
this? So possessed by life?

"Hello, Jens."

He stopped and darted a look upward. The moment he saw her,
something shifted in his eyes. His mouth opened as if he were about
to say something, but he didn't. He bounded up the last stair and
came forward until he was almost close enough for her to touch. His
eyes scanned her face.

"Is something wrong?" he asked quickly.

"No. I just need to talk to you."

Still, that gaze on her face.

"How did you get in here? Like a magic fairy you materialize
outside my apartment door."

She laughed. Saw his eyes watch her mouth.

"Your concierge let me in. I told him I was your cousin."

He smiled. "Did he believe you?"

"I think so. He said I could wait up here on the landing in the
warm instead of out on the sidewalk."

"Then the dolt is more stupid than I thought."

"Why?"

"Because you're far too beautiful to be any cousin of mine."

The words caught her off guard. He didn't laugh when he said
them, just tossed them out into the quiet dusty air and walked past
her to unlock the door of his apartment. The building was an old
one with ornate plaster moldings and a baroque extravagance of
carvings and cornices, but it was tired now, its glory days behind it.
Even the air tasted old and velvety, as though it had been breathed in
by too many people over too many years. Valentina found it appeal-
ing that a man with such modern ideas chose to live in such an old-
fashioned apartment house.

He opened the door with a flourish. "Would you care to step inside?"

She shook her head. "I think I'd better not."

"Of course." He inclined his head courteously. "We wouldn't want to compromise your reputation, would we?"

He was laughing at her beneath that polite manner of his.

"Maybe," she said with a flick of her dark hair, "it would be permissible . . . as your cousin, you understand."

The green eyes grew greener. "As my cousin," he echoed.

She walked past him into the apartment.

ಆ

IT WAS LIKE NO OTHER ROOM SHE'D BEEN IN. THE FURniture was all pale honey-blond with such plain straight lines that for a moment she thought it was unfinished. The floor, made of sanded pine boards, was strewn with colorful rugs, and in front of the fire lay a large long-haired fur rug, as creamy as a dish of milk. On the walls were hung framed pictures of reindeer in snowy landscapes. It was hard not to stare.

"So, *cousin*, may I offer you tea?"

"No, Jens, thank you. I mustn't stay long."

He took both her gloved hands in his and studied them. "Such small hands." His finger touched her palm. "Yet so much talent in them."

She shook her head. Her lungs felt as if they were overheating.

"So," he said, "what is it you need to talk to me about?" He didn't release her.

"You said you have a friend who is a doctor."

"Yes, that's true."

"I need his help."

His grip on her hands tightened. "Are you ill?"

"No, nothing like that."

"What kind of help then?"

So she told him. About the hospitals. It all came rushing out, the scornful eyes across the desks, the rejections. She told him that all of them regarded her as *unsuited to nursing*. Despite needing nurses, none of them trusted her.

"Not even my own family doctor will help."

She told Jens how angry it had made her and how she'd wanted
to put her head down on the table and shout with frustration, but
instead she'd walked all the way across town to this tree-lined avenue and waited for him. He listened without interruption, and when
she'd finished he didn't tell her to give it up. That was what she'd
feared, that his voice would join all the others, would try to wrest
her future out of her fingers without realizing how important it was
to her. But he didn't.

"Come," he said briskly. "We'll go and speak to Dr. Fedorin."

"*Spasibo*. Thank you."

"He will help. Even if it means I have to promise to let him beat
me at cards for the next month. But"—he leaned closer and studied
her face intently—"are you sure this is what you want?"

She nodded. "I'm sure."

"Very well. Let's go and talk to the old quack."

"May I have my hands back?"

He glanced down at them, surprised. As if they were somehow
his now.

"If you must." He raised one to his lips and gave her a formal bow
over it. "To the future of *Sanitarka* Ivanova."

Nurse Ivanova.

She was finding it hard not to love this man.

❧

D R. FEDORIN WAS SEATED ON THE FLOOR OF HIS DRAWING
room playing cards with his five-year-old daughter when they
arrived, scratching at his whiskers in an effort to concentrate.

"Excuse me if I don't get up. My little Anna is thrashing me."

The child grinned up at them, holding her cards pressed against
her small chin. "I let Papa win one game." But she crowed with
delight when he played his last card and she promptly trumped it.
Her eager little hands scooped up the pile of sugared almonds with
which they had been betting and Jens laughed, ruffling her feathery
blond hair.

"Anna, your father is the worst card player in Petersburg and you
are going to be one of the best."

She popped an almond in her father's mouth, patted his cheek
consolingly, and scampered off to the window seat with her win-
nings. The doctor ordered wine to be served.

"Now what can I do for you?" He inspected his guests with interest.

"This is Valentina Ivanova," Jens introduced her. "She needs your help, my friend. She wishes to train as a nurse but the hospitals have turned her down as *unsuited*."

"Are you?" the doctor addressed Valentina.

"Am I what?"

"Unsuited to the task."

"No."

"Maybe that judgment is not yours to make."

The words sounded harsh, but she didn't object. How could she object to anything said by this man who, in his olive green trousers, sat sprawled like a long-legged grasshopper on the floor with his daughter and let her beat him at cards? She didn't know fathers did that.

"Let me tell you why I believe I am suited to nursing. I have helped nurse my paralyzed sister for the past six months. I have learned the anatomy of the human body, and"—she cast about for something else that would decide it for him—"I play the piano."

He blinked. She smiled. "I'll teach your daughter to play 'Für Elise' right now."

Against the far wall of the room stood an upright piano with books piled on top of its lid, obviously never opened. The child abandoned her sugared almonds and stood stiff as a soldier, holding her breath.

"My wife used to play," the doctor said softly. "The piano hasn't been touched since."

"I am sorry about your wife, *Doktor*. I would be proud to play her piano and to teach her daughter. Is it a deal?"

His gaze lingered longingly on the mahogany piano stool where his wife used to sit. He nodded.

Anna skipped across the room to remove the books.

༄

"THANK YOU, JENS."

He had driven her home in his carriage, but they had spoken little as the skies darkened and the lights on the bridges sprang into life. Winter afternoons were short-lived in St. Petersburg. Jens and Valentina stood on the gravel drive outside her house, their shadows shuffling awkwardly side by side. The words for *good-bye* wouldn't come.

"I am looking forward to the visit to your tunnels on Friday," she said brightly. The darkness stole parts of his face from her. "It will be exciting to see what you have engineered."

"Good."

The way he said it. It wasn't right.

"Is there a problem?"

"Nothing I can't deal with."

She caught a glimpse of the weight he had to carry on his broad shoulders, the expectations he had to fulfill.

"It's a responsibility, isn't it?" she murmured. "Each day."

"You will find the same when you're nursing."

"I look forward to it."

That brought a smile at last. "I can't wait to see you in your uniform."

She laughed, but she could feel something wrong, like a knot in a smooth-running thread. "Thank you anyway for saving me from a fate too awful to contemplate. I would have died of tedium if I'd had to spend an afternoon watching grown men play with swords."

"Épées. Not swords."

She shrugged. "Both are boring."

"And tunnels aren't?"

"No, tunnels definitely aren't. They have a purpose."

He took a small step back. Away from her.

"Valentina."

Her pulse slowed. She waited.

"Valentina, what did that Hussar want to speak to your father about?"

"Captain Chernov?"

"Yes, Captain Chernov."

"He's nothing to me. Forget him." She trailed her fingers through the crisp air as though to flick any trace of him from their tips. No stars to gaze at. No moon.

"It's not hard to guess what he wanted to speak to your father about. You."

"He's nothing to me," she said again, more deliberately this time, and she stepped forward. "I will have nothing to do with Captain Chernov. Nothing."

His fingers cradled her chin, tilting it directly into the beam of lamplight from above the door. "You promise?"

"I promise."

"I'll hold you to that."

She wanted to say, *Hold me*. Just *Hold me*.

The sound of a car's engine rumbled its way into the silence, and the crunch of wheels dug into the gravel. Her father had arrived home.

"Valentina," Jens said in a low voice, releasing her chin, "don't let others decide your life for you."

The car door banged and her father came striding toward them. Valentina's eyes caught those of the chauffeur sitting in the driver's seat in his uniform, observing her sharply, but she turned her head away as though he were invisible.

"Good evening to you, sir." Jens gave a courteous bow to her father and received a curt nod in response. Wrapped in his thick fur coat, General Ivanov resembled a bear lumbering into its den as he threw open the front door with a grunt of satisfaction.

"Inside, Valentina. Now, please. I wish to have a word with you."

He walked into the house without waiting for a reply. She stood where she was until the car moved away toward the garage at the back of the house, and for a brief moment they were alone again.

"Jens," she said, "don't forget what I have promised you."

"No," he said in that low voice that burrowed under her skin, "I won't forget. Have nothing to do with him."

She nodded, and in the slash of light from the doorway she saw his mouth curve into what might have been a smile. But now he was out of reach. She watched him move with long easy strides toward his carriage, and the horse whinnied a soft welcome. Valentina knew she couldn't stop the words that had to come next.

"Jens."

He halted. The lamplight caught the edge of his jaw and a twist of his hair.

"Jens, will you do the same?"

"What do you mean?"

"What about the woman who wears green gowns and who sinks hooks into you with her eyes? The one who walks as if she owns the world."

He frowned. "Countess Serova?"

"Ah yes, she looks like a countess. That one."

"What about her?"

"Will you have nothing more to do with her?"

She heard his intake of breath.

"Will you?" she insisted.

He started to return to her, one hand extended, palm up, the way he would hold out an apple to a horse. "It's complicated," he explained, "not so easy to . . ."

"I see." She clamped her teeth together.

"No, you don't see at all. I do promise that I will have nothing to do with her in the way that you mean, but I still have to visit her because . . . Valentina, don't . . ."

It was too late. She had vanished into the house.

༄

*IT'S COMPLICATED. WHAT DID HE MEAN BY THAT? HOW* could he still be intending to visit Countess Serova? Surely he realized that . . .

"Valentina," her father was saying, "I want to start by stating that I have good news for you."

He was going to agree to the nursing. She relaxed and gave him a grateful smile. "Thank you, Papa."

"You've met Captain Stepan Chernov?"

*"Da."*

"A handsome man, I'm sure you'll agree."

Valentina nodded. She was trying to be agreeable. She had not forgotten *Number 4* on her list. *Make Papa forgive me.*

"His father is Count Chernov," he expanded, "head of one of the most distinguished families in Petersburg. The captain is an extremely wealthy young man. Are you aware of this?"

"Mama mentioned it to me."

"I want you to marry him."

The words cut her. Razor sharp.

"Papa." She didn't shout. Didn't beg. Instead she spoke quietly. "I don't intend to marry anyone. I intend to take care of Katya."

For a moment he wouldn't look at her. "Captain Chernov has asked my permission to pay his attentions to you. It is a great honor." His cheekbones were working, as if he were chewing on something hard. "I don't want any more of this foolishness from you, Valentina. Your mother and I are in agreement about this. As your father, believe me, I know what is best for you. You will thank me when you are older."

She stood immobile on the Persian rug. "Papa, I don't wish to cross you, honestly I don't, but neither do I wish to marry Captain Chernov. I've explained that . . ."

Color rose to his cheeks in a dark flush, and his heavy brows bunched together over disappointed eyes. She knew he felt she was letting him down.

"Please don't disobey me, Valentina."

"Or what, Papa? What will you do?" She tried to smile. "Horse-whip me?"

He walked over to her, put an arm around her shoulder and kissed the side of her head. "Thank you for saving Katya. Now I need you to do this for me. It's as simple as that."

❧

H ER ROOM WAS COLD BUT VALENTINA DIDN'T NOTICE. She slipped out of her clothes, dropping them on the floor, but she couldn't slip out of her skin. She crawled into bed and pulled the quilt over her head. Shivers came.

*As simple as that.*

Nothing about this was simple. Not with her father and not with Jens.

"Jens, I made a promise to you. *Nothing to do with him.* I swore it to you."

Outside the wind tapped at the window.

"So why, Jens," she whispered, "why wouldn't you make the same promise to me?"

She stilled her pulse, waiting for that low voice of his to murmur in her mind. Minutes ticked past but no voice came, so she threw off the quilt.

❧

W HAT ARE YOU DOING OUT HERE?" Valentina jumped. "Nothing."

She could just make out the looming bulk of Liev Popkov in the darkness. He was ten paces away, leaning against a wall of the house, and her eyes would not have picked him out of the dense layers of black if he hadn't spoken.

"How long have you been standing there?" she asked.

"Long enough."

"Spying on me? For my father?"

He grunted. She heard him spit.

They were outside on the gravel at the back of the house, where by day the sun barely reached at this time of year and by night it froze hard. Ice and snow bunched in treacherous ruts. Valentina was scraping them with a stick, prodding at them, sliding her gloved fingers over them. With great care she examined them inch by inch in the light that fell from the music room window. She wanted to ask Liev to help her but the words stuck in her throat, so she continued her search alone and in silence. For a full five minutes neither spoke.

"Looking for something?" he asked at last.

"Yes."

"What is it?"

"That's my business."

"It's cold out here."

She said nothing but continued to scrape at the ice. Another five minutes of silence.

"Is this what you're looking for?"

Her head snapped up. He hadn't moved from the spot but he was holding out his hand. She walked over, wary of the ice, and stared at his big paw. In the center of it lay something that gleamed, something metal. She snatched it from him, closed her fingers tight on it. It was the key to the piano.

"You bastard!"

He laughed, loud and boisterous.

She slapped his knee with her stick, then tossed it aside and started laughing with him. A strange isolated sound, their laughter echoed in the freezing folds of the night air.

"You bastard," she said again.

And stalked back into the house.

❧

VIKTOR ARKIN WATCHED POPKOV AMBLE BACK TO THE stables. He'd seen the big man skulking in the shadows for hours, indifferent to the snow and the raking wind, waiting to see if the girl would come in search of whatever it was she'd lost. He'd observed the way Popkov baited her, teased her till she lost her temper with him, and he envied the careless ease of it. As if Popkov didn't give a damn. She'd called him a bastard but they had laughed. Together they had laughed. Arkin couldn't work out why.

He felt awkward with women, tongue-tied and mystified by what it was they wanted to talk about. The women at his political meetings and on the committees were all vociferous and aggressive. Wanting to be men, it seemed to him. He sometimes felt the urge to talk to Valentina and her mother, to stop the car and really talk to them, to find out what was in their minds. There was something about Valentina that didn't quite fit in. That was why she had startled him so much when she caught him unloading the ammunition in the church, because he had no idea how she would react. It was obvious she was suspicious, but would she voice her suspicions to her father? Would she ask him to call for the Okhrana?

He would have to be more careful, more than ever now. He walked silently back to the garage, let himself in, and closed the door behind him. His nerves tightened, but hardly anyone else came in here. It was safe. Always it was the same, this fire that was consuming him, this need to march forward into the new tomorrow. Impatience plucked and pulled at him, and he tried to quiet it by moving to the back of the garage behind the car. Against the wall he had arranged a tidy stack of cardboard boxes containing engine parts, oil cans, polishing cloths, spare tools, machine bits and pieces, all things that belonged in a garage. No one would suspect, no one would delve deeper.

Only he knew of the crate that lay at the bottom of the boxes. Only he knew what it contained.

## Sixteen

Nurse Sonya was to be Valentina's chaperone for the afternoon. Her bulky figure sat upright on the seat in the Turicum in her best black coat and gloves, and Valentina noticed that her hat with its red velvet band was new.

"We are very privileged," Nurse Sonya said, eyes bright. "To see the tsar."

"That's true."

It *was* true. Valentina was acutely aware of that fact. But Arkin was sitting in front of her at the wheel of the car, and she wondered what thoughts were crowding through his proletarian brain. When the car drew up, the place wasn't remotely as she had been expecting. She had imagined a wooden hut next to a giant hole in the ground and a rusty metal ladder fixed to the inside of the hole. She'd been nervous about climbing down and had abandoned most of her petticoats to make leg action easier. She wore a fox fur coat and hat at her mother's insistence, as she would be in the presence of Tsar Nicholas, but underneath she'd chosen a simple wool dress with a high neck for warmth and a loose design for freedom of movement.

"Excited?" she asked the nurse as they stepped out of the car.

"To meet Tsar Nicholas will be one of the best moments of my life." Nurse Sonya shook her head in astonishment. "I never thought I would live to see the day that I would receive such an honor."

Arkin was standing beside the step to help her out of the car, and Valentina glanced up at his face. But she saw nothing there. He was wearing his usual bland expression, but she would bet her sable muff that he was listening to their conversation.

"Arkin," she said.

"Yes, Miss Valentina."

"When you have parked the car you may come back here to cheer the tsar when he arrives." She looked straight into his impassive gray gaze. "If you wish."

"Thank you, Miss Valentina."

She gave him a small smile. A tiny victory in return for that rifle shot. Then she inspected the building they were about to enter. It wasn't a wooden hut of any kind, quite the opposite in fact. It was an imposing three-story structure built of brick with an entrance framed by elaborate stonework. Most striking was the way its façade curved outward, as though imitating the curves of the tunnels that crept like thieves under the city's streets. No giant holes in sight, not yet. No uniformed Cossacks either, the tsar's personal bodyguards.

The doors swung open as she approached, and her pulse lost its rhythm when she saw Jens standing in the entrance. One hand was already stretched out toward her in greeting, as though impatient with the immaculate manners of the rest of him.

"Ladies, good afternoon, *dobriy den*. You have arrived. I thought you may have had second thoughts about coming out in this foul fog."

Did he really think that she wouldn't come?

He bowed over the older woman's hand first and said, "You brighten my day, Nurse Sonya, with your glorious hat. It's my pleasure to meet you."

Her cheeks flushed. "This old thing. I thought its brim would protect me from any drips in the tunnels."

"How perceptive of you," he smiled.

Valentina wanted to snatch the nurse's gloved hand from his, but when he finally turned to her she forgave him. Forgave him anything because he looked at her as if he had been waiting for this moment all day and counted the minutes all night. He let her see this, didn't hide it from her. She thought that in today's fog his eyes would be dull and colorless, but they shone as vivid as the first shoots of spring grass. He took her hand and for a moment she thought he was going to raise it to his lips, but he restrained himself. He bowed low over it instead, so that she saw the top of his head, the way his hair sprang from his scalp as though it had somewhere to go. She resisted the urge to touch it.

"Good afternoon, Jens," she said quietly.

Their eyes held. Her fingers curled in his for a moment before she withdrew them.

"Is everyone here?" she asked him. "Ready for Tsar Nicholas's arrival?"

His mouth tightened. "His Imperial Majesty has been unavoidably detained, I'm afraid. He will not be accompanying us on the tour of the engineering works after all."

A squeal of disappointment came from Nurse Sonya. "Oh," she said in a long, drawn-out sigh.

"I apologize for the unforeseen change of plan, but there are many calls on His Imperial Majesty's time. Minister Davidov and his wife are here."

"But no tsar?" the nurse wailed.

"No tsar."

"Don't be foolish, Nurse," Valentina said sternly. "It's the engineering accomplishment we have come to see. It will, I'm certain, make up for your disappointment."

"Are you also disappointed, Valentina?"

It was Jens who asked, his question so sharp, so direct, it took her by surprise.

"No."

"Truly?"

"I came to see the tunnels."

"Then I'd better take you to them."

He offered her his arm and they walked through the door together. There must have been an entrance hall and other people, but she didn't notice them. She was aware only of the strong straight bones of his forearm under her hand and the warmth of his shoulder against hers.

*The tunnels*, she reminded herself. *That's why I'm here.*

❧

S HE'D BEEN WRONG ABOUT THE RUSTY LADDER. THEY'D descended in a heavy mechanical elevator, more suitable as an animal cage than a transporter of humans. The iron door slammed shut and Valentina's stomach clung to the ground floor while the rest of her sank into the bowels of the earth. She'd greeted Madam Davidova, remembering her from the ball the other night, and been introduced to the other guests, but her thoughts were only with Jens and his tunnels.

They were distinctly menacing, The air underground smelled like a dead animal. Water dripped down the walls, and pockets of darkness hid from the string of lamps that looped along the arched roof.

There were twelve guests, including herself. Four officials from the project: an engineer, a surveyor, the foreman of the works, and lastly a water specialist. All of them moved through the tunnels as naturally as moles, ducking their heads without thinking when the roof level lowered, turning their faces automatically to one side when they passed an offshoot tunnel with its onrush of dank air.

Up in the entrance hall there had been speeches. Jens had given a talk on the aims of the project, on the need for drainage and sewer system to improve the health of the city. Two thousand dead last year, cholera rampant in the slums. So many millions of gallons pumped out each day. The low water table caused flooding because St. Petersburg was built on mosquito-infested marshes. So many million bricks, fired in Moscow and transported. A workforce that labored in twelve-hour shifts, night and day. Sewage pipes running arrow-straight all the way north to the Gulf of Finland.

Valentina stopped listening to his words. She stared at his mouth, watched the way his lips moved. He was wearing a leather hat that flattened his hair and thick rubber-soled boots that squelched through water, making slapping sounds. She liked the way everyone listened when he spoke, even the sour-faced Minister Davidov, and that when he eventually stopped speaking, he maneuvered himself into a position next to her.

"Interested?" he asked.

"Yes, very."

"Frightened?"

"Yes, very."

"I don't believe you."

She laughed. "Your achievement is spectacular," she added. "You must be very proud."

He nodded, smiling at her, examining her face. Nurse Sonya was busy in front of them conversing at length with Madam Davidova about the use of camphor in rooms to rid a house of stale smells. She was just turning to advocate its use underground to Jens, when a sound like the crust of the earth cracking open roared through the tunnel, ripping at eardrums. The ground splintered beneath Valentina's feet.

Lights blacked out as people's screams echoed, only to be swallowed by the crash of rocks and bricks spilling down from above. Valentina stumbled, caught up in the panic, and would have fallen if a hand had not seized her wrist and yanked her against a wall. She groped for direction in the darkness. Blind and choking on dust, she had the sense to keep her mouth shut.

"This way." Jens's voice at her side was harsh and angry.

He pulled her along behind him. She couldn't breathe, couldn't think. Her ears hurt. She lowered her head as he dragged her into a smaller offshoot tunnel.

"This way!"

Valentina's mind struggled. But she reached behind her, found someone else's hand and pulled it along with her. Together the group stumbled forward. But ahead of her, even in the suffocating blackness, Jens seemed to know where he was heading, and his fingers had latched around her wrist tight as wire. He wasn't going to let go of her. She clung to that single thought.

༄

SILENCE. IT CAME IN THE END. THE SILENCE THAT ONLY exists underground. Jens knew it well, that total absence of sound. Sometimes he wondered if death was like this, not a burning raging hell but a cold and implacable absence. No life, no sound, no fresh air to breathe. A grinding ache gripped his skull. He lit a candle and only he saw the tremor in his hand. Around him he heard the whimpers of relief as the flame flickered into life. It was his rule never to venture underground without matches and a candle in his pocket.

"How many of us?" He counted heads. "Eight."

Eight out of seventeen. Dear God! Minister Davidov was here and his wife, as well as Kroskin, the young surveyor. But no assistant engineer. No Prutz, the water specialist. Who else? He raised the candle higher, sending shadows scrambling through the thick dust-ridden air.

Valentina was here, crouched on the floor. For one sickening moment he feared she was hurt, but no, she was helping the nurse, both of them tending Kroskin, the young surveyor, who was stretched out on the damp ground. One of his trouser legs was shredded, and the flesh on his shin gleamed wetly. Two others stood trembling, a whiskered member of the Duma parliament and his wife. He was crying, deep hacking sobs, and she was rocking him in her arms, whispering sharp little instructions. "Hush, no tears, Jakob, hush now, wipe your eyes."

"We're going to die here." His words came in short gasps.

Valentina raised her head. Her hat was gone, her dark hair coated in dirt. She turned steady eyes on Jens.

"Are we?" she asked. Just a straight question. "Are we going to die?"

All eyes fixed on him and Jens felt the weight of them as heavy as the layers of rock above their heads.

"No. *Nyet*. Of course not. Take a look at where we are. It's what is called a passing chamber. Two sluice gates, one beside the other to channel and control the flow of water through the open gully over there." He gestured into the darkness beyond the reach of the candle's glow, and hot wax dripped onto his fingers. *Keep talking. Keep crowding their minds with words to flush out their fears.* "But over here"—he walked away from the huddle of figures—"on a hook, ready for emergencies, is this."

He held up an oil lamp, like a magician producing a rabbit. He lit it from the candle flame and watched its light paint the ashen faces a sickly yellow. Their eyes grew rounder, no longer flat and stunned.

"We must give the aboveground engineers time to assess what has occurred," he continued. "Everyone will be in shock up there at the moment, as we are down here." He forced out a smile. "We're safe here," he told them. "Be thankful."

"How do you know there won't be another roof collapse any moment?"

It was Minister Davidov. Damn the man. Everyone scanned the curve of bricks three feet above their heads at its highest point, seeking cracks. Jens could smell their fear slinking around the chamber.

"The tunnel is strong and solid."

"So strong it crashed down on us." Davidov's lean face was hollow with tension.

"No."

"What do you mean, Friis?"

"The tunnel did not collapse because it was weak."

Valentina rose to her feet, a small figure in the gloom of the cavern. "There was an explosion. I heard it."

"Don't talk rubbish, young woman. The roof was weak. It crashed down on—"

"She's right," Jens cut in.

Such sharp ears. She was alert, she listened. Most people didn't listen.

"What the fuck are you trying to—"

"Andrei," Madam Davidova said pleasantly as she laid a firm hand on her husband's arm, "not now. Let's get through this the best we can. Leave the recriminations till later." She looked around her and smiled. It wasn't a particularly convincing smile, but it helped. The tension slid down a notch.

"Madam Davidova, what you say is true. We must remain calm. The most important thing now is to check on everyone's wounds." Jens walked over to Kroskin, the surveyor on the floor. The young man's arms were curled across his chest to hold in the pain. "How bad is it?"

Kroskin grimaced. "I'll live."

"We'll all live."

The nurse nodded encouragement. "The flesh is stripped off one leg below the knee but fortunately the bone isn't broken." Already in her hands was one of her voluminous petticoats, pressed hard against the wound.

"Here." Jens pulled a pocketknife from his belt.

Kroskin's eyes widened.

"We're not going to hack your leg off, boy," Jens reassured him. "Just cut up bandages." He placed a hand on the nurse's shoulder. "Do your best," he murmured. "Davidov, come and slice up some bandages here."

He passed the knife to the minister.

"Any more wounds?"

No one spoke. He looked around at his companions, trapped in this alien nether world of near-darkness, and he was impressed by their fortitude. He felt a rush of respect for them, even for that bastard Andrei Davidov, who had set to work on the petticoat with quick efficient strokes.

"We've all got bangs and bruises, I know, but"—they weren't going to like this—"if there's nothing else major, I'm going to leave you."

"No. Don't."

It was Valentina. He noticed a graze on her neck.

"You're going back there, aren't you?" she said.

"I have to."

"Because there might be others who are wounded."

Wounded. Crushed. Pinned under rocks. Bleeding and dying. Maybe already dead. Everyone saw images in their heads.

Valentina said quickly, "It's too dangerous to go alone. Take someone with you."

*Take me with you.* That was what she meant.

He glanced across the chamber. "You." He pointed to the Duma man, the frailest of them. "You come with me."

Valentina made a soft noise in her throat. This close he could see the dirt caked on her eyelashes. But he couldn't take her. He didn't know what mangled limbs they might have to tread on down there. He relit the candle and took hold of the Duma man's elbow, steering him back toward the mouth of the tunnel. He could feel the man's arm trembling.

"Wait!" Valentina stopped him. "Take the lamp, you'll need it more than we will. Leave us the candle." She removed the lamp from beside the wounded man and carried it to Jens. She held it out. "Take it."

"Thank you," he said. *"Spasibo."*

"Take care."

He nodded. "Minister Davidov," he called out, "watch out for the women."

"Jens," Valentina said in a low voice, "don't you know that it is the women who watch out for you men?"

"So I should be taking you with me?"

"You should."

"I can't."

"I know. No stars to look at this time."

He couldn't help a smile. Then he was gone, swallowed by the black tunnel so effortlessly that for a bleak moment he doubted his existence.

∽

THE LIGHT, WHICH NOW HAD DWINDLED TO A MISERABLE candle flicker, made people more anxious, nervy as cats in a wolf cage. But for Valentina, the loss of *him*, that strong center of him, was the worst. Without Jens the chamber felt much emptier, the air fouler, the people smaller. The rescue that only minutes ago had seemed likely, abruptly became unlikely. She was frightened he wouldn't come back.

She'd seen how he moved in the darkness as if he owned these tunnels, as if they were his, not the city's. The way you own a house. And for the first time it hit her forcibly what this collapse of his beloved tunnels must mean to him. A groan came from the young surveyor, and she switched her thoughts. She had done all she could to make Kroskin comfortable after Nurse Sonya had finished binding his leg, but it wasn't much. She had placed a scarf under his head and her fur coat over him, tucking it around him, trying to keep out the pain. His groans were muffled by the arm he had draped across his face and though she held his other hand between hers, he didn't speak.

"Is your family here in Petersburg?" she asked.

He nodded, nothing more.

"I have a sister," she told him softly. "Her name is Katya." *Katya, I'm not dead. Don't believe them if they tell you I'm dead. And don't be frightened for me. I'll come back, I won't abandon you, I promise.* "She's blond like you and loves to play cards. Do you have a sister?"

A nod again.

"What's her name, your sister?"

Nothing. His shivers grew worse.

"They have safety systems," she told him. "Rescue procedures. They'll get us out of here, don't worry."

His arm fell from his face. "Is that true?"

"Of course it is."

"She's lying." Davidov stood beside her, his sharp-angled shadow resting on her. "Just like she lied about hearing an explosion."

"Why would I lie?" she demanded.

"To protect Friis. He'll be hauled up for incompetence if we get out of here alive."

She looked around at the others. "Did anyone else hear an explosion?"

Nurse Sonya shook her head. Madam Davidova was standing motionless, close to the candle on the floor as though nervous of leaving it. Its flame sent her shadow scuttling up the walls. She stared at her husband with a bemused expression. Only the Duma man's wife, who had sunk down on her heels, nodded vehemently.

"I heard it," she stated. "My ears still hurt from the blast. Don't yours?"

"Yes," Valentina said, and looked at Madam Davidova.

Slowly the minister's wife nodded her head.

"An explosion," Valentina repeated. She knew the sound. It had been blasted into her brain at Tesovo. "A bomb."

The word splintered the fragile shell they had been sheltering under.

"Why would anyone attack the sewers?" Nurse Sonya whispered. Tears were running down her cheeks.

"It's not the sewers," Davidov snapped. "Are you too foolish to see the target?"

"The tsar," Valentina stated bluntly. "They meant to kill the tsar."

❦

SHE WATCHED THE CANDLE, THE WAY THE HOT WAX pooled. Watched time burn. Still he didn't return. She wanted to go after him. Instead she listened to the ever-present swirl and rush of water. She tried to assess the damage to the five faces huddled around the flame. It kept her mind off Jens's absence.

Nurse Sonya was steady. She had seen death and damage before. Yes, there were tears, but her hands were steady as she tended her patient on the floor. The surveyor was crumbling. Sweating. Pain and fear too much for him. But Madam Davidova was harder to judge because she was schooled in self-control. Just a small crease between her eyebrows, pulled tight the way Mama did when she had a headache.

*Mama? Don't worry about me.*

The Duma man's wife was different. She couldn't keep still. She sat, she stood, she paced, fingers fretting at her clothes, at her hair, at her throat. She was a thin woman. In the darkness she looked more like a shadow than a person. "The men have been gone a long time," she said.

"Searching for others," Valentina assured her. "It takes time."

"But more rocks could fall."

"We'd hear if they did. And, don't worry, the men would shout to us."

Davidov stepped between them. "We should not be too alarmed because we have among us someone who is the guarantee of our rescue."

"Who?" the woman demanded.

Davidov directed his gaze at Valentina.

"Me?"

"Yes, you."

"Why me?"

"Because you are about to become the jewel of St. Petersburg."

"What do you mean, Andrei?" his wife asked.

He paid her no heed. "Is that not so, young lady?"

"No."

"Valentina Ivanova is about to marry," he announced. "Into one of the finest families in the city."

"No." Valentina wiped her hands on her filthy skirts. "It's a lie."

"Your father himself informed me of the match. Congratulations, my dear. And because of you, the Chernov family will move heaven and earth—and rocks—to get you out of here. They'll send the army in if necessary."

Valentina felt the air around her change. Hope fluttered faintly. Eyes brightened and hearts beat faster.

"Do you have matches, Minister?" Valentina asked coolly.

He frowned. "Yes, I do."

"The candle is disappearing fast. We should save it."

"What?"

"We must blow it out."

❧

THE DARKNESS WAS TOTAL. SHE LIKED IT THAT WAY. SHE could hide in it. She couldn't believe she had ever been frightened of Jens's tunnels.

Jens. *Come back to us.*

All six of them were seated on the cold ground in a circle, feet touching, so that all were anchored to each other. No one would feel that he or she had been cut adrift in the blackness, alone with the scurrying sound of rats slinking from tunnel to tunnel.

Valentina felt, rather than saw, the minister on her right lean close. "You are a bright and lovely creature, my dear," he said under his breath, "far too intelligent to bow to the will of others when you so clearly have one of your own. Take this advice from an old campaigner. Use your weapons."

"Weapons?"

"The greatest of all, my dear. Your beauty."

"Do you know what the strongest weapon is?" she asked him in the pitch darkness. "One I will never possess."

"What's that?"

"Being born a man."

He chuckled, low in his throat. She sensed him nodding acknowledgment that she was right.

❧

WAS SHE DEAD? ARKIN WONDERED.

He had asked himself that question a thousand times.

He didn't want her dead. Or hurt. Or frightened. It shocked him how much he wanted her to be alive. Before this he had killed only strangers and always to further the cause, but this time it was different.

He glanced up at the window of her room, but she wasn't there. He was waiting in the cold beside the Turicum outside the front door. Waiting. Half his damn life was spent waiting. When finally Minister Ivanov and his wife descended the steps, both wrapped in heavy furs, both stiff and silent with each other, they seated themselves on the blue leather and didn't speak. They stared out at opposite sides of the street. It was a familiar routine, but it saddened Arkin that at a time like this, with their daughter missing, they couldn't find something to hold them together. Was there so little left to their marriage?

As he drove, his mind replayed his conversation with Sergeyev.

"Tsar Nicholas is paying a visit to the new sewerage tunnels," Arkin had told his friend. "This is our chance, Sergeyev."

"Are you sure?"

"Yes. The nurse in our household can't stop jabbering about it. She's been invited along as chaperone to the older Ivanov daughter. It's the perfect place for a trap."

Sergeyev groaned. "Fuck this arm of mine. It means I'm no use to you. I'm not working underground again yet."

Arkin had slapped him affectionately on his good shoulder. "No, my comrade, I know that. But your brother is."

Together they started to distribute rifles, and for the first time in many months Arkin allowed himself to get drunk that night. Tension was a creature with claws and fangs, living in his guts, eating him alive.

෨

M INISTER IVANOV DEPARTED WITH NOTHING MORE THAN a curt nod to his wife and headed into the ministry on the Embankment, while Arkin turned the car around and drove back up Nevsky. Outside Madame Monique's fashion house, he opened the Turicum's door and though it was not his usual custom, he offered his hand to Elizaveta Ivanova to steady her on the car's steps. To him she looked frail, the firm lines of her face blurred and uncertain. She accepted it, and before walking under the blue-and-white awning over the shop she thanked him.

"I'll be an hour," she said to him. "No longer."

"Yes, madam."

He bought a newspaper and read it in the car. But it told him little. An accident, they were calling it, a tunnel roof collapse. No mention of a bomb. No mention of an attempted assassination. Fuck the bastards. He cursed Tsar Nicholas for his fickle mind. Without the tsar, the corrupt regime would crumble because it had nothing to prop it up. When Minister Ivanov told him that His Imperial Majesty had gone ice skating that day with his children at Tsarskoe Selo instead of inspecting the tunnels, he'd wanted to howl. Where was the uprising? Where was the start of the brave new world Arkin had sold his immortal soul for?

Finally Madam Ivanova emerged, and he cranked up the engine. He waited for a tram to rattle past before pulling out in front of a monogrammed carriage, but the sight of all the extravagant shops and restaurants only deepened his sense of disappointment. He had truly believed these places would belong to the ordinary people of Russia today. He drove fast, needing to be away from there.

The noise, when he first heard it, startled him. For a second he thought he must have run over a cat. It was a single loud shriek that made the hairs on the back of his neck stand up. Abruptly it ceased, but by then he'd realized it had come from behind him. He turned in his seat and saw Elizaveta Ivanova slumped forward, her elbows tucked into her lap, her face in her hands. She was moaning.

Arkin pulled into a side street and stopped the car. "Are you unwell, madam?"

The fur coat didn't move. Just the low moan that went on and on. He stared at her crumpled figure and found himself breathing awkwardly. He climbed out of the driver's seat and stood on the icy pavement, the wind snatching at his peaked cap.

"Madam?" he said.

The moaning broke off. Still the sable coat remained hunched forward, but quivers ran through it and quiet sobs began to leak between her fingers. Instinctively he slid into the seat beside her. It broke all the rules, but to hell with the rules. He sat next to her, not touching, not speaking, just being there. When the quivering finally ceased and one of her gloved hands reached into the small gap between them, he placed his own hand over it. Glove on glove, the faintest of comforts, and they remained like that. Minutes passed. Several pedestrians glanced at them with a surprised expression, but Arkin ignored them.

"Thank you," she whispered.

Slowly, Elizaveta Ivanova hauled herself back to an upright position and took a long shuddering breath. She didn't look at him or remove her hand, but her back was ramrod straight once more and the tears had stopped.

"She may still be alive," Arkin said quietly.

"I can't believe it."

"Don't give up hope."

Her mouth pulled into a faint parody of a smile. "I gave up hope years ago."

"There's no need to. Hope is what keeps us going."

"Hope for what?"

"For a daughter still alive. For a life worth living."

She turned her face toward him, and he saw the cold loneliness in her blue eyes. Her fur hat was crooked and a strand of fair hair had come unpinned, hanging in a curl across her cheek. He wanted to straighten both for her. To straighten her life for her.

"Is your life worth living?" she asked.

"Of course."

She inspected him, taking in as if for the first time the dark spikes of his hair under his hat, the line of his mouth, and the careful expression in his eyes. Still her hand lay under his.

"Thank you, *Spasibo*," she said again.

She sat back against the seat and closed her eyes. Beneath the almost transparent skin of her eyelids he could see her eyes moving, restless as his own heartbeat, and he waited quietly while she found in herself whatever it was she needed to go on. When it started to snow, he removed his hand, returned to the front seat, and drove her home.

❧

JENS FRIIS CAME BACK TO THEM. VALENTINA WAS THE FIRST to sight the faint glow of the lamp, the first on her feet, the first to greet him and to see that the Jens who returned was not the same Jens who'd left them. His face had changed. In some indefinable way the bones sat differently, as if they had been taken apart while he was gone and reassembled by an unfamiliar hand. His eyes had sunk deeper in his head and a hard line ran down from each corner of his mouth. He was brusque. Unapproachable. He explained in brief sentences what he'd seen.

"The tunnel is completely blocked back there by rocks and rubble."

Valentina studied his hands. Gloves in tatters, blood oozing down his wrist.

"It is too much to remove. The roof is unstable. No rescue teams will be coming that way because more of the tunnel roof could come crashing down at any time."

"Did you find anybody?" Nurse Sonya asked.

The Duma man backed off to the gully and vomited into the water.

"There were bodies," Jens acknowledged. His mouth was tight. No one asked for more.

"Now," he said, "we wait."

⁂

"DO YOU SWIM?"

Valentina's stomach flipped over. "Yes." In the creek in the summer, back in the days when her sister could kick. "Yes, I can swim."

"Good."

"Will it come to that?"

"It could."

She imagined the cold water. "I don't think my nurse can swim."

"Then we shall keep her afloat between us. Don't look so worried. It most likely won't be necessary."

"I hope not. Will the water be filthy?"

"Probably."

⁂

WHEN THE OIL LAMP WAS LIT, THEY LIVED IN ONE KIND of world. Valentina paced up and down the cavern to the limit of the lamp's range, but she didn't venture beyond it. That would be too much. She was thirsty, her throat dry. The older women remained seated on the damp ground, quietly discussing the desirability of a hot bath. Jens stood by the gully water and smoked cigarette after cigarette. His leather hat had disappeared and his red hair had turned a dirty gray, flattened to his head by the weight of brick dust. At intervals he walked over to the young surveyor, studied the flushed face, and exchanged a few words with Nurse Sonya.

When the lamp was off, they lived in a different kind of world, one that released the demons that fled from daylight. The small group sat in a circle again, feet touching.

"Try to sleep," Jens ordered.

He crouched down beside Valentina, took off his coat, and draped it over her.

"*Spasibo*. Let's share it," she said.

In the total darkness she felt the touch of his hand as he spread the heavy coat over their laps. As time crawled past and voices quieted, the incessant swirl and flow of the water filled her mind and she pictured it rising, slowly, implacably, until she was drowning in her sleep.

"Hush."

Jens's voice in her ear. Jens's hand on her chin. Her eyes jerked open but met only blackness.

"Hush," he murmured again.

She was aware of his body leaning over hers.

"You were whimpering. Bad dream?"

"Yes."

"This place invites bad dreams."

The blackness was thicker than pitch. She could make out no trace of his face, but she heard him swallow and felt the soft brush of his lips on hers. There one moment, then gone. So brief she wasn't certain. Tentatively she touched his face and her fingers found the high forehead, the straight line of one eyebrow, and slid down to explore his eyelid and the dense fringe of eyelashes. She had never touched a man's face before.

"When will the water come?" she whispered.

"Soon, I imagine. They have to evacuate the tunnels that we need to escape through and rid them of water."

She breathed carefully, drawing in the air they shared.

"Do you know what I would like now?" he asked.

"What?"

"Four slices of cool refreshing pineapple, sweet and tangy. Two for you, two for me."

She laughed with surprise.

"Sleep now," he murmured. "No more dreams. Don't worry, I'll listen for the water."

❧

THE WATER CAME, JUST AS JENS HAD KNOWN IT WOULD. His sharp ears picked up the change in its voice, a sudden shift in note long before it reached them: a distant sound rattling through pipes and tunnels far off in the system. Water was being redirected, sluices opened and closed. Certain tunnels had to be emptied before the trapped group could escape, and now the sound of the water grew louder.

"Just remain calm," he told them. "As soon as the water is through this chamber, we can all climb up into the higher tunnel and walk our way out. Watch your heads; the ceiling height will be low. Keep together and take a firm hold on the rope." It wasn't a rope. It was their belts fixed together into a long line to stop anyone being swept away.

"How deep will it be?" the nurse asked. Her teeth were chattering.

"Not deep at all. Hold on to the rope."

They stood in a line behind him. The wounded surveyor was belted onto Jens's back, just conscious enough to grip around his neck. He was a skinny young man, not too much weight, but Jens worried about the open wound on his leg in the foul water. Next to him stood the nurse, dropping prayers from her lips like rosary beads. Jens raised the lamp in one hand and took a grip on her arm with the other. On the far side of her stood Valentina. He would have given much to be able to seize her hand and not release it, but he had given his word to help her nurse. One on each side of her, he'd promised, but all the time he'd be watching Valentina. He'd put Davidov behind her, then Davidov's wife, followed by the Duma couple.

When the water came, it rose out of the gully and sneaked across the floor of the chamber as black as oil, but no one panicked. There were raw gasps as the icy flow increased to a flood, crawling over their feet, sliding up their shins, and swirling around their knees. When it reached Valentina's thighs, billowing her skirt around her, her eyes sought his. Her hands held tight onto the rope and onto Nurse Sonya as a rat swept past them, swimming frantically.

Jens judged it carefully. "Now," he shouted.

He raised the lamp and set off. They followed meekly, up the four stone steps to the higher-level tunnel where the outflow had slowed to a knee-high slick of freezing filth. The stench was suffocating and the roof level low. Davidov crunched his head against bricks and swore, but Jens led them as fast as he dared, pulling the makeshift rope behind him. Once in this channel, it was not far to an exit.

"All well?" he shouted out.

"Da."

"Not much farther."

"How long?"

But Jens's ears had caught a sound, a rumble. Above the noise of legs splashing through the water came a distant but distinct rumble.

"Faster," he ordered.

He lengthened his stride. "Almost there," he called out.

"What's that noise?" Davidov yelled.

The panic swept out of nowhere. One moment they were orderly and then suddenly they were running through the filth, stumbling and sprawling, all realizing what the rumbling heralded. The rope was abandoned. The surveyor tightened his grip till he was throttling Jens, but Jens still clutched the nurse and saw that Valentina had an arm around Madam Davidova, who was having difficulty breathing. Her husband was up ahead.

"Take that opening up there on the right. You may see daylight from it," Jens called to him.

Daylight. It was only a word. *Daylight.* Jens had saved it till now. It brought hope in its wake. They hurried, scrambling and splashing to the side recess, turned the corner into it, and immediately Jens heard shouts. He came through last, dragging Nurse Sonya with him, and immediately saw what he'd known would be there. An iron ladder, a metal trapdoor above it. Daylight seeping through the small holes, air that was clean. A cheer went up, and tears were rolling down Madam Davidova's cheeks.

The rumble of water burst into a roar right behind them.

"Up," Jens ordered sharply.

Davidov climbed first. He raised the metal trapdoor with his shoulders, so that it clattered open onto the roadside and white air billowed in, making those in the tunnel squint as they stared upward. Quickly Jens hoisted the surveyor off his back and onto the ladder, so that Davidov could haul him up, followed by the Duma man and his wife. The water was rising fast now, up to Jens's waist already.

"Valentina, climb!"

But she pushed the nurse onto the lowest rung. Nurse Sonya was shivering so fiercely her plump hands could scarcely hold the metal.

"*Bistro!* Quickly!" Jens shouted.

He hooked an arm around Valentina's shoulders and lifted her onto the rung as a surge of water cascaded through the tunnel.

"Go," he said. He gave her sodden boot a push.

He seized Madam Davidova's wrist and placed her hand on the ladder. Saw her fingers curl around it. A dozen more steps and it would be over. But that was when the torrent hit. A great churning wall of water crashed into them, ripping the ground from under them, leaping up the ladder, tearing fingers from metal. The lamp went. The world blacked out. Jens was hurled into the water. Filth in his mouth. His head cracked against a wall. His lungs burned as he fought his way up toward the square of light, but something or somebody crashed against him, submerging him again.

He seized a flailing arm underwater and dragged it back to the surface. For a brief moment he held it and caught a glimpse of a terrified face before the roaring current ripped it away. It was Madam Davidova. Valentina was screaming at him. Her dark figure leapt over him, into the water.

"No!" he bellowed, "Valentina, no!"

He lashed out and caught her long hair; his fingers twisted into it and yanked it toward him against the rush of the current. Her body was small and slight, but Valentina was kicking at him. "Let me go," she screamed, dragging them under. He didn't let her go; he would drown before he let her go. A hand stretched out from the ladder, hurling a coat onto the water's surface. He snatched at a sleeve and was hauled in toward the metal rungs by the Duma man.

"*Spasibo,*" he grunted.

Valentina was quiet now, locked in the circle of his arms, staring back along the path of the water's torrent. Madam Davidova was gone. A low moan seeped out of Valentina, an animal sound of grief, but she didn't resist when he lifted her up the ladder. In the cold gray light of a winter's morning, they stood in a battered huddle, wet and exhausted, in the empty road. Davidov dropped to his knees, his face in his hands. Jens was not ready yet to look at the extent of his own failure. That time would come, when he was alone, away from the eyes of the world. For now he held Valentina's trembling body against his and stroked the filth out of her hair.

"I could have saved her," she whispered, the words shivering on her tongue.

"No," he said. "You couldn't."

In the distance he could hear cars speeding toward them. But the future he had prepared for himself was speeding away from him, as out of control as the raging flood in the tunnels below St. Petersburg.

# Seventeen

VALENTINA LAY SUNK DEEP IN HER PILLOWS. DRIFTS OF snowflakes buffeted the window as icy patterns clung to the corners of the glass, delicate as spiders' webs, cold and unwanted as the thoughts in her head.

Time was passing. She wasn't sure how long. Two weeks, three weeks? More? She'd been ill, the days blurred; a fever burned inside her, drenching the bedclothes with sweat, tying her limbs in knots in the sheets. She'd welcomed it. In her more conscious moments she knew it was a lung infection from the sewer water, but in her wilder spasms she was certain it was a punishment. Madam Davidova had drowned, her body washed up against a sluice grid, while Valentina had survived because she had climbed that ladder ahead of her.

At times the woman's gentle face came to Valentina in her dreams and said sweet words. But other times, at night when the darkness grew too hot and heavy inside her head, Madam Davidova came like a fiend out of hell. Eyes blazing fire. Mouth spitting obscenities. Then Valentina screamed. Nurse Sonya was always there, telling her, "Ssh, *malishka*, quiet now."

Something cold on her brow, a sip of liquid on her lips. Sometimes the bitter taste of laudanum.

The door opened quietly and there was the whisper of wheels on carpet. "Are you awake?"

"Yes. Good morning, Katya. You're looking well."

It was true, Katya did look well. Her skin had color, her hair was freshly washed, and she was sitting more upright in her chair.

"I've brought you some pineapple. Look."

She placed a dish on Valentina's side table. Inside a bowl lay two slices of canary-yellow pineapple, their fragrance drifting around the wintry room and turning it into summertime.

"How are you feeling?" Katya asked.

"Better."

"Good. Will you come downstairs today?"

Valentina closed her eyes. "No. I have a thumping headache."

"Nurse can give you something for it. You could get up and—"

"No. Not today, Katya."

There was a long silence. The window danced and rattled in its frame. Valentina felt her hand lifted by Katya's fingers.

"Valentina, you can't go on like this."

More silence. Thicker this time, harder to breathe.

"Nurse tells me," Katya said gently, "that your fever is cured. That you are better."

"But I feel weak." Eyes still closed.

"Too weak to walk downstairs?"

Valentina nodded.

The small fingers soothed her own with soft feathery strokes. "I hear you, my sweet Valentina, I hear you every night."

"I don't know what you mean."

"Of course you do. I hear you creep past my room every night when you think the whole house is asleep. You go downstairs and you play the piano. Sometimes for hours, even for most of the night."

"No."

"Yes. You creep back just before the servants start to stir. Admit it." Katya squeezed her hand hard, jerking Valentina's eyes open. "So," Katya said, "now you will look at me?"

Valentina looked. This wasn't her Katya, this was someone who had slid under her sister's skin. The blue eyes were cold and pale as moonstones. This person was masquerading as Katya, getting it all wrong.

"Valentina, what is the matter with you? What is it that has paralyzed you as totally as the bomb paralyzed me? You're not hurt. You're not ill. Yet you're hiding away up here. You didn't even bother with your birthday. Where has all your spirit gone?"

"It was washed away in the sewers."

"You're alive. You weren't crushed and you didn't drown, nor did you lose part of your leg like the surveyor did."

"The surveyor? Lost his leg?"

"Below the knee. Amputated."

Valentina recalled his young face. Sweat-covered. Frightened. His arms around Jens's neck, tight as tentacles.

"He'll be able to walk with a crutch," Katya said.

"Madam Davidova will never walk again."

"No."

"I saw her die, Katya. I watched this good woman drown."

Katya's hand slackened its grip, and her tone grew gentler. "Grieve for her. Yes, that's your right, but don't stop living because of her."

Valentina slumped against her pillows. "Katya, it should have been me. She should have been on that ladder, not me."

"But she wasn't. She died; you didn't. So get on with your life."

"Jens put me on the ladder."

"Thank God for Jens Friis. Though he shouldn't have invited you down there in the first place."

"Shut up, Katya. It's not his fault that bloody revolutionaries meant to murder us."

"Good." Katya was smiling. "A spark at last. You owe it to Jens to come back to life."

But Valentina yanked the quilt over her face. "Go away, Katya."

The quilt was wrenched from her grasp. "Look at you!" Katya shouted.

Valentina looked down at herself. A grubby nightdress, her hair lank and knotted. She started to close her eyes, to shut it out, when she felt a quick sharp slap on her cheek.

"Get up!" Katya yelled. "Get out of that bed."

"Don't!"

"Are you just going to stay in your pit and rot?"

"Yes. Leave me alone."

"Look at yourself. You have everything. Everything. You have no reason to hate the world. None."

Valentina said nothing, in case she said too much.

"Poor Madam Davidova would give anything to be you right now," Katya cried out. She sat back in the wheelchair, holding her hand to her throat as if holding something in. "Valentina," she said in a harsh whisper, "*I* would give my eternal soul to be you."

A swirl of wheels and she was gone from the room. Valentina gave a long moan and turned her face to the wall.

❧

S HE FELT SOMETHING MOVING INSIDE HER HEAD. SOME-thing slithering like a snake around her thoughts until it was throttling them as efficiently as a rope around a pickpocket's neck.

Guilt was crushing her. Breaking her back. Pressing her face down in the dirt. Katya. Her mother. Her father. Madam Davidova. The amputated leg of the surveyor. Even her beautiful discarded horse, Dasha, still unridden since the day of the explosion.

And a thought kept intruding, like a voice murmuring in her ear, so low she could barely hear it. If it hadn't been for her, would Jens have arranged the visit to the new sewers at all? If he hadn't wanted to steal her away from Captain Chernov, would all those others still be alive? Was it all her fault?

Staring blank-eyed at the wall, she slowly took herself apart.

Piece by piece she attempted to put herself back together. It took a long time to make what was left fit together.

It was the pineapple that finally drove her out of bed. With each breath she inhaled of its fragrance, something of Jens imprinted inside her. She could feel it seeping through her lungs and into her bloodstream, pumping along the twisting paths of her veins. Because only Jens would have brought her a pineapple. He must have been here. Called at the house. He wasn't curled up in bed like a wounded animal. She threw off the quilt and swung her feet to the floor.

Pulling off the nightdress, she picked up a segment of pineapple and slid it onto her tongue. A burst of sunshine in her mouth. She walked over to her writing table, unlocked the drawer, and took out the list. Pen in hand, she started to write.

*11. Come to an arrangement with Papa.*

❧

THE STREET WAS DRAB. A RAW WIND OFF THE SEA SWEPT along the dirt road, chasing the falling snow so that it flounced in lacy swirls through the air, as grubby as a whore's petticoat. Jens paced along the stretch of scrubland, his thoughts busy, jotting down his calculations. He almost didn't spot the lone figure hunched in a heavy overcoat that seemed to belong to a broader man. Jens tucked his pad and pen in his pocket, stamped the ice from his *valenki* boots and moved forward.

"Good morning, Minister Davidov, *dobroye utro*."

Davidov did not even attempt to look pleased to see him. These days nothing and nobody pleased the widowed minister. Least of all himself.

"We are making progress," Jens announced.

"Is the sale of the land agreed?"

"The papers are drawn up and ready. Did you arrange the bank transfer?"

"*Da*."

Jens nodded, satisfied. That was what he needed to hear. This tract of wasteland and the jumble of shabby shacks next to it would soon be under new ownership and ripe for rebuilding. He glanced at the shacks, no better than dog kennels.

"When it's signed and sealed," Jens said, "I shall announce the extension of the sewers to this district next spring."

Davidov sank his fists into his pockets and sniffed the air. What was he expecting to smell? Money? Fat greasy roubles lining the plot of land? A woman in a headscarf and shoes made out of rope came out of one of the shacks with a zinc bucket full of liquid waste and tipped it into the dirt road. Jens turned his head away. The street stank of piss. The woman stood in the cold and watched them, shoulders slumped.

"So?" Davidov asked.

"So you will have steered the committee into voting by then." He stepped forward, crowding just a little, his height an advantage.

Davidov murmured something, more to himself than to anyone, but the wind carried it away.

"Is there a problem?" Jens demanded.

"I am sick of sewers. I don't want anything more to do with them now; neither does the committee after—"

"Minister, we agreed. It is your duty to correct the misunderstanding of the committee."

He reached into his pocket and pulled out his cigarette case, a gift from Countess Serova, exquisite silver work from Fabergé. He handed a cigarette to his companion, took one himself, and lit them both with a match, cupping its flame against the wind, drawing Davidov into an intimate closeness.

"Minister, don't lose your backbone now. You are the one who decides what the committee thinks; we both know that."

He saw Davidov swell slightly, as though the flattery slid like cushions of fat under his skin.

"The committee's idea is that—"

"To hell with the committee's ideas," Jens snapped.

He turned, sent his cigarette case arcing through the air, and watched it land with a clatter at the feet of the woman in the home-made shoes. She jumped, startled, dropped her empty bucket, and snatched up the silver case. She scurried back into her kennel like a dog with a bone.

"We have an agreement," Jens continued. "When the ownership of the land is in your name, you will order the release of further government funds for next year's extension to the sewers."

Davidov drew on his cigarette and stared at the empty waste-land scattered with rusting metal and broken bedsteads. "It's not the same," he said with an ache in his voice. "Not without her."

"I hear," Jens said quietly, "that it's certainly not the same. For you, I mean."

Something in his voice alerted Davidov. "What?" he demanded. "What have you heard?"

"That your wife's brother had extravagant gambling debts. That in her will she left her money to him to pay them off." He spoke gently. "That you, Minister, need to invest wisely to recoup such a loss. It must have come as a blow."

He meant the money. He didn't mean her death. Couldn't mention her death. It stuck in his throat like glass.

Davidov exhaled a plume of smoke into the snow and watched it curl around the falling flakes. "You are remarkably well informed," he said stiffly.

"Minister, do as we agreed. You can bend this committee to your will. You're good at that."

He left it there. Enough had been said. He returned to his pacing across the wasteland, jotting down numbers with cold fingers.

❧

I S SHE ANY BETTER TODAY?" JENS ASKED.
        "Come with me."
    Katya spun her wheelchair with deft hands and set off at a fast
pace along a wide corridor lined with antique silk tapestries.

    He strode along behind her between the thin wheel tracks on the
dark-green-and-gold carpet. It was always visible, where she had been.
Always audible, where she was going. Never able to move silently. No
privacy. A world where people looked down at the top of her head
and she had to crane back her neck to meet them eye to eye. He had
no concept of how to live in such a world. "Katya," he said cheerfully,
"you have the speed of a wolfhound. What strong wrists you must
possess. I'll have to get you welding my metal joists for me."

    She laughed and speeded up, so that he almost had to run to
keep up with her, but he stopped dead when he heard the music. It
hit him in the center of his chest like the flat of a hand. It came rippling under the door, a bright fluid Russian folk song bursting with
energy. Katya glanced over her shoulder, shaking her blond curls at
him with a grin.

    "Come on, she doesn't bite."
    "I don't want to disturb her."
    "You won't," she said, and pushed open the door.

❧

V ALENTINA ROSE FROM THE PIANO STOOL. SHE WAS WEAR-
        ing a pale silvery dress that hung loose on her because she had
grown painfully thin. She extended a hand. He took her fingers and
felt a knot of pain at the base of his throat.

    "Jens," she said, smiling at him.
    Her dark eyes looked huge in her face, the lines of her cheeks
hollowed into shadows, her skin so transparent he could trace the
fine veins. But her hair swayed in soft waves that he found hard not
to touch.

    "Jens?" she said again.
    "*Dobroye utro*, good morning, Valentina. I'm delighted to see you
recovered from your indisposition."

    "Indisposition?" She raised an eyebrow at him. "Is that what it
was? I did wonder."

He smiled and her gaze lingered on his face. If he scooped her into his arms and pressed her fragile skull close to his chest, would she slap him? *You overstep yourself, you Danish tunnel builder. You drowner of women. You gazer at stars. Take your hands off me.*

Is that what she would say?

And what would she say if he were to sweep her up, tuck her under his arm, and run from the house like a thief stealing a carpet? Would she roll her eyes at him and laugh?

"Valentina, please play for me?"

"I'll need my hand."

He looked at the delicate hand in his own, kissed its fingers, and released them.

"What would you like me to play?"

"You choose."

"Play some Chopin," Katya suggested.

Valentina gave a small shake of her head. "This one. I think it might suit you."

She sat down at the piano and turned her back to him, but he picked up a chair and moved it so that he could view the side of her face as she played. Katya parked her chair by the window as though it were her usual place and gazed out at the skeletal trees. The room was large but muted in its colors, so that it felt surprisingly intimate, dominated by the large grand piano. It dwarfed the small figure of Valentina, and for a moment she sat quietly, unmoving, her hands stilled, as though silence were part of the piece.

When she finally began, she played something dark and complex, something he had never heard before, a difficult piece, and her fingers flew with a rhythmic assurance that stirred him, raking his emotions and drawing out of him thorns that were buried deep. Yes, she was right. It suited him. Suited his mood these days. Dark and deep and as twisting as the tunnels he had built that almost buried them both alive.

Abruptly the music ceased in midflight. Her hands were poised above the keys, eager to plunge into the music once more, but she held them back.

"Did you tell her?" she asked.

He didn't ask who.

"Yes, of course. I told Countess Serova."

"So it is settled?"

"Yes."

"Good."

Her eyes scanned him from head to toe as if seeing something different in him, and then she swung back to the music.

*Did you tell her?*

*Yes, of course. I told Countess Serova.*

*He'd told Natalia. In her garden on a cold sunlit morning, deep snow on the ground. They were walking down the path, Natalia's arm through his, and she was talking too much. Unlike her. As though nervous of any silences. Ever since the bomb she had been like this, tense around him. But his gaze was fixed on Alexei, who plowed through the snow with his new puppy. The dog would grow into a good hunter, he was certain. He wondered if the boy would too. His noise disguised the silences; his laughter filled the chill air with warmth and made Jens smile. Recently he wasn't good at finding smiles. The tunnels had seen to that.*

*"It's good to see Alexei so happy," he said.*

*"You were right, I admit it. The puppy is already his best friend." She tapped her fingers on his sleeve. "Jens, whatever it is you have come here to say today, spit it out. I'm tired of the wait." She pulled her fur coat around her like armor.*

*"Natalia, I'm sorry." He was frank with her, brutally frank. It was the only option with a woman like the countess, so used to having her own way in everything. "It's over between us."*

*Her hand didn't move from his sleeve, but for one brief moment her jaw dropped. He heard a moan before she gathered herself together once more and gave him a cold stare.*

*"I see," she said. "How dull of you. Who is she?"*

*"She?"*

*"Don't play games."*

*"Her name is Valentina."*

*"Ah! The little snippet of a pianist. The one in the tunnel with you. That Valentina?"*

*He nodded curtly. He did not intend to discuss her. Gently he removed Natalia's arm from his and called to Alexei. He threw snowballs for the pup to chase and a flurry of them at Alexei, who squealed with laughter. Jens was giving Natalia time to become a countess again, but when they reached the wide steps into the house he stopped.*

*"Won't you come in?" she asked. "For a warm brandy."*

*"I think not."*

*She nodded indifferently. "Very well."*

*"But I will call again, if I may."*

*"For the boy. You care more for him than you do for me." An edge of hostility had crept into her voice. "Some put it about that you are his father,"* *she said coolly. "It's the green eyes."*

*"You and I both know they are mistaken."*

*"So why bother with him at all?"*

*He looked her full in the face, at the arrogant set of the mouth, at the intelligence behind the blue eyes, and a flash of anger shot through him.*

*"Because if I don't," he said, "no one else will."*

Jens lost track of time. The music enthralled him. When it finally ceased, he drew a deep breath. He felt as he did after a long hard ride through the forest. Exhilarated. More alive.

"That was wonderful, Valentina. Thank you."

She sat very still on the stool, and he could see the rise and fall as she breathed. Without looking at him she asked, "How is the surveyor?"

"He is recovering well." He said it briskly. "I still employ him because there's no reason the fellow can't do desk work."

She turned to study him. What had she heard behind his carefully chosen words? With an abrupt shift of mood she swung back to the piano and broke into a lively Russian folk song bouncing with energy.

"Look!" Katya said pointing to the window.

"Good God!" Jens almost fell off his chair.

Outside in the snow a massive young man was dancing a wild Cossack dance. He was crouched down on his haunches, kicking out his legs in traditional style with his arms across his chest. Then up on his toes on one leg, spinning and kicking and leaping.

"It's Liev Popkov," Valentina laughed.

When it ended with an outburst of laughter and applause, the Cossack bowed politely and departed, the falling snow filling his footprints.

They looked at each other, smiling. Jens could not remember a moment when the rest of the world had seemed so far away. Valentina's cheeks were flushed and she was laughing, when abruptly the door burst open and Elizaveta Ivanova entered the room.

"Ah," she said stiffly as her gaze settled on Jens. "I had no idea you were here."

"Good morning." He rose to his feet and bowed.

"Jens came to inquire after Valentina's health," Katya said quickly.

"I am happy to find her so well," he smiled. "She has been well cared for."

Elizaveta Ivanova noted the color in her daughter's cheeks. "You have a visitor," she announced.

"Tell whoever it is that I am busy, please, Mama."

"I will do no such thing. It is Captain Chernov. He is waiting for you in the drawing room."

Valentina stiffened.

For a second Jens expected her to refuse her mother's request. She had promised him, *I will have nothing to do with Captain Chernov.* But he saw the fractional moment in her dark eyes when she made the decision to break her promise.

"What an unexpected pleasure," she said coolly, and walked out of the room. "Thank you for the pineapple." Five words trailing softly behind her.

# Eighteen

Dᴀʀᴋ ᴘᴀʀᴀʟʟᴇʟ ʜᴀʀᴍᴏɴɪᴇs.
     In music. In life. Valentina could sense them. In her finger-
tips. In the secret cavities of her heart. Vibrating sounds that belong
together yet fight each other, pushing apart. She sat upright on the
edge of her chair in the drawing room, and her cheeks ached with
the effort of smiling. *Yes, Captain. No, Captain. How interesting, Captain. How astonishing. How clever you are.*
     *How unforgivable is your intrusion into my life.*
     Caught like a hook in her mind was the look on Jens's face when
her mother came into the music room with the name of Captain
Chernov on her lips. No harmony there, parallel or otherwise. Just
darkness. His broad shoulders pulled back, dragging him away from
her as though the sight of her jarred on him, jangled his nerves. A
clash of chords. She folded a crease into her skirt, crushing the material beneath her fingers.
     "Are you feeling unwell?"
     The expression of concern on Captain Chernov's handsome face
did little to dull the edges of her thoughts.
     "No, I am much better, *spasibo*."
     "I am extremely pleased to hear it. I was disturbed when—"
     "I am recovered now."

"Good."

He was running out of words. Maybe his head could only hold so many at a time, filled as it was with sabers and rifles and military rules. His uniform was stiff and shiny, a bright scarlet and glittering with braid and brasswork, his boots polished till they shone like mirrors. His white gloves lay like a spare pair of hands on the seat beside him and he kept touching them, twitching them, as if he could provoke them into life. He was nervous of her. His mouth under its blond mustache was hidden and gave no clues.

Small silences. Brittle breaks in the conversation. She could almost snap them with her fingers.

"Captain, tell me this. If there is something you want, really want, how do you set about getting it for yourself?"

"That's easy. I just put my mind to it and go for it the way I would ride a saber charge. No distractions. Single-minded. Go for the kill."

"I can imagine that."

He twitched at a glove. "I didn't mean . . ."

She smiled. "I understand what you mean."

He flushed and looked like a schoolboy instead of a twenty-three-year-old officer in Tsar Nicholas's great Russian army.

"And women. Should they do the same?"

He slapped his thigh with a laugh. "No, if a woman really wants something, she should ask a man."

Valentina lowered her eyes and stared at her hands.

"Is there something," Chernov asked with an eager voice, "that you would like me to do for you? I'd be honored to."

"No." She made herself look at him. "Several weeks ago I saw the factory strikers marching up Morskaya."

"Troublemakers, the lot of them. We've received new orders for a harsher response. We'll ride them down next time they try it. Don't let them upset you; they're just ignorant peasants."

She waited for him to finish. "Among the marchers were quite a number of women."

"So I've been told."

"Women who were single-minded. No distractions. Going for the kill to get what they want." She spoke mildly and eased herself back into her chair, interested in him at last.

"They do what their men tell them to do. Don't you concern

yourself with them. They won't be bothering you anymore. We cannot allow anarchy to threaten the stability of our nation. How much more are these strikers going to demand? They've been granted their own Duma, and that should be enough for them. But instead it turns out, as my father prophesied, that the more you give these people, the more they want."

"Thank you for explaining that to me, Captain. So when you ride them down next time they march, will you take your saber and rifle to the women as well?"

His face suddenly grew somber. "I don't think this is a suitable discussion for me to be having with you. A young lady should not have to listen to talk of such things." His fingers stopped fiddling. "A young lady should have other pleasanter occupations on her mind. I came today to invite you to supper."

"Captain," she said demurely. "I am honored."

❧

H E'S NOT HERE."
      "I thought he'd wait."

"Why would you think that?" Katya asked.

"Because"—Valentina looked around the music room as though Jens might be hiding under a chair—"because I wanted to explain."

"You should have thought of that before."

"Did he say anything?"

"He gave me this letter for you."

Valentina tore it open, read the few lines.

"Good news?" Katya asked.

"Yes. It's from a doctor friend of his."

"So he said."

"I thought it would be from Jens himself."

She walked over to the chair he had used and sat on it. She closed her eyes.

❧

T ODAY VALENTINA WAS DETERMINED TO PLEASE HER father. She sat in front of his desk, which was drowning in a tidal wave of papers and files, and wondered how on earth he could possibly keep track of it all. To one side lay a large envelope with Tsar Nicholas's gold crest embossed on it.

"You asked to speak to me?"

"Yes, Papa."

"Be quick, please, I'm busy." He was always busy.

She started cautiously. "Is there anything I can do to help, Papa? I know you have your assistants and secretaries at the ministry, but maybe here at home I can help with this." She waved her hand toward the paperwork.

He had been scanning a sheet of figures in his hand, but now his focus shifted to her. His fingers pulled absently at the collar of his frock coat, and she felt the familiar tug of affection when she noticed yet again that his nails were like Katya's, round and pale.

"*Spasibo.* Thank you for the thought, but no. So what is it you want to discuss?"

"I thought you might like to know that Captain Chernov has invited me to supper."

His dark eyes widened with pleasure, and he gave her a broad smile. "*Otlichno!* Excellent!" He let the paper float down to the desk and pressed his hands together in a gesture of prayer. "Thank God," he muttered, then suddenly grew tense and leaned forward. "You accepted, I hope?"

"I did."

"Well done. He is an important young man and his father is a powerful influence at court, so don't make a mess of this, Valentina. I need you to handle it carefully."

She smiled sweetly and shook her head to set her hair dancing. *Use your weapons*, Davidov had told her. Her reward was to see the crease between her father's eyes relax, and she knew she had made him happy, if only for a brief moment.

"I won't disturb you any longer, Papa." She rose to her feet and started to walk to the door, but halfway there she stopped and looked over her shoulder as though she had just recalled something. "One other thing, Papa."

He had picked up his pen, his large head already bent over another sheet of paper. "What is it?"

"I am applying for nurse training at St. Isabella's Hospital."

The words were out.

"No!" His fist slammed down on the desk so that papers slid from their piles and his pen clattered to the floor. "You will do no such thing."

"Papa, listen to me. Please. *Pozhalusta*. I want to do this because—"

"Valentina, I've already told you, I need you to forget this foolish idea." There were beads of sweat on his brow.

"I thought," she said mildly, "that we might come to an arrangement."

"What kind of arrangement?"

*Tread carefully.*

"I need your signature on a form because I am under twenty. Please, Papa, sign it for me. In exchange I will dance with your charming and *important* Captain Chernov. I will smile and laugh for him and flutter my eyelashes along with my fan like an empty-headed ninny. I will do exactly what you want." In the pause that followed she presented her father with a soft compliant smile. "If you sign."

"I will do no such thing."

"Papa, imagine it. By day I will be quiet and unseen, an unknown nurse in an unknown hospital. But by night I will become the darling of Petersburg society for you, with all the champagne and caviar and dancing you could desire." She swayed her hips as though swept up in a waltz. "Your name, Minister General Nicholai Ivanov, will be spoken at court, your position envied. That's what you want, isn't it? That's what I want for you, too." She smiled at him. "It would suit us both. Agreed, Papa?"

He extracted a large white handkerchief from his pocket and dabbed at his face. There was a pause. "Agreed."

"Thank you, Papa."

She left before he could change his mind. As soon as she reached her bedroom, she removed the key from her pocket and unlocked the drawer. Lifting out the sheet of ivory paper, she read it through carefully before placing a line through the last point: *Number 11.* The arrangement with Papa was made.

She knew her father would not like her for it, any more than she liked herself for it, but it was the only way she would be allowed to set foot in a hospital. Slowly she unfastened the pearl buttons on her sleeve, peeling back the material to look at her pale skin and to imagine Jens's fingers on it.

*Please, Jens, please understand that I have to see Chernov.*

She tried a smile for him, but it faltered on her lips. *I want this job as a nurse. I need it. Please, don't take it from me, Jens.*

⁂

"DID YOU EVER POLISH SHOES LIKE THAT?"

Arkin was surprised by the question. He was driving Elizaveta Ivanova alongside St. Isaac's Cathedral, and its glorious golden dome immediately brought to mind Father Morozov. Such a bright well-read man, yet condemned to live in a damp shack and to wear homemade boots with holes in them.

"Did you, Arkin?" Elizaveta Ivanova asked again.

"No, madam." They had just passed a row of four shoeshine boys in the square, busy with their brushes and impudent smiles, hungry for kopecks. "I was brought up on a farm."

Behind him he heard a small sigh of approval, as though life on a farm were something to be desired.

"What made you leave?" she asked.

"The lure of the big city."

"Petersburg is very beautiful, I admit. Did it live up to your expectations?"

"Yes," he lied. But her ears were sharp and she laughed.

"I hope you're happy here," she said after a moment's thought. "And happy working for my husband."

"Of course. I couldn't ask for better."

"I hope that's true, Arkin, and that you're not just saying it to please me."

"It is true."

He half-turned his head, one eye still on the road, and caught a glimpse of her in her black fur coat, sleek as a panther's pelt. She was smiling. Oddly, it pleased him to see it.

"I have a favor to ask of you."

The way she said it, he knew immediately it had nothing to do with chauffeuring.

"Madam, I am always at your service."

"Stop the car a moment."

He pulled into the curb and it happened to be opposite a fish stall so that the smell of dead fish on the slabs drifted into the car. He swiveled around in his seat and noticed the tiny lace handkerchief in her hand. She dabbed at her nose.

"How can I help you, madam?"

Her eyes considered him for a moment, and he saw uncertainty in them. She was wondering how far could she trust him.

"It is . . . a delicate matter," she said, and her cheeks colored. She glanced away, and the black feathers on her hat bobbed as she moved. "I don't know who else to ask."

"I am discreet," he said quietly.

He thought of the times he had collected any of Minister Ivanov's young mistresses in the car or even driven his employer to his favorite brothel down by the Golden Apple nightclub where the French gypsy girl, Mimi, awaited the minister's favors. Oh yes, Arkin had learned to keep his mouth shut.

"I will help you if I can," he offered.

Her gaze studied his gloved hand where it lay on the back of the seat as if it held an answer for her. She swallowed awkwardly. "I want you to find out whether my elder daughter is seeing . . . someone."

Arkin almost laughed. She wanted to turn him into an Okhrana spy. It was ironic.

"Who is this person?" he asked, genuinely interested.

"The Danish engineer she was trapped with in the tunnel. His name is Jens Friis."

So that was it. He suddenly felt sorry for this proud woman, reduced to such snooping on her daughter.

"I'll find out what I can," he agreed, and immediately her eyes lifted from his hand to his face.

"We understand each other?" she asked.

"Perfectly."

She smiled at him, but he reminded himself who she was and what she stood for. He didn't want to like her.

"Shall I drive on now, madam?" he asked, suddenly formal.

"Yes." But as he turned to the snow-covered road ahead once more, she added in a low voice, "I'm grateful, Arkin. For this . . . and for the other day when I was . . ."

"You are welcome, madam," he interrupted.

He preferred not to think about it. It did not help the cause to feel sorrow for your class enemy. It was dangerous. Yet he couldn't help it.

༄

THE MORNING WAS BRIGHT AS POLISHED GLASS. NO HINT of fog today, just an endless arc of sky and the smell of the sea in the air. It made Arkin restless. He was waiting beside the car outside the front steps for Valentina to emerge, with the Turicum gleaming as gaudy as a kingfisher in the sunshine.

"Good morning, Arkin."

"*Dobroye utro*, Miss Valentina, good morning," he said as she crossed the gravel. She looked thin and pale. She was dressed in a plain coat and headscarf, yet there was a nervous energy in her step as though she were in a hurry.

"Miss Valentina, I'm glad to see you have recovered and are looking so well."

The comment took her by surprise. "Thank you, Arkin."

"I hope Miss Katya passed on my good wishes to you when you were ill."

"Yes, thank you."

Still he stood there, forgetting about the car. She moved to climb the step into its interior, but he raised a hand that, even without touching her, made her stop.

"What is it, Arkin?"

"The men who caused the explosion in the tunnel would not have wanted to harm you in any way. Those people are fixed on a goal. You were in their path, that's all." He wanted her to know.

"So tell me, Arkin, what is their goal?"

He dropped his voice. "Their aim is to build a new and fairer society. They want to bring down the tsar. Not to endanger young women."

"Is that what you believe in too, Arkin? In bringing down our tsar?"

"No, Miss Valentina."

"Good. If you believed in that, you would be arrested."

She stepped past him into the car and sat on the sleek blue leather, staring straight ahead. He started the engine with the crank handle and jumped up in front of her. Neither of them spoke.

❧

VALENTINA WAS THANKFUL TO CLIMB OUT OF THE CAR half a mile from the hospital and send it back home for her mother's use. She enjoyed the short walk and tried to fix her mind on what she was to say, rather than on all that had been said last time. She entered St. Isabella's Hospital and went through the same procedure as before, the name checking at the window hatch and following the green trail of worn linoleum down the corridor to the door marked GORDANSKAYA. She knocked.

"*Vkhodite.* Come in."

Whatever she had been expecting, it was not what she found. The large figure of *Medsestra* Gordanskaya seemed to have ballooned further inside her white uniform since their last meeting, and she was leaning against a row of filing cabinets with a pair of long-handled tweezers clenched between her fingers. Her attention shifted to Valentina for no more than a second.

"Ah, yes, the little aristocrat who thinks she has the makings of a nurse." She grinned into the mirror propped up on the cabinet, but it had nothing to do with humor. Valentina realized she was inspecting a side tooth that was black and broken.

"Good morning, *Medsestra* Gordanskaya."

"Know anything about teeth?"

"No, *Medsestra.*"

"Not much use to me then, are you?"

"I'm good with tweezers."

"Here." The woman thrust the instrument at Valentina.

Valentina took it and wondered whether the *medsestra* initiated all her would-be nurses with this exercise. But then she wouldn't have a tooth left in her head.

"Friends in high places, I gather," Gordanskaya said, but without rancor, as though it were a fact of life. "But of course you would have. Look at you." She laughed a deep laugh that wobbled her cheeks. "You can't hide behind a headscarf and a servant's mended gloves. I know what you are."

"I'm not hiding."

"Aren't you?"

"I want to be a nurse. To do something more with my life than arrange flowers and drink tea. I promise you I know how to work hard, and I am already familiar with Dupierre's book on human anatomy. I've nursed my younger sister and practiced bandaging."

"You talk too much. You educated ones always do. Learn to keep quiet."

Valentina nodded. "Yes, *Medsestra*."

"If you were applying to be a soldier, I'd call you cannon fodder, but instead I call you—and all the other chits like you—bedpan fodder. That's what you'll be dealing with most of the time, and that's what will finish you off in the end. Bedpan fodder, the lot of you. Dear Mother of Christ, why don't they send me some young women able to work? Not just these whey-faced milksops."

Valentina didn't make a sound.

Gordanskaya snatched up one of Valentina's hands, turned it over to inspect the palm, and prodded its pale pads with her thumb. Valentina felt like a farm animal in the marketplace.

"Skin as white as a piglet's tits." The *medsestra* shook her head. "But there's muscle in there. What is it you do with them?"

"I play the piano."

Gordanskaya burst out laughing. "Dear God, give me strength." Abruptly she opened her mouth wide and pointed to a black tooth that was hanging half loose. "Pull it."

One quick jerk with the tweezers and the black stump slid out like a nail from rotten wood. A tail of blood followed it and a whiff of pus. A flicker of relief passed over the nurse's broad face, and she pointed to the chair in front of her desk. Valentina sat down and she placed the tweezers, still clutching the tooth, within Gordanskaya's reach.

"You've been recommended to me for training by Dr. Fedorin," Gordanskaya said briskly. "I will need your parents' consent as you are under twenty. Now read this form and get them to sign it," she ordered before adding with a sly lopsided smile, "I take it you can read and write?"

"*Medsestra* Gordanskaya," Valentina said, "I can do whatever it takes."

# Nineteen

IT IS STRANGE, VALENTINA THOUGHT, HOW LITTLE IT TAKES to tilt the world. As she retraced her steps along the mottled green floor and down the front steps of the hospital, nothing looked the same. As though she had been viewing it through a distorting mirror before but now saw it clear and pin-sharp. Her heart felt tight, drumming loudly in her ears.

Before leaving she had stopped at the heavy swinging doors to one of the wards and peered through its glass panel, astonished at the huge size of the room. It seemed to stretch away forever with endless rows of beds like long white coffins. She was tempted to push open the door, to enter this unfamiliar world where pale faces lay on rumpled pillows. Some were talking; others lay flat and silent with eyes closed.

"Out of my way."

A young nurse barged out of the ward, holding an enamel bowl piled to the brim with bloodied bandages.

"What are you gawking at? Got your lover in there?" the girl grinned. "Don't worry, I give 'em all a kiss good night. He's in safe hands with me. I'm Nurse Darya Spachyeva, in case you don't know."

She was taller than Valentina and wiry as a weasel, with the broad cheekbones and swarthy skin of a southerner. Black stalks of hair escaped from under her headdress, but her hands looked capable, a peasant's large-knuckled hands. Her smile was open and easy.

"Got a tongue in your head?" she demanded.

"I'm going to be training as a nurse here."

The girl raised the bowl of bandages, thrusting it under Valentina's nose. It stank. "Get a whiff of that. That'll be your new perfume when you work here."

"I've smelled worse."

The untidy nurse rolled her black eyes in her head. "Don't say I didn't warn you."

Valentina smiled. "I won't."

"It's hard on the legs too."

"My legs are strong." All those years of horse riding. "If it's so bad, why are you here?"

The girl wiped a hand on her apron, adding a stain to the others. "It beats milking fucking goats halfway up a fucking mountain." She tucked the bowl in the crook of her arm as naturally as if it had been one of her newborn goats and scurried off on muscular legs.

Valentina had never heard a woman swear like that. She smiled and hurried down the front steps of the hospital, and that was when she saw Jens. He was standing stiff and stern in the shade of a lime tree, arms folded across his chest, face unsmiling. Waiting for her.

❧

THEY WALKED SIDE BY SIDE, NOT TOUCHING. SHE HAD TO quicken her pace to keep up with his long stride because he made no allowance for her, as though he didn't care whether she was there. Yet he had come to the hospital at the time of her appointment. She held on to that.

Jens looked a mess. A heavy gray dust was spattered over his coat and had burrowed into the black fur of his hat and into the red hairs of his eyebrows. She scarcely noticed where they walked, but there was a sense of purpose to his steps as he headed down Zagorodnaya Street. They barely spoke, yet she was acutely aware of him at her side. Aware of the crunch of his boots in the snow, and the sight of his breath spiraling out white and impatient into the cold air, and the triangular spot right in the corner of his jaw that clicked and jumped as though punctuating his thoughts. He looked directly ahead, shutting her out, and she wondered if he had forgotten her.

When they crossed the Moika Canal, she said, "Please thank Dr. Fedorin for me."

"You can thank him yourself. It's to his house we're going."

"Why there?"

"He wants to give you advice on what to expect at St. Isabella's. He'll explain how things are done and what you'll have to learn. He can tell you where to get your uniform and teach you how to ward off the advances of male patients. Fedorin is a good man. He spends a lot of his time in the missions for the poor and in the hospitals for the destitute. He's not just a doctor for the scented parlors of the rich and pampered."

She wanted to say, *Thank you.* She wanted to say, *See, you do care. You wouldn't be doing this if you didn't.* But instead she seized his arm, fixing her fingers on his dusty coat.

"Jens. Stop."

She meant, stop all the words that were blocking the space between them. Stop refusing to look at her. Stop the ache that the cold edge in his voice set up in her throat. Stop. Stop. But it was her feet that stopped. In the middle of the bridge they jerked to a halt, and her hand was still attached to him, a shackle that he did not try to throw off. For the first time that day he looked straight at her.

"You promised me," he said. "You swore you'd have nothing to do with Captain Chernov."

Standing there in the street, she slowly undid the buttons of his coat, one by one, and slid her arms around his waist.

"I promise," she said, "I promise on my sister's life that my heart will never have anything to do with Captain Chernov."

She rested her cheek against his chest, smelled the damp earthy odor of the dust on his clothing and felt the warmth of his body as he wrapped his coat around her, drawing her tight, pinning her to him. Below them on the frozen Moika canal, an elderly couple in matching beaver-skin hats skated sedately back down toward the Tauride, hand in hand. Valentina burrowed deeper, listening to the rapid beat of his heart.

THE DOCTOR WELCOMED THEM AND POURED JENS AND himself a glass of fine Georgian wine while Valentina and his little daughter, Anna, drank hot chocolate in front of the fire. She liked this man who was such a devoted father, liked his generosity and the way his bony fingers kept touching the diamond tiepin at his neck as he spoke. It was clear it meant something special to him.

"Now, young lady, let's discuss what lies ahead of you."

"I'm grateful, Dr. Fedorin, for your help. *Medsestra* Gordanskaya made it clear she expects me to fail."

He took her chin in his hand and inspected her closely in the way he would inspect his own daughter. "You'll do," he said. "If it's what you really want."

"It is. I've already studied anatomy and—"

"One step at a time. Let's talk first about the discipline of bed making, clean uniforms, and *Medsestra* Gordanskaya's filthy temper."

She sat and listened to him. He filled her mind with facts and figures about the hospital, its history, its rules. He told her the correct way to address a doctor, exhorted her to walk behind him at all times, and described with enthusiasm the wider range of drugs being developed, including the refinement of morphine to give more precise relief of pain. Again and again he emphasized the need for cleanliness, clean hands, clean linen, clean uniform. Sterile equipment. He talked about operations. Tested her knowledge with questions, all the time tugging on the ends of his mustache or stroking the bright diamond nestled in his cravat.

It was a strange sensation. In an odd sort of way she felt that his questions were opening doors within her that she didn't know were closed. Across the room Jens and Anna were perched on the window seat playing cards, Anna pouncing with the squeal of a kitten whenever she won a hand.

Finally Dr. Fedorin leaned back in his chair, tucked his thumbs into his waistcoat and exhaled a sigh of satisfaction. "She'll do, Friis. She'll do very nicely."

Jens smiled. "I know."

Something in the way he said it unbalanced her. It was as though he were letting go of her. She wanted to rush over to the window seat and sit herself on his lap to prevent him slipping away. She wanted to smile up at him and hear him say, *She'll do me very nicely.* She rose to her feet and took a step toward him.

"Jens . . . ," she started.

"Anna," Fedorin interrupted, "time for us to find your governess and see what she has planned for you today."

The child pulled a face but planted a kiss on Jens's cheek, bobbed a curtsy to Valentina, and scampered out of the room after her father.

"Jens," Valentina said softly.

He patted the window seat beside him and she sat down, nervous. But as soon as she felt the warmth of him—his leg next to hers, his hip touching her dress, his shoulder solid beside her—she knew she'd be able to explain everything to him.

"Jens, listen to me." She didn't take her eyes from his hand as she linked her fingers through his. "It is my ace, Jens, my only high card. It's all I have."

"Using Chernov?"

"Yes."

"To bargain with?"

"Yes. Without him I have nothing."

"You have me."

*You have me.* She tipped her head against his shoulder and let it lie there, the three words safe inside it.

"You have to trust me," she whispered. "It's the only way I can train as a nurse. My parents will not permit it unless I entertain Captain Chernov."

"Entertain?"

She rubbed her cheek on the material of his jacket. "A few smiles, a few dances, nothing more." His hands released hers, and her fingers felt bereft. "Jens, it won't be for long. He'll soon tire of me and my silences. You and I can still—"

"Still what?"

"Still talk to each other."

He made a sound, then wrapped his arms around her, lifted her onto his lap and tipped her back until she was cradled in his arms and looking up into his face.

"Now," he said, "let's *talk* to each other."

He lowered his head and kissed her lips. She raised a hand to his hair, twisting fiery strands between her fingers. "You see," she murmured as his lips brushed along the hollow under her ear and set a pulse racing in her throat, "I'm just like your tunnels."

"Dark and difficult?"

She tightened her grip on his hair and shook it roughly like the scruff of a stray dog. "Not easy to destroy."

༄

T HE REVOLUTIONARIES WORKED IN POCKETS WITHIN THE city, in individual cells that kept contact to a minimum to reduce the consequences of betrayal. Small furtive groups gathered in basements, huddled in back rooms that smelled of bad tobacco and bitter resentment. Arkin found it impossible to be patient. The food shortages were worse and prices were rising. Trade unions were being shut down, while all the time the gutters heaped higher each night with the sick and the homeless. The middle-class intellectuals continued to call for reform and needed to be taught that reform would never be enough. Only revolution would provide a decent life for Russians.

Beside Arkin sat Sergeyev. He was nursing his arm and smoking a pipe. God only knew what was in it, but it made the dingy room stink of horse dung. There were twelve of them at the meeting in the storeroom of a candle maker's shop, and the air was thick with tallow. Arkin could taste it at the back of his throat, slick and greasy. At the head of the table sat Krazhkov, a shaggy bearded man who had fought in the Imperial Army against Japan and who spat every time Tsar Nicholas's name was mentioned. He was older than the rest and had only one leg. He banged his fist down on the table and demanded silence.

"Arkin," he growled. "You are quiet tonight. What news?"

"The reprisals have started."

"The murdering bastards!"

"I overheard Minister Ivanov in the car talking to one of his assistants. He says that Stolypin has ordered the Okhrana to fill the prisons to overflowing."

Anger spilled hot onto the table.

It was Sergeyev who brought them to order. "Comrades, the harder they crack down on us, the more the workers rally to our fight."

"Sergeyev is right," Krazhkov agreed. "Each time we plant a bomb or toss a grenade, the Okhrana and the tsar"—he spat on the floor, just missing his dog—"see our strength and fear us. But the proletariat see our strength and respect us. More and more will flock to our side when they start to believe we have the power to crush the rule of the cursed Romanovs."

"Our problem is that we are desperate for funds," Arkin pointed out quietly. "Without more roubles, how will we equip this proletariat army?"

But Krazhkov would not be sidetracked. "What else did you hear?"

"The police intend to make an example of the union leaders," Arkin warned. "The minister was specific about that."

"We will alert them immediately," Krazhkov frowned. "We'll have to get some of them into hiding."

Sergeyev rapped the table with his pipe stem. "My nephew Yusev works at the Tarasov factory." The Tarasov brothers owned one of the largest toolmaking factories in Petersburg and drove around in a glossy Benz limousine while their workers begged for bread on the street. "He swears the apprentices are ready to revolt. Just yesterday two more boys died when an overhead gantry snapped." He pointed his pipe at Arkin. "One was the boy who did the train job with you."

"Karl?"

"No, the short kid, Marat. He's dead."

Arkin's rage was as thick and as stifling as the tallow in the air.

Krazhkov hunched forward with eager eyes. "What do you suggest, Comrade Arkin?"

"Tsar Nicholas may be ruthless enough to send his cavalry to hack and slash at his own people when they march on the streets, but not even he would slaughter the innocent children of Russia. It's time to use the apprentices of this city."

❧

THEY LEFT THE MEETING IN PAIRS. FIVE MINUTES BETWEEN each. Arkin and Sergeyev went first. They dodged quickly through the darkness along a series of back alleyways until they were far enough from the candle shop to slow their pace. It was snowing softly, and there was scarcely any wind, so that the flakes tumbled straight down from the black sky as gentle as feathers. Arkin welcomed the touch of them on his face. A pulse at the back of his eyes was throbbing, and he knew the dreams would be bad tonight.

"Viktor," Sergeyev said at his side, "don't blame yourself. For the danger to union leaders in retaliation for the attack on Stolypin."

"How can I not?"

"We always knew we would have blood on our hands. Trotsky warned us of that."

"Did he warn us of—" He stopped his tongue. His companion had enough problems of his own. "Tell me, my friend, how is your wife? Has she given birth yet?"

"Any day now."

Arkin could hear the pride in Sergeyev's voice and felt again that unexpected spike of envy. Like a nail hammered under a rib. *One day*, he told himself, *one day you'll have your own woman. And your own child.*

"Give her my best wishes," he laughed, "and tell her—"

A hand seized his shoulder. He was slammed against a brick wall, knocking the breath from his lungs. His own fist shot out, his knee rammed into a groin. He heard his attacker grunt, felt the hand on his shoulder grow slack, and a body slid to the ground. Another figure loomed out of the darkness.

"Stand still or I'll put a fucking bullet between your eyes."

Arkin stood still. He glanced quickly to his right to check on Sergeyev, but his friend was already motionless, his shoulders gathering snow. He was bent over, hugging his arm in its sling as if it had taken a beating.

"What do you bastards want?" Arkin demanded.

"We want some answers from you."

The man with the Mauser in his hand was broad chested with a beer belly and rolls of flesh instead of muscle. The other, shorter one was sprawled on the icy ground clutching his groin and cursing. They wore black leather coats, shiny as snakeskin, and possessed the cold focused eyes of hunters. They were the Okhrana. No one else.

"It depends," Arkin said politely, "what the questions are."

The one on the ground did not take kindly to Arkin's response, so he stumbled to his feet and slammed an elbow into Arkin's gut.

"Keep this bastard off me," Arkin growled, "or I'll tear his balls off."

"Vroshchin, back off!"

"What questions?" Arkin repeated.

"What are you doing roaming the streets at this hour of the morning?"

Arkin shrugged. "A card game. Nothing sinister. The only trouble is that my stupid friend here lost his rent money and is bleating like a lamb at the thought of telling his wife. Isn't that so, Mikhail?"

Sergeyev grunted. Arkin laughed and had the satisfaction of seeing the hard mouths of the secret police pull into a sneering smile. The trigger finger relaxed.

"He's in enough trouble already," Arkin added, and slapped Sergeyev on the back, straightening him up. "Let me take the poor idiot home." He tucked his arm under his friend's good elbow and started to swing him away a few paces. "Good night. *Spokoinoi nochi*, my friends. It's too cold to hang around here." The snow fluttered down thickly, and he was thankful for it.

"Wait."

A few more steps and the snow would swallow them. "Yes?"

"Stand against the wall, hands behind your head."

"But why—"

"Against the wall."

Arkin backed against the wall, drawing Sergeyev with him, but he noticed his friend was shaking. The Okhrana officers proceeded to search them with rough hands, turning out their pockets, opening their coats, and Sergeyev kept a protective hand curled over his sling. Arkin's mind was racing. Something wasn't right.

"Where have you come from?" demanded the fleshy one with the gun.

"I told you, a card game."

"Or one of the meetings of revolutionary scum?"

"No, *nyet*, of course not. I work for one of Tsar Nicholas's government ministers."

That made them blink, and the fierce grip on his sleeve loosened a fraction. Sweat trickled down his back despite the cold. In the thin ridge of light that fell from an upstairs window, cutting a yellow slice out of the darkness, he could see the misery on Sergeyev's face.

"Here! What's this?" The shorter policeman was yanking at Sergeyev's injured arm, dragging off the sling. "This fucker has something hidden in here." The man pushed his fingers under the top layer of bandage and drew out a small pistol that fitted in the palm of his hand. It gleamed pearl white in the falling snow.

*Damn you, Sergeyev. Damn you.*

The men in black coats showed their teeth. The one with the pistol slammed its butt against Sergeyev's arm, and he buckled with no sound, but Arkin seized him before he fell and swung him back like a battering ram against the two men. Their eyes opened in surprise as Arkin threw his weight behind the push, and they skidded backward on their heels, arms flailing. The ice underfoot won. Both crashed to the ground. Arkin heard a skull hit concrete, but he didn't stop to ask whose brains had been rearranged. He snatched the small gun from where it lay on the ground and seized Sergeyev's good arm.

"Run."

They ran. Skittering in and out of alleys, pounding down slippery banks, throwing themselves over railings and under archways, hearts straining in the freezing night air. Always they kept to unlit streets. Arkin was slowed by his wounded friend but refused to release his grip on him while behind them they could hear their pursuers' shrill shouts and foul-mouthed curses. Only once did Arkin risk a glance over his shoulder, and he saw that the shorter one was in the lead, face sharp as a hound on the scent. The fatter one was struggling to keep up but failing. Four shots rang out, but it was too dark and each time the bullet whistled wide.

They kept running and dodging, twisting and turning.

With Sergeyev in tow he scrambled down to a spot beneath a canal bridge and they crouched under its arch, lungs dragging in freezing air. Underfoot the ice crackled if they moved so much as a knee.

"Where are we?" Sergeyev whispered in his ear.

"No idea, but stay quiet."

For thirty minutes they remained immobile, no more than shadows, disturbing only a cat on its nocturnal run across the thick ice of the canal. When eventually they climbed up the frozen bank, everywhere was silent. The snowfall was heavier, stinging their eyes and gathering in mounds on the toes of their boots. They hurried through the streets, heads ducked down, keeping to the darkest areas of the city, and when they finally reached the Liteiny district they stopped.

Through the lace curtain of snow Arkin peered at his friend's strained face. "How's your arm?"

"It's still attached."

"Did those bastards do much damage?"

Sergeyev shrugged. "Wherever the Okhrana go, they do damage."

"You shouldn't have been carrying the gun. Why did you have it?"

"I swapped a good spade for it in a bar. I thought I'd be safer." He shrugged again. "I was wrong."

Arkin thrust the dainty pistol into Sergeyev's pocket. "Sell it," he suggested. "It will only get you killed. Buy some food for your wife instead."

"No." Sergeyev returned it to him with an apologetic grimace. "You keep it."

Arkin didn't argue. Sergeyev was less likely to get into trouble without it. "Take care, my friend." He rested a hand on his shoulder. "Tell your wife from me, good luck with the baby."

"It's what I'm fighting for. To build my son a better future. Thank you, comrade." He said it awkwardly. "For helping me. My wife will starve if I'm thrown in prison."

Arkin nodded, an image of her swollen belly vivid in his mind as he drifted away into the night, the snow so thick now that the air was almost solid. In his pocket his hand curled around the pearl-handled gun. Sergeyev was right. It did make him feel safer.

# Twenty

WELL, HOW DO I LOOK?"

"Like a nun." Katya inspected her sister with a critical eye. "It's the headdress."

Valentina twirled on the spot to show off her nurse's uniform from all angles. It was white and stiff and made her feel like someone else. In the mirror she stared at the tight wimple crossing her forehead in a straight line and at the neat linen folds hanging down to her shoulders, hiding every trace of her hair. It was her first day, and nerves scuttled like ants in her stomach. She patted the starched apron over the plain white frock and smiled at Katya.

"Take a good look."

"Why?"

"Because when I return from the hospital, I will be different."

Katya laughed. "Dirty and smelly and dead on your feet, you mean."

"Exactly!"

But the look that passed between the sisters lasted a long moment because both knew that wasn't what she meant at all.

S T. ISABELLA'S HOSPITAL WAS A RABBIT WARREN OF COR-
ridors. Its drafty wards seemed to suck all sound into its granite
walls, leaving the place muted and blank. The murmur of voices
remained subdued, the groans and coughs halfhearted, as though
life within these thick walls existed at a minimal level. The first day
altered Valentina's sense of perspective. It seemed that as *Sanitarka*
Ivanova she was no longer an individual, but an insignificant part
of an indifferent machine, and this realization took time to get used
to. She had expected other things but not that. The day started with
an inspection. A row of nurses lined up and *Medsestra* Gordanskaya's
small eyes narrowed with pleasure as she pointed out faults. She
picked on shoes, apron straps, frayed cuffs, fingernails. Valentina displayed her hands and heard the irritated puff of displeasure when no
fault could be found.

*Bedpan fodder.* Gordanskaya was right. She stopped even noticing
the stench of them. She was taught how to make envelope corners
on blankets and sheets, folding them around the thin mattresses,
told to make and remake them until she did it right. She practiced
turning patients in bed and maneuvering soiled sheets from under
them.

She was put on a female ward with rows of sad fearful eyes and
untidy hair. But Valentina learned not to walk quickly. She learned
to look, swiveling her head from side to side, seeing the patients
occupying themselves with small empty tasks. Playing cards, sewing, picking their feet, thinking about their next meal. Stiff bodies
and closed eyes made her nervous. She witnessed one young frizzy-
haired patient suddenly sit up, screaming that there was a worm
slithering in her heart and tearing the dressing off her chest so that
her breasts hung naked and bloody. Valentina ran to fetch help, calling out for assistance. For that lapse she was reprimanded and had to
face Gordanskaya in full flow.

"You don't run."

"You don't shout."

"You don't panic."

"You don't scare the patients."

"You don't make yourself look like the fool you are."

"You don't disgrace St. Isabella's."

"You don't."

Valentina stared straight ahead, unblinking in the face of

Gordanskaya's wrath, her hands behind her back, toes clenched in her shoes. "I'll do better," she vowed.

"You'll bloody well have to."

*She would bloody well have to.*

By the end of the day her hands were raw and her feet felt as if dogs had chewed them up and spat them out. But she had gotten through it without killing any of the patients. That was an achievement. She threw her navy cloak over her uniform, pulled on her *valenki* boots, and stumbled out into a dark and snowy world.

It seemed impossible that the city of St. Petersburg had continued its usual life, gone through the motions of a normal day when hers had been so completely abnormal. But the carriages rattled past, footmen shouting to each other as they held on at the back. Trams clanked. Boys trundled laden sleds and lights glimmered through the snowfall. Nothing had changed. Except her.

She pulled up her hood and hurried down the steps.

৵

J ENS WAS THERE. WAITING FOR HER AT THE CORNER UNDER the streetlamp, just the way he had promised. She walked into the circle of his arms and felt her fatigue and the dull shame of her mistake vanish. Her forehead rested on the damp wool of his coat and she could smell his sweat and exhaustion, a thousand times worse than her own.

"A good day?" he asked.

"Good, yes. The way having a painful tooth removed is good."

He laughed and pulled her tighter.

"And yours?" she whispered.

"It's good now. This is where my day starts. The rest I forget. *Sanitarka* Ivanova, you look tired."

"No, I'm excited." She snuggled against him. "And happy."

He curled an arm around her waist and together they started to walk across St. Petersburg, wrapped together, the snowflakes startlingly cold on their tongues when they laughed.

"Tell me more," she said, "about your day."

"Which do you want? Good news or bad?"

"Good."

"I heard today that construction of the new treatment station is going ahead this year, to provide the north of the city with clean drinking water. The funding is finally all signed and delivered."

"How do they make the water clean?"

"Long version or short?"

"Short."

He laughed, a contented roll of sound that spiraled out ahead of him. "The raw water is treated with a coagulant—I'm sure you're desperate to know which one, so I'll put you out of your misery by telling you it's aluminum sulfate—and then pumped to sedimentation tanks."

"Is that it?"

"No, by no means. This is 1911 and we use the most advanced modern technology there is."

"So what next?"

"This is the exciting part."

"I can hardly wait."

"It's then supplied to rapid sand filters and . . ." He paused for dramatic effect.

"Don't stop now."

"And ozonized. So," he said with a broad grin, "I hope you'll think of all that each time you drink tea in your refined ladies' drawing room."

"I swear I shall never look at the water running out of a samovar tap in the same way again." She brushed her cheek against his shoulder. It was damp. "Sand filters indeed!"

They walked the dimly lit streets together, her hip against his thigh. It pleased her, considering the difference in height, how easily and how naturally they fitted together.

"Now," he said, turning his head to look directly at her, "tell me, how did your day go?" There were snowflakes caught on his eyebrows.

"First, tell me your bad news."

He shook his head, and his mouth, always so expressive, turned down at the corners. A chill that had nothing to do with the cold air of the river ran down her tired legs and made her uneasy.

"Tell me, Jens," she murmured.

He hesitated, and for a moment she thought he was going to lie, to cover over whatever it was that was concerning him, but he didn't.

Instead he stopped and pulled her into the uncertain circle of light from a lamppost. The hood of her cape was raised over her nurse's headdress and he slid his hands inside it, tugging out the clips that held the white material in place so that he could touch her hair.

"One day," he said, "I want to brush out your beautiful hair." His fingers buried themselves among its waves. Strong capable hands. Hands that knew how to do things. "Valentina," he said quietly. "I'm frightened for you."

She placed her gloved hands on each side of his jaw as if she could manipulate the words in his mouth. "Why, Jens? Why should I be frightened?"

"Nurse Ivanova, haven't you heard?"

"Heard what?"

"That cholera is back."

❧

W ELL? HOW WAS IT?"
"It was good, Mama, thank you for asking. I learned a lot."
She'd been surprised to find her mother waiting for her in the doorway of the small reading room the moment she arrived home. She was dressed in a burgundy evening gown and wore rubies in her hair.

"Come in here, please, Valentina."

"I'm weary, Mama. Please let me wash and change first."

"No. I need to talk to you first."

"What is it that is so urgent, Mama? It's not Katya, is it?"

"No, it's not your sister." Her mother looked at her sadly. "You have to keep your side of the bargain." Her tone was gentle. "I know you're tired, but . . ."

Valentina realized what was coming next.

"You have one hour, Valentina. To get yourself ready."

"Ready for what?"

"To go out. Don't forget, Captain Chernov is calling for you to take you to supper."

"Mama," she said carefully, "would you ask the Captain to be so kind as to postpone the supper. I will be no kind of company for him tonight. Honestly, I'm too tired to think, never mind to entertain anyone."

"Valentina." Her mother's voice was flat. "You agreed to this. It's all arranged."

"Please, not today." She couldn't bear the thought of Chernov.

"You gave us your word. You must keep it. This is important. Do you understand me, Valentina?"

"Yes, Mama. I understand."

Her mother smiled, but her eyes remained watchful. "Thank you," she said, as she kissed her daughter's cheek and walked out of the room. Valentina closed her eyes. Slowly she lifted the shoulder seam of her damp cape, put her face to it, and inhaled. Was that Jens? That smell of something new. Or was that the hospital?

Quickly she ran upstairs, feeling her muscles twitch with fatigue. But the first thing she did when she entered her room was to take out the list and strike a line through *Number 5.*

*Obey Mama.*

Then with a smile she added another. A big fat line through *Number 3. Find employment.*

❧

CAPTAIN STEPAN CHERNOV ARRIVED IN A MAGNIFICENT shiny black rig that bore his family's crest on its doors and was pulled by two pairs of perfectly matched horses. He took her to Donon's, a fashionable French restaurant. When she learned he had booked a private room, she was alarmed, but she needn't have worried. He was unfailingly polite and courteous, at times even hesitant, uncertain what to say to her now they were alone. She didn't help him.

Over oysters and caviar there were long awkward silences, which she didn't attempt to break. At one point her eyelids turned into lead weights and slowly descended, but she managed not to fall asleep into her plate of baked sturgeon or into its mustard and olive sauce. Over coffee Chernov leaned forward and stubbed out his black cigarette with its gold filter, a quick impatient gesture.

"Am I boring you?" he asked.

The question was so unnecessary that she started to laugh. She didn't mean to, but she couldn't help herself, and once she'd started she couldn't stop. Laughter just bubbled out of her. It was tiredness. And the absurdity of what she was doing here with this man, the stupidity of her father if he thought she would be forced into marrying a blond mustache because it carried a high price tag.

Captain Chernov sat in his chair opposite her, watching her. She clamped both hands over her mouth to silence the sounds, but they still sneaked out between her fingers. Tears trickled down her cheeks.

"Valentina, please stop."

She nodded. More tears.

He took his time lighting a cigarette, observing her through the smoke. "So I amuse you, then."

His face drew nearer across the table, and she could see his blue eyes spark as he studied her. Was it bewilderment? Or just plain fury that she was behaving so badly? She had no idea.

"So," he said. With a sudden dramatic sweep of his arm, he brushed all the glass and crockery onto the floor in a crash that sent splinters of crystal flying around the private dining room. "Now we have a bare table in front of us. We can start again, you and I. You can put on it whatever you choose."

He watched her closely as he continued to smoke his strong-smelling black cigarette.

The laughter stopped, as did the stifling boredom. She lifted a corner of the white damask tablecloth, wiped her eyes, and hiccuped softly.

"Some rules," she said.

"Name them."

"If you have anything to say, you say it to me. Not to my parents."

He looked surprised, the pale freckles on his nose darkening so that they looked like tiny bruises. "Agreed."

"I know you have already spoken to my father, but I want nothing settled. Not for twelve months."

"A whole year! That's . . . inconsiderate of you."

"It's what I insist on." She was buying herself time.

"Then I agree to it."

"Thank you."

"Now my turn, Valentina."

She nodded.

"Only one rule."

"Which is?"

"No other men. I'll kill any other men."

She stared down at the smashed fragments lying around their feet like the torn feathers of some wretched bird. "You're not afraid of breaking things, are you, Stepan? To get what you want."

A dull flush crept up his cheeks and along the side of his nose. "I'm a soldier, Valentina."

As if that explained it.

"Stepan." He watched her mouth as she talked. "If I speak with other men or walk with other men or even dance with other men, I don't expect to find them dead at my feet."

"Of course not." He shrugged his shoulder, his epaulets shifting uncomfortably. "I didn't mean . . ."

Her lips formed a smile. "I know what you meant."

"So, what now? A nightclub? The Aquarium, I suggest. You'll like it there. It has fish tanks on the walls of its dance floor."

"No," Valentina said. "Now I go home and get some sleep."

☙

A T THE HOSPITAL, SHE LEARNED TO NOTICE THE SMALL things. Little telltale signs. A droop of a mouth, fingernails turning blue, a sudden rash on the skin, a mild shortness of breath. She learned to look for them. Even a change in the smell of the hated bedpans was a signal.

Her first death came at the end of the first week. It was a thin-haired woman who slipped away from life as unobtrusively as she had occupied it, and the sorrow that jumped into Valentina's chest was out of all proportion. She hid in the sluice room, angry with herself. She'd barely known the poor woman, yet tears flowed down her cheeks and she had to hold a wet cloth over her mouth to silence the sobs. She would die of shame if *Medsestra* Gordanskaya found her like this.

That evening when she came down the steps, Jens knew at once. "Valentina," he said, "it was never going to be easy."

"I know."

As they walked, his pace slowed. She didn't know if it was for her or himself, or just to delay the moment of parting. For today at least, winter had eased its grip on St. Petersburg and a fine drizzle trickled out of the dark sky, refreshing with its light touch and its tang of the sea after the cold dismal corridors of the hospital. Her nostrils burned from the stink of disinfectant.

"So," he asked, "how was the dreaded *medsestra* today?"

"A slave driver. Had me turning mattresses and swabbing floors."

"Good for her. It's what you young slackers need."

Valentina prodded him in the ribs. "I'll shut you up with an anesthetic injection if you say things like that."

"Oh, I'm impressed. You mean you've started giving injections already?"

"No, not yet. But"—she tilted her face up at him—"I could practice on you."

He chuckled and tucked her arm through his, holding on to her hand. "You can practice anything on me."

She liked the way he said it. A horse cantered past and the rider called out, "*Dobriy vecher*, good evening," as if they were any ordinary couple wending their way home to cook schnitzel and read aloud to each other in front of the fire. That thought did odd things to her heart. She wondered if he felt it too.

"How is Katya?" Jens asked. An unexpected question.

"She's cross. Thoroughly bad-tempered."

"Why?"

"Because she's better at the moment. In less pain."

"Isn't that cause to be happy?"

"No. It means her tutor comes every day and makes her do mathematics, which she hates."

He laughed. She loved his laugh. It was as much a part of him as his red hair and his long rangy limbs. The sound of it came to her sometimes at night and woke her. In her dreams, he sat on the end of her bed, his red hair shimmering in the moonlight, and told her things while his black shadow shifted from wall to wall. She was certain that what he told her was vital for her to know, yet each morning it all vanished the moment she raised her eyelids.

"Jens," she said as they crossed a bridge, "how is progress on the collapsed tunnel?"

"Too slow."

"It must be frustrating for you."

He shrugged, but she wasn't fooled.

"I'm taking this opportunity," he added, "of using the Duma's outrage to channel more funds into replacing another section of the old wooden sewage pipes and improving the gradients into Neva Bay."

They had stopped at a crossroad, pausing as two heavy horse-drawn wagons trundled past, rain gleaming on the animals' thick coats.

"Jens, why is it you care so much for your tunnels?"

"It's my job."

She laughed and shook her head. The hood of her cape slid down. She had removed her nurse's head covering but was still wearing her hospital uniform. "Yes, it's your job, but it's obvious the tunnels mean more to you than that."

She fastened both hands on his arm, holding him there on the curb though the road had cleared. The rain was growing heavier, streaking through the darkness, coating the roofs and puddling on the roads. Later it would turn to ice.

"What makes you want to build tunnels? Instead of bridges, like your Isambard Brunel in England. He built the beautiful Clifton Suspension Bridge, didn't he?"

"I am impressed."

She stood on tiptoe and kissed his chin. A slight stubble felt rough against her lips. "Do you know what I think?"

"Tell me what goes on in that convoluted mind of yours."

"I have a theory. I think you like to impose order on chaos."

"Hah! That's quite a theory."

"A pile of bricks, you turn them into a tunnel. A city that needs pipes underground, you work out the gradients. A row of houses sinking in filth and flooded basements, you give them a sewerage system. Order out of chaos."

His face was still, eyes intent on hers. Only his breath moved, lacing in and out of the raindrops. He lifted his head and stared up at the roofs of the city. Above them a blanket of low clouds blacked out any hope of stars. "Petersburg itself needs cleansing. Not just its water supply."

"Come with me, Jens. I want you to see something." She seized his hand and together they ran across the road.

৲৶

ARKIN PEELED HIMSELF OFF THE WALL OF THE SHOP DOOR-way. He slid out of the shadows into the sleeting rain as the headlights of a car picked out the figures of Valentina and her engineer. They were running, her cape flapping like wings, as if they could sense him stalking behind them, even though he was certain they couldn't. He was too careful.

The rain served him well. People scuttled along the sidewalks under a wave of umbrellas that created a black barrier for him to duck behind. He tracked Valentina and Jens easily, following their twists and turns. He waited patiently in dark corners when they stopped at shops, curious about what lay in the bundles under their arms when they emerged.

He saw more than he wanted. The way they touched each other. The way they could not stop looking at each other, again and again, so often they could have stumbled on the road. The way their bodies never lost contact, as though drawn together by an invisible thread. He saw it all.

They were moving fast now, choosing unlit roads. Making it easy for him.

# Twenty-one

IT TOOK VALENTINA SOME TIME TO FIND THE RIGHT ROAD, but as soon as she turned into it she recognized the place. The wind had picked up, driving rain into their faces.

"This is the house."

Jens showed no inclination to knock at the door where she had stopped. In fact he showed no inclination to be taking part in this expedition at all, but she had steered him into these backstreets, aware of his disapproval. His shoulders were set in a hard line.

"This is no place for you, Valentina. Your nurse's uniform is not a disguise, you know. It doesn't hide what you are. It's not safe for you here."

She laughed at him, provoking a frown. "Of course it's safe. I've got you with me. Look, this is the door."

Jens pushed at it, and it swung open with a grating sound. He led the way over the threshold and they were hit by the rank smell, so strong this time that Valentina lifted her handkerchief over her nose. The door to the left was closed, but this time there were no children to challenge her, so she walked over and knocked. There was no response from inside. Jostling his bundles, Jens tried the handle and it turned easily. The room was freezing cold and lay in semidarkness, just one stub of a candle spitting out a reluctant light. Valentina grew wary, knowing that the woman with the damaged skull had not welcomed her the first time.

"Varenka?" she called.

As her eyes adjusted to the gloom, she took in the silence. There was no bustle of children or squawk of a baby. No noise at all except a hot harsh breath like the sound of a wheezy horse. The smell in the room was worse than in the hallway.

"Varenka?" she said again.

There was a movement on the bed. A hand tugged at a blanket and a face grayer than ash stared at them through slits of eyes. It was Varenka. She wore no scarf on her head, the scars visible in the semi-darkness, but she roused herself to a sitting position.

"Get out," she hissed. "Leave me in peace."

Valentina dropped the bundle of kindling she was carrying and hurried over to the bed, shaking out the thick folds of the woolen blanket she had brought. But Jens seized her arm and jerked her away from the bed.

"Don't," he said sharply. "I'll light the fire and then we'll leave."

Valentina yanked her hand away. "No. Now I'm here I want to cook her some eggs and—"

"Go away." The woman sank back down. There was no pillow. Just a bare soiled mattress and a patched blanket that stank of vomit and worse.

"I'm a nurse now," Valentina pointed out. "I can help."

She'd never lit a fire before. Never cooked eggs before. But she was determined to do so now. She calmly set about looking for a pan while Jens organized the fire. He was efficient in his movements, spreading kindling in the stove, using the paper bags that he'd carried the food in to catch the flame from his match. Instantly the fire's glow cast more light into the room, and Valentina shuddered. The place was filthy, worse than filthy, with a metal bucket overflowing with excrement in one corner and yellow trails of dried vomit across the floor. She felt bile rise in her throat.

"Jens," she murmured. "I expected that we would present her with the food, thank her again for her help with Katya, and leave. Debt canceled." She looked around her. "But now this."

His face hardened as he looked at the woman on the bed. "She's sick, Valentina. You can smell how sick she is. If you stay here, you're taking a risk. We don't know what she's got and you could catch—"

She put a finger to his lips. "Just a few minutes, Jens. We'll be quick."

"I know," he said. "You won't leave this sick stranger any more than you will leave your Katya. That's who you are."

He wrapped his arms around her as though the woman weren't watching with envious eyes. He kissed Valentina's forehead. It silenced the chattering of her teeth. "We'll be quick," she promised.

"You're a nurse." His smile, when it came, did something extraordinary to her insides. It made them hum, taut as piano strings.

∽

THEY WORKED TOGETHER, SIDE BY SIDE WITH SCARVES looped around their noses and mouths, their hands safe inside their gloves. They took shallow breaths, gulping in air only when they ducked outside into the street. The night air tasted sweet by comparison, though in reality it was acrid with factory waste and God only knew what else.

The worst came at the start. Valentina approached the bed.

"Where is the baby?" she asked.

The woman seemed to convulse, her limbs twisted in pain. "Dead," the woman said flatly.

"I'm so sorry."

Valentina squinted into the gloom of the far side of the bed. Only then did she make out the three small bundles under the edge of the blanket, so thin and flat they looked no more than rumples in the material. She leaned closer. So there were the other children.

"Stay away," the woman snapped.

Valentina took a quick look at the small bluish-gray faces and turned away. "I'll find some water," she said. "There must be a pump somewhere in the street."

She snatched an earthenware bowl from a shelf and hurried outside. She only just made it. In the darkest corner she vomited up her day's food, wiped her mouth on her sleeve, and stood in the rain, her face turned up to the clean cold blast of it. The children in the bed were the ones who had accepted her coins with such eagerness. Now they lay there beside their mother, still and stiff. All dead. By

the time she had found a water pump and was making her way back
to the house, a stray dog was gobbling up her vomit.

❧

THE DOOR SLAMMED OPEN, STARTLING VALENTINA AS SHE
was boiling up another can of water on the stove. Even after
boiling, the liquid still looked gray and brackish.

"Who the hell are you?" A man in an army greatcoat with the
insignia cut off, dark at the shoulders from the rain, had kicked his
way into the room.

Even without the swaying of his stocky figure, it was obvious he
was drunk. He threw his cloth cap onto the floor, revealing a shaven
head and skin that was mottled with brown speckles like birds' eggs.

"What the hell are you doing in my house? Get away from my
wife."

Jens moved immediately. He took the skillet out of Valentina's
hand and swung her cape over her shoulders. "We're just going." He
threw a hefty handful of rouble notes on the table. "Get your wife a
doctor and your children a decent burial."

"You." The man was trying to focus on Valentina but had to blink
hard. "Who are you? What's a pretty thing like you doing in—"

"She's leaving," Jens said. His voice was as cold as the dog in the
street.

"We came to help your wife," Valentina said. "You should be
here helping her yourself."

"Shut up!" The man lunged for her.

She sidestepped him with ease. But before he could unscramble
his feet, he was slammed against the wall with a crash that cracked
the plaster and Jens's forearm was jammed across his throat.

"Don't push your luck," Jens growled.

"Ivan," the woman on the bed wailed. "Please, don't hurt my
husband."

Jens released the man. "You are of no interest to me," he said
sourly. "Your wife once helped my friend here, and she wished to
return the favor. That's all."

"You bloodsucking parasites."

Jens shrugged and moved away, keeping himself between Valentina and Ivan. He pulled out a cigarette and lit it, tossing another to
the man, who caught it and pushed it between his lips.

"Do you work?" Jens asked.

"Yes. *Da*. I work fucking hard every bloody day."

"Where?"

"In the Raspov foundry."

"Foundry work is tough," Jens commented.

"So am I."

"Ivan," the woman called. "They've helped. Look at the fire."

For the first time the man's bloodshot eyes shifted around the room, and his gaze took in the food package on the table and the new candle on the shelf. Finally it settled on the flames in the stove, and the sight of them seemed to sober him. He shuffled over to the candle flame and stuck his cigarette in it, drew on it with satisfaction, and held his callused palms out to the warmth of the fire.

"You've come from one of the meetings, haven't you?" Jens gestured at the pamphlet sticking out of the man's coat pocket.

"*Da*, I have. What's it to you?"

"What are they saying now?"

"They're saying we'll soon be rid of the lot of you. Justice for the proletariat is so fucking close we can taste it. We stand shoulder to shoulder, comrades in arms. We are organized."

"More strikes?"

"*Da*."

"I hear the Bolsheviks and Mensheviks are at each other's throats."

"You hear wrong."

Valentina sensed Jens being drawn in. He'd said, *You are of no interest to me*, but it wasn't true; she could see it in his eyes.

"Jens?"

He nodded but didn't shift his gaze from this Ivan, this man of committees and strikes whose wife lay sick. This man whose house she had just scrubbed, whose excrement bucket she had helped empty, whose children lay dead and unheeded on his bed while he drank himself stupid.

"Time to leave," she said.

Still Jens didn't move.

"It needn't be like this, Ivan," he said. "There are people working for change within the government, men like Garyatan and Kornov. The Committee of Industrial Development is meeting with factory owners, forcing changes that improve the conditions for the workers."

"Lies."

"No, it's true."

"They tell you lies. The factory owners pay off the bastards on your committees with fat bribes. Nothing is changing." The man's face sank into folds of despair. "Nothing. You are fools, people like you, if you believe this can be settled with talk."

"The alternative, *comrade*, is rivers of blood on Nevsky."

"So be it."

Valentina strode over to the door and yanked it open.

"Who are you?" Ivan asked her. "A dainty little rich girl. I bet your father is someone important. Corrupt and worthless, but important."

"How dare you?" She wanted to slap the loose smile from his face. "My father is Minister Ivanov, and he is an honest and upright man."

Suddenly Jens took a grip on her shoulder and hurried her into the street. The freezing rain sank like ice picks into her cheek.

"Valentina," he muttered as he marched her away from the house, "you should not have said that."

"But it's true. My father is an upright man."

"You should not have said your name."

❧

A RKIN WATCHED THEM DISAPPEAR UP THE RAIN-SODDEN street, the engineer's arm clasped around the girl's waist, her head on his shoulder. As if they owned each other. He watched them until they were out of sight, and then he strolled across the road to the front door they had just left.

It didn't take much. A quick nudge of his shoulder and it sprang open. No lights. A filter of night sky through the cracks of the door. So he stood for a moment, listening, waiting for his eyes to adjust. Why this hovel? What made her come here? What the hell was she doing? He wondered what her mother would say when her daughter came home laden with lice and fleas.

From the doorway of the house opposite he had watched the pair of them go in and out with buckets of stinking shit and of water; he had seen the girl lean over and vomit against the wall in the pouring rain. She had marched right back into the hall and turned to the door on her left. It opened at the touch of his knuckles, and he stepped inside.

"Get out!"

A big man with a shaven head was slumped at a table, glaring at him with bloodshot eyes. A woman lay on the bed, and her lifeless gaze sent a shudder through him.

"I'm here to talk to you, comrade," he said to the man, "nothing more."

It was the use of the word *comrade* that did it.

"Talk about what?" the man asked suspiciously.

"Your visitors."

"Them!" Dirty fingers tore a chunk off the loaf of black bread and pushed it into his mouth. "What about them?"

"Why were they here?"

"Bringing bread and blankets to my wife. When what we really need is a decent wage so that we can buy our own bloody bread." He sank his head on his arms on the table.

Arkin took a few paces nearer the bed. It smelled bad. "Did they say anything?" he asked the sick woman.

*"Nyet."*

"They just brought you gifts?"

*"Da."*

"Why?"

"She is my friend," she whispered.

He almost laughed out loud. This woman and Valentina. But he recalled again how she'd stood in the rain. And then, still, she'd returned to this place. As if she cared.

"Who are you?" the woman croaked.

"I work for her father."

"The minister?"

So she'd told them that much.

"She came once before," the woman mumbled. "With her sister."

Now he understood. This must be where Popkov tracked them to the day of the march on Morskaya, and Valentina had not forgotten the kindness.

"Where does your husband work?" he enquired.

"Raspov."

The foundry on the edge of the city. Immediately he went back to the table, lit a cigarette for himself and one for the husband, then prodded him awake.

"Here." He offered the smoke.

The man took it with ill grace and sat up bleary-eyed. "You still here?"

"You work at the Raspov foundry."

"So what?"

"You have many apprentices there."

"What of it?"

Abruptly the woman started to retch, and Arkin rose quickly to put a zinc bowl in front of her. He reached over to pull up the blanket but jumped back in shock. Three faces, tiny and gray as stone.

"Leave them." Her voice was a faint whisper.

Sorrow for her lay like lead in his chest. "I know a priest," he said softly. "May I bring him here?"

Her wretched eyes clung to his as she nodded. He headed quickly for the door, stopping only to shake the man by the shoulder. "Sleep it off, comrade. I will be back and I shall want to talk to you about your Raspov apprentices."

The man looked bemused. "Why?"

"Because I have a job for them."

# Twenty-two

Valentina didn't go straight home. She said she couldn't, not yet. Jens bundled her into a *drozhky* and took her to his own apartment, but he was acutely conscious of the impropriety of doing so. A young woman after dark without a chaperone, but neither of them could bear to face a public place right now, with strangers' eyes inspecting her disheveled and stained appearance.

"Valentina," he said, "let me dry your hair."

She was seated in a deep armchair, and its high sides swallowed her small frame. Her hands lay white as bone in her lap. He approached her with a towel, and she looked up at him for the first time, a quick flash of her dark eyes. He let her hold on to her silence while he unpinned her hair and stroked its damp strands with the towel, slow rhythmic sweeps that ran from the crown of her head where the hair was wettest. It fell in a dense mass of waves that clung to her scalp, outlining the elegant shape of her skull. He dried them right down to the tips where they danced and curled, teasing his fingers.

The intimacy of the task was immense, more intimate than a kiss. He perched on the arm of her chair and she sat with her head slightly bowed as he dried it, so that time and again the strands would fall forward, revealing the pale slender stem of her neck. At one point he cupped her chin in his hands to hold it steady while he rubbed gently at the top of her head, but still she said nothing. Just let her chin sit in his palm, as if it belonged there.

He continued to stroke the dark mane long after it was dry, first with the towel and then with his hand. It sparked within its shimmering depths as he lifted it and entranced him with the way the light rippled within it like moonlight in a restless night sky. He relished the silky sensation of it on his skin and the way it slid smooth as ink between his fingers.

He leaned his head down and kissed the nape of her neck.

ᘉᘉ

Η OW DO THEY LIVE LIKE THAT?"
    She was talking now. He had fed her *pirozhki* and a glass of hot chocolate, tempting her out of the dark place she was hiding in. He was seated on the sofa opposite her, his legs stretched out and crossed at the ankles, enjoying a glass of red wine. He was trying to distract her.

"Do you know," he asked, "that over half of the wine produced in France is freighted to Russia. Can you believe that? We drink more wine than any other nation on earth."

He often caught himself using *we. We Russians. Our country.* As though he were one of them, someone from Perm or from Tver.

"I couldn't live like that," she said staring into the fire. "Not like that."

He knew she was not going to let it go.

"We all live," he responded quietly, "the best way we can."

"I would rather be dead."

"I doubt that. And anyway," he added, "I would come each day and light your fire for you. And dry your hair whenever it rained and brush out the tangles when the wind caught it."

She lifted her head.

"Then when the summer came," he continued, "instead of attending glittering balls at Anichkov Palace or lavish meals at Donon's or nights at the ballet in diamond-studded evening gowns, I'd walk you in your rags down to a quiet spot on the banks of the Neva and we'd eat boiled eggs and dangle our feet in the river."

Her head turned. Her eyes met his. "And music?" she asked in a solemn voice. "In this new world of yours, would there be music? Or no piano for me, no opera, no ballet?"

"Of course there'd be music," he smiled at her. "You would sing for me to the music of water lapping around our ankles, and I would accompany you on my violin."

Her mouth dropped open. "You play the violin?"

"Not play exactly. More like scraping out a few squawky notes that make a tomcat sound musically accomplished by comparison. But," he hurried on, "I would improve, I promise."

She laughed. "You warned me before to beware of the Neva River," she pointed out. "You told me it was polluted."

"Well, that's the advantage of having a sewage tunnel engineer to steer you to the right spots. I know all the secret nooks where the fouled currents don't reach."

"Is it really so polluted?"

He didn't want to have this conversation. He shrugged. "It could be cleaner."

"Tell me about it."

"I'd rather play my violin for you."

Her eyes grew round as coins, and he was embarrassed. Only a visiting mouse had ever listened to his playing. She scooped up her knees to her chest and balanced her small chin on them with a stubborn tilt. He was tempted to pick her up and pop her in his pocket.

"Play," she commanded.

He stood, gave her a deep bow with an elaborate flourish as though doffing his cap to one of the Romanov grand duchesses, and said, "I am totally at your service, mademoiselle."

He meant it. But he wasn't sure she knew that yet.

❧

DON'T!" JENS INSISTED.

"I can't help it."

"It is unkind."

"I know." Valentina collapsed into great whoops of laughter again. "Unkind to human ears!"

"That's not what I meant."

Jens frowned at her sternly, bounced his violin bow against the neck, and tapped his foot with mock impatience on the polished floorboards. He was standing in the middle of the room, violin tucked under his chin as comfortable as an old friend. He'd been performing a section of Bizet's *Toreador Song* for her, but paying it scant attention. It was lively and made her laugh; that was all he cared about. She'd seen too much today. Now he wanted her to laugh. She did so with the total abandon of a child. Her nose turned pink, her lovely mouth burst wide open, and her eyes scrunched up, bright with tears. And the dark glossy wings of hair that he had dried and smoothed so lovingly broke loose and took flight around her as she rocked with noisy laughter.

She was still young; he had to remind himself of that. Young and vulnerable.

He placed the violin and bow down on the table with a clatter, glared ferociously at his audience of one, and stalked over to the sofa where he sat down, stiff and offended, arms folded across his chest. But she wasn't fooled for a moment. She flung herself out of the chair and pounced like a hungry cat on the patch of sofa beside him. She laid a hand on his wrist and tugged his arms apart.

"We must teach these fingers," she laughed, holding up his left hand, "these culprits!" She threw back her head with delight and rolled her eyes at him, then tenderly pressed the tip of each culprit to her lips as though forgiving them. "Teach them to know what they're doing."

Did she know, he wondered, what she was doing?

"I shall find you a teacher," she declared.

"Can't you teach me?"

"No, no." She grinned at him. "Anyway we'd only end up shouting at each other."

He tweaked her pink nose. "That might be fun."

"I don't shout at Anna, Dr. Fedorin's daughter, when I teach her the piano but that's because she's well behaved. I have a feeling you wouldn't be well behaved."

Their eyes held, and he knew the moment lasted too long when he heard a tiny gasp seep out from between her lips. He looked away because she'd seen too much of what was in him.

"Valentina, it's time I took you home."

She half-lowered her lids, looking up at him through her dense eyelashes, and he was certain that if he didn't get to his feet now, he would never do so. He retrieved his hand as a first step, but the look on her face froze him to his seat. It was naked. Openly revealing her need for him, dark and desperate.

"Jens," she whispered, her eyes fixed on his, "I am frightened of losing you."

"You will never lose me, my love. You and I belong together. Don't you realize that?"

He curled an arm around her, drawing her closer, and she leaned into him, snuggling her head on his chest as though trying to listen to his heartbeat. He held her there. Only their breathing sounded in the room, light and even, as they matched each other breath for breath. For a long time they sat like that, watching the light from the fire throw shadows that crept nearer, nudging their knees and hiding in their shoes. Jens kissed the top of her head, warm and musky.

"Jens." Her voice was thick. "Tell me who you are."

No one had ever asked him such a question before. He thought about it and started to talk. About his childhood spent on boats and beaches in Denmark, about building things, with pebbles, with rocks, with driftwood. About a bridge design that won him a prize, about a boat that sank and nearly managed to drown him and his dog in the gulf. He owned up to his passion for engines, for machines, for anything that possessed moving parts. He talked about the Wright brothers in America and Louis Blériot in France.

"Aeroplane flight," he said. "That's the future. You'll see."

He felt her smile. She didn't believe him.

"Your parents?" she queried.

He kept that part short. His father's printing business in Copenhagen, their arguments when Jens informed him that he wanted to study engineering instead. The disappointment in his mother's kindly brown eyes. He still wrote to them once a month, but he hadn't been back to Denmark for five years.

"I am Russian now," he declared.

"As Russian as a giraffe."

He told her more about his hopes for Russia and his longing that it would find stability through talking and compromise, not through violence. But he didn't mention the war he was certain must come; he kept his fears locked away from her. Gradually he felt the weight of her head on his chest increase and sensed the melting of her body into the lines of his own. Her hip molded against his hip.

"Tell me about the countess's son."

So it was then that he told her about Alexei.

"Alexei is Countess Serova's son, only six years old. You'd like him, Valentina. He has such courage." His fingers stroked her slender shoulder. "Like you," he said under his breath. "Just like you.

You have to understand, my love, that I can't desert Alexei. I can't turn my back on the boy. His father, Count Serov, cares only for his own gaudy life at court and his mistress in her lavish apartment on the English Embankment. The countess is angry. She resents the boy because . . ."

He let his words trail away. Natalia Serova's emotions were far too complex to untangle so simply. He put his lips to Valentina's cheek, inhaling again the hospital smell rising from her uniform, and wrapped both arms around her, rocking her, holding her. "Be generous, Valentina," he whispered. "Let me keep Alexei. I have grown to love the boy, and he is not to blame for my mistakes with his mother. She and I are finished. Don't ever doubt that."

To his surprise she let the subject lie untouched. Instead she lifted her mouth to his and kissed him fiercely, erasing all memory of other lips, imprinting her own. Laying claim. Her fingers undid the buttons of his shirt, stumbling over them, and her palms brushed his skin, tentative at first. But when he ran a hand down her spine, seeking out the delicate curves under her uniform, she grew bolder. Her hands caressed his naked chest and her lips tracked down the beat of his heart.

He kissed her neck, tasted her skin, felt her hair trail like threads of silk over his ribs and smelled the musky scent of her. Not of her uniform, of her, the slender hungry creature inside it. His desire for her raced through his veins and he forced himself to his feet.

"No, Valentina." The words came out roughly. "No, my sweet love, you are too young. You must go home." The words cost him dear.

Her gaze fixed on him so intently that he had to force himself to look away. Yet her voice was soft and teasing.

"How old were you when you first made love to a woman?"

"That's not the point."

"I think it is. You made the decision for yourself. Now I am doing the same."

She stood up slowly and without hesitation proceeded to undo the many buttons on her cuffs and bodice. She didn't look at him but concentrated on what she was doing as if she were alone in her room. He stood there, his back to the fire, and watched her. Watched her when her arm emerged from a sleeve and he saw for the first time the pale secret skin of her shoulder, the way it gleamed in the firelight, fresh and smooth as buttermilk.

He watched while she untied the laces of her stays and he could see clearly the form of her ribs under her camisole. He watched as she removed her wool stockings, balancing on one leg with the ease of long habit, rolling down each stocking with care, revealing slender white thighs. He must have breathed, but he was not aware of it. His heart must have continued beating, but he was sure it had stopped. It was as though for this moment he lost all ability to do anything but watch her.

She dipped her head, allowing the sleek veil of her hair to fall forward so that he could not see her expression when she slid out of her last garments. She stood naked before him and, God forgive him, he wanted her more than he wanted his own life.

"You are beautiful," he said softly.

She lifted her head and smiled at him. Her cheeks were flushed and her eyes darker than he'd ever seen them. Her breath came in short swift gasps. If he put his lips to hers, he knew they would be hot.

"I love you," she said.

The nakedness of her statement was more overwhelming than her beautiful body. Naked in its simplicity. In its trust. He stooped, picked up her cloak that was drying in front of the fire, and walked over to her. So close he could see a faint sheen of moisture between her young breasts.

"Valentina, if you don't wrap up in this right now," he said sternly, swinging the cloak around her shoulders and fastening it under her chin, "I shall ravish you in front of the fire." He refused to look at the expression in her eyes. "Now dress your exquisite self once more while I fetch us a drink."

He walked from the room. In the kitchen he leaned over the sink, ran cold water, and splashed it over his face and throat. He poured himself a shot of vodka and drank it down.

"Valentina," he murmured, "what is it you've done to me?"

He gave her time. After a few minutes had passed, when his pulse was steadier and he thought she'd be dressed, he refilled his own drink, poured out a lemonade for her, and, with a glass in each hand, walked back into the room. Immediately a long groan escaped him. The light was off and she was stretched out on the reindeer rug in front of the fire, the glow of its flames dancing over her skin, painting her naked body golden. A wide smile greeted him.

"Are all Vikings so slow to ravish their women?"

❧

Was her skin dead before? It must have been. Pale, lifeless, and limp. Because it came alive on the reindeer rug in a way Valentina didn't know was possible. She no longer recognized this extraordinary covering on her body as hers. Each pore, each fine layer, each smooth unexplored part of it possessed a separate existence of its own that only needed the touch of Jens's lips to bring it to life. The hollow of her throat, the inner curve of her elbow, the thin coating over each individual rib. Now they vibrated with life. When he kissed the underside of each breast, his tongue warm and moist as it circled up toward her nipple, it was as if her skin started to re-form. To become something other than skin.

Her fingers twisted his shirt from his shoulders, and she laid the flat of her hands on his chest, on his back, feeling the ridges of muscle. Exploring the structure of him, the sinews, the hard lines of his bones, her hands learning the intimate shape of him. She could feel the heat within him. Or was that radiating from herself, from the blood racing from her heart to the tips of her fingers?

When she tasted with her tongue the path of coppery curls that rose from his belt buckle to his throat, he uttered a sound she'd never heard before. It ricocheted up from somewhere deep in his lungs and somehow became a part of her, drumming in her head.

Quickly he slid out of his clothes and, with a noise like Thor's hammer resounding in her ears, he carried her to his bed.

❧

Valentina didn't want to leave. But Jens made her. She didn't know how she persuaded her body to rise, to abandon the sheets that smelled of him, to lift her head out of the warm curve of his pillow. Her skin still felt his touch and her body was still shaking with pleasure as he lifted her into his carriage and drove her back to her father's house. When the footman opened the door, she was certain he could see the change in her, smell the musk on her, and she hurried across the hall.

"Valentina!"

She stopped, one foot on the bottom stair, acutely aware of her untidy appearance. She had thought to reach her room unseen. "Yes, Papa?"

He was standing in the doorway of the drawing room, his face flushed. He was in full evening dress and in his hand he brandished a glass of champagne, which he jabbed in her direction, sending golden spills down his white waistcoat.

"Valentina, it's late."

"Yes, Papa."

"Where have you been?"

"At the hospital, at St. Isabella's."

"Till this hour?"

"There was an emergency. An accident in one of the factories." She wasn't any good at lying.

He viewed her uniform with distaste. "So you cleaned it up with your apron, by the look of you."

"No, Papa."

She didn't want to provoke him, not this time. The smile that wouldn't leave her lips was not for him, but he was not to know that, so he advanced toward her with an amiable expression. His gait was unsteady.

"I have something for you." He fumbled in his pocket and eventually produced a letter folded small. "From Captain Chernov."

She wanted to turn, to run up the stairs, to fling herself on her bed and refuse to allow Captain Chernov anywhere near her mind. It was too full of someone else. Her fingers hung at her side.

"Take it, girl."

"I don't want it, Papa."

"Take the damn letter."

It hovered between them, pale and insistent. Her fingers didn't move.

"I'll read it tomorrow, Papa. I'm too tired tonight."

"I'd like you to read it now, in front of me."

She didn't look at him. She stared at his black patent shoes, the spiky lights of the chandelier reflected back at her from their gleaming surface. She held out her hand and he thrust the folded paper into it. She let it lie there.

"Read it, please."

Slowly she opened the letter and words in a bold black hand reared up in front of her eyes, but they remained a blur. She refused to focus on them.

"Well?"

She shook her head.

He took the letter and read it aloud. *"My dearest Valentina, . . ."*

"I am not his *dearest*." Her voice came out low and disconnected.

Her father didn't notice.

*"My dearest Valentina,*

*I took the liberty of calling on you today but you were not at home. I hope you are well and not inconvenienced by the military presence that is patrolling the city, dismantling street-barricades and breaking up unruly gatherings. Don't worry, dear Valentina, I am making it my personal mission to keep you safe during these troubled and troubling times.*

*There is to be a grand imperial ball at the Winter Palace and I would be greatly honored if you would accompany me to it next Wednesday evening.*

*Thank you for the delightful pleasure of your company the other evening.*

*Yours devotedly,*
*Stepan Chernov."*

Her father nodded and his contentment spread pink streaks across his cheeks. His chest swelled. She could see he was pleased with her. "You've done well, Valentina."

"Papa, I know every father wants his daughter to make a good marriage."

He raised his glass to her. "Indeed they do."

"So I understand that you intend the best for me."

"Good girl."

He stepped forward and draped an arm around her shoulders, and the image of her list flashed through her mind. She thought of how easy it would be to make her father forgive her at last.

"But Papa, please don't force me into—"

He laughed and tickled her cheek with the corner of the letter. "Hush, child, hush." He came close and kissed her cheek.

"Papa"—she moved away and pulled her cloak tight around her body, isolating herself from him—"please inform Captain Chernov that I'm sorry, but—"

"Nicholai, are you ever coming back in here?"

It was a woman's voice, light and faintly slurred. It issued from the drawing room and was followed by a soft enticing laugh and the chink of a bottle against a glass. It was not her mother. But her father showed no sign of embarrassment, and his dark eyes gleamed with amusement as he observed his elder daughter. He patted the back of her wrist where she clutched the edge of her cloak, an affectionate fatherly touch.

"Don't look so shocked, Valentina. It's how marriages work. When you and Stepan Chernov are married, you'll soon get used to the idea, like your mother did. No, don't—"

But she was gone. Up the stairs two at a time, leaving him with his letter and his woman.

৵

HER DIRTY CLOTHES LAY ON THE FLOOR, JUST AS SHE'D dropped them a thousand times before for the maid to pick up. But this time when she looked down at the soiled uniform lying like a dead person on the carpet and pictured the clean one hanging crisp and ironed in her wardrobe, she frowned. She stooped, picked up the dirty clothes, folded them, and placed the pile neatly on a chair for Olga to find when she came in. The little things. They made a difference. She was noticing them now.

It wasn't until she was curled up in bed, hugging her knees, that she allowed her mind the luxury of slipping away. Her eyes closed and immediately she was on a different pillow, in a different bed, in a different life. Her body ached for Jens, a sharp driving ache that drew out a raw moan from her throat. The heat of him was still inside her, making her thighs restless, unable to keep still.

She had no idea it would be like this. The wanting. The recall of his every touch. His lips so tender on her breasts, his hands caressing and coaxing till her body became his instead of hers. The desire to please him, to taste him, to own him. Her lips claiming him. Her body and soul so in thrall to him that lying here on her own was like being only half a person, having only half a life.

"Jens," she whispered into the darkness. "I'll never be able to give you up."

Not even for Katya.

# Twenty-three

SNOW FELL IN CURLING WHITE SHEETS, BILLOWING FORWARD in sudden bursts of violent energy, then retreating like an army gathering its troops before the next attack. The roofs and roads glittered white and the city that had been created out of a dingy swamp so many years ago by Peter the Great looked as graceful and elegant as one of the tsar's own swans.

Arkin did not notice its beauty. It was the dark police uniforms that held his attention. They were gathering in twos and threes on street corners, their eyes watchful as wolves. He hadn't expected them yet. They had moved fast, which surprised him, and they were nervous. The Raspov apprentices were on the march, stomping through the streets, noisy and rowdy as boisterous dogs let off the leash, chanting the slogans he had taught them, shouting and waving their handmade banners.

"Give us justice!"

"United we fight! United we win!"

"We demand a fair wage!"

"Victory for the workers!"

Again and again their united voices shouted out the words that were dearest to their hearts, "Give us bread! *Khleb!*"

Scrawny skeletons, that was all they were, a jumble of skin and bones inside coats too thin to keep out the Russian winter. So young and yet so resigned to their fate. It angered his heart. It had taken all his persuasive powers to convince them that they could change the terrible conditions in their foundry if they worked together. Flat white faces had stared back at him at first with helpless, hopeless eyes.

The person who helped him put fire inside their hungry bellies was Karl, the engine driver's young son who'd collected the crate from the train with him. Only sixteen and already he understood.

"Comrades, things can change," Arkin had told them. He was standing on a box in the icy yard of the foundry, and he could feel their excitement mingling with the snow that blew in their faces. "*You* can change them. You workers are the ones with the real power—if only you have the courage to wield it."

"Brothers," young Karl had shouted out, "listen to our comrade. We are treated worse than rats by our masters. Yesterday Pashin lost half his hand, last week Grigoriev lost the skin on his neck. Who will be next?"

"The hours are too long," Arkin declared. "Mistakes are made."

"No safety at work," Karl added.

"No right to complain."

"No water. It's hot as hell in there."

"Do your masters care?" Arkin punched a hole in the white air with his fist.

"No," the young voices shouted back.

"So let's teach them to care," Karl yelled.

That was when they started to march. Ivan Sidorov had stood at the foundry gates, eyeing him with respect. He looked a very different figure when he wasn't drunk and sprawled over a table, a man Arkin could use. Sidorov was the one who'd gathered the apprentices together for him in the yard. They exchanged a look, that was all. It was enough.

❧

WORD SPREAD FAST. AS THEY SWUNG PAST THE SHOE FACtory on Strechka Ulitsa a string of young boys burst out, still in their leather aprons, and hurled themselves into the Raspov crowd. Apprentices from the Tarasov toolmaking factory swelled their numbers to well over three hundred, marching shoulder to shoulder and shouting their slogans. Behind them strode Sergeyev, his arm still in a sling.

"Good work," he commented to Arkin.

He nodded a greeting. "How's your wife?"

"Concerned about how today will turn out."

"Tell her we are rolling a stone downhill, gathering speed. Nothing can stop it."

Sergeyev clenched his fist in agreement, but he looked tense and tired.

"Go home," Arkin urged. "Your arm is clearly bad today, my friend. These apprentices hardly need us now that they can scent victory."

"Hah! They are blind to the battles ahead."

"This is just a skirmish, Sergeyev. It's a beginning. Let them have their day of glory." He studied him with concern. "You go home. Tend to your wife."

To his surprise, Sergeyev clapped him on the shoulder, gripping it hard. "Good luck, *udachi*, comrade." He peeled back from the line of marchers and was gone. Instantly the place at Arkin's side was taken by the lanky figure of Karl, a grin on his young face.

❧

THEY FLOODED INTO THE RAILWAY SIDINGS, AN OPENING windswept soulless place where rail carriages were shunted to die. Boots stamped on the ice-packed earth. Arkin listened to them and felt his blood quicken. It was the sound of the feet of Russia on the march. Not even the tsar on the imperial throne would dare to slaughter these innocents. He felt hope, hot and liquid, surge through his gut at the thought of the future for Russians.

"Arkin, good man, you've fired up their young minds."

It was Father Morozov. He grasped Arkin's hand. Snowflakes had settled in a halo on the priest's tall black hat, diamond sharp, at odds with his shabby coat.

"This is my young comrade, Karl, from the Raspov foundry. He has already proved he is one of us, valuable to the cause."

The priest held out his hand in welcome. The boy took it, dipped his head over the gloved fingers, and pressed them to his lips. "Father," he murmured with respect.

The simple gesture annoyed Arkin intensely, but he gave no sign.

Didn't they realize? That was exactly the kind of automatic subservience the Bolsheviks were trying to eradicate. There was no place for religion in the future of Russia, where all would be equal. No obeisance, no knee bending. Not even to God.

"Are they coming?" Arkin asked urgently.

Morozov smiled. *"Da."*

"When?"

"They're on their way now."

"Good. They've kept their promise."

Karl looked from one to the other. "Who? Who's coming?"

"The rail workers," Arkin informed him. "This depot has gone on strike in support of the apprentices."

"It's starting," Karl said quietly. "Isn't it?"

"Yes."

The boy straightened his back and puffed out his bony chest. "Comrade Arkin, Comrade Father, I am proud to be a part of this great—"

"They're here!" a voice in the crowd cried out. "The rail workers are here!"

Immediately the air filled with eager shouts, and a phalanx of about a hundred or more men in navy caps and work jackets crowded into the sidings, fists punching the air.

"Father," Arkin murmured under his breath, "give thanks to your God from me."

The priest closed his eyes and smiled. One of the rail workers, a big burly man with a voice to match, climbed up on a rusting flatbed and launched into a rallying speech that swept the apprentices into a frenzy of excitement. Not even the icy curtain of snow could chill the heat that roared through their veins or the anger that built into something as hard and sharp as the Admiralty spire. Arkin was satisfied with his morning's work.

"Horses coming," an apprentice near the back called out.

They'd sent in the army. The apprentices and rail workers were slow to react, but Arkin leapt up onto the steps of a decrepit carriage. "Get ready. Troops are coming."

From under jackets and coats, iron bars suddenly appeared. The sound of hooves grew louder, clattering over cobbles, until the veil of snow seemed to part like the Red Sea to reveal the platoon of scarlet uniforms on horseback, capes flying out behind. They halted and spread out in a long line, blocking access, leaving no chance of escape.

Panic started. It flickered from boy to boy, quick gasps and nervous shouts, but they took their lead from the railway workmen. They regarded the sabers with wide eyes as each soldier held his sword out in front of him, its blade flat to the sky. Snow settled on them as if to soften the threat.

"Disperse immediately!"

The order came from the captain at the head of the line. He sat astride a magnificent stallion that was eager to charge, its forefoot scraping at the dirt, raking through the trampled snow. The rider fixed his gaze on the rail worker on the flatbed.

"Disperse immediately!" he ordered again.

Arkin moved. He threaded his way through the apprentices and emerged at the front of them, nearest the soldiers.

"The boys are doing no harm." He spoke calmly.

The captain glanced at him, and something in what he saw made him stop and look again.

"Who are you?" he demanded.

"A comrade of the apprentices. Captain," he said sharply, "do not provoke trouble here today. We do not want bloodshed."

The captain's mouth curved at one side, revealing a satisfied smile. "Don't we?"

"No. These young boys are—"

"—dangerous."

"No. They are voicing their dissatisfaction and demanding to be listened to."

"We want justice," Karl insisted at his side. He was clutching an iron bar with his two fists.

"Then, young troublemaker, justice you shall have."

With no warning the captain stretched forward and flicked his saber through the air. A faint whistle, that was all. Arkin was fast, but not quite fast enough. He yanked his young friend back on his heels, so that the saber strike intended to open up the boy's pale throat just caught his nose and split one side of his nostril. Crimson spurted down his chin.

The railway workers surged forward. Angry words were hurled at the horsemen. Tempers flared. Metal bars and tools were brandished until the demonstration was on the edge of violence. It was to avoid exactly such violence that Arkin had involved the apprentices in the first place, but now he dragged Karl back from the front line. He inspected the boy's face. He was holding a hand to his nose, blood twining around his fingers, but his eyes were on fire. Fury, not fear, was making his arm shake in Arkin's grip.

"Get behind the railway workers," Arkin ordered. "Prepare the apprentices to give support."

The boy disappeared. Snow fell heavily in dense white veils and voices grew louder. The Hussars' attack, when it came, was lightning fast. The horses sprang forward, sabers scything right and left, silent and brutal. Screams rang out in high-pitched voices, and the snow on the ground turned crimson as feet skidded under hooves. Metal bars crashed down on the troops, crushing bones and twisting heels out of stirrups until uniforms vanished under a mass of workmen's boots. Yet the sabers continued to strike with expert skill, again and again, laying bare a back, slashing open a cheek, a throat. Charge, regroup, charge. Even the snow in the air turned scarlet as the horses wheeled in formation up and down the railway siding.

Arkin snatched Sergeyev's small pistol from under his coat. Six times he took precise aim, six times slamming a bullet into a scarlet chest. The strikers fought back with fury. Horses crashed to their knees. Helmets fell to the ground. Arkin threw himself into the battle, dodging blades, parrying blows, all the time working his way nearer to the tall blond captain on the devil-black stallion.

Arkin found Karl's body. His young eyes were wide open, staring up at the falling snow, but glazed and lifeless. Flakes settled in his lashes and melted on the warm eyeballs like tears. Arkin broke the neck of the soldier standing over him with his saber still dripping on the snow and dropped to his knees beside the boy. He closed the young eyes. Nothing was sacred in this world. Not even the innocents. He snatched up the saber and with a roar of rage went to work on the scarlet uniforms.

❧

THE WOMEN WORKED HARDEST. VALENTINA QUICKLY became aware of that fact. In St. Isabella's Hospital the women worked hardest and were paid the least, yet they didn't complain. They just treated the male nurses with a deference Valentina felt they didn't deserve and the doctors like gods incarnate.

She worked hard and spoke little. She didn't mind that she spent most of her time in the sluice room scrubbing things and sterilizing equipment. That was a good part, the instruments. She handled them with respect, finding unexpected pleasure in their fine steel edges and baffling shapes. She liked the way each one had a specific purpose: a clamp, a probe, a syringe, and many that she could only guess at. Each day she and her fellow novice nurses were given an hour of instruction in which she focused her mind with the same intensity as when she learned a new piece for the piano. During her time in the wards, she asked clear questions and paid close attention to the answers.

"You're a good listener," one of the patients told her.

St. Isabella's was a hospital for the poor. It had been set up more than one hundred years earlier at the insistence of Catherine the Great, but there were never enough beds and never enough wards. An unending stream of the sick and the dying stumbled through its doors, but many were turned away with no hope of finding treatment elsewhere. But Valentina was learning to lock things out of her head. Like the man this morning lying on the steps outside, dead as a dog. People with money didn't use hospitals. They were places you went to die. Doctors would come to the houses of respectable people, numerous times a day if necessary, and treat patients in their own bed. They even performed minor operations there. Only for a major operation did a wealthy patient enter a hospital.

Valentina plunged her hands deep into soapy water and started scrubbing a speculum, but after a minute she lifted her hands and inspected them. Red and raw, with hairline cracks around the knuckles. She felt a ripple of shame. A nurse's hands, not a pianist's hands. She hated herself for caring.

A door swung open behind her. "Ah, there you are. We need you."

Valentina turned, suds dripping to the floor. It was young Darya Spachyeva, the nurse she met the day she came for her interview, the one with black hair and the swear words. Her wide smile was missing today.

"Do you know," Valentina asked, "that you have blood all down your neck?"

"You have to come," the girl said. "Quickly."

☙

T HE AIR LAY THICK AND HEAVY. WALKING INTO THE MEN'S ward was like wrapping her face in a stale blanket. Blood and fear and a deep raw anger packed the room so full that there was little space for anything else. Bodies lay everywhere: on beds, on mattresses on the floor, on thin blankets, on bare boards. Too many, far too many.

"What happened?" Valentina demanded.

"The Hussars."

"An attack?"

"Well, they weren't playing with their nice shiny sabers for nothing."

Valentina could see their smooth unlined cheeks. Young men with dreams that had been shredded. Blood streamed from their heads; gaping wounds yawned open on their shoulders. They had fought, on foot, against men on horseback.

"*Chyort!*" Valentina swore.

Captain Chernov had kept his promise.

"Darya"—her pulse was thudding in her ears—"where do I start?"

❧

N URSE IVANOVA, TAKE THESE. BE QUICK."
*Medsestra* Gordanskaya thrust a pair of shears into Valentina's hand and moved with calm efficiency to the other side of the ward, where Darya was struggling to prevent a man with a bandage over his eyes from crawling toward the door. Valentina laid a gentle hand on the patient in front of her. He was lying facedown.

"Hello, I'm *Sanitarka* Ivanova."

She kept her voice firm and reassuring. With the shears she snipped through the material of his jacket from its hem right up to its collar, then the same with his shirt. Two long parallel cuts ran down his back like scarlet tram tracks. She bathed them with antiseptic, but as fast as she mopped up the blood, more flowed onto his white flesh. It needed stitches. All the time she worked, she talked to him. His frightened eyes, as he tilted his head to one side, kept darting up at her.

"The doctor will be here any moment," she assured him. "A few stitches, that's all you'll need." She placed a dressing pad on the wound and pressed hard to stem the flow. "You'll soon be back at work."

"They were waiting for us. Determined to finish us off this time."

"Were you marching?"

"*Nyet*. No, just gathering in our factory yard. Me and the other apprentices."

"The soldiers attacked you in the factory yard?"

"No." His eyes fluttered closed and opened again, small fragmented movements, and a smear of vomit slid from his mouth. "We went down to the railway sidings to have talks with the rail workers. Their foreman was . . ." He started to sob, raw animal sounds.

"Hush, you're safe here." She touched his hair on the back of his head and it was stiff and matted with blood. She stroked his cheek. His neck.

"Nurse," he whispered, eyes closed, "I can't move my arms."

❧

"*B*ISTRO! QUICKLY!"

A doctor in a white coat summoned her. All day it had continued, the young men dragged in on carts, on shoulders, on makeshift stretchers. Valentina steeled herself to the moans and the tears. She learned to hold a man's hand against her own throat because the strong pulse there somehow gave them something to hang on to. She learned not to say *Hush*. She let them talk or cry or shout. Whatever gave them respite. She wrote brief notes for them to their loved ones, held water to their bruised lips, and bound so many reels of bandage that the gauzy white strips seemed to become extensions of her own skin, skimming over arms and legs and heads. Holding their young bodies together.

"*Bistro!*"

"Yes, *Doktor?*"

"One grain of morphine here."

"Yes, *Doktor.*"

A young boy, dark as a gypsy and not much older than Katya, was lying on his back in a bed with his thin arms crossed over his chest. His skin was slick with sweat. He smiled at Valentina while his lips continued to form his prayers. She measured out two drops of the painkiller from a vial into a small glass and held his head while he sipped the liquid. His pupils were pinpoint specks.

"*Spasibo.*" The word was so faint it was barely there. "*Do svidania.* Good-bye."

"He was crushed," the doctor murmured. "By their horses."

"Is there a priest?" Valentina asked quickly.

"He's in the next ward." He exhaled an exhausted sigh. "His services have been much in demand today." He raised his head and looked properly for the first time at the young nurse at his side.

"Valentina! My dear girl, I had no idea it was you. Your uniforms turn you all into—"

"I know, Dr. Fedorin. We nurses all look the same."

"Hardly." He brushed the back of his wrist across his eyes. "You and *Medsestra* Gordanskaya are scarcely the same species."

She smiled, and it was such a relief to untie the knots in the muscles of her face that she almost slipped an arm around his neck, the way she'd seen his daughter do when she was pleased with him.

"You should take a rest, *Doktor*."

He shook his head. "This wasn't exactly the kind of nursing I had in mind for you when I recommended you to St. Isabella's." For a moment Dr. Fedorin took his eyes off the wounded in the ward and studied Valentina's face. She wondered what he saw there. "A baptism of fire," he said quietly.

The boy on the bed lifted one hand and carved the sign of the cross in the air. "A baptism of blood," he corrected, eyes on Valentina.

"I'll find you the priest," she said, then squeezed the boy's hand and vanished.

࿐

BUT THERE WAS NO PRIEST IN THE NEXT WARD. SHE BROKE the rules. Picked up her skirts and raced down one of the corridors, searching for a figure in black. She refused to let the boy die without the comfort of absolution. *You need to be tough,* Jens had told her. *To deal with the blood and the wounds.*

A hand fell on her shoulder, so heavy she felt her bones sag, and she jumped away, startled.

"Child, don't be frightened."

She stopped running and regarded the man who seemed to have appeared in the corridor from nowhere. He looked like a priest of some kind. He was an impressive broad-shouldered figure, imposing in a plain black tunic. And yet there was something about him that made her want to step away. His eyes were large and round, a striking pale blue and set deep in their sockets. They didn't blink, just stared at her. They seemed to burn. She could find no other word for it. They fixed on her and burned right into the coils of her mind till she longed to look away, but couldn't.

"I need a priest," she said quickly.

"Child," his voice was deep, his words measured. In the cold corridor they resonated with conviction. "Child, the whole of mankind needs a priest to show them the pathway to God. I see you are troubled. Let him cleanse you."

She almost laughed out loud. This strange man was anything but clean. She dragged her eyes from his and focused instead on his long straggly beard, which was filthy and matted with spilled food. His tunic was stained and his hands thick with grime. Worst of all, he stank. The only clean thing about him was the jeweled crucifix that gleamed on a chain around his neck.

"Maybe you should ask God to cleanse yourself first," she suggested. "But come quickly, please. You're needed in—"

He reached for her. Huge dirty hands. He clamped one on each side of her head and fixed his powerful gaze on hers. "You're the one in need, *malishka*, little one. I can bring you the peace you crave. In the Lord's name."

He lowered his head as though to give her the kiss of Christ on her forehead, but at the last moment he ducked down and placed the kiss on her lips. Shock and distaste shook Valentina as his mouth, huge and cavernous, swallowed hers. She lashed out. Her hand struck his cheek, the sound of the slap muted by his wiry beard, and all the hardship of the day poured into her anger.

"You are no man of God. You are an impostor, a disgusting, lecherous—"

He laughed, a delighted rumble of pleasure, as though the words she poured on him were words of praise. She was tempted to slap him again but couldn't bear to touch him. She scrubbed at her mouth with her hand and kept a safe distance from him.

"You're needed by a boy who is dying," she told him.

"He doesn't need me. You are the one who needs me."

"You are not a real priest, are you?"

"I am just a poor *starets*. With humility I offer myself to souls in suffering, souls like yours. Souls who don't know how to find their way."

"My soul is my own affair," she said. "You are not a *starets*, not a holy man. This boy needs a proper priest." His pale eyes held hers and she felt her tongue grow heavy in her mouth, her mind start to drift. With an effort of will she forced herself to turn away from the dark figure and hurry back down the corridor. She struggled to make herself dismiss him from her head.

"Nurse," he called after her in a deep voice. "*Malishka*, we shall meet again, you and I, and when we do you will offer me a kiss in exchange for your soul."

❧

Valentina found a priest at last, a real priest. He was dressed in a hand-woven cassock that was frayed at the hem, with a prayer stole around his neck, and wearing a tall black hat that had seen better days. At first sight she took him for a peasant priest who must have traveled to the hospital from an outlying village when he heard of the carnage, but when he responded to her shout, raising his head from intoning prayers over a wounded man, she recognized him at once. He was the priest she'd met with Arkin, the one she'd stumbled across when the chauffeur was unloading sacks of potatoes into a church.

"Father, I need your help."

"What is it, Nurse?"

"A young man is dying."

His reaction was not what she expected because, though he walked with an outward calm at her side when she led him to the other ward, his boots kicked out at the frayed hem ahead of him in a gesture of fury.

"Father, do you know what happened?"

"The apprentices work in terrible conditions." His words were controlled, even if his feet were not. "They held a meeting after one of them lost a limb in a machine, but there are always police spies everywhere." He shook his head and raised the Bible in his hand so that it was fixed in front of his eyes as he hurried along the corridor. "May the Lord God have mercy on the souls of those soldiers, because I can find none in my heart for them. I would damn the lot of them to hellfire for all eternity." He shook the Bible fiercely as though his fingers could provoke an answer from its black cover. "The apprentices are little more than children."

"But they joined forces with the rail workers, I was told."

"Yes."

"So that must mean it was well organized."

As she pushed open the swinging doors the priest stopped, and she was forced to look back at him.

"Who are you?" he demanded.

"Just a nurse. Trying to help save the lives of your apprentices."

*Just a nurse.* Simple words. They seemed to calm him.

His eyes became gentler, and he moved forward again. "Of course, I am distressed. What I saw today when the sabers slashed down, no man should see." He clutched his Bible to his chest like armor.

She put out her hand and touched the cross embossed on its surface. "You were there?"

"Yes."

"Tell me, Father Morozov, was Viktor Arkin there too?"

The bones of his face slackened. "Who are you?"

"Was he hurt?"

A shake of his head, so slight it was barely a movement.

"Tell him," she said, "to remove the box he has hidden at the back of the garage. Before the Okhrana come for him."

## Twenty-four

"*SANITARKA* IVANOVA."

*Medsestra* Gordanskaya stopped Valentina as she was leaving the ward at the end of the day. The older nurse looked tired, something bruised about her eyes as though the day had taken too harsh a toll.

"*Sanitarka* Ivanova, you did well today. You have the makings of a decent nurse." Her features softened. "I admit, you surprised me."

"Thank you, *Medsestra*."

"Now go home and wash today away with scalding hot water and a slug of vodka, if you know what's good for you."

"Yes, *Medsestra*."

*A decent nurse.* She pulled her cape over her shoulders. *A decent nurse.*

On the steps outside she bumped into Nurse Darya and immediately asked her, "Do you know the priest who was here today?"

"Father Morozov? Yes, he's often here. Can't stand his preachy stuff myself"—she pulled a face and snatched off her headdress—"but he brings the patients food as well as comfort. They love him."

"No, not him. Another one. Dirty and repulsive. With hypnotic blue eyes and a very expensive-looking crucifix."

"Oh shit, that bastard. Didn't touch you, did he?"

"No." The lie slipped out.

"Don't worry, that creep isn't here often. Only when he feels like slumming it for a change."

"What do you mean? Where does he normally spend his time?"

Darya poked Valentina in the ribs. "Jesus Christ, don't you realize who that stinking bastard is?"

"He claimed he was a *starets*, a poor holy man."

"Like hell he is. I wish I was that poor."

"Who is he?"

"That's Grigori Rasputin. The so-called miracle worker who spends his time at our fragrant empress's side. Tell me you didn't let him put a dirty paw on you."

"Miracle worker?"

"That's what he calls himself."

༄

J ENS, WHAT KIND OF WOMAN IS THE EMPRESS?"

"Why do you ask?"

"I was wondering what kind of person she is."

"Tsarina Alexandra? She has a cold and aloof manner and behaves like the arrogant German princess she is. But I'm not so sure how deep it goes."

He swept his hand up the delicate curve of her naked hip and walked his fingers one by one up her ribs. He was sitting upright beside her on his bed because he loved to let his eyes feast on her. *Feast.* It had always struck him before as an absurd word for eyes, for how could eyes feast? But now he understood. His eyes felt hungry when she was not with him. No woman had ever done this to him, made him hoard the images of her like jewels inside his head. He tried now to work out what it was that had triggered this interest in the tsarina.

"I believe," he explained, "that a part of it is that she's shy. The tsarina may be an aristocrat, but she has no idea how to make small talk, so she shuns the court's social life and they resent her for it. But there's no doubt that she's a very determined character."

"Determined in what way?"

"She keeps Tsar Nicholas shut away with her down in Alexander Palace at Tsarskoe Selo most of the time. He works from there. I know it's only twenty miles from Petersburg, but it's twenty miles too far when there is so much unrest in the city. He has a duty here."

She nodded as though this were something she had given thought to. "Their four daughters, the young grand duchesses, they are shut away as well?"

"Oh yes. Everyone says they all enjoy family life together, riding and sailing and playing games. They love tennis. And of course taking care of the boy. He's the center of their universe."

"Yes, the boy, Tsarevitch Alexei."

He lowered his head and planted a gentle kiss on each of her knees. She buried her hand in his hair, drawing his face closer to hers.

"What are you staring at?" she frowned.

"You. I'm trying to work out exactly how you are put together."

"Why? Are you thinking of taking me apart?"

He kissed her lips. "As an engineer, it would be an interesting challenge."

She sat up facing him and coiled her legs around his waist. He scooped his hands under her buttocks and pulled her closer. Her skin smelled faintly of carbolic soap.

"Tell me about the monk, Rasputin," she said.

"For heaven's sake, Valentina, why on earth do you want to know about that vile man?"

"Tell me." She was serious. Her forehead rested on his collarbone so that he couldn't see her face, but he could feel her breath on his naked chest, small shallow puffs of warm air. "He came to St. Isabella's," she told him.

"Keep away from him. He's done enough harm."

"What kind of harm?"

"Grigori Rasputin is widening the divide between the tsar and his people."

"Jens, my love, don't be angry. Tell me about him." Her tongue touched a patch of his skin.

"He claims to be a holy man of God, sent by Christ to guide the people of Russia, particularly to guide the tsarina. And through her, to guide the tsar himself." This was a subject that roused him to despair. "Tsar Nicholas is a fool. The monk is meddling in politics, turning His Imperial Majesty against his appointed advisers and—" He halted.

"And what?"

He shrugged. "Forget about him. Let's have no more of Petersburg's problems. The battle lines will form soon enough."

"Are you so sure it will come to that?"

He tumbled her back on the pillows. "None of us can be sure, so . . ."

"Don't placate me, Jens. I'm not a child."

The way she said it chilled him. Her eyes had witnessed too much today in that damn hospital of hers. Where was the girl who had gazed at the stars with him on a cold winter's night in the forest? He caressed the smooth slope of her shoulder. He sat back against the pillows, reached over to the bedside table, and lit himself a cigarette.

"Valentina, my love, the tsar's court is a corrupt melting pot. It is dissolute and degenerate." He kept his voice matter-of-fact. "Grigori Rasputin is a failed monk, but he struck lucky. Tsarina Alexandra has few friends other than the mild-mannered Anna Vyrubova, and he gained power over her. Some say that he has healing powers that help her son. Or that he hypnotizes her. Maybe even a sexual bond between them."

Valentina blinked. "How could anyone want to go to bed with such a repulsive man?"

"You'd be amazed. The women at court scratch each others' eyes out to oblige him."

"But he smells."

Jens's laugh was harsh. "A strong-smelling peasant, a ragged *moujik* who doesn't wash or change his clothes. Clearly a man of God!"

"Jens"—Valentina took the cigarette from his fingers and inhaled its pungent smoke—"do you think Rasputin really has healing powers?"

He removed the cigarette from her hand and stubbed it out. "No. So don't even think of taking Katya to him."

"I wasn't thinking of it."

But the lie hung in the air as transparent as the smoke.

❧

VARENKA WASN'T DEAD. THAT WAS SOMETHING, AT LEAST. The street was no better and the front door was still split, the odor as overpowering as ever in the unlit hallway. But she wasn't dead.

"I've brought more food," Valentina said as she placed a bag on the table. Beside it she tucked a purse. Neither mentioned it.

"So I see." Varenka smiled. It was nothing like a real smile, just a shifting of facial muscles, but it would do.

"I'll make us some tea, shall I?" Valentina suggested.

The woman with the scarred scalp was slumped on the floor,

wrapped in a threadbare blanket. A whisper of flame struggled in the stove and she hunched in front of it, mouth slightly open, as if she would devour the yellow flame.

Valentina yanked a bundle of kindling from the bag. "Here."

The woman eagerly extracted three sticks and laid them with care in an arch above the flame. When they crackled at her, the thin face smiled back at them as if they were friends, while Valentina boiled a kettle and provided tea. The dainty cakes from her mother's kitchen looked ridiculous in this setting, but the woman didn't seem to notice. She ate three of them before she spoke.

"What have you come for?"

"To make sure you are still here."

The woman made a strange noise in the back of her throat, and it took Valentina a second to realize it was a laugh.

"You think I could be anywhere else?" Varenka asked.

"Do you work?" Valentina asked.

"I did." The woman shook her head. "In a mill. But I was fired when I took a day off because my boy was sick." Her eyes were hard. No tears.

"I know a dressmaker who is looking for a cleaner. I could speak to her. If you want the position."

"Of course I want it."

There was a stillness in the room, each expecting something of the other. Valentina spoke first.

"Then I shall ask her. But you will have to be clean."

Varenka looked down at her filthy hands. "The water pump in the street is frozen again. I melt snow for tea."

Valentina's stomach turned as she looked at her own half-drunk cup. "Dogs piss in the snow."

Once more the rusty chuckle rattled out. Varenka looked at her new friend. "What is it you want? You're not here just to feed me."

Valentina removed a pot of apricot conserve from the bag, and a loaf of black bread. If Jens knew she had come here alone, he would be angry. "I want you to warn me."

"Warn you of what?"

"When the danger is coming."

"What danger?"

"This revolution of yours."

It was as if she had spoken a magic word. The deadness vanished and Varenka's eyes, her mouth, her dull skin, all changed. It shocked Valentina that one word could have such power.

"This is my address." She pushed a sheet of paper across the table.

Varenka didn't even glance at it. "I can't read. And anyway I wouldn't come near the kind of mansion you must live in. Even your servants would spit on me. Think of something else."

"There is a notice board I've seen by the bus stop in St. Isaac's Square. Pin a piece of a scarf on it to let me know."

"A red scarf?"

"If you want."

Varenka nodded. "Whatever the men say, it will not be soon, this revolution of theirs."

"I once saw an army of stinging ants swarm over a vole and kill it," Valentina commented. "Maybe your ants aren't ready to be an army yet."

"Tell me, what is it you do to make your fingers look so strong?"

"I play the piano."

Varenka prodded Valentina's fingers as if she could coax music from them. "I've never heard anyone play the piano."

Her words made Valentina want to weep.

❧

It was an accident. Jens had not intended to call on Katya. It happened because he had spent an evening playing poker at a friend's house. Dr. Fedorin was there, and between losing hands at cards he told him of a new treatment for spinal injuries that was being tried out at the spa resort of Karlovy Vary. He had heard good reports. Fedorin had in mind the apprentice boys whose brittle young backs had suffered the brunt of the saber blades, but Jens immediately thought of Katya.

When he was out riding the next morning and spotted Valentina's wild Cossack prancing through the watery fog on the back of a jittery mare, it was only natural to comment on his mount.

"She's an elegant creature, Popkov, that's certain. But not exactly your style, I'd have thought."

The Cossack swayed his head from side to side, like a horse himself. "The animal is not for me," he said gruffly.

"Ah! A surprise for Miss Valentina perhaps?"

"*Nyet.*"

Jens kicked his own horse into a longer stride, but the young wheat-colored mare had taken a liking to Hero and quickened her pace to keep abreast of him. The Cossack loosened her reins, allowing her to toss her mane at Hero and pick up her feet as prettily as a ballerina.

Jens couldn't resist a laugh. Even the Cossack cracked a smile indulgently and they rode side by side through the damp streets, Jens placing Hero between the mare and the traffic, giving reassurance when the crossroads made her nervy. The fog wrapped its thin gray arms around them all the way to the Ivanov house.

❧

POPKOV WAS RUBBING DOWN HERO'S COAT, AND HE HANdled the big horse well. Jens liked a man who could sense an animal's mood through the tips of his fingers and knew where to scratch a fold of skin to produce the wide-nostril whicker of a contented horse.

"I won't be long," he told the Cossack.

The man grunted.

Jens filled up a bucket from a tap in the yard and placed it in front of Hero, who pushed his great black nose into it with relish. Jens stood and watched the animal for a moment.

"Popkov," he said, "you are in a privileged position in this household." He glanced around at the big man with a wry smile. "As a thick-headed Cossack, I can't image why you are permitted inside the house or given access to the young Ivanova ladies." Jens ran a hand down Hero's muscular neck. "It must be because of your natural charm, I suppose."

The Cossack's mouth split open in a wide grin, revealing white tombstone teeth. "Go to hell."

❧

I'VE NEVER SEEN VALENTINA SO HAPPY."

Jens smiled at Katya and balanced the tiny teacup on his knee. "It's working in the hospital that has done it. She has gained a sense of purpose."

"That's what Mama says."

"Your mother is probably right."

"Mama does not know her as well as I do."

"What is it," he asked carefully, "that you know, that your mother doesn't?"

"Jens, I may not have the use of my legs but I can still use my eyes."

"So what is it you see?"

She laughed. "I see the way her skin glows when it should be gray and weary from long hours at the hospital, how her step grows heavy when she is forced to spend the day at home. I see the way her mouth smiles a secret smile when she thinks no one is watching, and the way her breath catches. She'll be in the middle of a sentence and suddenly she can't speak." Katya's voice grew wistful. "I believe it happens when she has just remembered something."

"What kind of thing?"

"A moment. One that invades her mind."

"Katya, what an acutely observant girl you are."

"She's my sister. I love her."

Their gaze held. "So do I," he said softly.

She nodded, bouncing her blond curls. "I know."

"How do you know?"

"Because I know Valentina. She is in love, and she is loved."

"I will take great care of her, Katya."

She smiled at him. "I believe you will, Jens. But be careful. If Papa finds out that she prefers you over Captain Chernov, he will deny you entry to this house."

"Thank you for the warning."

It could not be easy for Katya to give him her sister so readily.

❧

JENS HEARD THE UPROAR FROM THE STABLES BEFORE HE reached them. Fearing for Hero, he moved quickly. Shouts and crashes were reverberating off the wooden walls, and he found five men beating the hell out of Popkov. The big man was lumbering and lunging like a drunken bear, blood pouring from a gash above his eye. The other grooms had fled, and that meant only one thing. They knew exactly who these men were in their black coats and polished boots, and knew enough to keep away. But five against one struck Jens as harsh odds.

He seized one attacker's shoulder, spun him around, and received a fist in his stomach as a thank-you. He grunted. Before another fist could come his way, he rammed his head into the other man's chest, knocking the bastard off balance. A quick upward jerk of Jens's neck and his head cracked the man's jaw. A scream ripped through the damp air, setting the horses into a frenzy of kicking and whinnying. Curses and crowbars crunched down on Popkov's shoulders till he hit the ground, but he took two men with him. Boots thudded and chests heaved with effort.

"For Christ's sake," Jens shouted, "stop this now. You'll kill him. What's going on here?"

One head half-turned. A face with heavy features and a mulberry birthmark glared at him from eyes that were nothing but dense black pupils, deep greedy pits of enjoyment.

"Get lost. Unless you want some of the same."

A crowbar swung from the side and threatened to smack against Jens's skull. He had no idea what this fight was about, but he no longer cared. He ducked, snatched the knout from a hook on the wall and unleashed it. Its lash was tipped with metal barbs.

The first crack of the whip ripped open a man's back; the second sliced a strip of flesh from an unguarded neck. Blood spurted onto the straw. The two men, who were still standing, abandoned their Cossack prey and turned on Jens, but another flick of his wrist curled the length of rawhide through the air in elegant swinging loops. They backed off. Too late they became aware of the wounded man on his feet behind them. The stolen crowbar in his fist slammed down first on one head, then on the other, and they dropped like stones.

"Fuck them!" Popkov bellowed.

"Fuck you!" Jens muttered, breathing hard. "What the hell did you do to start this fight?"

They were both looking at each other, trying not to grin. Unexpected blood brothers.

"Damn it," Jens said, "what have you gotten me into?"

A quiet voice came from behind him. "Put down that whip. And you, oaf, drop that metal bar." No threat in it. Just a quiet statement. "Or I will put a bullet in your brain."

## Twenty-five

FEAR COMES IN MANY GUISES. FOR JENS IT CAME IN THE form of a pen, the pen in his questioner's hand. When his questioner was calm it lay still and somnolent between the man's fingers, but when he grew agitated it adopted a fast *flick-flick-flick*. Jens's heart rate echoed its beat.

"Ask Minister Ivanov," Jens said for the twentieth time. "It's his house, not mine. I came to collect my horse, that's all."

"Why was the horse there in the first place?"

"I told you. I was visiting the minister's daughter."

"Or were you using that excuse just as a cover to give you access to the stables?"

"No."

"To retrieve the box of hand grenades from where you'd hidden it."

"No."

"When did you secrete the grenades in the stables?"

"I didn't."

"Who asked you to collect them?"

"Nobody. I know nothing about them."

"You attacked my agents with a whip."

"They were killing the Cossack."

"So you admit this Liev Popkov is your accomplice in an anti-government plot."

"No. I hardly know the man. He is a servant there; that's all I know of him."

"You're lying."

"No."

They danced around in circles. *Flick-flick-flick.* Jens sat as though indifferent to it all as he replied to the same questions again and again. Yet it was all so civilized. No bare interrogation room, no harsh lights, no handcuffs tearing his skin. A chair with padded arms, even the offer of a cigarette. Which he declined.

They were seated in an ordinary office with manila folders and a flourishing potted plant on a shelf. A smart new carpet on the floor. No bloodstains, Jens noticed. His questioner was a small balding man with a patient face and large ears, which he fingered in moments of uncertainty. Each time Jens said, "Speak to Minister Ivanov. He is a loyal servant of His Imperial Majesty," the fingers sought out an earlobe. The questioner was treading with care, feeling for how thin the ice was under his feet.

The damn Cossack was a fool. Nowhere was safe, nowhere unobserved by Okhrana eyes. If Popkov thought the stables of a government minister would be a clever place to hide antigovernment weapons, he knew nothing about the way the secret police worked. Nevertheless he found it hard to believe that Popkov was a Bolshevik. Damn it, it gave him the shivers to think of Valentina anywhere near such a lethal package.

"Where is Liev Popkov?" he asked abruptly.

"The revolutionary is being interrogated."

Jens's blood chilled. *Interrogated.*

"I don't believe Popkov is a revolutionary. Anyone could have put the grenades there to endanger the minister."

"Including you."

"No, not me."

"What you believe is irrelevant."

The man's eyes were hungry. He wanted to unleash his teeth and devour Jens, but something was holding him back. Jens realized it was the title beside his own name on the front of the folder on the desk. JENS FRIIS: ENGINEER TO HIS MAJESTY THE TSAR.

ENGINEER TO HIS MAJESTY THE TSAR.

He would make use of it, that title. Why not? His pulse drummed in his ears. He knew there were a hundred reasons why not, a hundred interrogation cells in the basement nowhere near as cozy as this one. Ones with chains attached to the chairs and dried blood on the tiled walls. He spoke pleasantly to his questioner.

"Where is Liev Popkov?" he asked. "I want to see him."

It was plain the man was annoyed by the request but struggled not to show it. After a long silence during which the pen flicked back and forth he rose to his feet, walked over to the door, and swung it open with such force that it banged off the wall.

"Come."

❧

JENS GRIPPED ONTO THE EDGE OF HIS FURY. STOPPED IT FROM banging its fist against the metal door, prevented it from seizing his escort's neck and ramming it through the narrow observation flap. He stood outside the prison cell and called Popkov's name.

Inside the cell he could make out a broad back, blood pouring from fresh wounds. He moved closer and through the rectangular peephole in the door saw the Cossack chained by his wrists to the opposite wall. Stark naked but still on his feet, face pressed to the filthy tiles. The massive muscles of his buttocks were black with bruises; electrodes trailed from his genitals to a battery. Feces slithered down the back of his legs.

Stink. Sweat. Blood.

❧

# one.

THE NOISES OF THE CITY WERE MUTED. IT WAS LATE EVEning when Jens arrived at the imposing residence of the Ivanovs and he half-expected to find it locked and shuttered, soldiers on guard outside, its windows black and lifeless. But no. Lights blazed. That was a good sign. He was admitted immediately by a footman whose eyes skipped away, small nervous eyes. Whatever had gone on here between Minister Ivanov and the police, after he was carted off with Popkov, had left its mark.

Jens carried his own mark too. His right shoulder throbbed where one particular bastard had been too free with his rifle butt during the arrest. The footman led him to the blue salon, the one where he had sat with Valentina that first time, but he didn't expect to see her tonight because her father would have shut her away. Her name had to remain untainted by the scandal in his stables.

"Jens Friis," the footman announced.

Jens entered the brightly lit room and took a moment to adjust. To his surprise they were all there. General Ivanov looked formal in a dark green frock coat, his back to the fire, his bushy eyebrows pulled together over weary eyes, one foot tapping the marble hearth. Elizaveta Ivanova sat as unmoving as a doll on the ottoman, hands in her lap, a glass of water at her side.

But Jens hardly noticed either of them because Valentina filled his eyes. She was seated on a sofa next to her sister. Both were wearing cream dresses but the contrast between them could not have been greater. Katya's face was streaked with tears, although she smiled at Jens at once. She looked relieved by his arrival. But Valentina gave him no such welcome. Her brown eyes were almost black with rage, and he could see it was not her father with whom she was furious, it was him. Her hair was tied back from her face, and this time it was not her beauty that struck him so forcefully, but her strength. A fine steel mesh under the skin. He had sensed it before but never seen it so clearly. He wanted to sit down and explain to her why he'd gotten into a fight with Okhrana agents, but instead he turned to her father.

"Minister Ivanov, I am thankful to see you all safe."

"Friis, what the hell do you think you were doing in my stables? Lashing out at the police with a whip? I'm amazed they've released you after a display like that.

"The police were mistaken," Jens said firmly. He didn't look at Valentina. "They were killing one of your servants. Don't you care?"

"Damn you, man. I care that there was a box of grenades in the stables that could have blown us all to hell." Ivanov started to pace back and forth in front of the fire. Shoulders tense, fists clenched.

Jens remained where he was near the door. He was not invited to take a seat.

"Popkov was not the only one who could have been killed," Valentina said in a flat voice. "You took a terrible risk."

"I couldn't leave him there to be kicked to death in the straw."

"I know." Valentina shook her head as if to rid it of something. "Where is Liev now?"

Jens directed his response to her father. "He's in a stinking prison cell. That's why I've come. He needs your help tonight or I swear to you he will not be alive in the morning."

Katya moaned. "Papa! You must help him."

Ivanov ignored his daughters, his attention still on Jens. "Why did they release you?"

"Because I had nothing to do with the grenades. And because"—he paused, considering how far Ivanov could be pushed—"I have friends at court. You and I both know, Minister, this city functions on who you know and on what favors you are owed."

Ivanov blinked, considering exactly what that meant. He took out a cigar from a silver humidor on the mantelpiece to give himself breathing space but didn't offer one to Jens.

"So do they know who planted the grenades?" Jens asked.

"It was Viktor Arkin," Valentina told him. "Our chauffeur."

"Did he confess?"

"No," Ivanov growled. "My daughter saw the box at the back of the garage last week—without realizing what was in it, of course. He must have moved it in case the Okhrana came sniffing around. I'll have the traitor shot if ever they track him down."

"Has he disappeared?"

The minister inhaled heavily on his cigar. "He's run off. A damn revolutionary. In my own home. God curse the man, I hope his body is washed up in the Neva and his eyes are eaten by crabs."

"He was a good chauffeur. I liked him."

All attention turned to Elizaveta Ivanova with her water glass in her hand. It was the first time she had spoken.

"He was never impudent," she continued, "the way the Cossack horseman is. Or as filthy."

"Papa?"

It was Katya who called for him. She held out her hand, a pale thing that lingered in the air, and her father came quickly to her, taking her hand in his. "What is it, little one?"

"Do as Jens says, Papa. Please. Help Liev."

Jens witnessed the struggle within the man. His desire to please his younger daughter over a worthless servant, in the balance against his ruthlessness in political maneuvers. But there was something more within the man, something that intrigued him. It was fear. *What is this minister of the tsar so afraid of?*

"Katya, my dear child, you don't understand," Ivanov said sooth-ingly. "I know you are used to this ignorant Cossack, but—"

"*Used to?*" Valentina interrupted. "*Used to?* It is a little more than that, Papa. This *ignorant Cossack* has worked in your employ all his life; he watched his father die because of who you are and because he rode out to find me that day. Liev Popkov detests this infestation of Bolshe-viks the way he hates an infestation of rats in his stables. Yet you are going to leave him to die in a stinking Okhrana prison cell?"

"Yes."

"You can't." She leapt to her feet, breathing hard. "You must make a telephone call to the chief of police to demand his release right now," her voice was shaking, "or I—"

She glanced at Jens and something unguarded in her expression alerted her father. He turned on Jens immediately. "What the hell are you doing here, Friis? Why are you interfering? Is something going on between you and my daughter?" He did not wait for any response. "Get out!" he shouted. "Get out of my house! Stay away from her, do you hear me? I forbid you ever to enter my house again."

Jens turned to Valentina. "Come with me? Now. Leave this house with me."

It was a murmur but it echoed through the room as if he had shouted. His words seemed to pull something loose inside her. Her limbs grew soft and the rigid muscles of her face slackened as her gaze held his. The rage gave way and in its place a look formed in her eyes as languid and tender as any she'd given him in the privacy of his bed-room. For one foolish moment he believed she would come.

Her lips parted, and he drew her wrist into his hand. "Come with me," he said again.

She let her wrist lie between his fingers, but her head turned back to her father. He could see the effort it took, the tension in her neck.

"Papa," she said, "if you do not demand Popkov's release imme-diately tonight, I will ask someone else who will."

"And who might that be?"

"Captain Chernov."

"No," Ivanov spoke quickly. "Valentina, listen to me. I can-not permit our name to be beholden to the Chernovs or they will think you too weak and insignificant to be worthy of the agreed marriage."

*Agreed marriage.* The words scraped against Jens's mind. It had gone that far. *Agreed marriage.* He released Valentina's wrist abruptly. A curt bow to her mother, that was all, and he strode from the room.

❧

"WAIT!"

Jens was swinging up onto Hero's back and closed his ears to her shout. He needed to ride fast, to pound the image of her sweet treacherous mouth from his skull. *My heart will never have anything to do with Captain Chernov,* she had promised. On her sister's life she had promised. Not her heart maybe, but her marriage bed.

"Jens!"

She came flying through the darkness into the stable yard and hooked an arm around his foot in the stirrup, so that if he rode off he would drag her with him. He looked down at her pale upturned face, at her shoulders shivering in the cream silk, and he felt his heart turn over.

"Good-bye, Valentina."

"Don't go."

"I have no reason to stay."

"Jens, I love you." Her eyes blurred and tears strayed down her cheeks. "Only you."

He smiled at her sadly, bent down and kissed the top of her head. "It seems love isn't enough for you."

With a kick he urged the horse forward, so sharply that it broke Valentina's grip on his leg and at the same time snapped something within him. As he cantered from the yard he didn't look back.

❧

HER FATHER'S STUDY WAS EXACTLY THE SAME, HIS DESK full of papers, his cigar box open. Out in the hall she could hear the whisper of a broom over marble flooring. The cough of a footman, the creak of a stair. The same sounds. As though nothing had changed. As though her world didn't lie in pieces on the cobbles in the stable yard. She tried to concentrate on what her father was saying, but all her ears could hear was the deadness in Jens's words: *I have no reason to stay.* All she could see was the look in his eyes. The imprint of the hard muscles around his shinbone was embedded in her hands, and she couldn't unclasp her fingers in case she lost it. It was all she had left of him.

"Papa," she interrupted, "there is no *agreed marriage*."

He placed both his hands on his desk and leaned his weight on them, in need of support. "Valentina, please don't make more trouble for me than I have already." He spoke so quietly it unnerved her.

"Very well, Papa. But first, deal with Popkov. Please make the telephone call."

He didn't argue. He walked over to the black telephone on the study wall, wound the handle, and requested the number from the operator. Whoever it was he talked to, it was brief, a few curt commands. Valentina heard the words *chief of police*, but that was all. When he returned to his desk he sat down heavily, placed his elbows on its surface and his chin in his hands. He looked at her with dull dismayed eyes.

"It's done," he said. "Now go."

"Papa, we couldn't leave Popkov in the hands of the Okhrana."

He gave a grunt and lowered his face into his hands. The patch on the top of his head showed where his hair was thinning, and the sight of that small human weakness triggered in her a sudden rush of sorrow for him.

"Papa, I want you to understand that I will not marry Captain Chernov. Nothing will make me go to the imperial ball at the Winter Palace with him."

The stifled grunt came again, but he didn't look up. "I need you to."

She shook her head. "I'm sorry, Papa." She walked toward the door.

"Valentina," her father muttered, "he has no money."

"Who has no money?"

"Your engineer."

A pulse thudded in her chest. She stood with one hand on the door. "He has enough."

"Enough for you perhaps, but not enough for me."

His heavy chin was bunched in his hands, his eyes were observing her, and she could see where his gold signet ring had made a dent in his flesh.

"Papa, why would you want his money?" She gestured around the room at the fine English rifle on the wall, at the French landscape paintings, at the leather-bound books on the shelves. "I don't understand. Why?"

His eyes blurred. They changed from brown to mud. The veins on his whiskered cheeks drained of blood, and she saw his mouth go slack. For a second she thought he was having a heart attack.

"Papa?"

The moment seemed to stretch until it touched the walls.

"Papa?"

She moved toward him, but he pulled himself up straight. "Very well. I will tell you why I need the money, Valentina. It's simple. I am bankrupt. Don't look so shocked. I'm in debt. To banks. To money lenders. Even to thieving Jewish merchants. To anyone who would take my promissory note. Let me tell you that if you don't marry Captain Chernov, I shall go to prison for embezzlement. Your mother will die in a pauper's grave and your beloved sister will be turned out on the streets."

He released a long sour breath, as though it had been building up inside him for months, and fastened his gaze on her.

"Is that what you want, Valentina?"

❧

A RKIN LAY ON THE FLOOR. HIS BED CONSISTED OF A COUPLE of sacks flung down on flagstones and his blanket was a priest's ceremonial vestment. A candle burned in a tin lid at his side. It was ironic. Here he was, seeking refuge in the house of the God he despised and finding it hard not to feel grateful to him, just the way his mother had always done. He lay on his back and imagined the church with its icons and its glut of prayers towering over him. Protecting him. *Spasibo*. Thanks. The word grew hot in his mouth and he parted his lips to let it escape.

A rat scuttled in the shadows, its feet scratching like saber tips on the stone floor. Saber tips haunted his mind. Sharpening themselves on it whether he was awake or asleep. The pain in his shoulder was less now, the wound beginning to heal, but the pain in his heart grew worse each hour he lay here. He stared up at the great black timbers above his head and tried to think. The room was unheated and the air so cold now that it was impossible to sleep, but he had no wish to, not while his mind was like this.

"*Spasibo,*" he said aloud. "Thank you."

It was not for God this time. It was for Father Morozov, for giving him refuge. Morozov claimed he was a servant of his God, but he was wrong. He was a true servant of the people of Russia, and no tsar could rule such a man.

Against Arkin's hip lay the small pearl-handled pistol, warm and loaded. Betrayal was not something he could forgive.

～

"V IKTOR ARKIN, *VKHODITE*, COME IN."
Sergeyev's wife opened the door and treated Arkin to a warm smile of welcome. She looked . . . Arkin sought for a word . . . she looked transformed. The way a gray shapeless caterpillar is transformed into a vivid and vibrant butterfly. She was full of color and it all came from within. Her hair was unwashed and her clothes were as drab as ever, and yet she shimmered. Is that what having a child did to you? Satisfied something that hungered deep inside. For her sake he wanted to turn around and walk out, but he didn't.

"Hello, *privet*, Viktor. It's good to see you."

Sergeyev stuck out a hand, but Arkin couldn't bring himself to take it. Instead he leaned over the drawer that lay in pride of place on top of the table and looked down at the pink infant swaddled inside it. Everything was too tiny to belong to a human being: its fingers, its nose, its pointed little chin. Ears like a bird's soft feathers and minuscule gold threads for eyelashes. A pain nudged his chest and he breathed awkwardly.

"Her name is Natasha."

"Pretty."

"She is wonderful."

"I congratulate you." He studied her mother with an odd sense of awe. She was thin but her breasts had swelled, and he felt an unexpected desire for her. Quickly he turned away to Sergeyev. "May we speak in private?"

They lived in only one small room. Bed and table squeezed together around the stove. The place was clean and smelled of pinecones with bright handmade *poloviki* on the floor, but the plaster on the walls was crumbling and cracks ran back and forth like rail tracks across the ceiling. Privacy was not to be had.

"Anything you have to say, you can say in front of Larisa. It's too cold to go outside." Sergeyev sat down in a chair to emphasize the point. "She knows what we are doing."

"Does she?"

"Of course."

Sergeyev seemed on edge, unwilling to be alone with him.

"How's the arm?" Arkin asked mildly.

"A bloody nuisance."

Larisa stood beside the drawer, oblivious, one hand resting on it as if she couldn't bear to let it go, a contented smile on her face. Arkin looked away. He'd had enough.

"You are fortunate, comrade," he said quietly. "You missed the apprentices' battle against the army."

"I'm sorry. I heard it was bad."

"It was worse than bad."

"I'm sorry," Sergeyev said again. His gaze was on the drawer. "Were you hurt?"

"A few cuts, nothing much."

"We never thought the bastards would attack such young boys, did we?"

"No. We were wrong."

A sad silence sucked the air from the room. Sergeyev was breathing hard.

"Why did you do it?" Arkin asked.

"Do what?"

"Betray them."

Larisa gasped. "Take that back, Comrade Arkin," she said fiercely.

But Sergeyev said nothing, just stared at the drawer.

"Why?" Arkin asked again. "The soldiers were waiting for us. Ready to charge. Why did you do it?"

"Because of the baby," Sergeyev whispered.

Larisa clapped a hand over her mouth.

Sergeyev didn't look at her. "The Okhrana caught me again that night when we had our run-in with them. After you and I parted, Viktor, they cornered me like a rat. Beat me in the gutter till my arm was in pieces once more. They threatened to throw me in their fucking prison to rot. What about Larisa? What about the baby we were about to have? I had to do it." His eyes shifted to Arkin's.

"My friend," Sergeyev said harshly, "you don't know what it is to love someone more than your own life. Even more than your own beliefs. I couldn't let my wife and child be tossed out onto the street to freeze to death."

Larisa was crying silent tears. The baby sensed her distress and started to wail.

"Comrade," Arkin said in a stiff voice, "let us continue this discussion outside. Your wife and child do not need to hear it."

He reached out and dragged Sergeyev to his feet. As they left the room Larisa lifted the baby into her arms, tucking its head under her chin and crooning soft sounds to quiet its cries. Arkin turned his back on the image, but it stuck in his mind. Out on the street the two men walked some distance without speaking. The snow had stopped, but it hung in heavy blankets from the roofs, trying to slide down on unwary pedestrians as they passed. Russia was like that. It pounced on you, smothered you, destroyed you if you let it.

"My friend . . . ," Sergeyev started.

"I am not your friend."

"Viktor, please, I—"

"You betrayed the apprentices. They trusted us, and that trust got them killed. And you betrayed me. You informed the Okhrana that I had hidden the grenades in the Ivanovs' garage."

"No, no, not you, Viktor. It was the Ivanovs themselves I meant to get the blame."

"Don't fuck with me, *comrade*."

They were passing one of the narrow dark alleys that snaked between the backs of the houses, littered with frozen filth and dead rats. Viktor stopped. With no change in expression he drew the small pistol from under his coat, put it to Sergeyev's head, and pulled the trigger. He swung the lifeless body into the alley and walked away. The image of Larisa clutching the baby went with him.

## Twenty-six

VALENTINA FLUTTERED A WHITE SWAN-FEATHER FAN AS she walked up the Jordan staircase. It was official. She was a whore. For sale to the highest bidder. Money on the table? Take her, she's yours.

The imperial ball at the Winter Palace was a carefully choreographed display of grandeur and extravagant wealth, one of the highlights of the St. Petersburg season. The stiff vellum invitations embossed in gold with double-headed eagles became the most desirable possessions in the city, and the competition to secure one was fierce. Hundreds of chandeliers and candelabra flooded the palace with light that sprang at her from mirrors and flashed from gold vases. At her side Maria, the niece of Countess Serova, whispered that the orchids had been transported from the Crimea by special trains, but Valentina could not bring herself to care. She had come to the ball. Done as her father asked. Maria was making small breathy noises of excitement as they walked through the Nicholas Hall.

"Valentina," she said, "I think we've died and gone to heaven."

"I've died and gone to hell."

"Don't be ridiculous. Look at all those handsome officers just waiting to be snapped up."

The crowd of guests seemed to sway in one scintillating shimmer in front of Valentina's eyes. Lush displays of orange and lemon trees and tall wispy palms swirled through her mind. She fanned her cheeks and paid no attention to the parade of princes and princesses, to the dukes or counts, or to the bishops in their purple robes and long white veils.

*I'd rather be dead than here.* The thought invaded Valentina's head. It made her think of Katya and the night of the scissors skewered into her wrist, and she shivered despite the heat.

Maria clutched her arm. "Nervous?"

"No, why should I be nervous?"

"Because your Stepan will be here. As well as his parents, Count Chernov and his wife."

"My Stepan." The words clung to Valentina's tongue.

"Why do you say it like that?"

"To force it into my head."

Maria looked at her oddly. "Is he here yet?"

Valentina made herself focus on the uniforms. The military strutted through the magnificent halls in their gaudy plumage, officers from all regiments. Cossacks in scarlet. Lancers in blue. She couldn't see Captain Chernov.

"Maria," she said, "I'd like a drink."

❧

THE VODKA HELPED. IT HAD CRANBERRIES IN IT. THAT amused her. She had chosen it from a row of chilled glasses of vodka flavored with either lemon peel, peppercorns, cranberries, or buffalo grass. She had wanted to try the buffalo grass but didn't have the nerve because the footman almost spilled the drinks down his gold uniform when she stopped him and removed a glass from his silver tray. Maria was sipping cordial and staring at her friend wide-eyed.

"Valentina," she hissed, "you'll disgrace yourself."

Valentina laughed, astonished that she could still make such a sound. "I have already disgraced myself, don't you realize that?"

She found herself a pillar, a massive Italian marble one that wasn't going to topple over in a hurry. She stood with her back to it. Not leaning against it exactly; only men were allowed to lean against pillars or door frames. But she touched the white pillar with the back of one satin shoe and with the tip of her elbow, just enough to keep her standing straight. Her body's tendency to sway without warning alarmed her.

Maria had gone. Valentina wasn't sure when that happened, but as soon as she noticed her friend across the room talking to an officer, she turned her head and found an empty space beside her. Valentina had become expert at spotting the silver trays circulating throughout the hall and summoning them with a lift of an eyebrow. She felt surprisingly warm and comfortable. Not drowsy exactly, but on the edge of it, and the terrible black abyss that had yawned at her feet only moments ago seemed to have vanished like Maria. All she could think of now was Jens. His smile. Her cheek against his naked chest, his heartbeat drumming through her mind until it became the rhythm of her thoughts.

"Valentina, I have been searching for you."

"Captain Chernov, good evening."

She held out her hand to him, and he turned it over and kissed her palm. As if he owned it. She became aware of music playing, the *Dance of the Cygnets* from Tchaikovsky's *Swan Lake*, and she glanced over to one of the galleries to find an orchestra in full flow. The lilting sound of it brought to life a sharp pain in the center of her chest, a pain she thought she had drowned in the vodka.

"Valentina, my dear, how lovely you look this evening."

His face glowed with energy under the chandeliers, and she tried to imagine what it would be like to look at this face every day for the rest of her life.

"Captain . . ."

"Please call me Stepan."

"Stepan, shall we walk through the halls until Their Imperial Majesties arrive?"

He extended an arm. "Delighted to have the honor."

With misgivings she released her contact with the pillar, but she transferred her arm to his quite safely. Walking through the halls was a good idea. It meant she wouldn't have to look at his face.

STEPAN CHERNOV WAS COURTEOUS AND ATTENTIVE. FOR a whole half-hour she allowed him to steer her through the rooms, all the time delivering his opinion on military matters. "The tsar should kick out General Levitsky, he's too old and forgetful, and

replace him with . . ." Her ears grew tired and shut down. He introduced her to Makarov, the Minister of the Interior, and to Prime
Minister Stolypin, a big man with a domed bald head, a neat little
beard, and quick intelligent eyes. She smiled at him and he beamed
with delight.

"What a jewel you have here, Chernov. Take good care of her."

As though she were a possession, to be polished and paraded
for others to view before being locked away safely at night. When
Stepan led her over to his parents, she held on tight to his arm as
she bobbed a shallow curtsy, feeling the backs of her eyes rolling
around in her head as she did so. But she recalled little else about the
encounter. On the stroke of nine o'clock in the evening Tsar Nicholas and Tsarina Alexandra, emperor and empress of all the Russias,
were announced by the grand marshal of the imperial court, Baron
Vladimir de Freedericksz. He startled Valentina out of her skin when
he banged a ten-foot ebony staff on the polished floor three times
and cried out, "Their Imperial Majesties."

Captain Chernov smiled at her and stroked her hand on his arm.
She thanked all that was holy that she was wearing long white evening gloves.

The imperial party paraded slowly past, glittering in all its cascade
of jewels and medals. A hundred or more in the procession, grand
dukes and grand duchesses strutting past as if they owned the world.
They certainly owned Russia. These people gripped it so tight in
their Romanov fists that she couldn't see how any pack of ramshackle
factory workers could possibly ever wrest it from them. Despite herself she was impressed. Russia was safe. No marauding revolutionaries had a hope of seizing control of the reins of government.

"You don't need jewels like that," Chernov whispered in her ear.
"You are more beautiful than any diamond."

She released his arm. "What do you know," she asked, "about
what I need?"

◦❧◦

THEY HAD BEEN DANCING FOR HOURS, BUT VALENTINA
would rather dance than sit down. The warmth of the vodka
began to ebb. Like the tide going out, leaving razor-sharp rocks
behind.

How could her father have done this? She wanted to rip off the dress she was wearing, cream silk studded with hundreds of pearls. Thousands of roubles, that was what it had cost. What about all the others in her dressing room? In her mother's dressing room? All on borrowed money. And there was that word that terrified her, that made her feet falter and her heart stop. *Embezzlement.* Her father was a minister of finance to the tsar, with his hands in the Romanov coffers.

"Why so serious?" Chernov asked with a squeeze of her hand. They were dancing a waltz, and his arm around her held her possessively.

"I was looking," she said, "at the different military uniforms here tonight. What a warlike nation we are."

He smiled at her indulgently. "My dear Valentina, you have to understand that Russia is a country that has always been held together throughout its history not by its laws, not by its civilization, but by its army."

"I thought we'd outgrown all that. What about our commerce and agriculture?"

He laughed, dismissing her opinion as if it were tinsel. "No. Russia is, and always will be, a military state."

He danced well, gliding across the room with easy control. But she hadn't finished. "I heard that some apprentices were attacked the other day in the railway sidings."

"Not attacked exactly, just taught a lesson."

"What were they doing wrong?"

"Valentina." He spoke her name sharply. "Not now."

"Stepan, were you with the Hussars who attacked the apprentices?"

Stiffly he brought his gaze back to her. "Yes, I was there." He paused, examining her face. "Do you have any comment to make on that?"

"No," she said quietly. "I have no comment."

༄

At midnight a buffet supper was served. Valentina ate almost nothing. Round tables had been laid out in the Concert Hall with gold cutlery and white damask cloths embroidered with the Romanov eagle. One chair was kept vacant at every table for Tsar Nicholas as he circulated among his guests. Halfway through the meal, the sight of all the *zakuski* and pheasant became too much for her, so she excused herself from the table and walked into one of the anterooms where a female figure in a pale gown stood at one of the tall windows staring out into the night. Valentina approached and stood directly behind her.

"Good evening, Countess Serova."

The countess spun around, and Valentina saw the brandy glass in her hand. "The piano player again, I do believe. What are you doing out here?" she asked.

"I was hot."

The countess took a sip of her drink, and a small smile of anticipation softened her lips. "Are you thirsty, too?"

"Yes."

"Come with me."

Valentina followed the elegant figure to a long table in the next room. At its center rose a leaping dolphin sculpted in ice, but Valentina gave it little more than a glance. An array of drinks in crystal glasses was arranged around it: cordials, lemonade, and fruit juices to the right, wine and spirits to the left.

"A glass of wine?" the countess suggested. "Or maybe something stronger?"

"Peach juice, I think." Valentina picked up one of the tall glasses and raised it to her lips. "So refreshing."

The blue eyes of Countess Serova clouded with annoyance. She nipped the edge of her lower lip with her teeth and walked away, clearly tired of the game. But Valentina remained. It was cooler here. She lifted a sliver of ice and held it to her temple while she sipped her drink. When the fruit juice was half gone she selected another glass from the platter of ice, a different one this time, and tipped it into the remains of her peach juice.

❧

You've been gone a long time." Stepan Chernov frowned, his blond eyebrows lifting as Valentina took her seat. "Are you unwell?"

"No, not at all." She smiled at him. "I met Countess Serova, and we were arguing about which of you military men have the most attractive uniforms."

"I hope you said the Hussar Guards."

"Of course." She trailed her hand down her throat just to watch his gaze follow its path. "As if I notice anyone else's."

He laughed and launched into a story about a bet on a cockfight, but Valentina lost track of what the point of it was.

"I'll just fetch myself another drink," she announced.

"Let me ask one of the servants to fetch it."

"Thank you, but no. I feel like a little exercise."

"Be quick." He gestured to where Tsar Nicholas was seated at a nearby table. "We have the honor of His Imperial Majesty's company next."

As she hurried through the huge gilded doors, a thought struck her. He liked telling her what to do.

# Twenty-seven

J ENS WAS SMOKING ONE OF TSAR NICHOLAS'S MONO-
grammed cigarettes. He tried to imagine what it must be like to
have your initials stamped or gilded or embroidered on everything
around you. It meant you could never forget who you were. He had
come to the imperial ball only to please Minister Davidov. Jens was
not in the mood for gaiety. But he had talked to the men Davidov
had gathered together in one of the more discreet anterooms, talked
business till the air was blue with smoke and had shaken hands at
the end of it. Even so, he didn't trust them. In Petersburg you didn't
trust anyone.

Not even a pair of dark laughing eyes. He grimaced and stubbed
out the cigarette.

"What's the matter with you this evening?" Davidov asked. "You
look ready to bite."

"I'm here. I've talked with your damn money men. Don't expect
me to smile at you as well."

Minister Davidov chuckled to himself and swirled his brandy
around in its glass. His hawkish face looked pleased, which was rare.

"It's got to be a woman," the minister declared.

"What makes you think that?"

"I've seen you at work, Friis, and I've seen you risking your life in one of your blasted tunnels. I've seen you bad tempered and bloody minded. But I've never seen you like this. Look at yourself."

Both men were wearing black frock coats with gold lapels, but Jens's was crumpled and he was slumped in the brocade chair, his limbs awry.

"I'm here to do business," Jens growled. "Nothing more."

He lit himself another cigarette, but as he did so he saw a woman enter the room. At an imperial ball the ladies were obliged to wear white or cream, so at a brief glance she was just one among many in an elegantly designed pale gown. But the way she walked alerted him, a haughty carriage that approached with an eagerness he did not welcome.

"Countess Serova." He rose to his feet and bowed over her extended hand.

"Jens, what are you doing burying yourself away in here? Don't you know that your little pet pianist is performing for His Imperial Majesty?" Her smile was as hard as a cat's claw. "You should hurry. She has drawn quite a crowd."

～

HE COULDN'T HELP HER. IT WAS LIKE WATCHING A KITTEN drown. The hands struggling. The mouth gasping for air. The waves of relentless scorn washing over her, the derision dragging her down. When he first walked in he thought Valentina was teasing her audience, joking with them by hitting wrong notes. But it was no joke. She was perched on the edge of the stool at a grand piano, and the sight of her wrenched the heart from Jens.

The performance was a disaster. Valentina could have burst into tears and rushed from the room, but she didn't. She sat there, teeth gritted. She kept playing. Her head and her hands seemed to have severed contact. She was playing Beethoven's *Ode to Joy* and nothing could have been more inappropriate: There was no joy to be found in this room. To one side on elaborate gold chairs the tsar and tsarina sat stiffly, surrounded by more than a hundred of St. Petersburg's elite who had gathered in this smaller hall where the Balalaika Orchestra had been playing earlier. Whispers slithered around the room.

*Valentina, my love, if I could give you my fingers, I would.*

Tsar Nicholas tugged with annoyance at his neat little beard, and his frown grew petulant. Finally, without a word he rose, offered his wife his arm, and walked out of the room. A trickle of guests followed, and Jens noticed that the countess was one of the first.

*Damn you all for your rudeness, she's still playing, still trying.*

At the front of the audience stood Captain Chernov, and his face was a mask of scarlet, as vivid as the uniform on his back. Jens felt a sick twist of his gut. What Valentina's father said must be true; the marriage must be arranged because already the captain was seeing her as an extension of himself, regarded her humiliation as his own. Jens loathed him for it. Not for the arrogant assumption that her behavior reflected on him, but for the fact that the man felt humiliated. Not sorry for Valentina. Not sympathetic for her plight. Not willing to cut off his right hand to get her out of the drowning pit she was in. Just humiliated. Ashamed of her.

The music came to an abrupt end and Jens led a ripple of applause, then strolled forward. "Valentina Ivanova," he spoke in a loud voice, "how generous of you to agree to play for us when you are unwell."

She lifted her eyes to his. There were no tears. She raised her chin, straightened her back, and rose from the stool with all her customary grace, placing one hand to her temple to indicate a slight headache. She smiled at him, and he gave her his arm. In no hurry, they walked together through the gathered finery and feathers of the guests toward the door. She didn't even glance at Captain Chernov.

❧

JENS HELD HER. SMELLED THE PERFUME OF HER HAIR AND the misery on her breath. He held her clenched against him until her trembling ceased and her head grew still, instead of banging itself over and over against the hard ridge of his collarbone.

"Valentina"—he kissed her burning ear—"forget them. Not one person there is worth a moment of your distress." He kissed the top of her head and drew her into a niche behind one of the marble pillars. "You were wonderful."

"I was terrible."

"No, you were magnificent. Drunk as a skunk and still able to make Beethoven sound like Beethoven."

"My stupid fingers made a million mistakes."

"No one noticed."

"What?" Her head jerked up, her eyes not quite in focus. It took a moment, but she registered his teasing smile and her mouth toppled into a crooked line as she started to laugh. "You don't think that the tsar noticed anything wrong?"

"Not a thing."

"Thank goodness."

Her body in its pale silky gown rested against his, warm and pliant, and his arm around her waist held her on her feet as she let her head tip back with all the joy that had been missing from her music. She laughed in a long luxurious release of tension.

"You liar," she breathed, a husky unfettered sound.

He brushed his lips along the curve of her throat. "Come away," he whispered. "Come away with me now."

She slid her arms around his neck as he gently raised her head and looked intently into her dark eyes. They were half-closed, just a gleam of brilliance beneath long lashes.

"Marry me?" he asked.

"Kiss me first."

He pressed his lips hungrily down on hers, and she responded with all the passion, fury, and joy that she had meant to pour into her music.

"Jens," she murmured, "let's go out and look at the stars. Ask me again under the stars."

It was cloudy tonight, but it didn't matter. He would describe each one for her, each blaze of light dazzling faraway worlds, and they would gaze at them together.

She stood on tiptoe and kissed his mouth. "Ask me again, Jens Friis," she whispered.

The slap on the side of his face snapped his attention away from Valentina. He felt the sting like a snakebite on his cheek, and his fist struck out at the uniformed arm as it swung at him again, a white glove flapping loose in its hand. As he stared at its owner, his heart sang with Viking blood. Thor's hammer pounded in his chest.

"Captain Chernov," he said, "you do me an insult."

The glove was tossed at his feet.

"Take your hands off her," Chernov shouted. His mouth quivered with rage. "Take your hands off her or I swear to God I will kill you here and now with my bare fists in front of the tsar himself."

"Feel free to try."

"Stop it," Valentina cried. "Stop it." She seized Jens's arm, and he couldn't bring himself to shake her off. "Please," she shouted, "someone help to stop them."

Other uniforms arrived, Davidov's dark frown, a stream of invective and angry voices gathered close. Jens paid them no heed.

"I demand satisfaction," Chernov snapped, while two officers in blue pinned back each of his arms. "My seconds will call on you tomorrow."

"It will be my pleasure."

"No." Valentina stood apart from them both, white faced. "I swear I will marry neither of you if you fight a duel."

Jens could feel her trickling away through his fingers like dry sand. He wasn't willing to lose her, not like this, not now. Slowly, with rigid control, he turned to Captain Chernov, clicked his heels in a curt bow, and held out his hand. Chernov hesitated, glanced uncertainly for a second at Valentina as though assessing her worth, then reluctantly shook hands. Neither spoke.

"Thank God." Valentina released a shudder of relief and shook her head. "What is it that turns sane men into brainless fighting machines?"

Neither man offered an answer, so she turned on her heel and walked away with as much dignity as she could muster.

"Tomorrow," Jens muttered brusquely under his breath the moment she was out of earshot. "I will expect to hear from you tomorrow."

❧

LIGHT AND MOVEMENT, THEY SPLINTERED HER BRAIN. THE next morning Valentina took each narrow stair with great care, her hands feeling for the walls on either side of her, her eyes squinting even in the gloom. If she could keep her head immobile on her neck, there was a chance she would make it to the top. But halfway up the wooden flight of stairs a mouse scurried across her shoe with such speed that she lost her footing and stumbled.

"*Chyort!*" she muttered. "Devil take you!"

"Who's there?" a voice bellowed from upstairs.

Her eardrums vibrated painfully.

"Ssh, don't shout." She scrambled up the remaining steps in an ungainly rush in case she toppled back down into the stables below. Once at the top she allowed the narrow slit of her eyes to open further and looked around with interest. She'd never been up here before in the grooms' quarters. There was a long dusty corridor ahead of her. Skylights on the left let in vicious amounts of sunlight, but on the right ran a row of small cubicles, each with a door. Only one was closed. She banged on it.

"Go away."

"*Chyort!*" she swore again. "I'm not coming all the way up here for nothing, damn you." She pushed open the door and walked in. The light was dim, thank heavens, the window small and unwashed. The room, if it could be called such, smelled of horses and sweat. "So you're still alive, Liev. They didn't manage to kill you off."

"Weeds never die."

"Here, I've brought you something."

From inside a shawl that was tied around her waist she drew out a full bottle of vodka and a packet of cigarettes. Popkov's black eyes gleamed. He was sitting upright on a hard chair beside the bed, but he didn't look good. His eye sockets were bruised deep purple, his nose was broken at an odd angle, and there were gashes on his forehead and lips. As he reached for the bottle she saw that one of his fingers was missing its nail, a black clump of dried blood in its place. She felt fury stirring up the acid in her stomach.

"It's good vodka from my father's cabinet." She put on a smile for him. "Not that rotgut rubbish you gave me."

He grinned and took a swig, breathing out heavily with contentment. "The only medicine I need."

"Liev, how are you? Really, I mean. Is the pain bad?"

He studied her through swollen eyes. "I'll live." He raised the bottle. "Want some?"

"No, thank you."

"You look like you need it." He chuckled, and she saw him wince and rub his ribs.

She was tempted, but looked away from the bottle. "Not much of a home, is it, this place?"

"It's enough."

A bed, a chair, a shelf, and some hooks. Enough? Liev was twenty-two years old, a grown man, and already he thought this was enough.

"Is there water here?" she asked.

"In the stable yard."

"I'll fetch some."

"Don't bother."

She thought of the stairs and her stomach cramped. "No bother. You need attention."

It took her a while and a trip back to the house, but she carried up an enamel bowl of warm water and a plate of black bread and cheese. Under her arm she'd tucked a pack of bandages and dressings from Nurse Sonya, who complained bitterly about wasting them on "that filthy Cossack." Popkov grumbled loudly while Valentina bathed his wounds, straightened his nose to the best of her ability, and bandaged what else she could, but he refused to remove anything more than his shirt.

"Don't be stupid," she scolded, "I'm a nurse. I'm used to—"

"You're a girl."

She smiled and let it rest. As she bound a long strip of bandage along the lash wounds on his broad back, she asked curiously, "Do you hate them now? The men who did this to you?"

"The Okhrana?" He spat on the floor. There was blood in it. "I've always hated the police. No different. Same with the murdering Bolsheviks." He spat again.

"But Liev, if you hate both sides, who can you rely on, who can you believe in?"

He eyed her with surprise. "Myself, of course."

"I should have known." She laughed and felt her head spin off around the room. She waited for it to return, and when she'd finished with the bandage she picked up the bowl and stood beside the door, leaning against its frame. She'd left a pot of ointment on his bed. "Better?"

He grunted and downed another mouthful of vodka. She turned to leave.

"That man of yours, the engineer. He saved my . . ." Popkov stopped. The words stuck in his throat.

"I know," she said gently. "I know. Jens Friis is glad you're still alive."

Popkov nodded his battered head. "He won't be alive himself much longer if you don't do something."

She froze. "Tell me."

"A duel."

"No, it's not true."

"Word is everywhere. About you. About the fight. The blond bastard with the fluff on his face has a taste for blood. He killed two men in duels last year."

"No, Liev. You've got it wrong. They agreed. They said they wouldn't."

Popkov slowly swung his head from side to side with disappointment. "I told you, you're a girl. They fucking lied to you."

∼

VALENTINA COULD HEAR THE CLANKING OF THE METAL elevator not far away, and the sound of it made her skin crawl. This was the first time she had returned to Jens's tunnel. She was wearing her nurse's cape and pulled its navy folds closer around her to ward off the memories that the sound dragged in its wake.

She didn't sit in the chair offered in Jens's office but chose to stand. She took up her position beside the window and focused her aching eyes on the yard outside. It was full of activity, of workers in cloth caps scrambling up from belowground, blinking like moles in the sunlight. The women wore headscarves and pushed trucks of rubble along metal tracks. All were thin, all were colorless, all coated in a uniform dirt color. It was impossible to tell them apart. Is this what Jens looked out on every day? He wasn't in the office when she arrived, so a runner had been sent to fetch him.

"Tea?" a clerk offered.

"No, thank you."

The clerk returned to his sheaf of papers and Valentina to her waiting. Outside the sky was a pale wintry blue, and a solitary bird slid back and forth on slender wings, riding the air currents above the city. She heard Jens's rapid footsteps before she saw him, and her pulse quickened. When he caught sight of her, he came to her side in two quick strides.

"Is something wrong?"

"Yes."

He turned to the clerk and waved a dismissive hand, so that the man left the office without comment, his head swiveling to catch a stray word or two as he closed the door.

"What is it?"

He was leaning over her, full of concern. She stepped back and regarded him fiercely. "You lied to me."

"About what?"

"The duel."

"Oh, that."

"Yes, that."

He moved over to his desk, a haven of order and neatness compared to the untidy paperwork on his clerk's desk. He sat down and looked at her with a guarded expression that she wanted to scratch off his face. "What about it?"

"You're going to fight?"

"Yes."

"No, Jens, no. Don't, you mustn't. Do you hear me? Are you out of your mind? He'll kill you. He'll . . ."

She was determined not to cry, not to be *a girl*. She had promised herself. But the thought of losing him tore at her heart and her throat closed on the words, as though to utter them aloud would be to give them power to become real. She looked away from him and concentrated on the window, on a spider spinning its intricate web in the corner. Her hands were shaking, so she hid them under her cloak.

"Please, Jens. Don't fight him. I want you alive."

That sounded better. More controlled. He would listen to that. But the silence that stretched between them was as gloomy as his tunnels, and in that moment she knew she would not win. She swung around to face him and found him examining her from behind his desk as intently as if it were for the last time.

"Trust me," he said in a low voice. He sounded tired.

"He might kill you."

"Or I might kill him."

"He killed two other men in duels last year."

"I am not *other men*."

"Jens, don't. For me." She kept her voice reasonable.

His mouth flickered with a hint of a smile. It startled her. It was so resigned.

"Why, Jens? Why do it? Just walk away."

He shook his head.

"*Chyort!* Don't," she shouted as she slammed the flat of her hand down on his desk. "Don't tell me it's something men have to do, to fight for what is theirs, to set down their mark. Don't tell me you're that stupid. Or maybe I'm wrong. Maybe you are as thick-skulled and eager for glory as all the rest of those mindless would-be heroes in their military peacock feathers. I thought you were different, I thought you were . . ."

She stopped. He had risen to his feet and walked around the desk. His hand seized her, dragging her to him, enveloping her in his long arms till her face was buried in the neck of his shirt. She couldn't have spoken even if she'd wanted to.

"Listen to me, Valentina. I am not eager for glory, but I am eager to have a life with you here in Petersburg." As each word came from his mouth, she could feel it hot on her hair. "Captain Chernov has challenged me. If I don't accept the challenge I will be labeled a coward, and that will be the end of my life and my work in this city. I would be dropped from the sewage project, cold-shouldered by the tsar and his courtiers, rebuffed by all decent homes. I would be a leper. A pariah." He lifted her face from his chest and kissed her pale forehead. "What kind of life would there be for us? No one would employ me."

She clung to him. "We could run."

"Run where?"

"To another city. To Moscow. Anywhere."

"My reputation would follow me like a sick dog. Russia may be a vast country, my Valentina, but word spreads faster than the plague from city to city. Wherever I go, as an engineer my reputation is my lifeblood."

"I'd rather have your lifeblood tainted than spilled on a forest floor."

He said no more, just held her. "I'm not worth it," she whispered at last.

"Who says so?"

"I do."

"Then you don't know what love is."

She broke away from him and returned to the window. She didn't want him to see any tears. "Have you ever killed a man before?" she asked, watching a child shoveling ice off the tracks outside.

"No."

"Do you know how to handle a pistol?"

"Of course. Don't worry, I'm a decent shot."

"But he's in the army. It's what he does all day."

"And chasing my woman. The bastard does that too."

But she wouldn't smile. "What kind of man has it in him to shoot another in cold blood?"

"None of us know"—she heard him step closer—"what we are capable of doing until we are faced with it. What about you, Valentina? What are you capable of?"

She swung around and found him standing right behind her, tall and unbending. "I love you, Jens Friis." She touched his face, rested a hand on his heart. "So don't underestimate what I am capable of."

# Twenty-eight

ARKIN PUSHED HIMSELF AWAY FROM THE WALL THAT WAS leaching the heat from his body and advanced warily down the crowded sidewalk at the lower end of Nevsky Prospekt. He had been waiting for more than an hour. The sky was overcast, a bruised purplish color that made the city feel fragile. People hurried in and out of the shops without looking up. A carriage with a coachman in maroon and gold livery pulled up at the curb with a rattle of wheels, and the coachman vanished into a tiny shop with a painting of grapevines over its front window. Arkin had performed the same task himself many times.

He dodged between shoppers and approached the carriage. She was there, alone as usual. Through its window he could make out Elizaveta Ivanova's profile and saw the expectant little smile on her lips. Every Thursday after her morning round of social engagements in the mansions of the wealthy ladies of St. Petersburg, he used to halt the Turicum here. He would return from the tiny shop with a cup of warm spiced wine for her from good Georgian grapes, and she would sip it slowly in silence. It had become a ritual.

Always there was a queue at the counter, so he knew he had several minutes now before the coachman returned. He opened the carriage door swiftly and slipped inside, taking the bench opposite her.

The maroon leather with its gold tassels and brass trimmings smelled of her perfume. He had prepared in his mind the words he would say if she started to scream and shout for help, but she astounded him. Her blue eyes grew wide, and for a split second her mouth fell open, and then she gave him a smile of such genuine warmth it unknotted something painful in his chest that had sat there under his ribs ever since that moment in the alley with Sergeyev.

"Arkin, I've missed you," she said.

Such simple words.

"Thank you, madam."

"I was worried that the police might have . . ." She let the words trail away.

"They haven't caught me yet, as you can see."

She frowned. "I know you wouldn't intend harm toward my family. Any of the servants could have planted the box of grenades in the garage."

He didn't contradict her, but let his eyes enjoy the sight of her again. She was dressed in oyster pink with a slate gray wrap trimmed with silver fox fur around her shoulders, and the appearance of her jewels and her cosseted wealth didn't anger him the way he knew it should have done.

"Madam Ivanova, I must be quick. There's something you need to know." He edged forward, his knees almost touching hers. "Something I've heard in the city's bars that I fear you may be unaware of."

"What is it?"

"That Captain Chernov is to fight a duel with the engineer, Jens Friis."

He had expected a reaction of surprise, but not this draining of blood from her face till her lips were the color of paper.

"Why?" she whispered.

"Because of your daughter."

"Valentina?"

"Yes."

"Dear God, no." Her mouth opened and a harsh sound issued from her throat. "My husband is ruined," she moaned under her breath, rocking back and forth on her seat, her hand clamped over her mouth.

The word astonished him. *Ruined?* What did she mean? Her reaction was so extreme he almost wished he hadn't decided to bring her this information. But he had taken the risk for a purpose. Sergeyev was dead. Many apprentices were dead. Before long, if the next plan worked well, Prime Minister Stolypin would be dead. Russian soil was shaking beneath the streets of St. Petersburg, and the edifices would start to tumble one by one. He could not stop himself from wanting to make certain that Elizaveta Ivanova was safe.

"Madam," he said softly, the way he would to a child he had inadvertently frightened, "Captain Chernov is a renowned shot. He will kill the engineer. There is no need for you to fear . . ."

"No, no, no. If he kills the engineer she will *never* marry Chernov—I know Valentina." In her distress she was thumping the heel of her hand against her small chin, and he could hear her teeth clicking together.

"Does it matter so much?" he asked. "If she doesn't marry Chernov?"

She didn't answer. Instead she swayed forward till her pale face was so close to his that he could see every detail of her eyes, the motes of lilac like patchwork in the blue of her irises. A thin scarlet thread on the white of one eye. Her breath smelled faintly of mint.

She wrapped both her hands around one of his and pulled it onto her knee. Her eyes fixed on him. "Help me, please?" she begged.

Even through the gray material of her gloves he could feel that her hands were icy. It was as though all the heat that belonged in her body had flowed into his, and he could feel the skin of his neck burning.

"How could I help?"

"You are a resourceful man, Viktor."

She'd called him Viktor. He didn't think she even knew his first name. He glanced out the window to check that the carriage driver had not yet emerged from the wine shop, but she lifted her hand, seized his jaw, and turned his face back to her. Her lips were quivering, parted in mute appeal.

He kissed her. A quick firm touch of his mouth to hers, an awareness of the fullness and sweetness of her lips.

"Help me," she breathed.

He knew he would help this government minister's wife. But he didn't know why.

༄

T HE *DROZHKY* DROPPED VALENTINA OUTSIDE THE MILITARY barracks of the Life Guards Hussar Regiment, and soldiers' heads turned as she was ushered through the courtyard into the visitors' room. She had dressed carefully. After much thought she'd chosen a flowered silk gown and with it a scarlet hat trimmed with pale ostrich feathers that fluttered in the lightest breeze. Her coat was cream, pulled tight to emphasize the narrowness of her waist and adorned with a black fur collar and small scarlet buttons. Her mother had ordered the coat specially because the colors of the Hussar Guards were scarlet, white, and black. Today it would come in useful. Because today she needed to entrance the captain.

The room was extremely male. Dark oak settles and table, a plain oak floor, and on the walls two portraits of severe-looking military gentlemen in full dress regalia, bristling with silver and gold galloon. Valentina frowned at them and wondered how many men they had killed. She did not have long to wait. She heard Chernov's footsteps crossing the hall, quick and eager, hurrying toward her in hungry strides. Her heart raced. Was this how a soldier felt before battle? With a life hanging in the balance? His energy burst into the room with him, and his smile leapt all over her skin. His lips claimed her glove. He didn't release her hand but kept it prisoner in his own, taking it hostage.

"Valentina, my dear girl, what an unexpected pleasure. And how well you seem."

Not in a stupor. Not flat on her back. Not tipping vodka down her throat. That was what he meant.

"I am very well, thank you, Stepan."

"And how utterly charming you look too." His eyes skimmed over her, and when his gaze came finally to rest on her face she caught a sound like a purr in the back of his throat. "Forgive my own appearance," he said, "but I am only just back from drilling on the Field of Mars."

"How appropriately named. The field of war."

"We are warriors, Valentina. That's what the army does. What else would you expect?"

She lowered her eyes. "The people of Russia are grateful to you."

Chernov kissed her hand once more in response. He was wearing a clean white shirt, open at the neck, and the Hussars' black trousers with a single red stripe down the side. His hair was wet, freshly washed and slicked back from his face. Strong golden curls glinted at his throat.

"I hope I am not disturbing you, Stepan."

"Not at all. Tell me, what has brought you here today? Without a chaperone." It was a mild rebuke.

"I wanted to speak with you. In private."

"Concerning what?"

"Concerning Jens Friis."

His mouth was still smiling, but his eyes had changed, suddenly pale and sharp as ice. She brushed her free hand down the length of his shirt sleeve.

"I want you to abandon this duel with him," she said softly. "It's not of any importance and"—she drew in a ragged breath—"I couldn't bear you to be hurt."

The triumph. She saw it on his face. An unmistakable rush of it.

"Valentina, why play games?"

Her heart thudded. "What games?"

"Pretending that you don't care for me and trying to rouse my jealousy by flirting with another man. Don't look so shocked. Look at you now; I can recognize your distress under your pretty feathers, and I know the reason for it."

She didn't blink.

"You are afraid for me, aren't you?"

She nodded.

"There is no need to be. I kill every man I duel with."

A sound escaped her.

"No need to be so surprised, my dear. I am a first-class shot, and I intend to teach that engineer what happens to anyone who attempts to steal what is mine."

"Stepan, I told you last night at the ball that I will refuse to marry you if you insist on the duel."

He laughed and drew her closer by the hand he still held. "Another of your little games." The laugh stopped abruptly. "No games now. The duel will take place. I have challenged Friis and that is the end of it. And the end of him."

"Stepan! No!"

He regarded her with surprise. "What now?"

"If you abandon the duel, I will marry you."

The words were out. Instantly his mouth was on hers, his tongue probing and tasting of beer. His breath was hot on her face and his hands squeezed her breast, but she didn't flinch. When she could stand no more of him, she drew back her head and stared up into his face. It was flushed, his pupils greedy black holes.

"Agreed?" she asked.

"Agreed." He pulled her back to him and kissed her once more. "Wait here."

He vanished from the room. She clasped a hand over her mouth to hold in any sound and within minutes he was back with a flat velvet box. With a flourish he dropped to one knee in front of her, presenting her with it.

"An engagement gift." He didn't smile.

She took it, opened it, and her heart sank. She was staring at a necklace on a bed of white silk, a solitary diamond set in a chased gold cradle on a heavy gold chain. The diamond was the size of a walnut. Beside it nestled a pair of matching diamond earrings. Her chest burned as if she'd swallowed acid. So this was her whoring price.

"It's beautiful."

He leapt to his feet and solemnly clasped the necklace around her neck, undoing the top button of her coat. Only when it was secured did he smile, the same way a man smiles at his dog when he's attached a collar and lead.

"It belonged to my grandmother when she was your age," he said. He rested a finger on the diamond, then on her pale skin. "Exquisite," he murmured.

She was bought and paid for.

"Thank you, Stepan."

"Is that all?" He moved to kiss her again.

"So you'll not fight the duel?"

"Don't worry, my angel, I shall not receive a scratch." His lips were almost on hers.

"But you agreed not to fight."

"I agreed to marry you, that's all." He pulled back and shrugged. "Of course I must fight the duel. It's a matter of honor."

"No!" She shook herself free of him and glared angrily. "I will not marry you if you continue with this absurd duel."

"Valentina, don't be foolish. We are engaged."

"No!"

Her hands struggled with the clasp at the back of her neck to rid herself of his chain, but he stepped forward and seized both her wrists. He lowered his face close to hers.

"We are engaged," he repeated coldly. "You cannot alter that."

She stopped struggling and rested her head on his shoulder. "Please, Stepan," she said in a low voice. "No duel."

He released one hand and lifted her chin so that his eyes were looking into hers. His grip hurt. "It's that damn engineer, isn't it? You want the bastard spared."

"Please, don't fight this duel. Don't kill him, Stepan. I said I'll marry you, isn't that enough?"

He kissed her roughly on the mouth. "I promise you, Valentina, I shall take great pleasure in putting a bullet straight through his heart."

❧

VALENTINA SWORE AT HERSELF. CURSED THAT SHE HAD for too long ignored *Number 9* on her list: *Buy a gun.* Instead she was forced to slink into her father's empty study and steal the hunting rifle that hung on the wall. From a drawer she pocketed a handful of ammunition and ran with them to the stables.

"Here." Valentina threw the rifle down on Liev Popkov's bed. "Teach me how to use it."

He was slumped in the chair, tobacco smoke hanging like mist in the air. He rubbed the back of one hand over the spiky stubble on his jaw.

"Ever used one?"

"Liev, if I'd ever used one I wouldn't be asking you to teach me, would I?"

"A rifle that size would kick a hole clean through your puny shoulder. You need a smaller one."

"It's the only one I could get. Please, Liev, teach me fast. How to load it and to hit a target."

But the Cossack didn't move from his seat. Just reached out, plucked the rifle off the bed as though it were no heavier than a whisker, and rested it across his knees. "It's English," he said. With reverent strokes he ran his hand along the length of it, from the base of its smooth stock along the blue metal to the tip of its gleaming barrel. He nodded while he did so, as if it were talking to him.

He took another noisy swig from the half-empty bottle on the floor. "I have a better idea."

❧

VALENTINA FLICKED THE REINS AND THE DUMPY LITTLE mare sprang forward, ears pricked. It was the first time she had ever driven a carriage. The horse was steady but quick to respond and to forgive her mistakes as she set it to a brisk trot along Bolshaya Morskaya.

*Thank you, Liev. You chose well for me.*

The carriage was old and creaky, a small two-seater with a curved hood and an open front. Where he'd dug it up from, she had no idea, but it served their purpose well. It was light and fast, and easy for her to maneuver. It had taken her by surprise when they both climbed onto the narrow bench seat inside the carriage and Popkov had handed her the reins.

"You drive," he'd growled.

She'd looked at his battered face and, taking the reins, clicked her tongue at the little mare. Popkov had hunched himself on his hip, twisting his body so that as little as possible of his buttocks touched the seat.

"Liev, you're in pain. You must stop this. I can do it alone. Go back to bed until you are well."

His black eyes had narrowed at her. "Don't spoil my fun," he'd grunted, and she had not argued.

❧

THE FOREST WAS COMING TO LIFE. THE FRAIL SKELETONS of silver birch trees shimmered in the last shreds of sunlight and an evening mist rose from the ground, wrapping itself around the slender trunks. Rustlings in the undergrowth marked the spots where nocturnal creatures were scenting the air, preparing for the night ahead. Valentina and Popkov had remained still for so long that they had become part of the undergrowth themselves. Valentina inhaled the musty smell of the forest floor and watched a pine marten rake its sharp claws along the bark of a fallen tree not ten feet away, digging out beetles.

The air grew so chill that her breath froze on the dead leaves in front of her face where she lay on the ground. She had tethered the horse and carriage a long way back in the forest and had unloaded the two heavy fur rugs. Liev carried the rifle. He walked so slowly it pained her to see it, but he refused help and she didn't offer sympathy because she knew he would hate it. When they reached the clearing at the top of a slight rise, Liev spoke for the first time.

"This is it."

"Pistol Ridge?"

"*Da.*"

How he had discovered that this was where the duel was to take place, she couldn't imagine. He had disappeared for a couple of hours, limped away dosed on vodka, and returned to announce, "Pistol Ridge. That's where we head for." She could only guess that he had gone drinking in the bars frequented by Hussars and oiled a few tongues with beer and vodka. She'd offered him morphine from Katya's medicine cabinet, but he'd refused it point-blank. She knew better than to insist.

He informed her this was a favorite spot for dueling, hence its name. It lay conveniently close to the city, yet private and safe from prying eyes, tucked away just on the edge of the forest. Valentina could not stop thinking about how many young men's blood had been spilled here, all in the pursuit of so-called *honor*.

Wrapped in the furs pulled right over their heads, she lay flat on her stomach next to Popkov among the undergrowth at the base of the birches. They had a good view of the clearing. It lay no more than forty paces away, sliced into strips by the shadows of the trunks as the last rays of the sun slid behind the trees. Fingers of mist crept closer. One hour passed, then two. Popkov was so still Valentina was convinced he had fallen asleep. Her own arms ached but she didn't move, not even when she heard the muted swish of carriage wheels on the dirt track. She whispered, "They're here."

"I hear them."

The pulse at the base of her throat jerked. "Don't kill him, Liev."

She'd said it before and he'd only shrugged, but this time he didn't even bother to respond. He was unwrapping the rifle from its pillowcase and sliding it into position against his shoulder. She was startled by her desire to use it.

First one black carriage swung up to the edge of the clearing, then within minutes of it, another. Out of the first one sprang four men, all in scarlet Hussar jackets, all full of nervous energy, but the front one was Chernov. She knew him instantly, by the way he walked, chest first. Out of the second carriage stepped three men, two in heavy coats, the third in a black cape. They spoke briefly in a huddle, then one of them, the one in the cape, detached himself and walked over to the men in red. To Valentina's horror she saw it was Dr. Fedorin. The sight of him, this man of medicine, brought the reality of what these men were doing, of the pain about to be inflicted, crashing into her head, and she couldn't swallow.

Popkov elbowed her in the ribs. She had uttered a moan because she had seen Jens. He was standing quietly in one of the last patches of sunlight, and it cut across his neck like a blade. She could make out his steady breath even from this distance, a billow of white in the graying air, no sign of panic. She wanted to scream at him, to beg him to give up this suicidal notion of male honor and reputation, but she didn't; it was far too late for that. Part of her believed deep down that Jens wanted to kill Chernov, truly wanted to kill him, and that was the reason he was here. She touched Popkov's hand on the rifle.

"Just wound the Hussar," she reminded him.

He stroked the engraved metal plate on the weapon with his thumb as fondly as if it were a horse's ear. "Which part," he hissed, "do you want me to stick a hole in? That strong black thigh of his?" He gave a low chuckle. "Thighs are good bleeders."

"No, please. His right shoulder, so that he cannot hold a gun."

He nodded his shaggy head.

Valentina couldn't believe she was having such a conversation. What kind of person was she turning into? All the figures in the clearing were standing in a circle around one of the Hussars, who was holding out a polished mahogany box, and she saw Jens reach in to remove something from inside. It was his choice of pistol. The sun suddenly ducked down as the two men took up their positions back to back in the center of the clearing, pistols in front of them, and the remaining men retreated to the far side. Jens was the taller, but Chernov made the process look as easy as a child's game, his confidence reaching out across the swirling mist to Valentina.

Both men were slow and precise in their movements. Thirty paces. She counted out each one under her breath and felt Popkov's shoulder grow tense. *Now*, she thought, *now, now. While Jens is still standing. Before they turn to face each other. Now, do it now, Popkov.* A shot rang out. But it didn't come from beside her, not from Popkov. Chernov dropped to the ground as though his legs had been chopped from under him, and almost immediately came the crack of another rifle shot. Jens fell.

Valentina's world shuddered to a halt. The two men in the center of the clearing lay slumped on the damp ground, crimson stains coloring the icy grass beneath them while on the fringe of the forest stood a row of ten dark figures like angels of death. Rifles in hand. Each one of them was aimed at the remaining members of the dueling groups.

"Jens!" Valentina choked.

She threw off the rug and tried to leap to her feet, but Popkov, rolling off his stomach, seized her by the scruff of her neck and slammed her hard against a tree. The sky spun around her. He rammed her down on the ground.

"Jens," she moaned. She could see his body, motionless. Leaking the lifeblood she had sworn to herself to protect.

Curses came thick and low from Popkov's mouth. "Don't move."

"I have to go to him. He needs—"

"Who are they?" He nodded toward the row of dark figures.

"Murderers," she said. "If he's dead, I . . ." If Jens Friis was dead, her own heart was dead. Her veins and bones and muscles might still be alive, still functioning, but with no sense and no purpose. "Jens, don't leave me," she moaned, as if she could summon him back to her.

"This is no accidental meeting." Popkov sighted his rifle on one of the men.

"Look, Liev, look at that one," Valentina pointed. Her arm was shaking. "The one in the front."

The dark figure standing at the head of the line of riflemen had turned his attention from the group of Hussars to contemplation of the two bodies on the ground, and it was toward Jens that he started to walk, stiff-legged and wary. His cap was pulled low over his forehead but as the mist shifted, a shaft of light caught him full in the face. Valentina knew him at once.

Viktor Arkin. The man who had been her father's chauffeur. With a shout of fury she darted away from Popkov's side and started to run toward the clearing.

## Twenty-nine

"JENS, DON'T MOVE."

Valentina was on her knees in the snow, her hand pressed flat on his chest to stop the bleeding. *Let him be alive. Let him be alive.* She dragged off her scarf and rammed it against the front of his shirt under his coat. A white shirt. Scarlet now. Her teeth clenched, holding on to him in her head, not letting him go.

"Jens." His name squeezed out between her lips. "Jens, stay with me." She leaned close and slid a hand under his head, cradling it, lifting it out of the cold grip of the snow. His cap had fallen off and his red hair still possessed a fierce life of its own. "Jens. Please, Jens, don't die." Her breath curled like a white shroud onto his lips, into his nostrils, and she willed him to live.

He didn't move. She pressed harder on his chest, feeling for his heartbeat. "Jens, damn you, don't you dare leave me." Her eyes didn't shift from his face as she watched the thick fringe of his eyelashes for the faintest flicker of movement. She shouted out in a loud voice, "*Doktor!* Dr. Fedorin! Come quickly."

Behind her she heard noise and dimly she was aware of raised voices, but they didn't even come close to getting inside her head. She could feel Jens in there, cold in her mind, heavy and listless, but somewhere, very faint, there was the whisper of his breath. She bent lower and kissed each closed eyelid.

"Jens, I hear you." She put her own warm lips on his cold ones. "I love you. You'll take my life with you if you die. Come back to me, Jens."

She felt rather than saw something change, a sudden sensation of warmth in the center of her palm where the back of his head lay, a fleeting pulse of life. Then it was gone. "Jens Friis," she said sternly, "open your eyes at once."

Nothing.

"For me. Do it, Jens."

A narrow slit. A flash of green as one eyelid lifted, no more than a hair's breadth, but it was enough.

"Dr. Fedorin," she yelled again. She rested her forehead on Jens's cheek. "Thank you," she whispered. *"Spasibo."*

Under her scarf she felt a light movement as his ribs began to lift and she murmured to him, soft private words that told him how much his life meant to her and what his death would do to her.

"Valentina! What the hell are you doing here?" It was Dr. Fedorin, his mustache coated with ice, his worried gaze already scanning his friend's body in the snow.

"He's alive," she said quickly. "But bleeding badly from his chest."

He knelt the other side of Jens, his leather bag open, and started to remove dressings. In that moment Valentina looked up for the first time, but what she saw barely imprinted itself on her thoughts. The soles of Captain Chernov's boots iced with compacted snow, the broad backs of Hussars in a cluster around his body. Scarlet everywhere. Scarlet and crimson. Crimson and black. The uniform hiding the blood. Was that why they wore such colors?

The doctor removed her hand from the wound, and suddenly with a jolt of anger she recalled Arkin. She twisted around to look over her shoulder. He was standing on the fringe of the forest observing her, legs planted wide apart, one hand on his hip, the other on the rifle, a look of satisfaction on his face. If she had a gun now, the one she had written down on her list, she would shoot him between those cold gray eyes. Slowly she rose to her feet, leaving Jens in Dr. Fedorin's care, and started toward the chauffeur. In her hand she clutched a scalpel snatched from the doctor's bag.

"Arkin!" she called across the expanse of snow that divided them. Her attention was fixed on the small patch of skin between Arkin's jaw and the frayed collar of his coat. "Arkin, if Captain Chernov dies"—the snow was deeper here, her feet were struggling—"the army will scour the backstreets of Petersburg and tear you limb from limb when they find you."

He was higher than she was, looking down on her from the low ridge, and clearly perceived her as no threat. The rifles of his companions were trained on the Hussars, not on her, and he made no attempt to back off as she approached. She saw his pride, like treacle on his lips, thick and dark and sweet. Her fingers tightened around the metal in her hand, hidden in the folds of her coat.

"Why did you shoot them?" she hissed. "Why both?"

"They are enemies of the people."

She took two more paces. "You're wrong. Jens Friis is helping you and your workers by bringing water to them."

His eyes suddenly narrowed, sensing danger as her hand started its swing. He ducked just as a shot rang out, but he was knocked back on his heels, blood trickling from a straight scarlet line on his forehead that tracked up into his hairline where a bullet had scored his skin. Valentina didn't hesitate. In that half-second of shock in which he realized what had happened, she swept her hand to his side. The short blade sank through cloth and into flesh. He uttered a groan but staggered back from her, yanked out her scalpel, and hurled it at her feet.

"You don't know what you're doing," he growled through clenched teeth, and before she could even begin to question what he meant, he was gone. Into the trees, lost in the gloom. His men vanished with him.

She swung around and looked across to the far side of the clearing. The burly figure of Liev Popkov was standing in the snow with her father's rifle at his shoulder, grinning at her.

❧

THEY TOOK REFUGE IN THE DOCTOR'S HOUSE. THE BULLET looked too small an object to inflict such damage. It sat in the jaws of the forceps, slimy with blood, before it rattled into the enamel dish beneath it.

"Well done, Nurse Ivanova. A good job."

Dr. Fedorin dipped his hands in a bowl of hot water as Valentina flushed the wound with an antiseptic solution of boric acid and dusted it with iodine powder. She watched carefully as he worked. As the needle threaded through the ragged edges of Jens's flesh, she assisted calmly and methodically, the way she had been taught at the hospital. Swabbing blood, passing instruments, keeping a close watch on Jens's thready pulse, ensuring that his tongue didn't roll back to suffocate him. He was only lightly sedated and released small pained growls at intervals, like a bitch giving birth. At one point when she raised one of his eyelids to check his pupil dilation, he looked straight back at her and, despite having a bullet in his chest with a pair of forceps rooting around under his smashed ribs, lifted the corners of his lips in a faint smile.

"I'll sit with him," she said, and took the chair by the bed when the doctor had finished stitching and the wound was dressed.

What she meant was *Leave us. Please. I need to be alone with him.*

Dr. Fedorin opened his mouth to speak, looked at her face, and shut it again. He rested a scrubbed hand on her shoulder for only a brief moment, tossed a towel over his arm, and walked out of the room with his tray of medical instruments in his hands. He would sterilize them in his kitchen. As soon as the door closed, Valentina rested her head on the pillow next to the shock of red hair. She touched it gently. Like a horse's mane, thick and wiry. His chest was naked except for the heavy bandage, and she studied the fineness of his skin and the gingery hairs that curled up toward his collarbones, the sunburst of freckles at his throat.

"Jens," she murmured into his ear, "if you ever try to fight a duel again, I swear I will shoot you myself."

The corner of his mouth moved. That smile again. She draped an arm carefully across his waist and curled herself around him on the bed, molding her body to the shape of his bones. She listened to his breathing, to the catches in the back of his throat when the pain was bad, to the ticking of the French marble clock on the mantelpiece, to the sounds of the city outside launching itself into the stride of its nightlife. She held him close. Only when she was certain that his pulse had settled into a steady though shallow rhythm did she start to hum to him, her breath brushing his cheek. Chopin's Nocturne in E Flat.

MAMA, MAY I SPEAK WITH YOU?"

It was the middle of the night but her mother was downstairs in the blue salon, dimly lit by only a small reading lamp at her shoulder. She was wearing an exquisite Oriental kimono that Valentina had never seen before and was playing cards, a game of solitaire on a card table by the fire. Her hair lay loose on her shoulders, and when she looked up at her daughter her eyes were alert and observant.

"What hour is this for you to return home?"

The words were a milder rebuke than Valentina had expected. "I was nursing someone."

She slid off her coat and stood in front of the fire. She couldn't imagine ever being warm again. Dried blood marked the front of her dress where she had held Jens in the snow, and they both looked at the stains in silence.

"The engineer's blood?" Elizaveta asked quietly.

"You know?"

"Yes." She didn't look up. "I know about the duel."

Valentina didn't ask how. "Mama, Captain Chernov survived the attack, though he is gravely ill. But I want you to understand that I am finished with him."

The words were out, like spitting stones from her mouth. "I refuse to keep up the charade of an engagement to that man for even one more second of my life." The image of Jens with a hole in his chest made her hand clench around the blood on her dress. "Chernov was the cause of this."

Elizaveta turned back to her cards. She gathered them up and shuffled them, but her hands were not as steady as she would wish. "Your father will be ill-pleased when he hears."

"I want to tell him myself."

"Not now."

"Is he at home? In bed?"

Elizaveta gave a sad smile. "No, he is not."

Valentina crouched in front of the fire, stretching her hands to its flames, and for once her mother did not chide her. "I want you both to understand, Mama, that I can't do it anymore. I don't mean to hurt you or Papa, really I don't. But this is . . ." She wanted to say, *This is killing me. Killing Jens*, but instead she changed it to, "This is wrong. There must be some other way to sort out Papa's finances."

"I understand." Elizaveta proceeded to lay out the cards once more.

For a while nothing more was said, and the fire sent shadows darting up the walls as they both lived with their thoughts. After a while Valentina removed a velvet case from her coat pocket and placed it on the floor as far away from herself as she could reach.

"I will give Papa this," she said.

Elizaveta flicked a glance at the blue box containing the diamond necklace, but Valentina did not choose to open it.

"It's from Chernov. The banks will advance credit to Papa on the strength of it."

Her mother sighed softly. "Thank you, Valentina. I am grateful."

"You would like it, Mama. It's very beautiful."

"Is that what you think of me? That I am so easily tempted by beautiful objects?" Her eyes remained on the cards.

"Why did you marry him, Mama? Why Papa?"

One of her mother's hands gave a little jump. She dealt the cards in a faster rhythm, but she spoke slowly. "When I was a little older than you, I loved a man whom my parents deemed unsuitable. They paid him money to leave Petersburg."

"They bought him off?"

"Yes. He went without saying good-bye. After that I didn't much care whom I married. They chose your father. It was a good match."

Valentina remained on the floor by the fire, staring intently at her mother until Elizaveta finally lifted her eyes from the cards and met her gaze.

"I'm so sorry, Mama," Valentina murmured. "Sorry for everything."

Her mother shrugged and concentrated on the cards. Valentina rose to her feet, moved over to a mahogany cabinet that contained an array of bottles on its shelves, and poured out two vodkas. She walked back, placed one glass on her mother's card table, and sat on the floor in front of the fire with her own. She gazed into the shifting flames and sipped her drink.

"Why tell me now, Mama?"

"I have my reasons."

"What reasons?"

"Firstly because I want you to know that men are rarely what you think they are. Don't ever forget that. Secondly"—she paused and played three cards in quick succession as if trying to bridge the gap between her thoughts and her tongue—"because tonight you have gone."

"Gone?"

"You have gone from us. I can see it in your eyes, in the way your feet touch the floor as if they know exactly where they are heading. I hear it in your voice. Tonight you have grown up and gone."

"I'm still here, Mama."

Her mother nodded. She drank her vodka in one quick movement and asked, "I assume he's alive, your engineer?"

"Yes." Valentina said it quickly, the single word tumbling off her tongue. For even the possibility that he might not be alive was too dangerous a thought to allow. Like her mother, she drank down the clear liquid, emptying her glass. She had dosed Jens on morphine, enough to knock out an ox, but in Dr. Fedorin's guest room his hand had clamped around her wrist, unwilling to let her go even as he slept. She had kissed his fingers. *Trust me, Jens. And I will trust you. Because Mama is wrong. You are the man I think you are; you have proved it to me.*

"You're smiling," Elizaveta commented.

Was she? She hadn't realized.

"You're smiling because you are thinking of him."

"Don't you still smile when you think of the man you love?"

Her mother's blue eyes widened. "Yes, I do." She opened her mouth to say more but closed it abruptly and swept all of the cards into her hand, squeezing them tight. Tears slid down her cheeks.

"Mama." Valentina hurried to her mother's side.

"Valentina," Elizaveta whispered, "I am so jealous of you."

Valentina wrapped her arms around her mother's stiff figure and rocked her gently by the light of the flames.

VALENTINA STOOD AT HER BEDROOM WINDOW, IMPATIENT for morning to arrive. The moment that lights started to appear and the servants roused themselves to the new day's activity, she wrapped herself in her coat and slipped out into the dark. The air bit into her lungs. The stable was swarming with grooms raking straw and rubbing down the horses, whistling snatches of tunes and breaking the ice on water buckets. The air smelled of oats and the sweet scent of hay, and she noticed that the sturdy little mare she had driven yesterday was safely back in her stall. One of the grooms rolled his eyes at her when she headed straight for the narrow stairs that led up to the sleeping cubicles, but she ignored him.

"Liev," she called, jolting open his door, "you are a rotten shot."

Popkov was lying flat on his back on the floor, clothed in the same filthy tunic as yesterday, and didn't make any effort to stand. His eyes were dull and filmy but regarded her with interest.

"The bastard ducked," he growled.

"You creased Arkin's skull, that's all."

"It was meant for his brain."

"What was he up to?"

"Revenge, most probably."

"Revenge can work both ways."

The Cossack bared his teeth and it was impossible to tell whether it was a grin or a snarl. Valentina sat down on his narrow cot and studied his muscular frame. "The rifle?" she asked. "Back in the study?"

"Of course."

"*Spasibo.*"

"Your engineer alive?"

She nodded. "Do you need morphine?"

"*Nyet.*"

She drew from under her coat the vodka bottle from the blue salon. Instantly his eyes lost their dull haze and gleamed black as sin. She handed it over.

"Try to make it last, will you? At least until after breakfast," she urged.

He laughed, a booming sound that shook the flimsy walls, and started to open the bottle.

❦

V ALENTINA REALIZED IMMEDIATELY THAT CAPTAIN STE-
pan Chernov was drugged up to his eyeballs. His pupils were tiny pinpricks at the center of misty irises and his mouth had lost its firm line. It was loose and pliant as though it belonged to someone else. Clearly his doctor believed in pain control for his patients as much as she did.

She sat quietly by his bedside and listened to his mother cry. Countess Chernova, a delicate woman wearing too many ropes of

pearls, was seated in a gilt chair on the opposite side of the bed, sobbing into a tiny lace handkerchief that struck Valentina as inadequate
for the job. She could find no sympathy in her heart for the mother
of the man who had sworn to kill Jens. She had come here for the sake
of her own parents, and it was the last time she would play the role of
fiancée. She refused to touch him. His right hand lay on the quilt,
but she would rather chop it off than pick it up. This was the offend-
ing hand that had gripped the dueling pistol with such relish. His
parents had announced their intention of whisking him away as soon
as he was strong enough to travel to their dacha on the Black Sea,
where the weather was warmer and the healing would be faster.

"Valentina," Stepan Chernov whispered, "come with me."

He tried to smile but it was beyond the strength of his drugged
muscles. He had lost a large amount of blood from a stomach wound
and had hung all night on the edge of survival, but this morning
he had rallied and was making improvement. That was what his
father, Count Chernov, had told her. *Rallied. Improvement.* She had
shut her ears.

"I can't come with you." She spoke clearly, so that there would be
no mistake in his foggy brain. "My sister is ill, so I can't leave Petersburg." She offered one crumb of comfort to the ghost-white face on
the pillows. "When you return, we will talk again," she said, and
rose to her feet. "I might even play the piano for you." She couldn't
quite hide the faint trace of a smile.

# Thirty

JENS HAD BAD DREAMS. IN THE DARK HOURS WHEN LIFE is stretched in some indefinable way, so that reality becomes flexible and consciousness is elusive, the wolves came. He knew he was in Fedorin's house and that wild animals did not roam the carpeted stairs and bedrooms in the heart of Petersburg, and yet they came nevertheless. At first he could just smell them, the same feral stink that existed in the house where the woman lay in bed with her dead children.

But when he tried to sit up to drive them away, they leapt on his chest with a snarl and sank their fangs into his flesh. He felt their tongues, hot and smooth, lapping the blood from his heart. Again and again he told himself it was a bad dream, but how could it be? He could see their red eyes. He could smell their oily breath. With an effort he punched one in the jaw and heard it grunt. That would teach it to stay away. He lay back, satisfied.

IT WAS DAYLIGHT WHEN HE WOKE, THE KIND OF DAYLIGHT that is so white and hard it pushes between the eyelids and prizes them open. It took a moment for Jens's battered brain to recognize where he was or to work out why the hell he was flat on his back in a strange bed, but everything slotted into place the moment he saw her. Waiting for him to come back to her.

Valentina was seated on a chair beside the bed, a small and delicate figure between its heavily padded arms, her dark gaze fixed on him. Something about the stillness of her made him think she had been there a long time. When she saw he was awake her eyes widened with a lift of her long eyelashes, and it made the damaged flesh of his chest tighten with pleasure. Her mouth curved into a slow smile that warmed the blood in his veins.

"How do you feel?" she asked in a gentle voice.

Still she didn't move. He wanted to touch her. "Like there's an elephant stamping on my chest."

Her smile grew. "Don't let Dr. Fedorin hear that. Elephants aren't allowed upstairs."

When he laughed, the muscles behind his ribs seemed to explode. He started to cough, blood seeping from his mouth, and she watched him with a rigid unreadable expression, her cheeks stiff and pale. When he finished, she used a red washcloth to wipe his lips.

"Don't talk," she ordered. "Don't laugh either."

He lay struggling for breath, fighting off the damn elephant, and let his eyes feast on her. She was wearing a warm green-and-russet-colored dress, like a forest nymph that had crept into his room by mistake. It had a high neck with twelve tiny perfect pearl buttons at the front. Her hair looked as if she'd been out in the wind, but maybe she'd just been running her hands through it. That thought, the idea of her doing so in distress, was like a cold finger placed at the base of his throat.

"Are you in much pain? Don't speak. Just nod or shake your head."

He shook his head. Their eyes held tight to each other.

"Good," she said.

"Kiss me," he whispered.

"Go to sleep."

"Kiss me."

He pushed his hand to the edge of the bed, but she did not move forward to take it.

"Keep still," she ordered. "You mustn't tear anything inside."

"Kiss me or I shall leap from this bed and chase you around the room."

"You don't deserve a kiss." Her face was solemn and her eyes fierce. "You almost got yourself killed."

With a wrench he sat up and seized her wrist, pulling her out of her chair toward the bed.

"Don't!" she shouted at him. "You'll do more damage and tear the stitches."

He drew her close and kissed her. Her lips were soft and yielding but her dark eyes remained open, furious with him.

"Valentina," he whispered, "I won't let him have you."

She gave a sharp shudder and nestled her head into the curve of his neck as though trying to burrow into him. "I was always yours. From the first moment I saw you. Now lie down."

He let her ease him back onto the pillows and wipe the trickle of blood from his chin with her cloth, but he did not release his hold on her. She sat on the bed close beside him, and for the first time he noticed a bruise the color of port wine on her cheek. He touched it with his fingertips. Touched her hair. Touched her ear and undid two of the pearl buttons.

"What have you been doing to yourself?" he asked.

"You mean this?" She fingered the bruise. "I slipped on ice."

But he knew her too well. He recalled the wolves. "Come here."

She leaned over him and allowed him to kiss it. The fragrance of her skin stirred something deep within him. Only then did she give him a wide teasing smile that spread to her eyes and drove away the dark shadows that haunted them. She planted a light effortless kiss on his lips before she sat up again.

"Jens, if you keep looking at me like that . . ."

"Like what?"

"As though you are about to eat me."

"I do believe you would taste good."

"If you don't stop it I shall lose my professional nurse's control and leap between the sheets with you."

He flicked back a corner of the quilt. "Come and ravish me."

For a second he saw her gaze on his face and he knew she saw more than he wanted her to, but his defenses were weak as a blasted kitten's. Gently she tucked the quilt around him.

"I shall entertain you," she smiled, "with music."

"What?" He could feel his head floating off up to the ceiling somewhere. "Are you going to whistle?"

"Wait and see."

She moved away from the bed. His eyes remained fixed on the spot where she had been sitting, where her small bottom had impressed itself, a perfectly round indentation. He rested his hand in it. It felt warm. From across the room music drifted to him, wrapping itself around the jagged chunk of pain embedded in his chest and blunting its edges. He looked up and saw her. His wood nymph was standing at the foot of the bed playing a violin, her slender arm sweeping up and down in such an exquisite curve he couldn't take his eyes off it.

"Sleep," she murmured. "Sleep, my love."

Reluctantly he closed his eyes and immediately found himself floating in warm balmy air, high above the reach of the wolves. She played like an angel.

❧

AFTER THE FIRST FEW DAYS JENS SENT HER BACK TO THE hospital. Valentina wasn't pleased.

"I don't need to be fussed over," he said with ill humor. "Go back to work and let me rest. When you're here I can't . . ."

"Ssh, my grumpy Viking."

She had placed a finger on his lips to seal the words inside because she knew they were lies. She understood, but she didn't like it. He was sending her away because he couldn't bear her to lose her position at St. Isabella's. Her absence from *Medsestra* Gordanskaya's instruction classes would not be tolerated, and they both knew it.

So by day Valentina wore the starched uniform of a nurse, and each evening she returned to Dr. Fedorin's house. She would burst into the guest bedroom and fling herself on Jens as if she were drowning. All day she'd been struggling in a sea of faces with no air to breathe, not until she entered this room and saw his green eyes waiting for her. They fixed on hers as though he too had not existed until this moment.

"Miss me?" She kissed his mouth, tasted his lips.

"No," he laughed. "I slept all day in peace and quiet, and then little Anna came and read to me. The doctor's cook made chicken soup for me."

Valentina gave him a frown. "You're turning into one of those fat lazy autocrats who has women dancing attendance on him all day. I shall bring an ostrich feather to fan you with next time."

"I can't think of anything better."

"I can," she said with a teasing smile.

Instantly his head lifted from the pillows, and she had to slip off the bed to avoid being caught.

"You're sick," she told him.

"And you're my medicine. I need you."

He said it with a grin, but the look in his eyes stopped her heart. He meant it. Every word of it. Something dislodged inside her, a cold fear that had been there ever since that day in his office when he had declared he would rather fight the duel than run to safety with her. Slowly she turned to the bed, lay down on the quilt beside him, inhaling his warm musky scent, and held him so tight he groaned with pain.

❦

THE CRACKED DOOR OPENED NO MORE THAN A SLIT.
"Oh, it's you again."

The greeting could have been warmer; Valentina hadn't traipsed all the way down here in the snow just for one of Varenka's smiles.

"Yes, it's me."

The door opened farther and she followed the woman into the room. It was looking better, cleaner and brighter. The fire muttered like an old man in the corner and there was the aroma of hot food in a pot on the table. Varenka was wearing a bright headscarf.

"So you got the job?" Valentina commented.

"*Da.*"

"I'm glad."

She waited for a smile. Even a thank-you. Valentina had kept her promise and recommended Varenka for the cleaning position at Madame Angelique's fashion house, but it seemed Varenka wasn't good at common courtesy.

"What's she here for?"

The question came from the bed. Ivan was stretched out on it, naked to the waist, his trouser buttons undone, and Valentina was embarrassed to realize the timing of her visit wasn't good.

"Good evening, *dobriy vecher*, Ivan," she said, her cheeks flushing.

At the hospital she was used to seeing men in states of undress, even fully naked when necessary, but this was different. There was an aggression in the ripple of his muscles as he clasped his hands behind his head, something so male in the dense mat of black hair on his chest and in the small bright eyes that glared at her with dislike.

"It's you I've come to see," she said.

He swung his feet to the floor but remained seated on the edge of the bed, elbows on his knees, without bothering about his trouser buttons. She could see more black hair curling in the gap down there.

"What about?" he demanded.

"I'm looking for someone. I thought you might know him."

He stared at her, interested. "What's his name?"

"Viktor Arkin."

"Never heard of him."

But there was a hesitation, so slight it was barely there. That split second that it takes a mind to decide to lie. She studied him in silence, but he didn't break it. Varenka did.

"Would you like some soup?" she asked awkwardly.

"What about you, Varenka? Do you know someone called Arkin?"

"*Nyet.*"

"You're a bad liar."

"Leave her alone," Ivan snapped as he stood up, fists clenched, and the room immediately felt smaller.

"I'll pay you for the information," she offered.

"Your sort think money is the answer to everything, don't you?" he snarled. "You think you can buy us as easily as you did when we were serfs and you were our owners. You treated us worse than your dogs." He took a step closer, head jutting forward. "But let me tell you, little rich bitch, things have changed. I won't take your dirty money."

"You took it when it suited you."

"Don't provoke him," Varenka muttered under her breath.

But Valentina was angry. She wasn't one of the factory bosses who abused their workers, or one of the wealthy landowners who ill-treated their peasants. She had helped these people, scrubbed their filthy floor and cleaned out their bloody bucket. Who was this man? *Rich bitch*, he had called her. *Rich bitch.*

She stepped right up to him and slapped his flat-nosed face, a determined blow that rocked his head back on its bull neck. But instead of knocking her to the floor, he laughed, his breath sour in her face.

"You've got guts," he admitted, "but you've got no brains. If you had any, you'd take all that you value in this world and leave Russia like your tail was on fire."

"Russia is *my* country as much as yours. I won't let you steal it from me."

"Wait till the revolution—"

"Shut up about your revolution! It won't happen. You people are all talk and no action."

"You call the apprentices' march *no action*?"

They were shouting at each other, face to face, the air hot between them, but the mention of the apprentices silenced Valentina. She turned away.

"Tell Viktor Arkin from me," she said coldly, "that I won't give up until I've found him. Tell him that."

Varenka nervously touched her hand. Her pale eyes were worried, but she gave a crisp little nod. Ivan grunted. That was all.

Valentina headed for the door, but before she reached it she swung around and tossed a small bag of coins onto the table. They chinked together as they landed, and the sound drew both Ivan and Varenka's gaze.

"I want you," Valentina said, "to buy me a gun."

❧

A SUDDEN SHIFT IN THE WIND BROUGHT A FUNNEL OF warm air from the south and rain fell, drenching her. The city shed its feathery frosting of snow and icicles and instead gleamed harshly in the light of the streetlamps, the roads a glossy black once more, the roof edges hard as flint. Jens was sitting in bed propped upright against an avalanche of white pillows when she arrived, a distinct improvement on lying flat on his back. He held a towel in one hand, a hairbrush in the other. His smile of welcome warmed her wet skin.

"Come here," he said.

She curled up at his side on the quilt and let him dry her, slowly and calmly, no rush, no effort, and the tension flowed from her aching limbs until her muscles grew soft and her cramped brain let go.

"What happened?" he asked.

"I've been thinking. About the duel."

They'd barely mentioned it. Until now neither had been willing to venture into what both knew was dangerous territory. It was like black ice, invisible until your feet shoot from under you and you find yourself flat on your back in the dirt. A silence wedged itself between them, but Jens brushed it aside and told her, "The duel is over and done with, my Valentina. Think about our future, not our past."

"Why did he shoot you? Why not just shoot the Hussars?"

She heard him sigh, scarcely audible, but the sorrow in it was solid and unrelenting, something that had set hard inside him.

"They regard us all as the oppressors," he said. "Chernov leads soldiers against strikers, and I lead a tunneling project in which workmen labor twelve hours a day, sometimes even fourteen when we are behind schedule. And what are they paid for that? Less than you would spend on tea and cakes with Katya. Of course they hate us. They have every right to."

"I don't agree."

"Of course you don't, my love." He ran the hairbrush through a lock of her hair, lifting it, stroking it and letting it float down onto the palm of his hand. "Let us both be thankful the man was a poor shot."

"I've been thinking about that too."

He leaned back against the pillows. "And what conclusion did you come to? That revolutions won't get anywhere until they learn to shoot straight?"

"No. But he was the same man who shot at us in the sleigh the night of the ball at Anichkov Palace."

"What?"

"It's true, Jens. I saw it clearly."

She felt his intake of breath and a wince of pain as he did so, but his hand continued to stroke her hair in a steady rhythm.

"Twice he shot at me," Jens muttered. "Twice he didn't kill me."

"I know who he is."

"Who?"

"Viktor Arkin. He was my father's chauffeur. He was the one who hid the grenades in the garage."

"For which I was briefly arrested, I remind you."

"Yes."

"So." He breathed carefully. "So this Arkin is determined to do harm. To you and to me."

"I stabbed him."

"You did what?"

"With one of Dr. Fedorin's scalpels. But it wasn't deep enough, so he ran away."

"Oh, Valentina!"

He drew her into his arms, her head on his shoulder, and tucked his quilt around her as though he could hold her safe. She could feel a quiver in his jaw where it lay against her forehead, words struggling to escape.

"Jens, when I was young we were told that the people of Russia loved the tsar. Where has all that love gone?"

"Eighty percent of Russians are peasants. They have an ancient tradition of devotion to their tsar even if they hate their own landlords. Many still feel that way despite all this unrest. Look at the revolt in 1905 when they marched on the Winter Palace with Gapon. It wasn't meant to be a revolt. It was to tell the tsar of their troubles. They were convinced that if he knew of their suffering he would help them and make their lives better." He gave a snort of anger. "Little do they know the kind of man this Tsar Nicholas Alexandrovich Romanov really is."

She rested her hand on the dressing of his wound. "Jens," she said lightly, "I think it's time you had some medicine."

She slid from his grasp and stood beside the bed, watching his green eyes grow greener as she started to undo her buttons.

ᕱ

HOW COULD HE KEEP HER SAFE?
        The scent of her skin filled the caverns of his mind. But even while her lips lingered on his throat as she tried to kiss away the pain, still his mind would not let go of the question. It lay like a bullet in his brain, jamming all other thoughts. How could he keep her safe?

And what did Viktor Arkin want?

With slow hungry movements he slid his hands up along the length of her naked thighs as she sat astride him. He traced the line of his hips and the tight curve of her buttocks, warm and yielding, cradled in his palm. He adored the angles of her bones, loved the way they moved against each other, creating hollows and shadows in her flawless skin. And he listened. Breathless. To the sounds escaping from her, the purrs, the whimpers, and the secret mews of pleasure.

She held him pinned to the pillows, whispering in his ear, her hair a wild curtain around him, its fragrance enticing, its strands intimate and familiar across his face. Her breath swirled in his damaged lungs as if she would climb inside him, and her touch stirred places deep within him that had lain cold till now. She moved him in ways he couldn't understand, excited him in ways he couldn't explain. And fired him with such strength, such desire for her that the weak and wounded body in its sickbed vanished.

There was a ferocity to her lovemaking that he had never found before, and as he kissed her breasts, tasting the firm sweet rise of her nipples, he was aware of the pulsing heat of their bodies molding them together, forging them into one. It was always like this for him. As if a lifetime of her would never be enough.

~

ARKIN WAS CAREFUL. IT WAS DARK AND ST. PETERSBURG'S roads were busy. He backtracked time and again as he made his way to the Hotel de Russie, ducking into doorways and dodging down side streets. No footsteps behind him, no quiet tread or quick turnabouts by agents in black raincoats. He skirted the broad boulevards, past Brocard's French perfumery, and doubled back over the bridges, crossing and recrossing the Fontanka. His collar was tucked up around his ears against the sleeting rain, and he cursed himself for a fool. This filthy weather made his journey across the city safe, but it didn't make it wise.

He had followed the girl earlier and he knew exactly where she headed each day when her hospital shift was over. It was to an elegant house on a tree-lined avenue, with wrought-iron gates and a coat of arms paraded on the gateposts. The kind of house his mother had always yearned to be a servant in. He had learned that it belonged to a Dr. Fedorin. He was one of the despicable intellectuals, part of the liberal elite who liked to count themselves among the upper classes but prided themselves on doing charity work with the poor. As if they could patch the wound that lay at the heart of Russia, place a frail gauze bandage over a ravine and hope that it would hold together.

When the revolution came, such people would be trampled underfoot by the boots of the masses. In the chaos that would surely follow the toppling of the hated Romanovs, people like this doctor would never understand that they could no longer be in control. That a grubby peasant from Siberia or a factory worker from the Putilov works would have the right to order them around. These people, whether doctors, lawyers, or teachers, would always be traitors to the socialist cause because their minds were incapable of believing in their own subservience.

He shook the rain from his face, dull anger digging at his gut. So what of upper-class women? What of them? They were used to being controlled and directed, told what to do and what to think by their husbands or their fathers. Was there any hope for them?

Damn such thoughts! He hated himself for wanting the answer to be yes. *Da!* Yes, they can be remolded. Yes, they can be taught to make themselves useful, like the Ivanova girl.

But what of the mother? Clinging to her pearls and her prejudices. How could she ever be of use to the cause? She'd been angry with him. When he told her how he'd stopped the duel, she had berated him. Sharp words had poured from her, her ivory cheeks filling with hot blood and her eyes glittering with fury. It had surprised him that this woman had such fire hidden away in her belly. It drew him to her against his will.

He had sat knee to knee with her in the Turicum, and when she had finished he took her quivering hand in his. But this time he undid the buttons of her calf-leather glove, so fine it felt more like silk than leather, and peeled it off. Her skin was unblemished, no marks on it of a life being lived. It lay cradled in his thick fingers like a bird, nervous and trembling. He'd had no idea a hand could ever be so soft.

A carriage barged past him in the darkness as he crossed Mikhailovsky Square and doused him in a slick wave of filthy water from the gutter. He cursed. He was irritable tonight. His thoughts jumpy, sharp as razors in his head. He should have killed that Hussar outright in the forest. It would have meant no more than aiming a notch higher. God damn his weakness. He should have done it, owed it to Karl, whose young life had been sliced open in the railway sidings. Instead he'd done as Elizaveta Ivanova asked.

God damn his weakness.

At the corner of the square stood the Hotel de Russie. He turned quickly down a side road and slipped unchallenged through the hotel's back entrance, past the busy kitchens and up the broad stairs. On the second floor he moved silently along the corridor and knocked on one of the doors.

"Come in."

His pulse quickened as he entered the room. In the shell-pink glow from the wall lamps Elizaveta Ivanova was standing there, without pearls, without gloves, wearing only a silk kimono, her hair curling like a haze of summer sunlight around her shoulders. The sight of her drove all thought of Chernov from his head.

## Thirty-one

THE DAYS GREW WARMER AND THE CITY DELIGHTED IN shedding its choking shroud of fog. It had grown tattered and stank like an old man's coat. The golden church domes began to gleam once more as skies brightened and palaces shook off their mood of gloom, throwing open windows so that sunlight could linger in the rooms, settling on armchairs and stretching out on rugs like a ginger cat. The Fontanka and the Moika thawed, allowing boats to set about their business of carting coal and logs to the outlying factories. The streets grew rowdier. Markets sprang up. Hawkers shouted their wares, traders thrust apples and cinnamon, shoes and paintbrushes under the nose of every passerby. St. Petersburg ruffled her skirts and started to smile.

Valentina smiled too. Jens was waiting for her. How could she not smile? He claimed that the walk to the hospital each day exercised his lungs and did him good, but she wasn't so sure. His breathing was still labored and at times made thin strange whistling noises as he stepped up and down the curbs.

Just the sight of his angular figure, his hair like copper in the last rays of sunlight, and the thoughtful way he leaned his head forward as he paced back and forth made quiet corners of her vibrate with life. This whole business of living became more vivid when she was anywhere near him, more important, more vital. Today in the hospital she had seen her first birth, and she had been stunned. That life should begin with such violence and yet at the same time with such beauty, the new infant so perfectly formed. She had wept.

But even that was pale and insipid in comparison with what happened inside her when she saw her Danish engineer waiting for her. She wanted to hurl herself at him. To wrap her arms around him and devour him. Every day it was the same. Instead she walked over to him, smiled up into his eyes, and took his hand in hers.

ᕙᕗ

B Y THE TIME THEY REACHED THE STREET IN WHICH HIS apartment lay, the sky had taken on a muted lilac haze that turned the buildings into dainty dollhouses. Jens had his arm around her shoulders and spoke little, needing to save his breath for walking, so she was entertaining him with a story of how *Medsestra* Gordanskaya and Nurse Darya had almost come to blows over the loss of a doctor's stethoscope, each blaming the other till the air in the sluice room was thick with swear words and Gordanskaya's grand bosom was threatening to pop the buttons of her uniform.

He chuckled, but abruptly she felt his body go rigid. She sensed the laughter draining out of him into the gutter and something darker sliding into its place as he tightened his grip on her shoulder. She followed his gaze and saw a smart carriage with a gilded family crest and liveried servants parked outside his house.

"Whose is it?" she asked, already certain of the answer.

"It's Countess Serova's." He halted his step and looked down at Valentina, his eyes intent on her face. "I'll tell her to leave at once."

"Why would she come?" she asked.

"Alexei might be ill."

Valentina felt a shiver flick up her spine. Countess Natalia Serova was clever. She was more than capable of using her son if she had to. The carriage and the hallway were empty, so Jens started up the stairs two at a time but halfway up he stalled, one hand pressed against his chest as he fought to drag in air. Instantly Valentina was with him, taking his weight on her shoulder. Her arms encircled his waist, and in the icy silence inside her head she cursed the countess.

"How touching."

The voice came from above. Valentina glanced up. Countess Serova stood on the upper landing in all her finery, a mint green gown with a black cape, a tall black hat with emerald feathers, and a boy at her side. About seven. Green eyes. Beautiful worried green eyes. Eyes that were too old for him.

"Jens has not been well," Valentina said sharply to the black hat. She did not care to look at the woman's eyes.

"*Dyadya* Jens! Uncle Jens!" The boy catapulted down the stairs and slid his young shoulder under Jens's other arm.

"*Spasibo*," Jens murmured. "Good evening, Countess." On the upper landing he disentangled himself and managed a polite bow. "To what do I owe this pleasure?"

"Alexei was concerned. When we heard you were unwell, he badgered me to bring him to see you."

Her smile was as smooth as a snake's tongue. Jens ruffled the boy's brown hair. "I'm fine." He unlocked the door to his apartment, but once inside there was an awkwardness that Jens did nothing to ease. He just knelt down in front of her son.

"What have you there?" he asked.

"A present for you," the boy grinned.

His mother pulled a face. "It was his own idea."

Under his arm Alexei was clutching a box the size of a shoe box, and he thrust it into Jens's hands. Carefully he removed the lid and then burst out laughing.

"Well, look what we have here!"

Inside on a bed of straw snuggled a large white mouse, its whiskers twitching, its pink eyes staring up at them with intense annoyance.

"While you're sick, I thought"—the boy's eyes shifted sideways to Valentina and quickly veered away again—"he could keep you company. In case you get lonely. His name is Attila."

"Attila?" Another roar of laughter came from Jens, sending him into a violent spasm of coughing and making the mouse chitter angrily with a display of yellow teeth. "He's magnificent. The heart of a Hun in a tiny fur coat. *Spasibo*, Alexei. Thank you. He and I shall be good friends."

He kissed the boy's cheek, and the small arms sneaked around his neck and stayed there.

"Don't cling," his mother ordered.

The arms vanished. Jens led him to the table and together they sat examining the wonders of Attila, while Valentina and Natalia Serova eyed each other with interest.

"I hear he fought a duel over you," the countess commented in a low voice.

"Not quite."

"So his wound is your fault."

"His wound," Valentina said stiffly, "is the fault of the man who pulled the trigger."

"I'm told that it wasn't the charming Captain Chernov. He is still recuperating in the enviable warmth of the Black Sea. Do you know who fired the shot?"

"What is this? The Spanish Inquisition?"

The countess gave a cold smile that went no farther than her lips. "I am curious. You know what Petersburg is like, so many wicked rumors."

"So many wicked people."

Valentina's challenging stare did not please the countess. She looked away, and Valentina took the moment to walk over and stand behind Jens, one hand on his shoulder as she bent and laughed at the mouse's antics. Alexei was giggling uncontrollably at the size of the animal's testicles. He and his mother didn't stay long, but before they left, Jens knelt once more, kissed the boy's cheeks, and promised to design the most elaborate mouse palace a rodent had ever possessed. He held the eager young body to him.

"Will you come when you're better?" Alexei asked shyly. "To take me horse riding again?"

Jens hesitated. Seconds ticked past in the room, seconds when the countess didn't blink.

Valentina stepped forward with a smile and patted the child's shoulder in the sailor suit. "Of course he will. Anyway he will want to bring Attila's new palace for you to see."

Jens looked at her for a long moment, then nodded to the boy. "Of course."

As the countess drifted from the room with a rustle of her silk skirts, there was an unmistakable look of triumph on her face.

❧

VALENTINA PUSHED OPEN THE HEAVY DOOR TO THE CHURCH and entered the building, accustomed now to its musty odor. The domed space should have pressed down on her with the weight of prayers but didn't. It felt empty.

"Father Morozov," she called out to the tall figure in black who was lighting a candle under one of the gilded icons to the Virgin Mary.

He turned with a patient smile. "Back again, I see."

"Back again."

She stood in the center of the marbled floor. Around her the murals and icons and votive candles glowed solemnly, the long sad eyes of saints directed at her as though *she* were the sinner, the liar. Not the man in the long black robe. But she knew different. Under the gentle smile and the kind words lay a tongue that dispensed lies more readily than it dispensed absolution.

"Have you seen him?" she asked.

"I tell you today what I told you all the other days: Viktor Arkin doesn't come here anymore. You are always welcome in this church, my child, but this is a place of peace and prayer, not of persecution."

"When did you see him last?"

"I told you. Not for weeks."

"Do you know where he is?"

"No."

"Are you sure?"

"I'm certain." His pale eyes folded at the outside edges, as crinkled as tissue paper, when he smiled. "I'm not lying to you."

"Have you heard anything new?"

"Only that he was injured."

"Badly?"

"I don't know. But I was told he'd left for Moscow. How true that is, I don't know." He touched the crucifix that hung from his neck.

"Tell him from me, Valentina Ivanova, that he cannot hide forever."

He smiled his priestly smile at her and blew out the lit taper in his hand. "This is the house of the Holy Lord, my child. Let him bring peace to whatever it is that is driving you to seek this Viktor Arkin so relentlessly." He made the sign of the cross with two fingers.

"Thank you, Father, but I would prefer it if he brought me the information I seek."

"I cannot help you there."

Valentina saw the watchfulness behind the gentle eyes, the bright mind that denied her help. She swung away and hurried from the church. Behind her the priest's voice echoed in the damp empty space. "May God bless you, my child."

❧

"Has she gone?"

Father Morozov nodded. "But she will be back, comrade."

Downstairs in a stuffy back room in the church, Arkin was seated at a table beside a mountain of red-printed pamphlets. He was folding each of them to hand out at the next meeting, running a thumbnail along the crease with a spurt of irritation. "Why doesn't she give up?"

"She is tenacious, that one." Morozov patted a hand on the heap of pamphlets that declared, *UNITE! POWER TO THE WORKERS!* "Like you," he added.

On a stool in the corner a nickel samovar burbled softly and an uneaten *pirog* lay beside it on a tin plate. The priest glanced over at it. He frowned.

"Viktor, if you want your wound to heal you must eat. You must sleep."

"Not yet, Father."

"When?"

Arkin lifted his eyes from the pamphlets. He was thinner—he had noticed that himself, his cheeks hollow between the sharp bones of his face—and the gray of his eyes had grown darker. Even Elizaveta Ivanova had commented on it. She liked to stare at his eyes for long periods, as though the secret of who he was could be found in them if she looked hard enough.

"When the job is done," Arkin said. "When the Romanovs are buried in a pit. Then I will lead a normal life again."

The priest's face folded into deep furrows. "It may be too late then," he said softly. "You may have forgotten how."

❧

A LETTER ARRIVED FROM CAPTAIN STEPAN CHERNOV. JUST the sight of its envelope with its crest crisply stamped on the seal made Valentina want to tear it into a thousand pieces. She took it into her father's study and handed it to him unopened.

He read it in silence. "The captain is in Switzerland," he informed her, "taking a spa cure for his injury. He doesn't expect to be back in

Petersburg till the end of the summer." She heard the relief hiding in his words. They looked at each other with understanding, and she nodded.

"Not long, Papa. You have till then. Whatever loans you have secured against the Chernov necklace will have to be repaid or relocated by the autumn because I will have to return the jewelry to him then."

"If you cared at all for your sister, you would marry the man." He crumpled the letter in his fist.

Valentina shook her head. "Please, Papa. It must be possible to find the money. Somewhere. Sell everything. Sell our house in Tesovo or even sell . . ."

Her father sank low in his chair behind the wide expanse of his desk, which was piled high with manila files and folders that threatened to topple on him. His cheeks were the dull color of overripe plums. "The banks already own everything we possess, Valentina. But I will try."

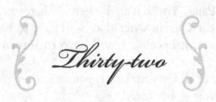

## Thirty-two

*DESPITE MY FATHER.*
  *Despite Arkin's disappearance off the face of the earth.*
  *Despite the wounds I bandage in the hospital wards and the patients I've seen die.*
  *Despite my mother being rarely at home and the heat of the city being worse than I can ever remember.*
  *Despite my hands looking like someone else's hands.*
  *Despite all this, it is the happiest summer of my life.*

❧

THE SUMMER WAS SLOW IN COMING. IT HUNG BACK LIKE a girl at her first ball. It started pale and tentative, the leaves on the lime trees reluctant to unfurl and the sun skulking behind clouds. St. Petersburg felt gray and tired. Factory smoke hung in a sooty pall above the roofs, too exhausted to move. But just when Valentina resigned herself to cold winds from the Gulf of Finland and no picnics with Katya this year, the season launched itself on them and transformed it into a gleaming glowing city of gold.

It was the first year of her life that they did not spend the summer months on their estate at Tesovo. Valentina did not inquire why.

It was obvious. Her father was preoccupied and spent all his time either at the ministry or locked away in his study with a crop of men in well-tailored frock coats and silk top hats coming and going all day with heavy attaché cases. But she had long ago determined she would never go near Tesovo again. How could she after what happened? How could Katya? And even sharper in her mind, Valentina knew she couldn't leave Jens.

It was a summer of walks, of arms brushing together, as his wound healed. The easy casual strength of him constantly astonishing her when he lifted her over streams or encircled her waist with his arm as she bent forward to pluck a ladybird from the surface of an ornamental pond. It was a summer of ice creams and dragonflies, of exploring the city, seeing it with new eyes because they were seeing it for the first time together.

She took him to concerts of Tchaikovsky and Stravinsky at the Alexandrinsky Theatre with its tall Corinthian columns, and he took her to Nikolaievsky Station to show her the wonders of the construction of its roof span and to explain in detail the workings of the shuddering steam engines. But she looked instead at the texture of his skin, at the dappled green of his eyes. Listened to the passion in his voice as he spoke, instead of to the labored breathing of the locomotives.

There was the day they sat with their feet dangling in the river, the scent of mown grass heavy in the air and a squall of mist over the water, as he explained plans for the dredging of Neva Bay to improve the water flow in and out of the city. Sharing an apple, bite for bite.

There was the day they took Katya to the forest, where a deer fed from her hand, and then to St. Isaac's Cathedral, where Katya cried because it was so beautiful.

There was the day he kissed her on the steps of the Hermitage.

There was the day she and her mother stood at a window, watching Jens in the garden with Katya. He was straightening a spoke on the wheel of her chair, and she rested a hand on his shoulder as he crouched. And her mother saying in her ear, "Do you realize how much your sister loves him?"

And just as the tail end of summer dipped into autumn she sat with Jens in an open carriage under the velvet darkness of a night sky, counting the stars, and she told him she was pregnant.

❧

WILL YOU MARRY ME?" JENS ASKED.
Valentina's heartbeat echoed in her ears. He took her hand and pressed it to his lips, turned it over and kissed its wrist. The moonlight sculpted his face into cold marble, but his eyes were burning with life.

"Will you do me the honor of marrying me, Valentina Ivanova?"

"Yes."

"Tomorrow?"

She laughed. Joy tight and unyielding in her throat. "As soon as you like."

"Now."

She closed her eyes. When she opened them again, he was still there. Still owning her hand.

"Jens, I swore to Katya that I would never leave her."

"Then she can come and live with us. My land deals with Davidov have done far better than I expected, so I shall buy us a splendid new house. With room for your sister as well."

He said it so effortlessly. As if it were such a small thing.

"Thank you, my love."

He held her face between his hands. "I love you," he murmured, and softly touched her lips with his own.

"I won't break," she laughed.

He drew her to him on the carriage seat and held her so close she could barely breathe. "I will speak to your father tomorrow."

"He won't like it."

"He shall have to get used to it." His hand found her stomach and started to caress its still-flat outline.

"A boy," she whispered. "An engineer to build a new Petersburg."

"A girl," he smiled. "I want a girl."

"With my hair and your eyes."

"And your talent for music. A girl who will fly high with courage and ambition. A girl with an agile mind. Like her mother."

A fretful wind tugged a strand of her hair across her face, and she shivered.

"You're cold," he said.

"No. Excited."

He sat up and wrapped her in the warm rug, tucking it under her knees and around her neck. "I shall drive you home at once. You mustn't catch a chill."

"Jens, I am not ill! I am pregnant."

He smiled at her, a look so tender in the silvery moonlight that her heart forgot to beat. But then he snapped the reins at the horse with a determined crack, and as he did so, she saw a pulse flicker at his throat. She would have reached out to touch it had her arms not been pinned under the rug.

"Jens, it is my father's birthday tomorrow. He has booked seats at the theater for the family and dinner at A'lours afterward." The words tasted like soap on her tongue. "Please let him have tomorrow. Ask him the day after."

He whirled around to look at her. "God, give me strength! Haven't I waited for you long enough?"

"No," she smiled at him.

"One day. No longer."

౭౭

THE FOLLOWING DAY A FAINT DRIZZLE BROUGHT TO AN end the stifling heat that had been gripping the city by the throat. The theater was a dazzling blaze of lights when the Ivanov family took their position in their box on the first tier, with its gilded scrollwork and plush velvet chairs. Below them in the auditorium the swell of voices rose. The elite of St. Petersburg society flashed their jewels and their gold medals at each other, competing with the glittering chandeliers for preeminence. The smiles were fixed, held in place beneath magnificent diamond tiaras that dragged many of their owners into such ferocious debt that it set grubby moneylenders rubbing their hands in anticipation. But to be seen at the opera in anything less would risk ostracism and scorn.

Valentina hated it, but the music helped. It always did. Once the lights dimmed and the opera *The Legend of Tsar Saltan* took flight, Rimski-Korsakov's dramatic arias gave Valentina something to hold on to. She closed her eyes and let the notes come alive within her. She breathed more freely, picturing the room in Jens's apartment. A reindeer rug soft as a kitten's paw in front of the log stove. The touch of its fur on her naked back and Jens's lips moving against the warm skin of her stomach, murmuring to the infant growing inside her.

"Valentina, my dear girl, how exquisite you look tonight. You outshine the chandeliers."

Her eyes flashed open. "Captain Chernov!"

His scarlet figure was seated right beside her. With a ripple of shock she realized that it was intermission and the others, including Katya in her chair, had withdrawn to the small anteroom to drink wine, eat caviar, and greet guests who had hurried in to pay their respects. He had not changed. All that pain and suffering, yet he had not changed. Just the teeth a little sharper, the eyes a little angrier.

"You didn't reply to my letters, Valentina."

"I am pleased to see you well again, Captain. I didn't know you were back in Petersburg."

"I wrote to tell you I would be here."

She had read none of them.

"I did write once," she said. "To inform you that the engagement was at an end."

He laughed, a quick bark of sound, and bared more of his teeth at her. He seized her white-gloved hand from her lap and trapped it between his own. "You young ladies like to tease."

"No." She tried to remove her hand, but he gripped it hard.

Slowly, never taking his eyes from her, he raised her hand and pressed the back of it against his lips. Even through the fine leather she could feel the individual bristles of his mustache.

"Let me go."

They were leaning toward each other, almost like lovers, their faces so close she could see a pink scar on his jaw that hadn't been there before. She lifted her other hand and grasped two of his fingers, prepared to snap them off if he didn't release her. Below in the theater, patrons were beginning to resume their seats and the hum of voices grew louder. Something made her look, a sense that she couldn't explain, but suddenly she knew beyond doubt that Jens was here. At the far side of the auditorium she saw him, his hair windblown, as though he had rushed in from the street to see her. And now, he was seeing her. With one of her hands at the lips of this captain of Hussars, the other clutching two of his fingers, her face flushed and close to Chernov's. She moaned and leapt to her feet, at last breaking his grip on her.

"Jens!" she called, indifferent to the surprised looks from below. But he had gone. "Damn you, Stepan," she said fiercely and ran from the box.

❧

SHE FOUND HIM IN THE BAR, SMOKING A CIGARETTE AND leaning against a marble column, indifferent to the crowd jostling around him.

"Jens, I didn't know you were here."

"Obviously."

"Captain Chernov was just saying hello."

"A friendly hello, it seemed."

"No"—she rested her fingers on the sleeve of his jacket, trying to find him—"it wasn't what it looked like. Jens, please, don't—"

A shout came from outside. A man in a cape and top hat that glistened with raindrops stood in the doorway.

"The prime minister has been shot!" He bellowed the words again and again. "The prime minister has been shot!"

There was a collective gasp in the bar. Jens wrapped an arm around Valentina's waist and barged a path through the throng of drinkers to the man's side.

"What happened?"

"*Bozhe moi*, my God, he was at the theater in Kiev tonight. One of those murderous revolutionaries drew a gun. He shot Stolypin in the chest. No bulletproof vest." Tears were running down the man's face.

"Is he dead? Tell me, man," Jens demanded.

"They say he's dying."

"Stolypin dying. God help Russia!"

"*Bistro!*" The man yelled into the smoke-filled room. "Get out of here. *Bistro!* Quick! They say that the revolutionaries are coming to every theater tonight. In Kiev. In Moscow. To massacre us even here in Petersb—"

He didn't finish. The crowd lunged, panic wrenching them from their stupor, as they dropped their glasses and fled.

❧

VALENTINA HAD NEVER SEEN PANIC BEFORE. NOT LIKE this. Screams and shouts, feet pounding and voices falling apart. On the pavement outside the theater, slick with rain, hats were trampled underfoot as the crowd grew desperate. Elbows pushed and barged as people rushed to their carriages, calling for the coachmen, indifferent to the shouts of police in heavy cloaks who appeared from nowhere. Valentina was buffeted by an officer as she ran, wide-eyed with dismay.

"Jens, it can't be true, can it?"

They were scouring the curbs for her family, but umbrellas hid heads from view, and top hats all looked alike in the darkness.

"That Stolypin is dead?"

"No." She shook her head, her shoulder tucked hard against his. "That the revolutionaries are attacking every theater. Surely it can't be true."

"It's most likely a rumor to create chaos and fear. But we can't take any chances, so stay close."

"Why?" She dug her heels in, so that Jens was forced to halt in the surging crowd and look down at her. "Why? What would they gain by causing such chaos?"

"Let's just find your carriage."

"No." She shook his arm. "Tell me, what is it you fear?"

He looked at her intently. "I fear that someone has organized this and is doing something under the cover of this panic."

"Doing what?"

"I don't know. Come, don't stop now."

He pulled her forward, and she pointed ahead toward the jumble of carriages blocking the road. "There. It's Papa's."

Jens shouldered his way through, until they found her father and mother standing beside their carriage in the rain. The wheelchair waited empty and forlorn in front of them.

"Where's Katya?" Valentina asked quickly.

"She's gone."

❧

WHO WOULD TAKE HER?"
      Jens had to ask the question twice. Elizaveta Ivanova was holding herself rigid, her eyes unfocused and her movements jerky as her fingers touched her mouth but her lips remained silent and unco-operative. Her husband was the reverse. Streams of anger poured from him; his feet stamped the ground and he jabbed a finger at one of the group of policemen who had gathered around them. "Get

out there, you fool, and find my daughter," he shouted. "She's been kidnapped."

They were all back at the theater standing in the rain outside a side door. It was the one from which the Ivanovs had first emerged, carried along by the rush for the exits, with Katya safe in her wheelchair.

"Madam Ivanova," Jens asked, "tell me again what happened."

She didn't look at him. Her mouth quivered but no sound emerged.

"Elizaveta!" her husband urged.

Jens placed himself directly in front of her, took both her elbows firmly in his grip, and drew her closer, so that she had to focus on him. "Was Katya hurt in the crush?"

She shook her head, blinked hard, and murmured, "*Nyet*. She didn't panic. Just held tight to her chair." She drew her fair eyebrows together, frowning at the images ransacking her brain. "She . . ." The words stopped.

Jens lowered his face to hers. "What happened?"

"My husband went off to find our carriage."

"Think, madam. Think. The minister left you and Katya here . . . and then?"

"Princess Maria and her husband came out behind me."

"You spoke to them?"

He was losing her. Her gaze grew glassy as she nodded. "She was screaming."

"Katya was screaming?"

"No." It was a whisper.

"Princess Maria was screaming?"

No answer. He shook her gently and saw her eyes roll.

"Yes. She'd fallen. Her cheek was . . ."

"You spoke to them?"

"Yes." She shuddered. "There was panic everywhere. When I turned back to the wheelchair, it was empty."

"Mama." It was the first time Valentina had spoken. Her voice was calm but sounded hollow, as if it came from far away. "Was Katya frightened? By the panic and the shouting."

"No. No, she was excited."

Valentina nodded. She seized Jens's hand and started to pull him away. "Quickly. Come with me."

"Where are you going?" her father demanded. "What about your sister?"

"Papa. I'm going to find her."

Rain was sliding down Valentina's cheeks, and the light of street-lamps and carriages skidded off her bone-white face, changing its shape. Her eyes were the harsh color of coal.

❧

SHE RODE ON HIS HORSE WITH HIM. IT WAS QUICKER BY horse than in a *drozhky* cab. The roads were crammed with traf-fic, lights streaked through the darkness, and the rain grew heavier, drumming on carriage hoods with impatient fingers. Tempers flared and accidents occurred, causing more confusion.

Jens's horse, Hero, sidestepped it all neatly, with Jens guiding him up onto the sidewalks when necessary, until they were free from the blockages and could canter unhindered through the center of the city. They rode fast. Jens felt the heat from her. Could smell her wet hair. She was tucked inside his riding cape in front of him, her body like a furnace against his chest and her grip on the horse's mane so fierce it almost tore the hairs from the animal's neck. She sat stiff-backed and tense. They had argued fiercely.

"Jens, it's the revolutionaries who have taken her."

"No, Valentina, think carefully. It could be just greedy kidnap-pers, holding her to extort money from your father." *Dear God, don't let it be the revolutionaries.* Their knives would slit an upper-class throat, male or female, as readily as they would slice open a chicken.

"No," she'd insisted. "No. It's them, I know it's them. They tor-ment my family and won't be satisfied until we are dead."

The air between them stretched thin, damp against their faces. He had come with her because he could not bear to let her go alone to the back alleys of Petersburg. But it was madness.

❧

THE FOUNDRY WORKER AND HIS WIFE—THE ONE WHO slept with dead children—were both at home. Jens looked around as he stepped into the room. At least it was cleaner than last time. They regarded him with narrow eyes, as though they would like to stamp on him the way he stamped on cockroaches. Both had their arms folded across their chests, the table between them, and he saw two mugs of beer on its surface. Drinking a toast? Drinking to success?

"He's dead," Ivan announced smugly. "Prime Minister Pyotr Stolypin is dead."

"Not yet," Jens corrected. "Wounded, I heard."

The woman was staring at Valentina. "What's wrong with her?"

"My sister," Valentina said. "Where is she?"

"The one in the wheelchair?"

"Yes. She's been kidnapped." Her voice was without emotion. "I believe your revolutionaries have taken her captive. I want you to go to your friends and ask where she is being held."

The couple shook their heads. Jens stepped forward and banged a fist on the table so hard that beer slopped onto it. "I will give you each six months' pay."

Their eyes brightened with hungry interest.

"Only if," Jens continued, "you find out where her sister is being held."

"Why would revolutionaries want to take her?" Ivan spat on the floor at his feet.

"To exert political pressure on her father, Minister Ivanov."

The man flexed his shoulders like a fighting dog. "And if we refuse?"

"Then I shall be obliged to insist."

❧

JENS WAITED WITH LESS PATIENCE THAN VALENTINA. THE room with its damp walls and cracked ceiling felt small and suffocating to his restless mind. Each time the woman threw a log on the fire, smoke billowed out, settling on the furniture and in their lungs. The truth was as hazy and insubstantial as the smoke, it seemed to him.

The truth of what a person believed and the truth of what they said were two different things. There was no hard-and-fast line to draw under it because it shifted between shadows and sunlight. A changing shape. The Bolsheviks and Mensheviks were forever tearing strips off their so-called truth as they jostled for power, worse than jackals on a carcass, crying out for justice and equality. Kidnapping a young girl. What kind of justice was that? What kind of equality, the weak devoured by the strong?

They sat at the table, Valentina's hand in his. The woman watched them, tightening her headscarf every now and again, as she crouched by the fire drinking her beer. For two hours they remained like that. He could see the thin shreds of tension in Valentina's eyes, could almost see her brain turning, hear the cogs and chains whirring, and he feared for her safety. At one point she squeezed his hand and stared at him, unblinking. His watch over her was vigilant, but not vigilant enough.

When four men in ragged jackets and sodden caps barged into the room behind Ivan, bringing the chill night air with them, Jens rose to his feet. Valentina didn't look at the men, as if she already knew what they would say. Ivan strode over to the fire for warmth.

"Well?" she asked mildly. Her eyes were on Jens.

"You," Ivan pointed at her, "come with us. You," he pointed at Jens, "stay here."

"No!" Jens moved purposefully toward her, but she jumped in front of him and seized his face between her strong hands.

"I'm sorry, my love," she whispered as her lips touched his.

That was when the floor leapt up at him and a noise like a firecracker exploded inside his skull. He could feel his brain fracture into a thousand glass pieces. When the pain of the blow reached him at last, it tipped him into an empty black pit.

# Thirty-three

RAIN DRIPPED INCESSANTLY. COLD RIVULETS OF IT BURST through the roof of the *izba* cottage and fell like gunshots into the zinc buckets. Viktor Arkin hardly noticed the sound. His feet paced the rotting floorboards and his mind chased a thousand answers to the questions that pounded through his head.

Were they coming?

How much did she know?

What had she seen?

Was the girl a pigeon laid out by the Okhrana to ensnare him?

Who could he trust?

It was always the same, this looking over his shoulder. It was the price he paid.

He had prepared the room. But she would not be like her sister. She would be a constant danger; he had to tread warily. He had perceived the strength behind the wide dark eyes and despite her young age he knew she would tear him limb from limb if he gave her the chance. Yes, he was prepared.

He ceased pacing and stared out of the small grubby window. Three o'clock in the morning, what did he expect? The blackness outside was impenetrable, drowning any other sounds under the relentless onslaught of wind and rain. The peasant's cottage was flimsy, its rooms small, but it did the job well enough. Far from anywhere, it sat in the middle of a flat ocean of marshy land through which ran one single dirt road that was raised above the level of the fields to avoid flooding.

For an hour he stood at the window, ears alert for the rumble of a cart, but all the time he could not keep their mother from his mind. She slid in uninvited. The secret pale hollows of her skin, the mound of glorious curls at the base of her stomach like a vivid splash of butter. The taste of it in his mouth. And now the memory of her blue eyes would not let him rest. Wide with glazed shock. Her voice calling his name as he ran from the theater through the rain with her daughter in his arms. He had to make her hate him, so that he could be free of her.

An hour later, they still hadn't arrived. Arkin lifted the kerosene lamp from its hook on the beam and unlocked the door behind him. The sulfur-yellow light leapt in ahead of him, crawling up onto the ceiling and tunneling into the solid blackness that lay like a wall across the room. The girl was huddled on the bed. He called her *the girl* in his mind, never *Katya*. It was better that way. Safer. That way he could look at her and not feel sick for her. *The girl.*

He raised the lamp high. Her eyes stared back at him, huge and accusing, her lips trembling.

"Go away," she whispered.

"Are you cold?"

She shook her head.

"In pain?"

Another shake. *Liar,* he thought.

"Go away," she whispered again.

If he went, the darkness would be absolute once more because he couldn't risk leaving her even a candle. So he leaned a shoulder against the door frame, put the lamp on the floor, and lit himself a cigarette, exhaling loudly to cover the soft panting of her breath.

"Don't die on me," he said.

She pulled the meager blanket up over her face. "Go away," she whispered a third time, and it came out as a muffled hiss, no louder than the hiss of the lamp. For a full minute he studied the unmoving shape on the bed, and he waited for her to shout at him. But she didn't, so he took up the lamp, left the room, and locked the door. It was easier that way.

❧

THEY BROUGHT IN THE OLDER SISTER FROM THE CART, handling her with a roughness that made him want to slap them. He'd chosen these three men for the job because they were not so hotheaded and would keep their hands off her. But they had been driving the cart in the teeming rain for too many hours, changing routes and doubling back through the forest to avoid being followed. Now they were wet and bad tempered, and they took it out on her.

She looked small, far smaller than he remembered. Soaked to the skin, hair plastered to her head, and teeth chattering, which she tried to hide. Yes, he reminded himself, this girl above all others would hate for him to think she was frightened. They pushed her into the chair at the table, the blindfold still in place, her hands fastened behind her back with a leather thong. He could see it biting into the skin of her wrists, carving red weals like candy stripes.

He took the chair opposite her.

"I know who you are," she said before he had spoken. "Don't think you can hide."

He waited. Imagining the things in her head. Blind and drenched, thrust into a room that smelled of men, listening for their breath to count how many. Her words were her only weapons. Somewhere she had lost her coat and had no idea how her wet evening gown clung to her body, its pale silk almost transparent, outlining her slender curves and turning her into one of those dolls that children dress and undress at will.

"I know who you are," she repeated. Her voice was controlled, but he heard the rage in it. "You are Viktor Arkin. You were my father's chauffeur."

There was no reason to add those last words, except to remind him that he was dirt. He yanked the blindfold from her face and watched her squint against the sudden light, long strands of her dark hair clinging like tendrils to her throat and cheeks as though they could protect her.

"As you see," he said pleasantly, "you are correct. How shrewd of you."

Her eyes adjusted, pupils slowly shrinking, but she could not quite keep the scorn from her face. "It wasn't hard."

"Count yourself lucky to be alive at all after that blade you stuck in my side."

"Where is she?"

"Who?"

Her mouth tightened with anger. "Where is she?"

"Asleep."

"I doubt that." She rose to her feet, and immediately two of the men seized her arms. They could have snapped them with no effort. "Take me to her."

"After we've talked."

"Please, Arkin." Her voice remained quiet. "Please take me to her. We can talk tomorrow when I am dry and you have had some sleep."

Did it show so clearly? That he had not put his head on a pillow for three nights. Each movement of his eyelids felt as though they were rolling over brick dust. He nodded curtly toward the door with the key in the lock. She was across the room, her forehead jammed against the wooden planks before he had time to give the order.

"Let her in," he snapped.

He walked into the other musty bedroom and lay down on a bare mattress in the dark, but he didn't sleep.

❧

KATYA!"
Valentina wrapped her arms around her sister on the narrow bed, aware of the animal smell of the sweat on her, though her skin was like ice.

"I'm all right," Katya said.

But Valentina knew that voice, the one when her back teeth were clenched against the pain. "Of course you are." Valentina pulled the blanket up around her. It stank of urine.

"Why are you here?" Katya asked, bemused. "Did they take you too? It's Arkin, do you realize that, the chauffeur? What is he going to do with us? Does Papa know? Valentina, you're wet, take your dress off, you mustn't . . ."

"Hush, my sweet, hush." She took her hand. "Calm down, we're together now. There's no need to be frightened. Arkin won't hurt us."

"He will."

"No. I will speak to him in the morning. When it's light. Tonight he wasn't . . ."

"Why us?"

"Oh, Katya, I don't know. He must intend to pressure Papa into doing something."

Katya groaned. "Papa will never do anything against the tsar, not even for us."

"Hush, we don't know yet. Let's wait until morning. It can't be long now. Try to sleep."

"You must take your dress off. You're shivering."

"No. Not with those men outside the door."

The room was in darkness, but a thin rat's tail of lamplight crept under the door and even squeezed between its planks in places where the wood had warped. Valentina slid off the bed, went over to the door, and banged on it with her fist.

"Open the door," she shouted.

No answer.

She banged again. "I want to speak to you."

"Shut the fuck up," an unknown voice growled.

"Open the door."

"Shut up, bitch."

She kicked the door viciously, and it rattled on its hinges. "I want dry clothes."

"Piss off."

"Dry clothes and another blanket. A bucket. And a candle." She kicked the door again and swore under her breath.

She waited. When she was sick of waiting she started with her fists again.

"Stop that." It was Arkin.

A key grated in the lock and the door swung open. At once the light bounced in and Valentina caught sight of Katya on the bed, her teeth clenched so tight on her lower lip that there was a trickle of blood, like a spill of black ink on her chin.

"Here," Arkin said sourly. "Clothes, a blanket, a bucket. No candle."

The door started to close.

"Wait."

It paused.

"My sister needs medication for her pain."

"No."

The door slammed shut.

"Damn you, Arkin," Valentina yelled, and kicked the door hard. "I hope you burn in hell."

❧

THE WINDOW WAS SHUTTERED. AND INSIDE A HEAVY grille had been bolted across it, but nevertheless the air in the room shifted from black to gray and a whisper of daylight trickled through its slats. They both used the bucket. Valentina had to support her sister on it. As she held her upright on the floor, she noticed that Katya was taller than she was. When had that happened?

They spoke in low voices. Hands clasped. Katya kept her eyes fixed on Valentina, as though she feared she might not be real, and let her massage her feet to keep the blood flowing through them.

"You shouldn't have come," Katya said. "It doesn't matter if something happens to me, but how will Jens survive without you?"

"Nothing will happen to us, silly. I wasn't going to let you run away from home without me."

Katya laughed, a soft bubble of sound, and rubbed the back of her neck. "You didn't want me to have all the excitement."

Valentina stroked the small hand. "Tell me, Katya, do you curse me every day for going riding that morning at Tesovo?" It was a question she'd never asked before.

"Of course not."

"You wouldn't have gone into the study if I had remained at home."

"Yes, I would. You're not the one who sent me there to fetch a pen."

Valentina's heart stopped. "Who did?"

"Papa."

❧

VALENTINA KEPT HER HANDS IN FRONT OF HER ON THE table as instructed. They were tied together with a leather thong, but not as tight as last night in the cart. It had made her fingers swell. She flexed them now, the flesh raised in white bars across the knuckles, and she let her mind escape for just one fleeting second to the ivory keys.

"Valentina!"

She looked at his hands, which had thick spade-shaped tips on the fingers and a wide hardened span across the palm. A worker's hands? A killer's hands?

"Valentina, you are not paying attention."

"I am listening."

She pictured Jens's hands. Long-boned and muscular, touching the skin of her belly.

"You understand what I'm saying?"

"Yes."

"I will be back this evening. One of my men will remain here in the meantime. I will know by then whether your father will pay."

"How much?"

"Half a million roubles."

She gasped. *Half a million roubles.*

"Arkin." Her eyes fixed on his face. It was tense, stubble darkening his jaw. "Arkin, you are crazy if you think my father has that kind of money."

He leaned back in his chair. He was smoking a cigarette and exhaled a curl of smoke with annoyance. "You forget," he said, "that I have been inside your house. I have seen the paintings and the statues, the silver and the gold that lie unnoticed by you in every room. I've seen your mother's diamonds as big as turtle eggs, so don't—"

"No. He has no money."

"The minister can sell a necklace or two."

"He can't."

"He'll have to."

"You are too greedy."

"It is you and your kind who are greedy. You want to own all of Russia and divide its spoils between you. The millions of Russian workers and peasants have nothing because you have stolen it all." There was no doubting the ruthlessness of this man's conviction.

"You are one of the Bolsheviks," she stated flatly.

He did not bother to answer.

"Is the money for the revolution?"

"Of course. To finance the socialist cause. Did you think otherwise?"

This time it was she who didn't answer.

"Why did you shoot Jens Friis and Captain Chernov at the duel?"

A faint smile crossed his face, and for a moment she saw something of the polite chauffeur he used to be. "That is not important now." He rose to his feet. "I will be back here by this evening." He nodded at the man beside the door, whittling a stick with a knife. "Mazhik will guard you." Again that slight tilt of the mouth. "Don't annoy him."

Mazhik grinned and cleaned his blade on his beard.

"What will you do, Arkin, when my father says no?"

"You had better hope he doesn't."

She didn't push him further. "Before you go, will you please order Mazhik to open the shutters of our room?" She added, "We cannot escape. The metal mesh is enough. The light would make this . . . this"—she gestured to the locked door of the bedroom—"more bearable."

To her surprise he nodded curtly. No argument. She stood up. *Gently, tread gently.* "And medicine? Would you bring back some morphine, please, for Katya? She's . . . desperate, though she doesn't show it."

He nodded again and rubbed a hand over his stubble. It was the gesture of a tired man. "I promise you this, if I get money from your father today, she will get her morphine."

"If not?"

He shrugged and moved to the door that led outside. The overnight rain had dragged itself northward, and an empty blue sky hovered above as though waiting for something. Silky shreds of mist hung over the flat landscape, trailing gray fingers in the marshes where waterbirds squabbled as they bathed. As he strode down the steps he glanced back at her to ensure she wasn't trying to escape, but she remained standing meekly by the table. He studied her slight figure in the rolled-up trousers and bulky checked shirt.

"Those clothes look better on you than they ever did on me."

She clamped her tongue between her teeth and managed not to spit.

## Thirty-four

T HE WIND WAS CHILL WITH THE STREETS DARK AS THE devil without lamps or sidewalks as Jens moved silently through a maze of backstreets. He kept alert as they twisted and turned, splitting into dingy alleyways and courtyards that spilled into one another with no warning. The main thoroughfares were designed by Peter the Great to be the showpiece of the Western world, but behind the palaces and the magnificent façades, these overcrowded hives of the underclasses had spread like sores. Bitterness and resentment festered.

In front of one of the shabby houses, Jens walked down a flight of stone steps to a basement, wet and slippery underfoot. This was no place to live. Down below the water level. The swampland on which St. Petersburg was constructed liked to reclaim its own when the rain was heavy or the tides high. Basements flooded throughout the city, yet here people still lived in them. It was either that or sleep on the street. He banged at a door. It opened warily, and a woman in a flannel nightdress stared up at him.

"I'm looking for Larisa Sergeyeva," he announced. "Is she here?"

The woman blinked rapidly and backed away into the room behind her, allowing Jens to enter. My God, *bozhe moi*, Jens put a hand over his nose. In the unsteady light of two candles, he could make out that the room was large and stretched away into darkness but was packed right up to the low ceiling with bunk beds and bodies huddled together for warmth. There must have been thirty to forty people. Scraps of sheet were draped over a few of the beds in an attempt at privacy, and children lay on grubby mattresses on the floor.

"Larisa!" the woman in the nightdress shouted. "A gentleman visitor for you!"

Voices jeered good-naturedly and a thin young woman stepped forward from the shadows, a baby asleep in her arms.

"Larisa Sergeyeva?" Jens asked.

"*Da.*"

"I'd like a word with you."

"What about?"

"It's a private matter." He flicked a glance at the rows of eyes trained on them. "Outside, I think."

She didn't argue. She handed the baby to the woman who had opened the door and followed Jens up into the street. He saw her shiver. Good. He wanted her to be nervous. He led her into the slice of murky light that fell onto the road from a nearby window and inspected her. Her face was gentle, with shy uncertain eyes and light brown hair cut in a line at jaw level. One of her feet was kicking at the dirt road with quick jabs.

"You are the widow of Mikhail Sergeyev?"

"Yes." Her voice was soft. Pleasant on the ear.

"I believe he was a friend of Viktor Arkin."

Abruptly her foot stopped kicking. Her eyes lowered. "I don't know."

He could shake her. Till her teeth rattled and her soft lying tongue fell out. Instead he dropped his voice. "I think you do."

She shook her head and fingered her lips in silence.

"He brings food to you," Jens stated.

"Sometimes."

"I want to speak with him. Tonight."

Her eyes lifted nervously to his. "Who are you?"

"My name is Jens Friis."

"*Direktor* Friis?"

"Yes. Your husband worked for me."

"You helped us when he broke his arm." She touched his hand. "Thank you. *Spasibo.* We would have starved."

"The baby?"

"She's well."

"I wish I could say the same of Valentina Ivanova."

"What? I don't understand. Who is she?"

Jens lowered his face to hers and said fiercely, "Tell Arkin I want to see him. Now."

She shook her head and scurried back down the steps.

❧

S HE WASN'T CAREFUL ENOUGH, NOWHERE NEAR CAREFUL enough. Larisa Sergeyeva kept looking back over her shoulder as she ran down the alleyways, but at the wrong times and in the wrong places. Ten minutes after he left her, she set off from the house with a scarf over her head and something bulky in her pocket. He could see the way it dragged at her coat. She was too easy to follow.

He tracked her to a narrow passage with high brick walls on either side from which footfalls echoed, but she was running and would only hear the beating of her own heart. He moved in the shadows and merged with the wall when she stopped at the end of the passage, scanning its length. When she suddenly turned into the rear entrance of a noisy bar, he hung back under an archway. Almost immediately she emerged again, and behind her loped a dark figure who was careful to avoid the lamplight from the bar. They drew into a doorway and spoke in whispers. This was the man, the one who had left his fingerprints all over Petersburg. Jens drew a gun from his waistband and checked the pool of darkness behind him in the passageway. Never before had he killed a man, but this one would rot in hell before the night was over. He moved forward to the doorway.

"Arkin! Where is she?"

Arkin made no sound, but Larisa Sergeyeva released a sharp gasp. "I didn't bring him here, Viktor, I swear."

Jens ignored her. "Where is she?" The gun was aimed at the bastard's head.

Arkin stepped away from the woman. He came into the open and regarded Jens with a watchful stare. "The engineer," he said softly. "If you kill me, she will also die."

Jens lowered the gun till it was pointing at Arkin's right knee. "Listen carefully. If you ever want to walk straight again, talk now. Where are they?"

Arkin looked down at the gun and for a moment said nothing. "How did you know about Larisa?"

"You are not the only one with eyes and spies in this city."

"What do you—"

His voice was cut off as a massive arm came from behind and encircled his neck. The woman screamed.

"Remember our friend, Liev Popkov?" Jens slammed the gun into Arkin's jaw and heard him grunt. "He was tortured by the Okhrana police because of you. And let's not forget the hole in my chest because of you. It would give us both a great deal of pleasure to put a bullet in you in return."

"Let me rip his head off first," Popkov growled.

Larisa whimpered.

"No," Jens said. "A bullet in the right knee first, then in the left."

Arkin struggled in Popkov's grip, but it was like trying to escape from a bear and when his arm was twisted almost out of its socket, he stopped. Jens stepped closer, his voice harsh. "One last time, Arkin. Where is she?"

"Fuck off."

"It's your choice." He aimed the gun.

"Let him go." It was the woman.

She was pointing a revolver of her own at Jens. Her hand was shaking and she was shifting nervously from foot to foot, but at this range she couldn't miss.

"Larisa," Jens said quietly, "don't do this. You will ruin your life and your child's. Whatever you decide, I am going to blow this murdering bastard's leg off right now if he doesn't tell me where he's hiding the Ivanova daughters."

"If you do, I swear I'll kill you," she said. "I need his help, if I am to keep my baby alive."

"That's a risk I'll take."

She tightened the grip on her gun. He looked away from her.

"Arkin, where is Valentina?"

Arkin stared at the woman and kept his mouth shut. Jens drew a breath but before he could pull the trigger Popkov suddenly released his stranglehold on his prisoner and moved back from him. Before they could blink, Arkin was gone.

"What the hell are you doing?" Jens shouted at the big man.

"The little mouse would have killed you. What good are you dead to Valentina?"

❧

*H*OW MUCH DO YOU GIVE? THE QUESTION HUNG IN VAL-entina's mind. *What is the price? What is the price one person should pay and where do you draw the line? When do you say no, enough is enough?*

*Who says where guilt starts and where guilt ends?*

Valentina stood with her face pressed against the window grille, breathing in the scents of the wetlands and listening to the birds as if this would be the last time she would hear their songs. She squinted through the mesh toward the open-sided hut outside, where logs were stacked in untidy rows. A rat with half an ear ripped off stared back at her suspiciously from the woodpile.

"Valentina, do you think we'll go home tomorrow?"

She turned and faced her sister on the bed. Gray lines like the footprints of tears ran from her nose to the corners of her mouth. Valentina smiled. "Of course we will."

❧

*I*T WAS LATE WHEN ARKIN ARRIVED BACK AT THE *IZBA* THAT night and pushed open the door. Valentina heard it slam on its hinges and caught the drag of his footsteps across the boards. Not a good day then. The rumble of male voices lasted no more than a couple of minutes before the outer door slammed again and she heard Mazhik swear thunderously as he stomped off across the yard. Arkin didn't knock, just unlocked the door to their room and walked in. He didn't offer even that courtesy.

"*Dobriy vecher*, good evening," Valentina greeted him.

"Here is bread and water for tonight."

"Morphine?"

"*Nyet*."

"My father didn't pay?" Katya asked from the bed.

"No."

Katya shut her eyes, draped an arm across her face, and took no further part in the conversation.

"Nothing for her?" Valentina asked.

"No."

Her fingers itched to tear his eyes out.

❧

T HE POOR ARE EASY TO BRIBE. JENS COULD BUY THEIR
words but he didn't expect to buy their loyalty. The night had
proved futile. He cursed again and again.

*Valentina.* As he stalked the smoky rooms of the city's backstreets
he kept catching a glimpse of her out of the corner of his eye, in her
blue dress with that graceful swing of her hips and the way she tilted
her head in greeting. Her dark eyes teasing him. But each time he
turned around, she had vanished. *Valentina. Don't vanish, don't give
up. Stay here. Stay. With me.*

He had spoken with her father, and it had been a heated exchange.
Minister Ivanov was a man who did not take kindly to being told
what to do, but it was obvious he cared for his daughters and for
them had suffered the humiliation of begging on his knees. But
banks, wealthy friends, fellow government ministers, and even the
Jewish moneylenders had all said no. Half a million roubles. It was
too much when he was already in debt. But Viktor Arkin would
not accept less, that was what he had demanded for his revolution.
Jens sought to raise the money himself from the land he owned with
Davidov, but it didn't come close. Elizaveta Ivanova had sat rigid and
silent, her face the color of ash.

It was only halfway through that terrible day that it occurred to
Jens that maybe Arkin didn't want the money after all, and that was
why he had set it so high. What he wanted was to hurt the Ivanov
family. To make the sisters suffer, he had plunged his revolution
right into their lives. That was when Jens ceased talking to banks
and started haunting the back rooms and smoky cellars where men
with red pamphlets in their pockets gathered and talked of rage and
destruction and a new order.

❧

T HERE'S A PLACE."
"Where?"

"Somewhere"—the man with the freckled face waved a hand
toward the window of the gloomy bar they were in—"out on the
marshland."

Jens placed a fifty-rouble note on the table between them. "Where on the marshland?"

"I don't know. Honest, I've just heard about it. A long way out."

Jens gave an exaggerated sigh and put the note back in his pocket, but poured the man another shot of vodka. "Where?" he asked again.

"Look"—the man's eyes were indistinct behind pale ginger lashes, his hand not quite steady on the glass—"they'd kill me if I shot my mouth off."

Greed did strange things to people. Jens laid two fifty-rouble notes on the table.

∽

K ATYA'S BREATHING SETTLED INTO A RHYTHM. WAS SHE asleep? Or pretending? Valentina decided she had to risk it and slipped off the bed without disturbing her. In the dark she found her way to the door and scratched it softly with her fingernails. She paused, listened, and scratched again. She heard nothing, no footsteps, but before she could do it once more a whisper came from the other side.

"What is it?"

She put her lips to the crack of the door. "I need to talk to you."

No sound. Maybe a sigh. She waited, bare feet curling on the boards, her heart slamming against her ribs. There was the familiar noise of the lock. She watched for movement in the soft mound that was Katya but saw none, and a strip of amber light sneaked in through the small gap at the door, making Valentina blink.

"May I come out?"

"What for?"

"Please?"

Arkin's voice sounded different, as though he'd been drinking. She thrust her wrists out through the narrow space between door and frame and felt a leather thong tighten around them. She stepped out with her wrists bound in front of her, and he locked the door behind her.

"Now what?"

It must have been the early hours of morning, but he had obviously been sitting at the table under the kerosene lamp studying a set of maps, beside which stood a bottle of vodka and a glass. The glass was half full. She walked over and drank it. He folded the maps before she could look at them and regarded her with appraisal. She was wearing her silk evening gown, which had dried out during the day, brushed free of dirt as best she could, and her hair swung in tangled waves on her bare shoulders.

"You look"—he sought for a word—"delicate."

It wasn't exactly a compliment but it would do. There was a bruise on his jaw, and his eyes were heavy as though ready for sleep. *Not yet, Viktor Arkin, don't you fall asleep yet.* She sat down at the table and refilled the glass but didn't pick it up. Every movement was awkward with her hands tied.

"So?" he asked roughly.

"Sit down, please. I want to talk." She smiled at him to show she meant no harm. *Use your weapons,* Davidov had said.

He took the other chair, and she pushed the glass nearer him. The room was small and mean, uncared for, and she wondered to whom it belonged. Not to him. It was far too untidy to be his. It had a low smoke-stained ceiling and timbered walls with shelves and an icon in one corner. The place smelled of rotting wood, but there were no drips into the buckets tonight.

"My father said no?" she asked.

He nodded.

"Did he offer you anything at all for us?"

"No."

"Did you speak to him face to face?"

He looked at her with a stare that made her feel foolish. "Of course not. Written messages were passed back and forth. I was very careful." He gave a slight snort. "No one followed me back here, if that's what you're thinking."

"No," she said, "I wasn't thinking that. I don't doubt your skill at avoiding capture. So what now? Will you release us?"

"No."

One word. Yet so much rage in it.

"So what will happen to us?"

He reached for the glass and drank it down in one swallow. His eyes were bloodshot. "You really want to know?" he asked tiredly.

"Of course." She licked her dry lips.

"Your father must be forced to open up his purse, so . . ." He stopped. Refilled the glass. A sinew was jumping in his neck. "So one of you will be killed tomorrow to demonstrate that we mean business, and then he will pay for the other's safety. It doesn't matter which one of you it is."

Something broke inside her. "I told you, my father doesn't have money. He is in debt to the banks, so it's no use expecting him to—"

"Shut up. No lies."

He placed the glass of vodka in front of her and she drank it down, but neither spoke for a long time; just the wind rattling the shutters kept them aware of a world outside the close confines of their own.

"Arkin," Valentina said, "I'm not lying. It needn't be like this. Have you no conscience?"

He didn't bother to respond but lit himself a cigarette. Even that task he did with precision despite the alcohol in his blood. When he rested his hand on the table she removed the cigarette from his grasp, inhaled on it, and blew out smoke in a thin line that stretched across the table to him.

"I promise you," she said softly, "you will get no money for your Bolshevik cause from my father because he is bankrupt. You will have to kill us both, Katya and me."

He took back the cigarette. "I have killed before."

That shook her. "It would be pointless. What would you gain except more police attention?"

He leaned his elbows heavily on the table. "What are you suggesting?"

She didn't let herself hesitate. "This." She reached forward with her bound hands and took his face between them, aware of the stiffening of his jaw as she touched him. She drew him toward her and kissed his mouth. It tasted of vodka and tiredness, lips hard and tight.

He seized her wrists and jerked her hands away. "What the hell are you doing?"

"You will receive no payment, not for my sister and not for me. So let Katya go." She paused and angled a teasing smile at him. "I am offering you a different kind of payment . . . if you will agree to release her tomorrow."

His eyes widened, and she couldn't tell whether it was astonishment or disgust. "You will sell yourself? Like a common street whore?"

"Yes." She flushed.

He stared at her so long she almost lost her nerve. It wasn't too late; she could snatch back the words, she and Katya could . . . could what?

Arkin stood up suddenly, swaying on his feet. "I agree. Both of you can go."

A tight sharp pain kicked inside her heart. "You promise?"

"I promise."

❧

S HE THOUGHT SHE WOULD THINK OF JENS. BUT SHE DIDN'T, and that made her want to weep.

She thought she would imagine that they were his lips nuzzling her thighs, his hungry fingers caressing her cold skin and delving into the dense mound of dark curls between her legs. She wanted to believe it was the weight of Jens's naked body pressing down on her, trapping her on the filthy mattress. But she didn't. Not even for one second. She could not bring Jens into this bed of betrayal. She banished him from her head so that his eyes could not watch what her legs were doing, how they entwined with those of this hated stranger, or see how her treacherous lips kissed the bare flesh of his shoulder.

Arkin didn't speak. He couldn't remove her dress completely because of the bonds on her wrists, but he undid what he could, stripped off his own clothes and lay down beside her at first. Touching her. Stroking her. Cradling her breasts but never looking at her face. Once he was on her and in her with her arms looped around his neck, he closed his eyes firmly and with each thrust released a mumbled jumble of words. But they were not meant for her. It was as if he were making love to someone else.

## Thirty-five

VALENTINA WOKE LATE. AN AX WAS CHOPPING SPLINTERS from her brain and her mouth tasted sour. Before she even opened her eyes she remembered the vodka, the full glass of it afterward. *Afterward.* The word lingered like oil on her tongue, and she longed to burn it off. A dull ache inside her reminded her of her body's resistance, but it was nothing to the other pain. The one that clawed at her heart.

"Valentina?"

She opened her eyes. Already it was light and Katya was leaning over her. "Are you all right? You were moaning."

Valentina sat up and waited for the room to stop swooping around her. "I'm fine."

"You don't look fine."

"Neither do you." Her sister's skin was a thin transparent film that looked as if it would tear if she touched it. "We'll be going home today. Arkin has promised to release us."

Katya frowned. "You believe him?"

"Yes. He promised. I'll call him in now."

Katya shook her head. "He's gone."

"Gone?"

"He left before it was light; I heard him. The other one is here, the one with the beard."

Something cold as granite tumbled into Valentina's stomach. Instinctively she put her hand over her unborn child. She raced to the door and hammered on it, shouting for Arkin, but Mazhik's voice swore at her and a folded piece of paper was pushed under the door. She snatched it up.

*You expect too much of life, Valentina Ivanova. I was drunk. My promise was worthless. Today I see clearly that you and your sister must be examples to your class and to all oppressors. It saddens me, but it must be done. Our small personal tragedies mean nothing in the storm that is sweeping through Russia. I would ask your forgiveness, but I know you have none in your heart for me.*

There was no signature. Valentina froze. Ice crawled through her veins.

"What is it?" Katya asked.

Valentina crushed the note in her hand, screwing it into a tight ball. "It's from Arkin."

Whatever was in her voice, Katya heard it. "What's the matter? Valentina, come here, what's happened?"

She didn't want Katya to touch her, didn't want Katya to smell him on her. "He broke his word," she said flatly. "He's changed his mind."

"You mean he isn't going to release us? Maybe Papa can find the money somewhere."

"No. I told you. He is bankrupt."

"Well, the police could be tracking us down right now."

Valentina gave a murmur of scorn. "They have no idea where we are being held. Arkin is too clever for them."

"I see." Katya's voice sounded far away. "So you think they will kill us."

Valentina wanted to lie, but she couldn't, not to Katya. "Yes, I believe that's why Mazhik is still here."

"To finish us off."

"Yes."

To her astonishment Katya's eyes brightened. She smiled. "So what are we going to do? Start another adventure?"

Valentina sat down on the bed. "I have an idea."

֍

MAZHIK!"
"What? I'm eating." His voice was surly. He hadn't bothered to bring them bread this morning. Why feed the dying?

"Mazhik," Valentina called through the door, keeping her tongue soft. "We know what is going to happen to us. We do not blame you for this, but we do not want to die with our souls impure, so we are offering up our prayers to our dear Lord Jesus Christ, savior of souls. We are asking the Blessed Virgin to intercede for us."

"So?"

"So, I beg you to let us have a candle to burn to consecrate our prayers."

"Fuck off."

"Mazhik, do not send us to suffer in hell for all eternity, I beg you. One candle. To cleanse our souls. It's a small thing to ask of a man of the people who will one day soon be in control of all Russia."

Katya's young voice joined hers in a piteous thin wail. "Please, Mazhik."

There was a grumbling outside, followed by the sound of a chair being pushed back. Valentina's and Katya's eyes fixed on the door. It opened a crack and the blackened stub of a candle was tossed in, and then the door banged shut again.

"A match?" Valentina called out.

After a moment a single match slid under the door. Valentina pounced on it. She picked up the pile of threads that they had shredded from one of the blankets and her silk gown in a bundle.

"It will burn well," Katya had pointed out. "You can wear the shirt and trousers."

"Ready?" Valentina asked.

Katya's blue eyes glinted with excitement as she clamped over her nose her handkerchief dipped in their drinking water. "Ready," she answered.

Valentina struck the match on the rough floor—they were committed now—and held the flame to the candle's wick. She waited for it to flare, then stood it in the heart of the nest of material piled against the inner wall of the room. It spat and crackled, but one lick of yellow flame was persistent and smoke began to billow from the planks. Valentina retreated to the bed beside Katya and draped the other blanket over their heads with just a spy hole to allow her to keep track of the fire's progress. She wrapped an arm firmly around her sister, who faced her with a wide smile.

"Valentina, I want you to know that there's no one on earth I'd rather burn to death with than you."

Valentina laughed grimly. "We won't die. I give you my word."

It didn't take long. In a matter of minutes they were both coughing and the flames were climbing like monkeys up the timbers. It was time. She held a strip of Arkin's shirt over her nose and took up position behind the door.

"Fire! *Pozhar!* Fire! Mazhik, come quickly. Help! *Na pomosch!* Help! *Bistro!*" Her fists hammered on the door the way her heart was hammering on her ribs. "Mazhik! Fire!"

Smoke filled the air, pouring under the door into the room outside, and she heard the key in the lock, Mazhik cursing her. Relief flooded her brain, making her light-headed. Or was that the lack of oxygen?

"You fool! *Dura!* What have you done?"

"Water!" she shrieked.

He turned and ran. In the few minutes it took him to seize a bucket and race to the water trough in the yard outside, Valentina had Katya wrapped in the blanket and hoisted her up on her back. Eyes stinging from the smoke, she stumbled through the door, through the living room and out into the crisp fresh air.

"Get a bloody bucket, you fool," Mazhik screamed at her. "If this house burns down, I shall kill you."

She almost laughed. He was going to kill her anyway. She sat Katya on the ground next to the woodshed and picked up a bucket beside the trough. Hurriedly she filled it, ran indoors, and hurled the water at the burning wall. Even she was amazed at how the flames were leaping to the roof rafters already, greedy in the speed with which they were devouring the *izba*. For several minutes she and Mazhik worked together with the buckets, back and forth to the trough, passing each other at a run.

It was on his fifth dash out the front door with his empty bucket that she stepped up behind him and brought a heavy log crushing down on his skull. He crumpled to the ground as though the strings working him had snapped, and she dragged him away from the house toward the store of logs.

"Is he dead?" Katya whispered.

Valentina crouched at his side and felt his neck for a pulse. "No."

"Thank God."

"The bastard would have killed us, don't forget."

"Valentina! We aren't like them."

"Aren't we?" Valentina looked across at her sister and asked again more thoughtfully, "Aren't we?"

But Katya was staring openmouthed at the house. The whole shabby building was on fire, flames crackling and spitting, punching holes in the misty air, painting it bright orange. The glow gleamed like sunlight on Katya's cheeks, and it struck Valentina that despite the pain she was in, her young sister looked more real, more engaged with life than she had been since that day in Tesovo. As though the fire in this dismal piece of deserted marshland had set something alight inside her. Time to move. Rope, she needed rope. At the back of the woodshed she found a length of it and quickly tied it around the man's wrists and ankles.

"Feel that," she muttered under her breath. "Feel what it's like to be helpless."

At the side of the shed was something else, something she had spotted from the window of their prison room: a small cart for shifting logs from the forest. It consisted of a large rectangular box on wheels with a long rope for towing it. She dragged it out and pulled it up to Katya.

"Your carriage awaits!"

Not once did Katya let a moan slip past her lips as her limbs were tucked into the cart.

"Let's go," Valentina said.

She fixed the rope around her shoulders like a sled dog in harness and set off at a fast pace. She didn't look back, but she knew the peasant cottage was still blazing fiercely and she was glad. She wanted it to burn. To become such a furnace that only ash would remain as she walked away, pulling her sister behind her over the rough road. All her shame, all her disgrace, all her betrayal, all of it, burned to nothing. Just dead white ash blown across the wetlands in the wind. No secrets. Nothing.

THE GOING WAS TOUGH. THE ROAD WAS STREWN WITH stones and potholes that jolted the cart but she didn't slow. The air tasted clean after the *izba*, though large areas of standing water on the wetlands had formed into mosquito-ridden ponds and stagnant channels on either side of the raised track. Feathery threads of mist clung close to its surface. The cart was difficult to maneuver and the rope cut into her shoulders, yet for no reason Valentina could understand, a fierce sense of joy possessed her.

Everything had changed. At the heart of her life now—at the heart of herself—Jens and their child were waiting. She knew he'd be angry with her for running off after Katya without him, and she fretted about the blow to his head, but none of that mattered when she pictured the life together that lay ahead of them. Years and years of it. Her head on his lap, his fingers combing her hair. Their thoughts interwoven. She wanted to be at his side long enough to watch his hair grow white and the lines deepen around his eyes as he smiled at her. To discover the secrets at the core of him and to know the intricate pathways of his strong mind.

What had happened in that *izba* behind her was over and done with, scorched away by the flames. In her mind she made herself lock the betrayal deep down in a dark and secret place where no one would ever seek it out. Only she would know where it lay, always able to find it by the smell of filth. But Katya was safe. They were both alive.

"Sing, Katya!" she shouted.

She heard a laugh and then her sister's voice reaching out into the morning air with a good army marching song. Where had she learned that? But almost immediately a shout stopped her in mid-stride, and the singing ceased abruptly. She whirled around to see that behind them on the road a man was approaching at a rapid pace, leading a long-eared white horse with a woman on its back, a heavily pregnant woman.

"Hey!" the woman called out. "Are you young ones in trouble? Out here on your own."

Valentina wanted to fling her arms around the horse and kiss its muscular neck. "We could do with a little help," she admitted.

The man was bearded, with a harsh guttural way of speaking and his front teeth missing, but his eyes were kind and his hands were gentle as he hitched the makeshift cart to the back of the horse using the rope.

"Look at you," the woman scolded. "Climb in with your sister. You look exhausted."

"No, thank you, I'll walk."

"It's three hours to Petersburg."

Three hours. No time at all. To walk into a new life.

～

ONE HOUR LATER THE FIRST RIFLE SHOT SLAPPED INTO the back of the cart and made Katya jump with shock. Valentina spun around and spotted Mazhik on the road behind. *Chyort!* He had found something to cut the ropes. By the time the second bullet snicked at the stones at her feet, she was pushing Katya's head down below the level of the cart's sides and the man had released his grip on the leading rein. He was dragging a gigantic ancient shotgun from the pack on the horse's back.

The roar it made as he pulled the trigger nearly ripped her ears apart. It startled the horse, which skittered sideways, ears flattened, but the shot stopped Mazhik in his tracks. He fired off one more wild shot, then shied away and retreated along the road, but that final crack of a bullet was too much for the horse. Its nerves leapt out of control, and with a loud whinny of panic the animal bolted down the track. The woman was a strong horsewoman and held on firmly, but the flimsy cart at the back was not built for such speed. Valentina screamed. She raced after the horse and her legs felt slow, too heavy, as though moving through mud, fighting for speed that wasn't there. She fixed her eyes on her sister's pale face. Katya's mouth opened but Valentina heard nothing, just the high-pitched eerie cry spilling out of her own mouth.

A wheel snapped off and the cart slammed one corner on the ground. Nails split, splinters of wood spiraling up into the air as the horse veered off to one side. The rope snapped. In Valentina's head everything slowed. She saw the moment piece by piece, as if it had shattered. The wheel whirling back toward her, the cart leaping like an unwieldy dolphin in a wide arc into the murky channel beside the road. The splash of water rising in a rainbow of colors, the awful sucking sound as mud and water seized their prize, and Katya's body sank under the surface.

"Katya!"

Valentina leapt into the channel. The water came only to her waist and she plunged her hands under the upturned edge of the cart, twisting it over. Immediately Katya's head bobbed above the water and though her face was covered in black slime like witch's weeds, she spat the filth from her mouth and cursed Mazhik when Valentina grasped her tightly in her arms.

"Enough adventure for you?" Valentina hissed.

Katya gave her a crooked smile. "I always liked swimming."

"Next time get out of the cart first."

"Next time I'll . . ." But she started to shake.

*"Bistro!"* Valentina shouted to the man to help her. His wife had the horse under control and was holding out a blanket for Katya. *"Spasibo,"* Valentina said gratefully.

The people of Russia were kind; Valentina felt it keenly. Something soiled and selfish corrupted their souls when they lived too long in Petersburg, but out here in the wide open spaces of this country the heart of Russia still beat strongly. It gave her hope.

In the distance ahead of them a lone horseman was galloping hard toward them, his cape flying out behind him. The bearded man murmured a word of warning and reached once more for his gun, but Valentina seized his arm.

"No!"

Even at this distance she knew who it was. Jens.

# Thirty-six

VALENTINA WALKED BEHIND JENS AS HE CARRIED KATYA into the house and up the stairs. Dimly she was aware of her mother crying, of Nurse Sonya fretting, of servants rushing to open doors. Words rebounded off the walls and off her skin. Sounds entered her ears but didn't reach her brain. All she saw was the long line of his back. His cape was wrapped around Katya, so that his jacket was what she saw and the way the blades of his shoulders shifted under the material. She noticed how his white collar nudged at his hairline, the width of his strong neck, the length of his limbs, the loose-jointed way of moving as he strode up the stairs.

She needed to draw all these things inside her again. As if she had lost them. Her eyes devoured them all. As soon as Katya was in her bed with people crowding around it, Valentina led Jens downstairs to the music room. He closed the door and took her in his arms. Held her fast against him. Neither spoke.

She rubbed her cheek against his cheek, her hair against his throat, even her legs twined around his legs like a cat, imprinting her scent on him and taking his scent on her. They stood together in the room, her body slowly molding to the shape of his bones once more, ousting the dents and hollows where someone else's weight had left its mark on her. When he kissed her mouth hard and she tasted him once more, she started to feel clean.

❧

SHE WATCHED FROM ABOVE AS DR. BELOI SHOOK HANDS with her father in the marble-floored hall below, took his top hat, and left. He must have made a joke of some sort because they both chuckled. A good sign. She hurried down the stairs.

"What did he say, Papa?"

Her father looked older. These few days seemed to have sucked the last strands of his youth from him, so that his shoulders slumped, but there was something softer in the lines around his mouth when he spoke to her.

"Katya's going to be all right. Dr. Beloi has given her something to make her sleep. A few days' bed rest and extra medication should bring her back to her usual self, that's what he says."

He smiled, surprising her. She smiled back. A tentative connection once more.

"I'm so relieved," she said, and started up the stairs again, but she stopped halfway and turned. "Papa, thank you."

"For what?"

"For trying to raise the money for our release. It must have been . . ." She sought for a word. *Humiliating? Degrading? Belittling?* In the end she just said, "It must have been difficult."

He nodded but brusquely, unwilling to discuss it. He looked up at her and fingered his side whiskers in a self-conscious gesture. "And you? I hope you are all right after your ordeal?"

"Yes, Papa. I'm all right."

"Nothing bad happened, except for Katya falling out of the cart?"

"No, nothing bad happened."

"Good. You did well to find her."

He walked back into his study and shut the door. It made no difference to her that he was the one who had sent Katya into his study at Tesovo, though he'd never voiced it. She knew that if she had taken Katya with her for that dawn ride to the forest, her sister would not have been at her father's beck and call. They'd have eaten breakfast and rushed straight down to the creek to swim. He may be as guilty as she was, but it altered nothing.

❧

THE FEVER STARTED THAT NIGHT, THE SICKNESS BY THE next evening. Katya's skin burned at first with a fierce dry heat that gave her cheeks a flush and made her eyes bright. But when the vomiting began, her eyes dulled to the color of the Neva Bay, and the hand that held a handkerchief to her mouth shook.

It was cholera. Dr. Beloi announced it and ordered Elizaveta Ivanova to take precautions. The house was quarantined, closed to all visitors, and Katya was moved to a room away from the family bedrooms. The servants were ordered to avoid that end of the house. Everything was scrubbed again and again, as Nurse Sonya ordered her assault on the illness with all the vigor of a military campaign. It was the stagnant water in the marshland channels, the doctor said, the infection lying in wait in the foul water like a spider in its web. She had swallowed it. And now it was swallowing her.

❧

WEAR THIS MASK, VALENTINA."
"Will it help?"

Jens cupped his hand over her nose and mouth as though he could guard them. "It's a surgical mask. Dr. Fedorin gave it. It is essential that you don't breathe her air."

She nodded, her eyes huge above his fingers, and he wanted to pluck her out of that house of sickness. They were by the stables, the sound of hooves on cobbles echoing around them.

"You promise me? You will wear it always?"

She nodded.

"Don't kiss her," he said.

Her eyes flinched, but she nodded and he released his hold over her face. She touched a finger to his cheek.

"I will protect our child," she promised.

"Protect yourself."

He leaned forward to kiss her, but she turned her head away. "Don't kiss me. Don't risk yourself."

He pulled her to him and pressed his lips to hers.

❧

VALENTINA WAITED OUTSIDE ST. ISABELLA'S HOSPITAL, impatient as she watched the nurses descend the wide steps at a leisurely pace at the end of their day shift. There was a smell in the air of something burning, but she took no notice. It happened regularly now. A shop burned down, a warehouse torched, to teach bosses not to shut down unions or enforce punishing work methods.

"Darya!" she called at the sight of the figure with the spiky black hair.

"Valentina! What are you doing here? Can't keep away even though—"

"Darya, listen. You know the empress's monk who sometimes comes to the hospital wards."

"Grigori Rasputin?"

"Yes. How do I contact him?"

Darya rolled her eyes and laughed. "*Durochka!* You idiot! Stay away from that mad—"

"How? How do I find him?"

"They say he has an apartment on Gorokhovaya near the Fontanka River and that the highest ranks of society flock to him there, when he's not twisting his filthy mind around the Empress's . . ." But she didn't finish. Valentina had gone.

❧

THE ATMOSPHERE WAS CLAUSTROPHOBIC. THE BIG UNTIDY man who swaggered into the room was wearing an expensive black satin tunic and high black boots, but Valentina recognized him at once.

"I remember you," he declared. "The little nurse who slapped my face."

Father Grigori Rasputin pointed his finger at her, his strange blue eyes fixed on Valentina as he strode toward her. She leapt to her feet. She intended to seize him before he could be distracted by anyone else. The room was large but stifling, as dust floated in bars of sunlight that bleached the carpet and softened the sweets and biscuits spread out on the oak table. Damask chairs lined the walls, jammed together to accommodate as many petitioners as possible, their faces tense and suspicious of each other, stealing sideways glances. They had stood in line hour after hour on the stairs outside the apartment and now waited nervously for their turn.

Except it seemed to Valentina that there was no certainty, no order in which they were invited to rise and enter the inner study, no way of knowing if their turn was next or in two hours' time. Or not at all.

"Father Grigori, I need to speak to you."

He gazed greedily around his room, examining the upturned faces, and smiled at a woman in a low-cut dress and ruby earrings that blazed in the sunlight. "All need to speak to me," he murmured, "because I am the path to the Holy Khristos."

"This is urgent."

"Come with me, my child of Christ."

He wrapped an arm around her waist and led her away to the coveted door of the inner sanctum. She heard the desperate sighs behind her. His study was long and thin with a striking icon of the Virgin of Kazan in one corner lit by a red lamp. An old desk, a battered leather sofa, not much else in the room except a large Bible open on a low table in the center. The place was musty, like Rasputin himself, unwashed and in some way uncivilized, though she couldn't quite work out why.

Rasputin sank to his knees immediately in front of the gilded image of the Virgin and bowed his head. His black hair was long and lank, his lips large and red. Valentina remembered those lips, remembered the sour taste of them on her own. She shivered, impatient to be away from this place, but had no idea whether he would be minutes or hours on his knees.

"Father Grigori, my sister is dying."

He responded in a way she didn't expect. He laughed and lumbered to his feet. "My child, we are all dying."

"Father, I have not come for such words. I heard that you can heal people. Please . . . heal my—"

"Child," he said in a slow sonorous voice, "you are in far too much of a hurry. You are trying to rush through life, but what you must take time to consider are your sins."

The way his strange eyes stared at her. She felt her thoughts loosen a notch. Felt her cheeks flush red.

"Sin," he said, his voice penetrating her mind, "is our path to Almighty God. We sin and we ask forgiveness, that is how we enter into his arms." He moved closer, and it was a wrench to make herself look away.

"I'm not here to talk of sin. Healing is what I need."

"We all need to be healed." He laid a heavy hand on her shoulder. "Can you help me, Father?"

"Yes. *Da*." He leaned down to kiss her forehead, but she was ready for it this time and stepped back. "Ah"—he smiled at her, his mouth a dark red cavern—"a nervous fawn." The smile widened. "I like those best."

She looked at the door. She could leave. "Father Grigori, they say you work miracles on the tsarevitch for his mother and father, the tsarina and tsar."

The eyes drooped, half-closed, and it was a relief. She flicked a tongue across her lips.

"God has granted me the honor of being the channel of his power and his love to that child, the next emperor of Russia." He turned abruptly and sat down on the sofa. "Come here."

"Will you help me? I have money, it's not much, but . . ." She placed a small pouch of gold roubles on the table.

"Kneel here." Rasputin's voice was powerful in the narrow room.

"I'd rather stand."

"Then you are no good to me because you are too proud."

"Katya. My sister's name is Katya Ivanova. She has cholera. Please"—she moved closer and sank to her knees on the bare boards in front of him—"please, help her." The weight inside her chest was crushing her. "Please, help Katya."

He placed his hand on the top of her head, heavy and possessive, and she felt a heat in her mind, churning her thoughts until she almost lost track of why she was here.

"No," she whispered and swayed back on her heels, so that his hand fell to his side.

"You are strong."

He made a sound, an odd growl in the back of his throat. Uncivilized. Lecherous. Unclean. A semiliterate peasant. He was all these things, but she could feel his power and touched his knee with her fingers.

"Help me, Father Grigori."

He stared at her for a long time, his lips moving in silent prayer, her fingers the only connection between them. His eyes grew rounder, became a more vivid blue, but then seemed to glaze over, and for the first time since becoming pregnant Valentina felt violently sick. He reached forward, took her face in his hands, dirty fingernails scratching at her skin, and his mood seemed to change.

"You would have been sweet and tender," he said with a sad smile. "You would have been luscious and fragrant, my tempting little fawn."

"I am not your little anything. But I need you to help my sister."

"She is beyond my help."

"No! Please!"

His face came so close to hers she could see the purple pockmarks on his nose and smell the brandy on his breath.

"The Lord God Almighty heals through my hands," he said, "and sends me visions to help lead sinners to the salvation of their souls. I see your sister. She is soon to be cleansed of all tribulations of this flesh."

"No! You're lying."

"But you." He slid out his tongue and touched her lips. "You have a girl growing inside you who will one day drag her father from the jaws of a fiery hell."

*No. How could he know? It was impossible.*

"A girl?" she breathed.

"Yes." He laughed. Loud and boisterous, shaking his wild hair, and he dropped his hands from her face. "And she'll be a good little liar, so you'll have to watch her carefully."

Blood pumped through her veins, scalding her skin. Her hands touched the spot where the child lay, and she prayed that it was a boy. Because if it was a boy, Rasputin was wrong. *Let him be wrong.* Wrong about Katya. She jumped to her feet. Enough of his lies. Enough of his games with her mind and his hands on her body. She picked up the pouch of gold and walked out of the room.

❧

KATYA DIED THAT NIGHT. VALENTINA HEARD THE SOFT rustle in her throat and saw the fractured moment of relief when her frail body gave up the fight. Valentina didn't utter a sound but continued to sit, knees jammed against her sister's bed, holding Katya's small hand wrapped in hers, denying it the ability to grow cold.

Her mother laid her head on the pillow and wept, harsh grueling sobs, while her father stood stiffly at the end of the bed and demanded of God what they had done to deserve such wrath. All through the day while priests came and went, while candles were lit and incense burned, and all through the next night while Sonya again washed Katya's body and clothed her in fresh garments, Valentina held her sister's hand.

Only when dawn fingered the black curtains on the third day did she lay the bone-white hand on the quilt and quietly leave the room. She never entered it again. She walked into her own room, unlocked the drawer, and tore up her list.

❧

T HE MUSIC WAS HARSH. NOTES THAT GRATED ON JENS'S ears. Chords clashed as Valentina's hands flew over the keys, darting and falling like broken wings. Sound filled every corner of the music room, stirring the air with rising crescendos and tender aching passages that broke his heart.

He sat there, hour after hour. Watching each vibration of her body and listening to the cries she didn't make. She played as if a tidal wave of music could flood every corner of her, crowding her veins, her bones, her mind, leaving no room, no space, no air left for grief or pain to breathe. And when he rose from his seat, walked over to the piano and wrapped his arms around her from behind, he pinned her against him so that her hands couldn't play. They fluttered in desperate empty movements. Her whole body shook until something snapped inside her. She spun around within the circle of his arms and clung to him.

# Thirty-seven

THERE WAS A LULL IN TIME. ARKIN COULD SENSE THE PAUSE as though Petersburg were holding its breath, and he took extra care to be on his guard, moving from place to place, never staying long in any, always rootless, always shadowless. Yet he could not bring himself to stay away from the Ivanovs. They drew him the way the summer draws swallows.

He watched them, their comings and goings, the mother tall and erect in heavy black weeds, her daughter by her side in black yet somehow not in mourning. There was an alertness to the young Ivanova's stride and a quickness to her movements, an anger in the slam of the carriage door. He remained out of sight, but his eyes followed her and he heard again her words in his head: *Have you no conscience?* Didn't she understand? The revolutionary severs all links with the social order and its moral codes because only the exclusion of such values can bring about radical change. The old order *must* be destroyed. She was part of the old social order, hand in hand with her mother.

So why could he not destroy them?

Carriages and motorcars came and went at the house, friends with condolences and young women who he presumed were from Katya's school days. The funeral itself disgusted him. A long line of carriages adorned with black crepe, horses with ebony plumes, mourning dresses that must have stripped the city of black silk and jet jewelry. If Minister Ivanov did not have money to pay the ransom for his daughter, where did he find the gold for this showy display of grandeur? More credit from banks? While working men and women were given hovels to live in, the rich were given palaces to die in. He spat on the ground outside the church. Death to them all.

Yet still his feet wouldn't walk away. As he leaned against a wall in the shadow of Kazan Cathedral he cursed that he had ever crossed paths with the Ivanovs. The father emerged first from the massive cathedral doors, but Arkin gave him no more than scant attention. He was the kind of man who called for revolutionaries to be hanged from lampposts as a warning to others. His day of reckoning would come.

Beside him stood his wife, head bowed, a heavy veil hiding her from sight. He wanted to rip the veil from her face, to look into her eyes. To see what lay in her mind. She moved slowly as if it were an effort, but behind her the daughter did not drop her head or lower her gaze. The moment she emerged into the autumn sunlight she stared intently at the crowd of strangers who had gathered outside the cathedral to watch. Her eyes scanned back and forth, clearly searching for someone she expected to see, and Arkin sank deeper into the shadows.

Because he knew that someone was him.

༄

ARKIN HID IN THE SECRET CHAMBER WHEN VALENTINA came to Morozov's church once more. It was a small airless scrap of space behind a panel in the basement room, and the moment he heard her voice with the priest at the top of the stairs he vanished inside it.

"You can see, my dear, it is exactly as I said. He is not here." Father Morozov's voice was gentle.

There was a long silence, and Arkin could hear her footsteps prowling the room. At times they stopped and he pictured her, listening for the faintest sound, scenting the air for any trace of him.

"The place smells of cigarettes," she pointed out.

"Many come here and smoke, but not Viktor Arkin. Listen to me, my dear, and believe what I say. He was in Moscow and returned to Petersburg for a few days, but now he has gone. I'm not sure where. He mentioned Novgorod, so maybe he's there. I gave him your message that you are looking for him. So now go in peace, my child, and forget our friend."

"Father," Valentina said, and Arkin smiled because he'd heard that tone before, "that man is not my friend. Tell him there are not enough days in the year or enough towns in this country for him to hide in, tell him I will find him, tell him . . ." Her words stopped, and the sudden silence seemed to bang on the walls. When the words started again her voice had changed. "Tell him," she said so softly he barely caught it, "that I need help."

❧

JENS DID NOT LIKE MINISTER IVANOV'S STUDY. IT WAS BOASTful and showy. Displaying success in trophies and swords and giltframed paintings of mammoth Russian battles, but like the man himself it was starting to fray at the edges. The impressive desk bore scars of cigar burns, there was an ink stain on the carpet, and a patch on one wall was paler than the rest where a painting had been removed. No doubt claimed by a bank. Jens was seated on a chair opposite Ivanov who sat on the other side of the desk, puffing with annoyance on a fat cigar.

"You cannot force Valentina into a marriage she doesn't want," Jens stated.

"The answer is still no, Friis. She has to marry into money; she knows that."

"I am not poor."

"The answer is no."

Jens controlled his anger and said coolly, "I work closely with Minister Davidov. I believe you know him."

"Yes. What the hell is he to do with this matter?"

"He lost his wife earlier this year."

"I know. A sad matter. So what?"

"So Minister Davidov has no interest in his private life anymore. Yet he is still ambitious, despite his age. Last month he inherited the extensive estates of his elder brother, who was killed in a motor accident."

Ivanov narrowed his eyes. "Go on."

"He is looking for ways to invest it in furthering his career, broadening its scope. I heard a whisper that he is interested in heading several of the committees that you control, so perhaps I could drop a word in his ear if . . ." He left it there.

Ivanov could not keep the greed from his eyes. Jens flipped open the mahogany cigar box on the desk, removed a cigar for himself, and held a hand out to the minister, who seized it like a lifeline.

Ivanov smiled and shook it hard. "Welcome to the family, Friis. I always wanted Valentina's happiness."

Jens lit his cigar. *Yes*, he thought, *I'm sure you did.*

～

JENS WAS WORKING IN HIS OFFICE WITH YOUNG KROSKIN, the surveyor who lost a part of his leg after the tunnel explosion. They were bent over a set of plans on his desk, discussing the latest expansion of the tunnels, when the telephone rang. Jens gave a grunt of irritation at the interruption, walked over to the wall, and lifted the earpiece.

"Friis here."

"Friis, you cunning bastard!"

It was Davidov. "What is it you want, Minister?"

"To congratulate you."

"On what?"

"On your engagement, for one thing. I heard it from Ivanov himself. And for a second thing, for arranging my deal with him. He's one hell of a greedy bugger, so it has cost me a fortune, but I shall enjoy . . ."

Jens stopped listening. Valentina was standing in the doorway of his office. "Excuse me, Minister, I have to go. Thank you for calling." He hung up.

Kroskin was staring at Valentina. "Miss Ivanova," the young man said, blushing, "I'm so pleased to see you. I always wanted to thank you for your help down . . . down in the tunnel."

She nodded, but her eyes were on Jens.

Kroskin gathered up his crutch and limped to the door. She let him pass, then entered the office, closing the door behind her.

"Jens," she said, and despite the black coat and hat that she was wearing, she brightened the dull room. "I know how we can do it."

❧

THEY WAITED TILL AFTER DARK, UNTIL THE FACTORIES spilled out their work shift and shops locked their doors at the end of the day. Valentina loved moving through the city at Jens's side, her shoulder feeling the solidity of him. He was not going to vanish. Not like Katya. Not like Arkin. Jens would be a part of her life forever.

The street hadn't changed at all; the door with the cracked panel was still unmended. Jens knocked loudly and when it remained shut, he knocked on it harder until the panel flapped loose. Only then did a man yank open the door no more than the width of his head, and in the dim light they could see it was a young man's face with quick curious eyes.

"Yes?"

"We're here to see Ivan and Varenka Sidorov," Jens said as he slid one foot into the gap.

"They've gone."

"No," Valentina insisted. *No. Not vanished.* "I think you're mistaken."

"No mistake."

Jens took a hand from his pocket, and between his fingers lay a five-rouble note. "May we see for ourselves?"

The note disappeared into the man's jacket. "Of course," he smiled, amused. Easy money. He stepped back and they saw that the door on the left stood open, a kerosene lamp burning inside, as the sound of a woman singing trickled into the hallway.

"Take a good look," the young man offered.

Valentina walked into the room. It was still dank and small, still with a cracked ceiling and mold on the wall, but it had been transformed. The furniture was cheap and worn, but a scattering of material in rich colors gave the place a life it had not possessed before. Golds and ambers, magenta and scarlet, colorful swathes of it were draped over chairs and table and bed. Valentina stared. In the middle of the room a young woman with long black hair and gypsy eyes was swaying as she sang softly, an old folk song that belonged in the wilds of the Russian steppes.

Abruptly Valentina turned and walked out.

༅

JENS LED HER DOWN TO A BASEMENT. HER FEET FELT FOR each step in the dark. It had started to rain and the air here stank of factory waste that burned the eyes, but Valentina focused on the blackened house in front of her and let herself hope that Arkin could be here. Beside her Jens stood silently. Ever since they'd left Varenka's old place, he had said little except, "I know someone else who might help." She had tucked an arm through his and slid the flat of her hand under his coat so that she could gently rub his chest as they walked. He seemed to have withdrawn.

The door to the basement swung open. It was not what she had been expecting. One large room was crowded with beds and bodies and the wail of a hungry child, while a short squat dog with fighting scars sniffed her leg as though considering whether to taste it. Jens put an arm around her, keeping her close, kicked the dog away, and approached a thin woman with a golden-haired baby at her shoulder.

"I came here before," he said to her. "Remember?"

"Of course I remember you." She smiled and let her eyes linger on him with interest. But it was the baby that Valentina could not take her eyes off. She wanted to touch the gossamer curls on its head, to feel their softness. Exactly like Katya's.

"Is Larisa Sergeyeva here?" Jens asked, his gaze probing the shadows of the room.

The woman laughed and rolled her eyes at him. "Gone off, that one has."

"Gone where?"

"How should I know? A man came in very early in the morning a few days ago and they spent an hour with heads tight together, talking and arguing. But all smiles in the end. She just picked up her bag, tied the babe on her back, and we haven't seen her since."

"A man?" Valentina asked. "What did he look like?"

"Tall, I suppose." She smiled at Jens again. "But not as tall as you. Brown hair, old clothes but neat."

"A face that knows what it wants?"

"Yes, that's true," the woman nodded. "That's him."

"*Chyort!*" Valentina swore. "He's ahead of us."

Jens walked her out and up into the street where he curled an arm around her neck, warm and intimate. "There are other places," he told her.

❧

At any time Arkin could have stepped out of the shadows and put a knife in her throat to make this hounding cease. But he didn't. He knew he couldn't. Any more than he could put a knife in her mother's delicate white throat. He despised himself for his weakness. They were his enemy; they were the oppressors.

The engineer too was his enemy, a far more dangerous one. If Arkin killed Valentina Ivanova, he would have to kill the engineer as well because if he didn't, one day Friis would find him. There was no question of that. And that day would be his last.

So for now, he let the girl live.

❧

Arkin walked along the hotel's long corridor, aware of the risk he was taking. He didn't for one moment think Elizaveta would be here in the Hotel de Russie. Instead Okhrana agents could be waiting for him in the room, but, even so, he didn't turn back. He stood silently outside the door and listened for a long time, but there was no sound. That meant nothing. At his touch on the handle, the door opened and he entered the room.

Elizaveta Ivanova was sitting on the edge of the bed clothed in sepulchral black, with a veil under a hat of glossy black feathers. An expression of bleak misery lay on her face, and a large gun sprawled like a lapdog on her knees. One gloved hand was stroking it. At the sight of him she picked it up. For a moment they stared at each other without speaking.

"*Dobriy vecher,*" he said at last. "Good evening, Elizaveta."

She rose to her feet and steadied the gun with both hands. No words.

He moved forward till he was close enough to touch it, but he kept his hands away from her. "I didn't mean for Katya to die," he said quietly.

She shook her head from side to side, a slow awkward movement, as though it were too heavy for her neck. "That's not what Valentina says."

He took a step toward her so that the muzzle of the gun was

jammed into his chest. He could feel his heart beating against it. "Pull the trigger if it makes you happier."

She closed her eyes behind the veil. He held his breath and counted to ten, but there was no blast of pain to rob him of life. Without comment he took the gun from her hands and tossed it onto the satin quilt, then gently removed her hatpin and let the hat fall to the floor. His arms encircled her trembling figure and he rested his cheek against her hair, her breath warm and quick against his neck. For ten minutes they stood locked together, the rigid frame of her body slowly melting into his.

"How can I not hate you?" she whispered. "How can I be such a bad mother?"

"I wish," he said, "that you and I had met at a different time and in a different place."

"There is only this time. There is only this place."

He kissed her hair, inhaled its familiar scent, unclipped a pearl grip, and watched a golden tress tumble to her shoulder.

"How did you know I would come today?" he asked.

"I didn't."

The words swirled in his mind. He pictured her, day after day, a lonely figure seated on the edge of the hotel bed with a gun on her lap. Anger in her heart. Waiting for him. It was too much. His tears fell on her hair.

VALENTINA HUNTED HIM, SHE AND JENS TOGETHER, WEEK after week. The way hounds hunt a fox, from den to den. She wanted him to feel her hatred pursuing him as he shifted from place to place, abandoning one safe corner after another as they ventured into bars and slums, churches and meeting halls. Always with roubles in their hands.

Twice they came so close she could smell him in the air they breathed, but each time he disappeared through a window or over a rooftop. By day she worked once more in St. Isabella's Hospital, but by night she and Jens stalked the backstreets. When her mother asked where she was going, she was honest with her. "I'm searching for Viktor Arkin."

"The police are handling that. There's no need for you to do so."

"They have failed, Mama. I don't intend to."

But instead of forbidding her to leave the house, her mother stared at her solemnly and warned, "Tread carefully, Valentina. An eye for an eye may seem like justice to you, but he has a ruthless mind and is quick to anger."

"What makes you say that, Mama?"

Her mother's cheeks flushed. "He's a revolutionary, isn't he? They are all in a rage that eats their hearts out."

"I know his mind, Mama. Don't fear for me."

❧

J ENS, WHAT IS IT?"
   There was something wrong. Valentina could feel it in the room, an unease that set her pulse pounding. Jens was standing at the window of his apartment, looking down at the traffic and at the people hurrying to escape the chill autumn wind. Behind him in pride of place on a long table stood an elaborate wooden mouse palace with turrets for the white rodent to scurry up and bridges for its tiny feet to balance on. At this moment the animal was running inside its wheel, making a steady whirring noise that was oddly comforting.

"It will snow soon," Jens murmured. "The cold will stir the workers into strike action again. There is no bread in the shops."

Valentina came to stand behind him and laid her cheek against his back. "What is it?" she asked again.

"Valentina, you won't catch him."

"Arkin?"

"Not like this. He's always one step ahead."

"Let's not talk of him right now." She ran her hands down his naked sides and tucked her body against his, the hard muscles taut against her ribs. She closed her eyes and pressed her cheek against his spine so hard it hurt. "Jens." She turned him around so that she could smile up into his dark green eyes. "You are right. We must think of something new."

❧

A RKIN TOOK THE LETTER FROM THE PRIEST IN THE CHURCH
   and for a moment could think of no one who would have sent it. It was a rule: put nothing in writing. It could get you killed.

"Where's Father Morozov?" he asked the priest, a man with a domed head and small wire spectacles.

"He's in his village. There have been police here, asking questions about him." He shook his head nervously.

"So he is keeping out of sight?"

"*Da.* Yes."

"He is important to us."

That was when the priest offered him the letter.

"Who brought it?" Arkin asked. On the front of the envelope was his name in large elegant lettering.

"A young woman."

He tore it open.

*You expect too much of life, Viktor Arkin. You expect too much of me if you think I will stay away. So let us be direct, let us meet face to face, just you and me, no one else. Let us say what there is to say. You can call me an oppressor, I can call you a killer. Meet me tomorrow in the courtyard at the back of St. Isabella's Hospital. Three o'clock. What then? Then I can tell you that our small personal tragedies mean everything in the storm that is sweeping through Russia and that I am carrying your child.*

Arkin's hand shook, so that the words blurred in front of his eyes.

❧

S HE HAD CHOSEN WELL. THE COURTYARD LAY IN FITFUL sunshine, neither private nor public. Arkin had inspected it just as dawn was breaking over the city, and he could see why she had settled on this as the meeting place. It did not make a good trap. It had too many escape routes. As well as the massive metal gates that stood open at the entrance for ambulances and delivery vans, there were also two doors into the hospital, another in the rear wall that led to a side street, and a metal hatch down into a cellar of some kind.

Both of them would breathe easier. He wanted to trust her.

He observed the courtyard for several hours. For much of the time it remained empty but at irregular intervals it filled with activity, so that at any point their meeting could be interrupted. That made it safer. A couple of brick storage huts along one wall gave him concern, but he had easily opened their locks and found nothing but stocks of kerosene and crates with equipment like bedpans and sterilizers inside. He took in which parts of the courtyard were in view of the rear of the hospital and which parts weren't. As the sun climbed he smoked a cigarette in a shaded corner behind one of the huts and knew he was invisible.

*Yes, Valentina Ivanova, you have chosen well.*

♐

VALENTINA WAS BUSY. THE WARD WAS FRANTIC. A FIRE AT the sailmakers' workshop brought in a stream of burn victims, mainly women. Time ran too fast. Whenever she glanced at the clock, the hands had leapt forward in huge unexpected jumps. One o'clock. She bathed a damaged limb with hypochlorite solution and helped a man with dehydration drink a glass of tea at the speed of a snail. Two o'clock.

Her mouth was dry. Would he turn up?

She thought again about the letter. She had been careful not to show it to Jens, just told him she had written it to ask Arkin for a face-to-face meeting. No mention of its last line about the child. Would Arkin believe it? She sat quietly with a woman who was confused about where she was and why her son had brought her here.

Two fifty-one.

She washed her hands, put on her nurse's cape. Two fifty-six. She began the long walk down the corridors to the rear of the hospital. She pushed open the double doors and stepped out into the sunlight, so bright after the somber interior that she had to screw up her eyes.

There he was. Viktor Arkin stood against one of the walls, taller than she remembered, noticeably thinner. His forehead and cheekbones jutted through his skin. Her eyes fixed on the gun held loosely in his hand, and for the first time she let into her mind the thought that he might kill her. No, not if she could make him believe she was carrying his child. She walked over to a brightly lit area next to one of the huts, but Arkin didn't move. A full minute ticked past and she could hear each second click inside her head, but just when she thought he would be tempted no closer he approached, up on his toes like a cat. He stopped five paces from her, and she saw his eyes adjust as he stepped out of the gloom.

"You've given me trouble," he said.

"I'm glad."

"Where is he?"

"Who?"

"Your engineer."

"He doesn't know I'm here."

He smiled politely, and she had no idea whether he believed her. He shrugged and lowered his gun to his side, watching her carefully. "That may be true. I can't imagine you would want him to know what a little whore you were in the *izba*."

She didn't answer.

"So what is it you want?" he asked, suddenly brusque and businesslike.

"Where are all your men? I'm sure they're hiding somewhere here, a whole army of them inside the huts and down in the cellar."

He smiled, but this time it wasn't polite. "No one is here except me. Don't think I didn't consider it. I could have taken you captive again and kept you locked up for nine months, then taken the child and slit your throat."

He had seriously considered such an action; she could hear it in his voice, and the thought made her legs tremble. "I'd have stuck a fork in your throat long before the nine months were up."

He laughed, genuinely amused. "I do believe you would. If the child is really mine, not your engineer's, have you considered marrying me instead, or even letting me have the child after it is born?"

"No."

"I thought not. So what is it you want? We're here face to face. Do you intend to try to kill me?"

"Don't think I haven't thought about it."

How could he smile? How could he laugh? How could this man not tear his hair out and rend his clothes into shreds after what he did to Katya?

She spread her cape, so that he could see under it. "Look, I am unarmed."

"That makes me more nervous." His glance darted around the yard. "I shouldn't have come."

"I want you to know, Arkin, that every day that I wake, I feel pain. I will miss my sister for the rest of my life. My mother is suffering, and my father. You and your Bolshevik *cause* have crippled my family."

She was observing him as she spoke. She saw something darken his face—it could have been sorrow or satisfaction—and tug at the skin around his mouth. She unbuttoned her cape at the neck and let it drop from her shoulders. It was the signal to Jens, and Arkin was far too accustomed to such things not to recognize it as such. Immediately he scanned the hospital windows, but he was the one in the sunlight while they were in the shade and he could see nothing. He started to run. He knew what was coming.

A single shot rang out, the sound like the crack of a whip in Valentina's ears. Arkin's right leg crumpled under him, flinging him to the cobbles, but even as he hit the ground he was dragging himself into the shadow of the hut. Valentina looked up at the row of windows on the second floor, at the one belonging to the sluice room where Jens had been hiding since last night.

"*Thank you, Jens. Spasibo,*" she whispered.

Arkin was binding his kerchief around a knee that was pouring blood, shards of bone spattered in grisly chunks down his trousers. Valentina stood over him and stared down at his face twisted in agony.

"You'll feel pain now," she said harshly. "Pain every day for the rest of your life. Death would have been too easy for you. I want you to suffer like Katya suffered. I want you to hate me every time you put that foot to the floor, the way I will hate you every day that I cannot speak to my sister."

He looked up at her, his eyes black holes of rage. "One day your engineer will pay for this."

She seized his hair in her hand and yanked back his head. "If you ever touch him, I swear to you I will destroy the child." Their eyes locked, and she knew he believed her. She released him and wiped her hand on her skirt. "I'll go and order a stretcher for you," she said, and walked into the hospital. By the time she came out with two orderlies Viktor Arkin was gone. Only his blood remained on the cobbles.

# Thirty-eight

JENS SAW A CHANGE IN VALENTINA AFTER THAT DAY IN THE courtyard. Some of the shadows left her eyes, and her limbs regained the fluid grace that they had lost since the death of her sister. They didn't talk about what had happened. Neither wished to mention Arkin's name. To do so would be to invite him back. But there was a new tenderness in their lovemaking and a deeper passion in her music that made him ache for her when they were apart.

Unknown to her he continued to search for Arkin. He dredged through the slums of St. Petersburg once more but found no trace of him, not even a whisper. The man had left the city, Jens was convinced of it. He even sent Liev Popkov to drink the backstreet bars dry, but still no word. *Neechevo.* Nothing. If there were any justice in the world, he'd be dead and buried from gangrene of the leg, but that was too much to hope for. Jens didn't believe in natural justice. You had to make your own.

Though the official period of mourning for Katya was not over in the Ivanov household, he spoke to Valentina's parents in private about the wedding, and the ceremony was arranged with a certain amount of speed. Jens was not a man for Russian weddings. They were too long and too solemn for his taste, the ritual too precise. But on the day of his marriage, he was mesmerized by the sight of

Valentina in her long white dress, holding her lighted candle, her dark hair twined up at the back of her head, clustered under a white veil with a scattering of pearls that could not begin to compare with the creamy texture of her skin.

As the priest in his *epitrachelion* robe performed the traditional liturgy, bound their joined hands with his stole, and led them three times around the *analogion* lectern, circling the Gospel Book, her eyes flashed at him with such a challenge and such desire that he considered scooping her up in his arms right there and then. He couldn't bear to share her a minute longer. When the golden wedding crowns were held over their heads and the priest in his finest robes chanted the *ektenia*, he saw the way her glance moved against her will to the church door, as though expecting someone else to slide in. A small crease of concern on her high forehead, a tense touch of her hand when they exchanged rings. The faintest sliver of fear behind the shimmer of her veil.

Not for the first time Jens cursed himself for not raising the barrel of his rifle that day in the hospital courtyard and blowing a hole the size of her crown in Arkin's chest. Like for like. A bullet for a bullet. But the revolutionary had been wearing body armor that day; Jens had seen the bulk of it clearly under his shirt, and that was why he could be so bold. Whatever lair the bastard had slunk off to now, that knee of his would take a long time to heal. Arkin would not be returning to St. Petersburg in a hurry.

When the ceremony and the elaborate celebrations were finally at an end, Jens whisked Valentina away and drove her at speed in a decorated carriage to their new home. It lay in a quiet avenue near Dr. Fedorin's house.

"It will be useful to have a doctor on our doorstep when the baby comes," Jens had pointed out, but she had laughed at him, calling him a worrisome bear, and promised to produce the child as effortlessly as a she-cat sheds kittens. He had chosen the house for her with care. The view of the river, with its surface looking as solid as steel, was for when she needed to sit and be quiet, and the height of the ceilings would form a perfect chamber for her music. The pale polished floors reminded Jens of the dense pine forests of Denmark, and he had brought his reindeer rug to lay in front of the fire. He intended to put it to good use.

He took delight in peeling her wedding finery from her body, while she stood smiling at him and proffering each tempting arm and each slender leg to be denuded. When she was naked and her hair was spread in a rippling fan of satin over her bare back, he led her to the new Erard grand piano in the drawing room and she played for him. Just for him. The lilting notes of Chopin's Nocturne in E Flat.

As her hands glided over the keys, his eyes traced each delicate notch of her spine. Every line of her was smooth and supple, the curve of her buttocks on the piano stool, the angle of her shoulder, the tip of her elbow. And the exquisite hollow above her hips that was slowly filling as the swell of her belly grew larger.

This woman, his wife, carrying their child. As essential a part of him as the lungs in his chest and the blood in his veins. He moved over to her and kissed the warm top of her head, then each rib on her back and the dainty bone at the base of her spine. All the time her hands kept playing but he heard her sighs of pleasure, and when his arms encircled her, cradling the child inside her, she let her weight lean back against him, as if it belonged there.

"I love you, Madam Friis," he whispered into her ear, and swept her up off the stool into his arms. "Time for bed."

She twined her arms around his neck, her eyes bright and laughing at him, swinging her bare feet, her fingers tight in his hair.

"We have forever," she promised.

❧

C ANDLES STILL BURNED AROUND THE BEDROOM. THEIR soft flickering light soothed Valentina's thoughts and turned Jens's skin golden on the sheets. She kept a hand on his head where it lay next to the curve of her stomach, and she smiled contentedly. Both were asleep—one beside her and one inside her—and she let her mind stretch into the future that was waiting for them. She filled it with new engineering projects for Jens and St. Petersburg's Conservatoire of Music for herself.

There would be no more St. Isabella's Hospital, not now, not without Katya to care for. No list to cross off one by one. She had different aims now. Instead she pictured concerts and walks in the park, a small hand tucked in hers, and the world's biggest mouse palace constantly being redesigned and expanded. Always the sound of laughter. Always the warmth of Jens's body next to hers at night and that look in his eyes when he lifted his gaze from his book or from his papers and caught sight of her. That moment. As though they were bound under one skin.

She stroked his hair. There would be problems; of course there would. The social order in St. Petersburg was unstable, but she had faith in the power of men like her father to bring it under control, of men like Captain Chernov to hold the line against the strikers. But above all she had faith in men like Jens to build a better world for the workers to live in. Arkin and his ferocious revolution would never succeed; it would just fade away to nothing, leaving the banners and the slogans to be pecked by the gulls that swept in silvery flocks low over the city.

She rested her hand on her stomach and imagined a delicate head with a mass of fine curls living inside her. To be a mother. The thought took her breath away. But it made a sensation that was warm and real beat inside her blood, a feeling that in a strange way she was now larger than herself. Not just physically, but in her love. She smiled, thinking of her own mother.

Elizaveta Ivanova had recently taken to traveling by train to Moscow to stay with an old school friend of hers. Sometimes for only one or two days, sometimes longer. She said she needed to escape from the city where her daughter had died, and certainly she always returned without the lines of tension on her forehead and without the dull sorrow in her eyes. Papa barely seemed to notice her mother's absences, he was so involved in deals with Minister Davidov, but he had embraced Valentina warmly at her wedding and kissed her cheek with his blessing. The gesture meant much to her. Only her sister wasn't there to share her joy.

Valentina turned on her side and curled herself around Jens's sleeping form, entwining her limbs with his and inhaling the scent of his skin. "My husband," she murmured.

Katya would have been happy for her.

❧

RASPUTIN WAS RIGHT. VALENTINA COULD ADMIT IT NOW and laugh. It was a coincidence, nothing more, she told herself. After a winter that was milder than usual and a spring of relative peace in the factories, she gave birth to a daughter. Not just any daughter. As she held the little bundle of snuffles and tiny clutching fingers, she knew that this was the most perfect being ever created. How could she not be? Look at her father.

Valentina could not stop smiling. Or crying. She touched each eyelid, each wrinkled ear. She gazed at the plump little lips and the tiny heart-shaped chin. She loved the way Jens didn't wait for Dr. Fedorin to open the bedroom door to him but entered with eager strides that stopped dead when he saw her and the child. She could see that however much he had prepared himself, he had no idea it would be like this. Like an earthquake inside him. And then the grin on his face, so wide she thought it would crack his cheeks. With the gentlest of movements, he sat on the bed.

"Valentina, are you—"

"I'm sore and battered," she interrupted, "not a bit like shedding kittens." She held his daughter out to him, and his arms enfolded the small bundle in a possessive embrace.

For a long time he held her, his head bent over, staring down at his daughter, at her flame-colored curls still damp on her head. Only when the tiny mouth popped open in a silent yawn did he laugh and look up at Valentina. The love in his eyes was naked and it felt as if they'd stepped out of this world.

"I hadn't realized," he said tenderly, "how my life was not complete before. Not without this child in it." His voice was shaking. "She's beautiful."

Valentina smiled. "Let's call her Lydia."

## Thirty-nine

ST. PETERSBURG, RUSSIA
FEBRUARY 1917

S TOP THE CAR!"

Valentina shouted the words to Jens as he steered the motor-car through the crush of traffic in St. Isaac's Square. Rain was sheeting down, bounding off umbrellas and off the car's roof, splashing in the gutters. Whenever it rained, Valentina noticed—even after more than five years of marriage—the way Jens's quick eyes checked each drain they passed to ensure that it was clearing the water flow efficiently.

"Stop the car," she said again. "Please."

"What is it?"

They were driving back across the city, returning from a visit with Lydia to Valentina's mother, but Jens had insisted they leave early because he did not want his wife and child on the roads after dark. She didn't blame him. In February the daylight hours were short, and the mood of the city had grown ugly. It was bitterly cold, and nearly three years of war against Germany had brought terrible defeats and humiliation for Russia, with wounded soldiers pouring back home, unfed and uncared for, begging in the gutters. Public fury at the tsar had erupted not just in strikes this time but in barricades in the streets. Shops were destroyed, bricks were hurled through windows, and firebombs reduced businesses to rubble.

"*Death to Capitalists*" was the shout that echoed through the city.

Rationing was severe. There was a shortage of bread, no *khleb* to fill the empty bellies of the workers, no flour, no milk, no butter, no sugar. Queues formed outside bakeries and butcher shops from dawn to dusk in the bitter cold.

Valentina could feel the hatred in the air. Taste it like acid on her tongue. Eight million Russian soldiers killed, wounded or taken prisoner in the trenches, Tsarina Alexandra labeled a treacherous German whore by the masses, and Tsar Nicholas so out of touch that at this critical time he had left Petrograd to go to army headquarters. *Petrograd.* Even after three years, the new name for St. Petersburg still did not fit easily into Valentina's mouth. It had been changed to avoid any contamination from the German-sounding word. Since the start of the war in 1914, anything and everything German was to be despised—including the tsar's wife.

As soon as Jens stopped the car, Valentina jumped out and raced across the square, her coat plastered against her legs by the driving rain. She ran to the *placati*, the notice boards with newspapers and posters displayed for people to read. In this foul weather there was not the usual crowd huddled in front of them. That was why she'd seen it.

The flash of red. The scrap of scarf that Varenka had promised as a warning so long ago.

She had prepared herself for this moment—*not yet, don't let it be yet.* Her hand reached out and she saw the rain spattering her glove, the wind snatching at torn posters that screamed POWER TO THE PEOPLE, and four crows hunched like black heathens on the cathedral dome behind. The strip of red material was nailed to the notice board, sodden and ragged, but it was there. Waiting for her to see it. She wrenched it off the board.

❧

MAMA, YOU'RE ALL WET."
As Valentina slid back into the car, Lydia's small hands patted at her cheeks, wiping away the raindrops.

"What was that about?" Jens asked.

"It's Varenka's." She held up the red piece of cloth. It dripped onto her lap.

Jens slowly shook his head. "After five years of nothing from her."

"Jens, it's a warning. She promised it as a sign of when the revolution was close. Remember?"

"Yes, I remember." He stared grimly ahead through the windshield at the blurred figures scurrying through the rain. "Dear God, now the bloodletting will begin."

❧

WHAT ARE YOU DOING?" JENS ASKED.
Valentina looked up from her sewing and smiled. He was on his knees on the floor, building a railway station out of wooden blocks with Lydia. At four years old her young face would crease with concentration as she balanced one on top of another, careful to imitate her father's technique. She was wearing a navy velvet dress with lace collar and cuffs, but she had pushed up the cuffs and tucked her skirt into her underwear to stop it from getting in her way as she worked. Valentina sighed indulgently. Her flame-haired daughter wasn't turning out quite as she expected. Tawny eyes that missed nothing and a determined preference for playing with model trains with her father instead of the magnificent dollhouse Valentina had bought for her last birthday.

"Valentina"—Jens sat back on his haunches and studied her with a lift of one eyebrow—"the maid does our sewing. What are you doing?"

Her needle froze midstitch. She lowered her voice. "Getting ready."

She slid a golden rouble from her pocket and pressed it into the section of hemline that she had opened up in the plain brown dress that was sprawled over her knees.

His eyes lifted from the stitching to her face. She saw his throat swallow. "My dearest Valentina, have we really come to that?"

"Yes. I believe we have."

Lydia laughed, crowing with delight as she abandoned her bricks. "Can I play too, Mama?"

❧

LENIN WAS COMING BACK. THE GLORIOUS VLADIMIR ILYICH Lenin was at last returning from his enforced exile in Switzerland. Arkin recognized the moment for what it was: the end of the Romanovs.

After five hundred years of tyranny, they were finished. Now that the people would have a figurehead to rally behind, nothing and nobody would stop them. Not the tsar. Not his troops. Not his pathetic attempts at silencing the outcry of the proletariat by dismissing the Duma. The air spat fury. The streets of Petrograd were on fire. Not just the shops and the capitalist businesses, but the ground beneath the feet of Russians. It was burning. Scorching away the old ways, ridding Russia of injustice and fear.

Arkin lit a cigarette, inhaled as he flexed and unflexed his damaged knee, and looked around his office. It was small, but it was all he required. Posters on the walls: WORKERS UNITE! and VICTORY TO THE PEOPLE! A huge image of a clenched fist and of a peasant stamping on the Romanovs' double-headed eagle. A desk, a telephone, a cabinet, a typewriter. And stacks of rectangular white cards. Hundreds of them. He kept names on cards, names and details.

On top of the pile in front of him was one name: JENS FRIIS— DANISH ENGINEER. He picked it up between two fingers and struck a match on the leg of his desk. The flame flared. He held it under the card and watched it eat it up as the card curled and crackled and died. He dropped it into the metal bin at his feet.

Very soon. He allowed himself a smile as the flames consumed the final remnants of the card. Very soon. Jens Friis would not exist.

❦

IN THE STABLE JENS WAS BRUSHING DOWN HIS HORSE, HERO, with quick angry movements. He'd just heard that General Krymov had arrived back from the front in the war against Germany. He'd brought tales of thousands dead and a woefully underequipped Russian army. Soldiers were perishing of cold and starvation, and those still alive were marching in boots held together with string, feet rotting in the trenches. Insufficient ammunition. Toxic gases blinding their eyes. No food. No blankets. With no faith in their commanders, despair and misery were making men desert in the thousands.

"Who can blame them?" he muttered, and just then heard a carriage draw up outside his house.

"Your countess for you," Liev Popkov called out with a grin on his face.

"She's not *my* countess, ox-brain."

The big Cossack liked to turn up in the stables sometimes and took acute pleasure whenever he could in goading Jens into losing his temper. The day Valentina moved out of the Ivanov household and became Jens's wife, Popkov had departed as well. No one knew quite where he lived now, or how, but in the last few years he'd grown a dense black beard and seemed to relish his newfound freedom. When Valentina was busy in the evening practicing a new piano piece for one of her concerts, she liked to be alone to concentrate, so Jens would wander out to check on Hero and smoke a cigarette under the stars. More often than not Popkov would be out there with a pack of cards and a bottle of vodka.

Only once did they come to blows, and that was over Valentina. It happened late last year just before Christmas, the night that Rasputin was murdered and thrown into the river. Popkov had wanted to tell her that he'd heard that Viktor Arkin had turned up again in Petrograd. Jens had told him no. On no account must he tell her. They'd argued. In the end Jens had used the only language that seemed to register in Popkov's stubborn brain and knocked him to the ground. Fists had flown.

"What on earth happened to you?" Valentina asked in alarm when he eventually stormed back into the house.

"Popkov happened to me," he had growled.

She'd laughed uproariously and shown absolutely no sympathy while she bathed his cuts. "You'll probably catch rabies from him," she'd teased.

But right now he was in no mood for a visit from Countess Serova. She had never come to his house before, so why now? He gave Hero a bucket of fresh water, and when he looked up he was surprised to see not the countess, but young Alexei, her son, standing awkwardly in the entrance to the stable.

"Alexei! *Dobroye utro*, good morning. Come on in. Is your mother here?"

The boy came forward eagerly. Hero lifted his head and whickered a soft greeting. The boy had grown tall; his limbs were lanky and at that stage where they are not quite under control yet. Twelve years old and with a clear direct way of examining the world from those quiet green eyes of his.

"She's in the carriage. Uncle Jens, I've come to say good-bye. We're leaving Petrograd, Mama and I, and I wanted to see you." He shrugged self-consciously.

"Leaving Petrograd?"

"Mama says it's not safe here."

"Where are you going?"

"Paris."

Jens didn't want to lose the boy. He placed a hand on the young shoulder, felt the tension in it. "I'll miss you, Alexei. I'll miss our rides in the forest."

The boy nodded, a quick unhappy gesture. "I don't want to go."

"Your mother is right. It's not safe here."

"What about you? You're not leaving."

Jens smiled. "The socialists won't be interested in me. I'm Danish, so don't worry, I'm not in any danger."

Alexei fixed his eyes on Jens. "Are you sure?"

"Quite sure," Jens lied.

The boy looked relieved.

"Anyway," Jens added, "I have to stay to look after Attila's sons." Two of the white mouse's offspring still roamed the mouse palace for Lydia's amusement.

Alexei shuffled his feet.

"What is it?" Jens asked gently.

"I've brought you this." The boy held out a brown paper bag.

Jens took it and let out a low whistle of surprise. Inside lay a diamond bracelet and a pair of gold earrings. "I'm not sure they'll suit me," he said.

"No." Alexei's cheeks were scarlet. "They are not for you to—" Then he saw Jens's teasing expression and laughed. He looked quickly around the stable, checking for eavesdroppers, but no one was there. Popkov had disappeared. "Mama has taken all her jewelry out of the safe and is packing it, scattered throughout her clothes and even inside her pots of face cream."

"Really?"

"Yes. She says they'll try to steal it."

"Your mama is probably right."

"She left out these because she had so many and says these are almost worthless." He stared at the paper bag. "They don't look worthless to me."

"No, Alexei, you're right. But your mama has jewels of such value, these mean little to her, I expect."

"So I want you to take them. Hide them. In case you . . ." He shrugged his bony shoulders again.

"Thank you, Alexei." Jens was touched and hugged the boy close. "I'll miss you very much." He stood back and held him at arm's length, impressed by the quiet dignity of his young mind. "Make sure you keep riding, won't you?"

"Yes." The boy blinked hard. "Thank you, Uncle Jens, for . . ."

Jens ruffled his hair. "Go and say good-bye to Hero while I have a word with your mother." Briskly Jens walked out to the carriage. She was sitting inside, dressed in green, her eyes sad and solemn. "So you are leaving Russia?"

"Yes."

"For Paris."

She smiled at him and shook her head. "That's what I'm telling people. But actually we're heading east."

"That's a long journey."

"But far safer than trying to skirt around the war front in the west."

"Nowhere is safe now. Take care."

She put out her hand and fingered his where it rested on the carriage door. "Listen to me, Jens. I've heard there is a plot among the aristocracy to oust Tsar Nicholas."

"Good God, have they come to their senses at last?"

"No. Six of the grand dukes have gotten together with Prince Georgi Lvov from the Duma to offer the throne to Grand Duke Nicholas Nikolaevich instead."

"To swap one Romanov for another! They are insane. Prime Minister Golitsyn is far too weak to keep order for them. Can't they see it's too late?"

"No, Jens, they love their country. They don't want to give it up, and they know they would have to leave immediately if the Romanovs lose the throne."

"You love Russia too, but it's not stopping you from going."

Her gaze swept away from him, focusing on the stables at the side of the house where Alexei had just emerged, sprinting toward them. She dropped her voice to a whisper. "His father is a Romanov. If ever it came out, Alexei would be in extreme danger." She shivered. "That's why we're leaving."

Jens turned, seized the boy's arm, and hurried him into the carriage. He slammed the door. "Go quickly," he urged. "Go today."

"Tomorrow," she murmured.

"I shall come to say good-bye in the morning," Jens promised.

The boy smiled at him. "We could go for one last ride."

❧

THAT DAY WAS THE START OF THE END. VALENTINA WOKE early, uneasy, too restless to sleep. She could hear the city even in their quiet leafy avenue, breathing hard. Her bones ached with tension, as if she had been running too fast and too far. There were stories everywhere of workers turning on their bosses, of postal workers who had beaten to death the man they had obeyed for ten years, a couple who ran a jeweler's shop thrown out of it by their employees. She was frightened for Jens. She had visions of workers underground rising up like blind moles from their tunnels and savaging their *Direktor* in his flimsy office.

Instinctively her hand stroked him beside her to ensure itself he was whole and safe, and immediately he pulled her on top of him. She made love to him fiercely, leaving her mark on him, small nips to his chest and the taste of blood in her mouth where she nicked his lower lip with her teeth. Today she needed more of him, more than just his muscles and his skin and the thrust of him hard inside her. She needed the blood from his veins. She needed the beat of his heart. And when finally she lay exhausted in his arms, he lifted himself up on one elbow and looked down at her.

"You seem hungry this morning," he laughed.

She sat up, tucking her knees under her. "Don't go in to work, Jens. Not today."

"Why not today?"

"I have a bad feeling about it. Stay home today."

"I have to, my love. I must say good-bye to Alexei. And there are big problems at the moment."

Her heart clattered in her chest. "With the workers?"

"No, though it's true the unions are shouting their demands in my ear. No, it's the old wooden water pipes. They are rotting. The water is contaminated in places and typhoid has broken out again. I've announced that people must stop drinking it. But what else can they do?" He swung his legs from the bed, his mind already on the day ahead.

She had lost her chance.

※

JENS DIDN'T RIDE WITH ALEXEI. THOUGH IT WAS STILL EARLY by the time he reached the Serov mansion, the countess's carriage was standing packed and ready outside the door, and Alexei was slumped on the front step. He leapt to his feet at the sight of Jens on Hero, but their farewell was brief.

The countess was irritated. "He wouldn't get into the carriage until he had said good-bye to you."

Jens shook hands with the boy, a formal recognition that he was an adult now. "Look after your mother, won't you."

"Yes, sir."

"Write to me. Tell me what you decide to do with your life."

"I've already decided. I'm going into the army."

Jens's heart sank. "You're still young yet. Good luck in your new life. We'll meet again, I'm certain, when all this mess is over."

The boy held back his tears. "I'd like that."

Jens hugged him close, kissed his mother's cheek, and promised to see that Alexei's horse went to a good home. Then they were gone in the black carriage with its golden crest removed from the door. Jens watched it until it was out of sight and could not suppress his anger at a nation that drives its fine young men from its soil. He felt the loss of Alexei keenly and swung up into his saddle, urging Hero into a brisk canter down the gravel drive. An ugly mean-eyed horse was waiting outside the gates and on its back sat Popkov, scratching his beard like a lazy bear.

"What the hell are you doing here?" Jens demanded.

"Your wife sent me."

"Why?"

"To keep you safe." He grimaced sourly.

"To hell with you." Jens kicked his horse into a gallop.

※

EIGHTY THOUSAND WORKERS DOWNED TOOLS AND CAME out on strike that day in Petrograd. There were riots on Vasilievsky Island and violent marches that barged their way through the city's streets. Plumes of smoke rose like fingers of hatred across the skyline, as trains and transport and production lines were paralyzed. Shops and factories boarded up their doors and windows as their workers took to the streets with banners. Jens rode through the heart of Petrograd, and he could smell it. The animosity and the anarchy, the desire to destroy. To burn. To break. To tear down and to rip apart.

Motorcars lay on their sides, fenders and windshields smashed; shop doors hung on broken hinges, and goods were flung into gutters, where they were scavenged. Crates of vodka stolen from liquor stores fueled the tempers of the marchers; the men with red armbands and bloodshot eyes clutched at Hero's reins and tried in vain to unseat its rider. Jens experienced an overwhelming sense of sadness. This was the country he loved, and it was slicing open its own veins until its lifeblood made the streets slick and slimy with grief. A thousand or so wealthy families had held this vast country in the palm of their hands for hundreds of years, but they had squeezed it dry. Now the whole of Russia would pay the price.

Jens rode toward his office, dismayed as he passed factory after factory being ransacked. It would not take much for a group of his workers to bring a tunnel roof crashing down. Workforces were running riot everywhere, destroying machinery and stripping glass from windows. And as he rode, all the time he heard the sound of Popkov's horse behind him.

"Go home," Jens shouted.

But the horse remained like a flat-footed shadow. When he turned into Lizhkovskaya Ulitsa, the street was crowded with men wearing red ribbons on their chests and carrying iron bars in their fists. It was the Raspov foundry, its strikers pouring down the road, shouting "Fight for justice" and "Death to the Oppressors." Beneath him Hero edged sideways, unnerved by the smell of hatred in the narrow street. Jens patted the animal's neck, felt the oily sweat on it, and started to swing him back the way they had come. But at that moment the screams started.

A splash of scarlet capes and the gleam of sabers flashed as they sliced through the air. There was the whinny of horses and clatter of hooves. Jens felt a sense of doom, black and suffocating. The troops had been sent in. So the tsar had decided not to negotiate. There was the sound of shots. Panic and fear took hold as the street burst into motion, people trying to flee from the sabers but finding no space. Jens saw a young boy stumble and disappear under trampling feet. He forced Hero forward, barging a path with the horse's broad chest, and opened a bubble of air for the boy to regain his feet.

He heard Popkov's bellow of warning behind him and spun around. He ducked just in time to miss the sword aimed at his head as the Hussars on their mounts were slicing their way through the crowd, crimson staining their blades. Jens saw Popkov cornered against a wall, still on his horse but his arm drenched in blood, and a blond captain was raising his saber to strike a second time. The captain was Chernov. Jens kicked Hero into a leap forward, scattering strikers left and right as he dragged the horse's head to the side at the last moment, slamming it into Chernov's black stallion. The arc of the blade shifted. Just enough. Instead of striking Popkov across the throat, it sliced across his face with a force that should have ripped his head from his body.

Jens's pulse was singing in his ears, and he sent his fist crashing into the captain's chest, snapping ribs and toppling him from his saddle. Popkov had sagged forward, blood pumping down his horse's neck, but Jens steadied the weight of him in the saddle with one hand and seized the loose reins in the other. His own horse needed no urging. Using the animal's strength, Jens shouldered a path through the strikers who were trying to stand and fight. Iron bars against sabers and rifles was no equal contest, but they had numbers on their side. More and more saddles fell empty.

In a side street Jens dismounted quickly and touched Popkov's shoulder. It shuddered. *Still alive, thank God.* Carefully he raised the Cossack's head from the horse. Jesus Christ, it was a bloody mass of gore. Rage and sorrow ripped a hole in his own chest, and yet his hands were steady as he removed his scarf and bound it tightly around Popkov's head, leaving just one good eye free. That eye, narrow and black, fought to focus, and the bulk of Popkov's massive body swayed unsteadily on the horse's back. He was barely conscious.

"Hold on, Popkov," Jens said firmly. "I'll get you home."

He unlooped his belt and tied the Cossack's wrists around the horse's neck, then leapt up into Hero's saddle with Popkov's reins in his hands.

"Still getting in my way, Friis."

Jens looked ahead. A man with a hard face and dressed in a long coat was standing in the middle of the road, rifle in hand, a small army of men behind him. All wore red armbands.

"Get out of my path, Arkin." Jens had no time to argue with the bastard. He started to ride forward, leading Popkov's horse behind.

Suddenly rifle shots sounded like thunder in the narrow street. It was the only sound Jens heard. No whinny. No squeal of pain. Hero just juddered, then collapsed under him in silence. Front legs first and then, after a brief struggle, the hindquarters.

"No, no, no!" Jens roared as he jumped from the saddle before it hit the ground and knelt at his horse's head. He held the long nose in the crook of his arm but the dark eyes were already dull, the breath gone from the wide velvet nostrils. "No," Jens bellowed, leapt from his knees, and threw himself at Arkin.

"I've been looking forward to this moment," Arkin said with an odd twist of his mouth as he slammed his rifle butt against Jens's head.

# Forty

VALENTINA'S HAND SHOOK. NOT FOR LIEV POPKOV'S EYE, which lay in an enamel bowl on the kitchen table. Not for the blood he'd lost or the bone that showed white across his forehead in a diagonal line. Not for the effort it must have taken for him to get himself and his horse back to her with the news of what happened, nor for the death of Hero.

Her hand shook for Jens.

She'd bathed Popkov's head and snipped out the smashed eyeball, swilling an antiseptic solution into the socket, and tipped enough vodka down him till he could speak.

"Arkin has got him," he'd slurred.

*Arkin has got him.*

Her hand shook and she pictured Arkin's knee in splinters from a bullet that came from Jens's rifle. She poured herself a vodka.

∾

JENS TASTED DRIED BLOOD IN HIS MOUTH. THAT WAS WHAT came first. Piece by piece more images slid back into place until his mind started to turn, slowly at first, then faster, gathering speed, racing ahead of him, crashing into things, wrenching his thoughts out of his head. He opened his eyes.

He was in a prison cell.

A dull yellow light was caged inside a metal grille on the ceiling. It never went out. A metal door with an observation hatch at eye level and a food hatch at floor level was the only thing of interest in the tiny room. Brick walls, a bucket in one corner, an enameled bowl in another, and the narrow cot he was lying on. A bare stinking mattress under him, one blanket on top of him.

His head hurt. The vision in one eye was blurred, and dried blood was encrusted down the side of his cheek like a black crab clinging to his face. He stood up and the room hurtled around him, but he made it to the door. He hammered a fist against it.

"Arkin, you fucking bastard, open this door."

He hammered for an hour. Two hours? He had no idea but his fist grew sore and the skin of his knuckles cracked. They'd taken his shoes and his belt, so he had nothing else to use for hammering. Slowly he slid to the floor, his back against the cold metal, and at last let his mind begin to think.

ॐ

ONLY ONCE DID ARKIN ENTER THE PRISON CELL. AS THE days passed, Jens could hear other metal doors clanging, feet shuffling along the corridor, shouts from the guards, and sometimes soft whimpers from prisoners that caused Jens to call out. If there were screams, they were always cut short.

Jens lived alone day after day in a twilit world. He never saw anyone. Food and water were pushed twice a day through the hatch in the door, watery kasha in the morning, broth in the evening. A scrap of gristle or cabbage in it became a source of celebration. Every morning his bucket was emptied, removed through the same hatch, and he washed using a tiny part of his water ration tipped into the enameled bowl. It became precious, the water. He dipped his fingertips in it and thought of all the times in his life he'd wasted water with such careless abandon. Now he was like the slum dwellers who huddled around a leaky pump in the courtyard, cherishing every drop.

Each day he expected guards to enter his cell, men with iron bars and heavy fists. But none came. No one. So when Viktor Arkin walked into his cell after four weeks of only his own thoughts and his own smell, he was tempted to smile at him. Instead he sat in silence on his mattress, back against the wall, and watched him carefully. Behind Arkin stood three guards in uniform, bars and restraining chains in their hands.

"Jens Friis." Arkin spoke his name as if it tasted sour in his mouth. "There's something I want you to know."

Jens rose to his feet. He was taller than Arkin and forced him to look up. "The only thing I want to know from you is when I'm getting out of this rat hole."

"Don't be so impatient. This will be your home for a long time to come." His eyes grew dark and he dropped his hand to his leg. "Like this knee will be my reminder of you for a long time to come."

"If I'd had my way, it would have been your brains spattered over that courtyard, not your knee."

Arkin's hand jerked, and for a moment Jens thought the man's control would slip. Underneath the mask of his face, under that hard arrogance, rage prowled. Jens could see its shadow.

"So what is it," Jens demanded, "that you came to tell me?"

"I want you to know that I slept with your wife at the *izba* in the marshes."

"You're lying."

"It's the truth."

"You are a filthy fucking liar. Valentina loathes you. She wouldn't let you lay a finger on her without clawing your eyes out."

"It was her idea. She loved it."

Jens went for him. Caught him by surprise and slammed his fist into the gloating mouth. The guards used their metal bars, but Jens had the satisfaction of seeing blood on Arkin's face and a twist of fury as he wiped it away with his wrist.

"I know her, Friis, I know every inch of her body. The freckle on her thigh, I kissed it, the tiny white scar on her ribs, I sucked it till she moaned, the thick black curls around the moist center of her, I licked them as I put my fingers inside her and . . ."

If three guards had not thrown their chains around Jens he would have killed Arkin.

"Get out!"

With a satisfied smile, Viktor Arkin limped out of the cell.

～

VALENTINA SEARCHED FOR JENS DAY AND NIGHT FOR EIGHT months. But people had vanished all over the city, friends and loved ones there one day and gone the next, so no one wanted to know, no one cared. They were all too frightened for themselves. Mobs roamed the streets, opened prisons, slaughtered police. They set fire to large houses at whim and torched a courthouse and the offices of the secret police. The Okhrana agents were hanged from lampposts in their turn. The city was ablaze with red banners and posters: DESTROY THE TYRANTS and VICTORY BELONGS TO THE PEOPLE OF RUSSIA.

Valentina took care. Such care that people stopped recognizing her. She wore plain peasant's clothes, handwoven dresses and shawls, a scarf around her head, and heavy cobbled boots on her feet. She grew thin, so that her cheeks became hollow, as pale and gaunt as the workers on the street. She let her shoulders droop and her spine sag and kept her eyes lowered, her gaze fixed to the ground so that no one would see the rage that burned within it. She would kiss Lydia and leave her with her toy train and her books shut in her room at home, but never did she find anyone who had heard a whisper about a Danish engineer called Jens Friis.

Tsar Nicholas had been forced to abdicate. He and his family were put under house arrest in Tsarskoe Selo and later taken by train to Siberia. Petrograd changed then. Valentina saw it happen. It turned red. Red armbands, red ribbons, red cockades in caps. Alexander Kerensky headed the new Provisional Government, but he panicked as the city continued to spiral out of control. General Kornilov, the commander in chief of the army, was sacked, and the war against Germany stumbled through defeat after defeat until the people of Russia were begging on their knees for it to end.

It was a summer of chaos.

❧

THE GREATEST CHAOS WAS IN VALENTINA'S HEART. IT FORgot how to beat. It forgot how to be something living, and instead lay silent and empty, the blood drained from it, a black brittle shell that felt as heavy as lead behind her ribs. Sometimes she tapped her chest with the tips of her fingers or even thumped a fist between her breasts, but nothing she did could set it going again. Was that what was meant by a broken heart? Like a broken watch.

The odd thing was that her eyes had remembered what her heart had forgotten. At night in bed without Jens they wept, as if her tears could release her pain in a way her heart could not. Her body ached for her husband, for the strength of him inside her. Her nostrils inhaled again and again his scent on the pillow. She wore his shirt in bed, his socks in her boots, his tiepin in the collar of her blouse. If she could have used the instruments on his desk she would have, but instead she carried his watch in her pocket.

She didn't see Liev Popkov again after the day she had bandaged his head. But she wasn't sorry. Although she told him she didn't blame him for her husband's capture and he told her he didn't blame her for the loss of his eye, they were both lying. So she searched for Jens where she could. She went to Varenka's old house again, but she wasn't there and the friendly man with the gypsy wife claimed he had never heard of Viktor Arkin. However much she paid him. She went to the basement room that stank of sewer water where Jens had taken her, but no one there had heard of Viktor Arkin, either.

She went to the church. The priest wasn't there, not the one who had lied to her. She was told he'd been whipped to death by tsarist troops in his village in front of his daughter. Not even that image made her heart murmur inside her. In her plain peasant clothes she went to meetings, pinned a red ribbon to her chest, and attended every political meeting in every church and every hall she could find. She smiled at eyes she hated, talked with men who wanted to shoot all government ministers, walked with factory women to bars, and even played the piano in one. Always she wore gloves to hide her smooth hands.

Nobody knew of Viktor Arkin. What had he done? Gone back to Moscow? With Jens?

*Where are you, Jens?*

Talking to him in her mind was the closest she came to feeling a flicker in her heart. That, and when she sat on his white reindeer rug with her daughter on her lap and read to her about Isambard Kingdom Brunel.

❧

SOMETIMES ARKIN WATCHED THEM, ELIZAVETA AND VALentina.

When he was sick of meetings. Tired of the shouting and the

arguments as each man tried to impose his will on the swirling rush of ideas, throwing up new plans, new schemes, new rules. Kerensky had turned on the Bolsheviks, smashed the printing presses of their newspaper *Pravda* and the offices of their Central Committee. He had ordered the arrest of Zinoviev and Kamenev for campaigning against the war and even of Lenin himself, who had been forced to flee into hiding again.

But the time was close now. This chaos could not continue. With a Red Guard numbering twenty-five thousand fighters in Petrograd and with the support of the Baltic sailors, they had already defeated the assault by General Lavr Kornilov. Arkin burned in his soul for the Bolsheviks to take over the country in one almighty bloody coup, to put an end to this pretense of government under Kerensky. And in a secret back room away from other ears, he had voiced to Lenin the need to stamp out the other revolutionary parties. No Mensheviks. No Socialist Revolutionaries. No Kadets. Only one could rule, and that one was the Bolsheviks. Russia needed an iron fist.

That was why Arkin had returned to Petrograd. To be at Vladimir Lenin's side and to make certain the opposition revolutionary leaders would end up rotting in the Peter and Paul Fortress. But sometimes when he was tired and his knee ached worse than usual, he let himself watch them in the street, Elizaveta and Valentina. Valentina was clever. She was a chameleon, hiding in her drab browns, merging with her background, thinking no one would see her. Did she really imagine that any man who looked at her face wouldn't remember it? She had grown more beautiful in the years he'd been away in Moscow, more sensual, even more desirable in the way she moved, just a turn of her head or a flick of her hair.

Elizaveta, still parading in her silks and furs, was an easy target for any red armband seeking revenge, yet still she walked out into the streets, head held high. He had warned her. He had even begged her. But she had smiled her quiet smile and kissed his mouth to stop his words.

"I am me. And you are you," she had murmured. "Let us leave it like that."

So he had left it like that. He could not bring himself to ask Elizaveta about the child, but he never saw the little girl with them. Valentina kept her hidden away.

～ঌ

V ALENTINA SAT WITH LYDIA AT HER SIDE ON THE CHAISE
 longue in her parents' drawing room and pleaded with them to
leave Petrograd while they still could.

"Valentina," her father said sternly, "this is *our* home. This is *our*
country. I will not leave."

"Papa, please, it is not safe."

He scowled, but not at her, at the carpet, his skin settling into the
downward lines that were now permanent on his face. He had lost
weight in recent months like everyone else. Valentina could see that
things were missing from the room. The pair of gold candelabra was
gone, and an antique mother-of-pearl fire screen. Was he secreting
them somewhere, hoarding them for better times? Or had they been
sold or used as bribes? Maybe even stolen by roving bands of Red
Army soldiers pushing their luck.

"They do not frighten me, these Bolsheviks," he said.

"They should." It was her mother who had spoken. She didn't
look frightened. She didn't even look annoyed at the mention of
their name. She was quietly dressed in somber silk, no pearls or jewelry of any kind, Valentina noticed. So she was also being careful in
her own way. "We should all be frightened, not at what they have
done but of what they have yet to do."

Ivanov looked at her, surprised. "How do you know what they
intend to do?"

"I read the newspapers, I hear talk. They are hunting us down
one by one. Taking over our houses. It's only a matter of time."

"Mama, don't you hate them?"

"No. They are fighting for what they believe in, just like we live
in the way we believe in."

Her husband snorted with annoyance, and Valentina went over
to his chair.

"Stay at home, Papa. Keep safe." She touched his hand and he
wrapped his fingers around hers. She bent and kissed his cheek. It
felt softer, as if an outer layer had been removed. "Look after yourself
and Mama."

"Is that what you're doing? In those ridiculous clothes? I never
thought a daughter of mine would wear such rags."

"Grandpapa," Lydia said with her father's smile, "you should wear a work shirt and cloth cap. You'd look funny."

They laughed, all of them together. Later, Valentina remembered that last laugh.

⁓

THINGS BECAME WORSE AS THE WEATHER GREW COLD again and Valentina started work on preparing her house. She summoned a furniture dealer and had most of their possessions removed in exchange for a fat pile of paper roubles. Immediately she exchanged it for gold coins and diamonds because the paper rouble would soon be worth next to nothing. Both the dealer and the jeweler robbed her blind, but she was in no position to argue.

She sacked all the servants, filled the house with worthless beds and chairs and cupboards, and locked all her and Lydia's belongings in two rooms upstairs. She kept Jens's engineering drawings, a few of his clothes, none of his books, a stout pair of shoes. Everything else she let go. Lydia clung tight to her toy train and her wooden bricks as she sat on her mother's lap and listened solemnly.

"We have to become one of *them*," Valentina explained. "We mustn't let *them* throw us out of our house, or how will your Papa know where to find us when he comes back?"

"Will he come back soon?"

"Yes, my angel. Soon."

The tawny eyes blinked hard. "I am five now, Mama."

"I know."

"That is almost grown up."

Valentina smiled. "Indeed it is."

"So you must tell me the truth, Mama."

"Of course."

"When will Papa come back?"

"Soon."

⁓

WORST WAS THE ERARD GRAND PIANO. LETTING IT GO was like chopping off a limb. She polished it till it gleamed and sat on the stool one last time with Lydia on the floor, her back propped against Valentina's leg. She played the Chopin and Lydia cried.

"It's Papa's favorite."

"Maybe he heard it."

Lydia shook her head, biting her lip. Then the piano was taken away in a cart.

People moved into the house. People who walked mud onto the polished floors and who did not know what a light switch was for or how to use a flush lavatory. Valentina shut herself away in her two rooms, curled on her bed wrapped up in Jens's cotton shirt that now smelled of herself instead of him. She'd lost his house, she'd lost his beloved books, and now she'd lost his scent. She turned her face into his pillow, dry-eyed, and a sound came from her lips, a low formless moan from deep within her.

On the top step of the stairs Lydia sat hugging her knees and watching two barefoot boys play football in the hall with her father's globe of the world.

୬

DON'T HURT HER, VIKTOR."

"Elizaveta, I will never hurt your daughter, I have promised you that. Her husband is still alive only because of you."

"Don't let them hurt her, the ones in gray that call themselves an army. Or the ones that roam in packs like wolves, administering their version of justice. Don't let them hurt her."

"I can only do so much. When you remove a dam from the river, you cannot tell it not to flow. But"—he lifted his head from the pillow and kissed her slender throat above him on the bed—"I will do what I can. To protect you."

She moved her hips in rhythm to his as she lay astride him, her breasts soft as satin as they brushed over his chest, and a low sigh punctuated her words. "I don't need protection." She pressed her lips hard on his mouth, and her tongue sought his as if she would starve without it.

# Forty-one

A SOUND LIKE THE HAMMER OF THOR POUNDED THROUGH the city of Petrograd and rattled the windows like bones in a grave. It startled Valentina from her book and woke Lydia, who scurried in her nightdress into her mother's bed with wide excited eyes. Valentina could feel her daughter's heart fluttering as she held her close. She looked at the clock. It was nine forty-five in the evening of October 24, 1917.

"Is it thunder, Mama?"

"No, my love. It sounds like a gun."

Lydia's eyes grew large as plates. "A big one."

"Yes, a very big one. I think it's a ship's gun."

"Which ship?"

"I don't know." But her blood froze in her veins. She was certain what it was: a signal for the revolution to start.

Arkin could have told her. It was the *Aurora*.

IT WAS FOUR O'CLOCK IN THE MORNING AND VALENTINA stood under the freezing night sky, watching her world burn. There were no stars, no comets, nothing spectacular to mark the event. But somewhere in the distance above the roofs of the city, a fire was burning a hole in the darkness and its glow stripped away any last shred of hope in her heart that Russia could pull itself back from the brink.

What did it mean? For Jens. For her daughter. For her parents. Their world had gone. The ground beneath her feet was shifting, and her hand gripped onto the wrought-iron gates of her house as if their flimsy metal could stop the universe from crashing down on her.

*Jens, are you here in the city? Did you hear the ship's gun?*

She was convinced he was still alive, still breathing in the same night air she was breathing. Why Arkin wouldn't put a bullet in the brain of the man who had crippled him, she had no idea, but nothing would convince her he was dead. Nothing. She tightened her grip on the icy metal of the gate. It was the way his thoughts seemed to seep in to her mind. She would be stirring kasha in a saucepan, morning porridge for breakfast, and suddenly she would hear him sigh and know he was picturing the way she tucked her hair behind her ear and clenched the tip of her tongue between her teeth when she was concentrating. She would swing around from the stove, but he was never there. Or when she was angry with the urchins downstairs for kicking a ball through a window when glass was impossible to obtain, she heard Jens thinking at that exact moment that the country's children were illiterate and that the first thing the revolution must bring about was free and compulsory education for all.

She clung to his thoughts. As each one slipped into her mind, she wrapped it carefully as one would a precious object in cotton-wool, collected them the way a lepidopterist collects butterflies. She took them out to listen to again and again while she lay in their bed at night, holding his pillow. Now she watched the fire push back the darkness of the city but her own darkness remained, solid and absolute.

"You'll not find him in those flames." The voice came at her out of the night.

"Liev?"

Liev Popkov's huge form stepped out of the shadows into a pool of lamplight so she could see it was him. Bigger than ever. A patch covered the empty eye socket and black corkscrew curls spilled down over the scar on his forehead. She was pleased to see him. That surprised her.

"No horses now?" He gestured toward the stables where he used to play cards with Jens, and it occurred to Valentina for the first time that he must miss his friend.

"No, I sold them."

Without even asking, whole families had moved into her stables as soon as they were empty, sleeping in the stalls, wrapped up in straw at night and eating oats from the tubs. She didn't object. She didn't care. She wanted to feel something for them, but she couldn't. People like these were the reason she had lost her husband. Lost her sister. These were the ones Arkin was fighting for. *Don't you see what you're doing?* she wanted to shout at them. *Don't you see that you're destroying all that is good about Russia, as well as all that is bad?*

Quickly she drew Popkov out of the light. "You have news?"

"Yes."

"About Jens?"

"No."

She made no sound, not even the faintest gasp, though disappointment was cracking her bones. "Who then?"

He gave a chuckle and she wanted to seize his beard and shake it. "Who?" she asked again.

"A man called Erikov. I've heard he has Comrade Lenin's ear."

"What's that to me?"

"His name is Viktor Erikov."

Her heart stopped. "Viktor Erikov?"

"Arkin has changed his name. That's why we couldn't find the murdering bastard."

"Why would he do that?"

The big shadow shifted. "Because of your family. Because the name of Arkin was too close to Minister Ivanov. He's putting distance between them."

She nodded. "Do you know where he is?"

"Not yet. But I will."

"You'll tell me?"

"*Da.* It will probably get you killed, but I will tell you. Stay indoors till then."

"Where are the revolutionaries?"

"Everywhere. The bloody Bolsheviks have occupied the railway stations and taken over the telephone exchange. They've even stormed the State Bank. They mean business, so stay indoors."

"Thank you, Liev."

A shrug and he turned to leave.

"Liev." She held on to his arm. It felt like rock. "I'm sorry about your eye. Take care of yourself."

He growled something inaudible, a deep rumble in his granite chest, and loped away into the night.

❧

S TAY HERE, LYDIA. KEEP THE DOOR LOCKED. DO NOT OPEN it to anyone."

"What if I want the lavatory, Mama?"

"Use the bucket."

The dainty nose wrinkled in distaste.

"I mean it, Lydia."

"Where are you going?"

"To find Papa."

The small heart-shaped face beamed back at her. "Can I come?"

"No. You must be good. Papa will only come back if you are good."

"I'll be good, Mama."

Her daughter put on her angel face, but Valentina wasn't fooled. "I mean it. Don't unlock the door. Promise me."

"I promise."

She kissed her daughter's wild hair and made herself believe her.

❧

V ALENTINA!"
        She stood in Dr. Fedorin's doorway but glanced warily over her shoulder. The city was quiet now. Like a wolf sleeping after a good night's kill. But that didn't mean it wouldn't kill again.

Fedorin pulled her into his house and shut the door quickly. "You shouldn't be out on the streets today, Valentina. It's too dangerous."

"I just came to find out what you'd heard."

"My dear girl, the city has exploded in our faces. The Bolshevik revolution is tearing Petrograd apart, and their Red Guard is arresting anyone and everyone who isn't one of their own. Factory bosses, bankers, and politicians of every kind are—" He stopped as he saw her lips turn white.

"My father is one of those politicians."

He shook his head in despair. "Don't go to him, my dear."

"I have to. What about you?"

"Don't worry, I'm safe. I'm a doctor. They are going to need me. I see you have your nurse's uniform on, so that should help to keep you safe, too."

She opened the door in a hurry. "That's what I'm counting on."

❧

IT HAD GONE WELL. BETTER THAN ARKIN DREAMED OF. Kerensky's government had rolled over like a dead sheep and allowed the Reds to seize power. But—he smiled to himself as he considered Kerensky's stupidity—tonight would come as a shock. Tonight at the Winter Palace they would all be arrested. Kerensky's cabinet would be locked in the cells of the Peter and Paul Fortress before the day was finished. He walked around and around his office to ease the ache in his leg and waited for the next prisoners to be brought in.

His mind turned to Friis. Every day he thought of the engineer. And of the Ivanova girl. They were thorns in his flesh that he couldn't cut out, however sharp his blade. He drew on his cigarette, drowning his lungs in smoke but unable to drown the image of the pair of them that was lodged in his mind, the memory of them running through the rain together, arms linked, unable to keep their eyes off each other.

She'd been right. Valentina Ivanova knew exactly what she was doing. He did think of her every day, just as she'd said he would, but the irony was that if he didn't have a crippled knee he would probably be dead by now. Valentina had saved his life. He would have been forced into uniform long ago and packed off to the front in the useless war against Germany. He would have been cannon fodder, mown down on a battlefield somewhere, and Valentina would have been free of him. Except for the child, *his* child, she would always have that part of him. If it was his. He could never be sure of that, could he?

He wiped a hand across his face and stifled the familiar drag in his guts whenever he thought of the child. He was tired. No sleep. Too many fears about tonight and about the knives that would be aimed at his back by his fellow comrades the moment he held a degree of power in his hands.

He sat down at his desk and snapped at the soldier outside his door, "Next prisoner!"

Arkin didn't rise from his seat. But it was hard not to show Elizaveta that much respect.

"Prisoner Nicholai Ivanov," he said, "I order you to be taken before the tribunal and tried as a traitor to your country."

"You sniveling little nobody, what do you and your kind know about this country? I served it loyally for—"

Arkin nodded at the guard, and a rifle butt jabbed at the minister's face. His hands were roped behind his back so he could not stop the blood dripping from his mouth.

"Don't." It was the first time Elizaveta had spoken. "Please don't."

He allowed himself to look at her. To gather into his mind the exact shade of the gold of her hair and the smooth texture of her cheek, of her throat.

"Madam Ivanova." He could hear the respect in his own voice, but he couldn't hide it. He focused on the two sheets of paper on his desk, one with the name of Nicholai Ivanov on it, the other with Elizaveta Ivanova. He picked up a pen but rested the tips of his fingers on her name. It was the nearest he could come to touching her. "You are also to be tried for treason because you assisted your husband in his exploitation of the proletariat to fill the Romanov coffers."

She said nothing. Still he couldn't look at her. "Take them away."

"Immediately, Comrade Erikov."

But when the guard seized her husband roughly by the arm, Elizaveta said, "Wait."

The guard hesitated, the habit of obedience running deep. With her hands tied behind her back, she turned to her husband and kissed his cheek. "Good-bye, Nicholai. God bless you. We won't see each other again in this lifetime."

"Elizaveta, my wife, I need—"

"Take him away. Let her remain," Arkin ordered.

"Elizaveta," Ivanov cried out as he was dragged from the room, "I love—"

The guard slammed the door behind him. For a long moment Arkin and Elizaveta gazed at each other, alone in the room.

"I can't save you," he said at last.

"I know."

She smiled at him as intimately as she had on the lacy pillows of the Hotel de Russie. No sign of sorrow or regret in the curve of her full lips as she stood in his office.

"*Chyort!*" He threw his pen down on his desk and moved across the room till he was close enough to touch her, but he kept his hand at his side. "Elizaveta, I would if I could. But you are a government minister's wife. God knows, I would save you if I could."

Her blue eyes glittered with pleasure. "I know. Don't worry about me." Her elegant clothes were dirty and ripped on one sleeve. He wondered what rough hand had torn it. "I want to look at you one last time," she said quietly.

He touched her then, his fingers on her pale cheek. She tilted her head and gently leaned into his hand. "Take care of yourself, Viktor. These are such dangerous times and I want you to"—she swallowed and turned her mouth to kiss his fingers—"to be safe. I hate all that you stand for, I hate what you Bolsheviks will do to my country, but"—she lifted her head—"I can't hate you."

"Elizaveta, I shall do all I can to save you from the tribunal's wrath, but—"

"No, Viktor, do nothing for me, I beg you." She spoke the words slowly and thoughtfully, as though to impress their meaning on him. "I have lived more in these last years than ever before in my life. Lived more and loved more. That is enough for me. You brought me a joy I didn't know existed. *Spasibo.*"

He smiled at her, a tender smile that did not attempt to hide from her the sharp ache under his ribs. "*Spasibo,*" he echoed.

"God keep you," she murmured, and walked to the door.

༄

WHEN VALENTINA RETURNED HOME, LYDIA WAS KNEEL-ing at the top of the stairs throwing dried sultanas one by one to the two ragged boys in the hall below. Valentina didn't waste time on scolding her but seized her wrist, pulled her into their room, and knelt down in front of her so that their eyes were on a level.

"Lydia, I have an appointment to see a man, and I want you to come with me."

"Is it Papa?"

"No. *Dochenka*, my daughter, don't look so sad. If we do this right, we'll be seeing Papa soon."

"You say that every day."

"Well, today it's true."

She dressed them carefully, plain dresses, plain coats, no frills, no furs. She tucked Lydia's fiery locks under a brown headscarf and then pulled a felt hat down on top of it. "You must look like a workman's daughter today."

They studied their drab clothes in the mirror.

"You look beautiful in yours, Mama. But I look ugly in mine."

Valentina swung Lydia up into her arms and kissed her forehead. "You couldn't look ugly if you tried, my angel. Now listen to me. There are things I want you to say."

∾

I THOUGHT YOU WERE DEAD," VALENTINA SAID.

Valentina had walked into Comrade Erikov's office and stared at Arkin's face, at his gray uniform, at the new arrogance in his eyes, and for the thousandth time wished she had stuck Dr. Fedorin's scalpel into his throat that day of the duel on Pistol Ridge.

"I thought you would have died of gangrene," she said.

"I am not so easy to kill." But his eyes were not on her, they were on the child.

"Viktor, this is your daughter, Lydia."

Arkin's face remained blank. Not even a smile for the child. Valentina shuddered inwardly as she released her daughter's small hand and saw her skip forward to stand like a little elf before the tall figure behind the desk. Valentina's throat tightened at the sight of her young courage.

"*Dobriy den*, good afternoon, Papa."

A pulse jumped into life at the edge of Arkin's jaw. His gaze faltered as he reached down and touched the top of the small head with tentative fingers. "How do I know she's mine?"

"Because I swear to you that she is. I was already pregnant when I married Jens Friis." Valentina thanked God that Arkin had not been around to know the date of her daughter's birth.

He took his hand away, but Lydia continued to stare up at him with round eyes.

"That means nothing," he said. His voice was flat. "She could be Friis's brat."

"No." She glanced away as if embarrassed. "Jens and I always took care that I wouldn't become pregnant."

"You could be lying."

"I am not lying, I swear it on my child's life. Look at her mouth, it's yours. Look at her chin. It's small but the shape is yours." It was a lie, but she could sense how much he wanted it to be true.

"Her hair?" His hand moved toward the hat.

But Valentina had told Lydia that her hat must not come off. Without hesitation Lydia seized his hand, clutching it tight, and rested her small cheek against it. Her gaze fixed on Arkin with the naked yearning that only a child can possess.

He didn't snatch his hand away but studied her intently. "Her eyes aren't mine. Nor are they yours, for that matter."

"Her eyes are strictly her own. Much of Lydia is strictly her own."

In the chilly office he crouched down on one heel, the other leg stretched out stiffly to the side, and examined her closely, his expression guarded. But he allowed his fingers to lie captive in the small hands.

"So you are Lydia," he said to her. His voice was kind.

"And you are my papa," Lydia said softly. She tipped her head to one side and smiled shyly, then suddenly threw her wispy arms around his neck, hooking them together as if she would never let him go. She uttered a low mewing sound. "Papa." She kissed his cheek.

Valentina watched. Stunned. She had not instructed her daughter to do this, but as she watched the man she hated, she saw him melt. His bones grew soft in her daughter's grasp, and a small part of her hatred melted with it. With the child's cheek nestled against his own, his eyes lost their hard-edged focus and his features seemed to blur as though the structure under them had crumbled. For a long moment man and child remained locked together, and then he kissed her forehead briskly, rose to his full height, and retreated behind his desk without looking at either of them. He took out a form, wrote on it, and held it out to Valentina.

"Here," he said. "A permit to leave Petrograd. Now go."

She read it. Looked at Lydia. Tore it up. "My husband's name is not on it."

"No."

"I will not leave Petrograd without him."

"If you stay in this city, the Red Guards will come for you

eventually, Valentina, however much you hide inside your brown coat. You are the minister's daughter and they will hunt you down. Don't risk our child's life."

"If Jens Friis stays, we stay."

"Don't be so foolish, Valentina. Think of Lydia."

"If he dies, we die."

"I cannot save you all."

"Put his name on the travel permit if you want your daughter to live."

The moment was agony. She thought she had lost him. He seemed to withdraw into himself, and the room became a dead and empty place. But abruptly he fixed his eyes on hers.

"Does your mother love Lydia?" he asked.

Valentina trod warily. "Yes, of course she loves her grand-daughter."

He nodded but didn't look at Lydia again as he wrote out another form and handed it to Valentina. "Take it."

Jens's name was on it alongside hers and Lydia's. "*Spasibo.* Thank you."

"But I warn you, after he is released, they will come for him whether his name is on the permit or not. You have an hour, maybe less, before others will override this permit when they know he is here in Petrograd. He worked for the tsar, and such treachery will not be tolerated." Anger kicked into his voice. "The time of reckoning has come for people like him, people who think they are protected because they are liberal minded and well skilled. As if his intelligence is enough of a shield."

"Jens worked for the people of Russia, to help them. What are you Bolsheviks going to do, destroy everyone with a brain who can think for themselves? What hope is there for Russia's future if you do that?"

"Russia has a great future ahead of it now. Without its tyrants at last."

Valentina took Lydia's hand and pulled her close to her skirts. "I hope we do not meet again, Arkin."

"So take the child and run. It's what you're good at. It's what you did so well in the forest, hiding from tree to tree."

She stared at him. "What are you talking about?"

He smiled with satisfaction. "Don't you know even now? I was in the forest with you that day you stumbled into our preparations. I was the one who bombed your house at Tesovo."

༄

"DID I DO WELL, MAMA?"

"You did very well, *dochenka*, my daughter."

"Will Papa be angry with me at home because I called that other man Papa?"

"No. He will kiss you a thousand times."

"So why are you crying?" Her small hand chafed her mother's. "Don't cry."

"Hurry! We must be quick. We have only an hour."

"For what?"

"To leave Petrograd."

# Forty-two

VALENTINA STOOD INSIDE THE FRONT DOOR, EYES CLOSED, listening. Two dark-skinned boys were sitting on the floor in the hallway playing cards for cigarette butts, but they were so intent on their game that they spoke little. They didn't disturb her. A narrow bed had appeared in the alcove under the stairs, and a bald man lay on his back within it and snored. Not even he disturbed her because she was concentrating. Listening hard. She didn't want to draw attention to herself by waiting outside.

Minutes ticked past. She held her breath as though she could slow time by doing so, but she could feel the weight of Jens's watch in her pocket, its hands moving relentlessly. She was listening for military boots striding up the path, her mind tense with each rustle of wind, each rattle of the gate. She knew she would not hear Jens until his hand touched the door.

Minutes ticked past.

There was the faintest sound of something on the step outside. Her fingers went to the lock and turned it, letting the door swing open a crack and a cold whip of air rush in, and then she threw it wide so hard it rebounded off the wall behind. The boys on the floor looked up with interest. Jens stood there, tall as ever, but his skin was pulled taut over his cheekbones and his eyes sunk deep into dark sockets. Covering the lower half of his face was a thick red beard.

"Valentina." It was a whisper.

She drew him to her, over the threshold into the hallway, and he kicked the door shut behind him. She held him, unable to speak, her heart clamoring against his, and she felt his arms around her, hard and unyielding. She wanted him so badly her body started to shiver.

"Valentina," he said again into her hair, as if it were the only word he could remember.

Her body wouldn't let go of him. She was aware of the watch in her pocket and time like a traitor racing away from them. But still it wouldn't let him go.

❧

THE BAGS WERE READY ON THE BED, TWO LARGE AND ONE small. She'd packed them weeks ago, mostly with canned meat and packets of oats and dried fruit, but also matches, candles, a blanket, socks, and an extra wool sweater for each of them.

"We will be traveling light," she had told her daughter. Lydia had sat cross-legged on the reindeer rug and clutched her train to her chest.

Alone in their room, Valentina stripped Jens's clothes from his body. Eight months in the same clothes.

"I stink like a dead boar," he muttered.

She kissed his chest. "You smell good enough to eat."

He laughed but it was a tight sound, and she knew those muscles had been long unused. Unlike the muscles of the body, which were thick cords down the length of his thigh and across the width of his chest, but that was all there was of him. No real flesh. Just skin and bones and twists of muscle. She tried to imagine what it had cost him to keep his body and his mind ready for escape while on the edge of starvation, but she couldn't. He washed quickly and she scrubbed his back, trimmed his beard with scissors, and didn't stop long enough for him to shave. In minutes they were out of the house and walking briskly down the icy pavement, their daughter's hands in theirs. Lydia kept nudging her father's leg with her shoulder to make sure he was real.

"The Bolsheviks have taken over the railway stations," Valentina told him, "so we daren't risk trying for a train."

"We walk," he said. "All the way if we have to."

"To where?"

"To China."

Her mouth dropped open. He was watching her, smiling at her reaction, and she knew that with this man she would walk to the North Pole if she had to.

"China it is," she said.

"Where is China?" Lydia asked.

"At the end of Russia where it falls into the sea."

"Not far?"

They both smiled at her. "You'll have to walk fast," Jens said, and she nodded, speeding up her small steps.

It was in the next street that they saw the first roadblock, manned by figures in gray with wide red armbands and nervous jittery rifles. Valentina felt her spine stiffen with dread, but Jens didn't break stride as he turned smoothly down a side road and doubled back to try a different approach. Each time it was the same. In every direction. Each time they were forced to retreat. Lydia sheltered in the folds of her parents' long coats and stopped chattering to her father about how she had learned to play poker from the boys downstairs. After an hour Jens stopped in the shadow of a church, its onion dome a dull amber under the overcast sky as ashes from last night's fires still swirled in the wind. They rested their packs on the ground.

"Jens, we're trapped. The travel permits are worthless here."

"The soldiers here are hard-bitten Bolsheviks. They'd take no notice of a signature on a form if they decide it's their job to put a bullet in one of the *oppressors*. It's too risky to use them here." He leaned against the wall for a moment, turning his head as though to check the other end of the road, but it meant she could no longer see his face. "Why did he agree to release me?" he asked.

Her mouth went dry. She laid her head against his shoulder. "Does it matter?"

For a long moment he said nothing, and Valentina felt a weight like lead in her chest. Then he rested his bristly chin on her head and released the breath he had been holding.

"No, my love," he said softly, "it doesn't matter. As long as we are together." He kissed her forehead. "And now let's move."

"Where?"

He tilted her chin so that her eyes met his. "Do you really think

I spent eight months in that stinking cell thinking of nothing? I planned our route and have trodden each step a thousand times."

He picked up his pack and swung his daughter onto his back. "There is a way out."

❧

J ENS BENT DOWN AND LEVERED UP THE METAL HATCH IN the middle of the road. Some of them were locked, but he knew the bolt on this one was broken.

"Quickly! Climb down." He saw Valentina hesitate. "It's safe."

The last time she was in a sewerage tunnel, she almost drowned. He climbed into the black hole himself, holding on to the metal ladder fixed to the brick wall, and from a shelf on one side he removed a kerosene lamp. The matches that were supposed to be there were gone, but Valentina had given him a box for his pocket. He lit the wick, and instantly a muted yellow glow made sense of the shadows.

"Lydia, come on, sweetheart, your turn next."

The small face appeared over the edge warily, and then she slid her feet onto the first rung and scampered down the ladder like a monkey. When she saw the black tunnel stretching ahead, she didn't whimper but edged herself close against him, staring unblinkingly into the darkness.

"It's quite safe," he said, patted the top of her felt hat to reassure her, and reached up to help Valentina. Without being asked, she drew the hatch back over the opening as she descended, and the darkness swallowed them whole. The solid silence was punctuated by the sound of water dripping and a distant murmur that he knew was a nearby pumping engine.

"How far?" Valentina asked.

"As far as we can."

He raised the lamp to look at her face because he couldn't help himself. And he could see changes there that were new, but he kissed her lips and set off with Lydia on his back. At first Valentina sang to them as they walked, a clear sweet sound in the oppressive darkness, but as the going grew harder and they had to crawl on their hands and knees, dragging their bags through icy, foul-smelling water, it became impossible to do more than force themselves forward.

Jens was annoyed that he found it hard to focus in the shapeless tunnels because it was so long since his eyes had enjoyed the luxury of darkness. He stumbled time and again but refused to let Lydia climb down from his back despite Valentina's urgings. His daughter clung to his neck and to his hair with an eagerness that satisfied something dried and parched within him.

They didn't talk of what they were doing, of what they were giving up and what they were leaving behind. Now was not the time. Only once did he ask, "Your parents? Where are they?" She'd looked at her daughter who was listening to every word and shook her head. He didn't ask again. When they passed under another metal hatch Jens climbed the ladder and peered through the small holes in the cover. He saw feet running, hundreds of them, maybe thousands. After eight months of only his own company day after day, the concept of such numbers seemed almost incomprehensible to him. When the tunnels forked and he took the left-hand one without hesitation, Valentina laughed with astonishment, startling him.

"How can you possibly know your way around this maze of openings and inlets? It's impossible."

"They're *my* tunnels, Valentina. I built them. Of course I know how to find my way around them."

Lydia had been silent for too long. He turned to her, trudging behind him through the water ankle deep, and saw that her eyes were huge.

"Papa," she asked in a whisper, "where does the dragon sleep?"

"There's no dragon down here, *malishka*," Valentina said quickly.

"There is. I can smell its breath."

Jens took his child's hand in his. It was cold and clammy. "I think," he said, "it's time to go up into the light."

❧

THEY WERE NOT FAR FROM THE NEXT HATCH. THE TUNNEL ceiling was higher here, and he raised the lamp to cast its faint glow as far ahead as possible. The water reflected slick and oily.

"It's not in front of us, Papa," Lydia whispered. "The dragon is behind us."

"No, Lydia, my sweet, there's no—".

"Listen," she hissed.

He listened. Valentina put a warning hand on his arm. From somewhere behind them came the unmistakable sound of feet slushing through water, moving fast. Immediately Jens blew out the lamp.

He pulled Valentina and Lydia behind him and they stood in silence, waiting. After a minute he heard voices.

"The light has gone." It was a young boy's voice.

"They've vanished. Listen."

An elderly man speaking. And for a moment the feet were quiet. They had no light but must have been following Jens's. When the feet started again they were slower and grew louder until they were almost upon them, and Jens felt Valentina press something cold and heavy into his hand. It was a gun. His pulse kicked. He aimed the gun at the blackness.

"Whoever you are, stop right there," he called out.

The noises ceased.

"Who are you?" Jens demanded.

"No one," the boy answered. "Who are you?"

"Travelers."

"Maybe we're on the same journey," the older man suggested.

"Maybe we are. Do you have a light?"

"We have a lamp but no matches."

"Stay behind me, Valentina, and light our lamp."

She did so while he kept the pistol pointing in the direction of the voices, and the light swayed onto the two figures of a boy around twelve, beside a man with a waxed mustache and bemused regretful eyes. His hands were soft and he had the look of a banker or lawyer. Jens lowered the gun and threw his box of matches to the boy, who pocketed it smoothly. Jens heard Valentina curse behind him.

"I paid fifty roubles for those matches on the black market," she objected.

"Thank you, friend," the man said. "Do you have food to spare too?"

"*Nyet,*" Valentina said quickly.

"My grandson and I were forced to flee with nothing." He pointed to Valentina's pack. She started to back away. At that moment the boy whisked a huge heavy pistol from under his coat and aimed it straight at Valentina's head.

"Give me your pack," he shouted.

"You'll have to shoot me first, you worthless little thief," she answered.

Jens stepped in front of her, his gun aimed at the old man. "Tell him to put it away," he ordered. "I helped you. What kind of mind does your grandson possess?"

"A greedy one." He turned wearily to the boy. "Save your bullets for those who deserve them."

The boy swore and lowered his gun.

"We're leaving now," Jens said. "Don't stay down here too long. I warn you that Lenin and his Reds will sweep through these tunnels eventually when they realize what an escape route they are."

"Thank you for the advice."

Jens nodded farewell and lifted Lydia into his arms. She was trembling, teeth chattering like mice. But Valentina hesitated, and with a reluctant shake of her head, she opened up her pack and removed two cans of meat. She swore under her breath as she threw them to the boy and set off up the tunnel.

"Friend," the old man called after her, "there is a train."

She stopped and slowly swung back. "What train?"

"A train that skirts the land of my country estate east of the city on the edge of the forest. It is a small freight train that runs once a week, only shifting wheat and cattle."

Jens put down Lydia, reached into the bag on his shoulder, and pulled out the map and compass Valentina had packed in it. "Show me." He held the lamp high, and the man stamped a finger on the spot. He was wearing a signet ring containing a large diamond.

"See that bend in the river. That's where the train slows. That's where you can get on if you are quick. All the village peasants ride it."

"But I thought all the trains were on strike," Valentina said.

"Not this one. It runs just a small local service."

"How far does it go?" Jens asked.

"Not far but far enough. It meets up with the Trans-Siberian Railway to offload its freight."

"Is that where you're heading?"

"*Nyet.* Not yet." The old man pointed his finger up above his head. "First I have to find my wife. She is still in Petrograd." He looked at Jens and they both knew it was probably already too late, but neither voiced the thought.

"I wish you luck," Jens said. "Thank you for the information."

"Thank you for the food. God protect us all."

"It'll take more than God," Jens murmured as he scooped up his daughter and led his wife up out of the tunnels.

THEY FOUND THE SPOT, THE BEND IN THE RIVER. IT wasn't hard. On the outskirts of the city they had been stopped by a patrol of fresh-faced young soldiers, young enough to be easily impressed by an official stamp. So Jens had risked waving Arkin's travel permits under their noses, and the small family had been permitted to pass.

The forest had come as a welcome refuge. They had fallen into its shadowy world with relief and trekked along its animal trails for two days. The temperature dropped abruptly and fat lazy flakes of snow started to drift down, covering their tracks. Several times they saw other pale figures flitting between the trees like ghosts in the distance, but no one trusted anyone any more. No one approached. Strangers had become dangerous in Russia. If a person wasn't your friend, he was your enemy. She told Jens at last about her parents, how they had been condemned by a Bolshevik tribunal, and he held her in his arms, kissed her tears.

They camped among the trees at the bend of the river, wrapped in their blanket and coats, not risking a fire except briefly to heat water for tea. They watched the railway line. Hour after hour, day after day. The silver tracks carved a route through their minds to the future.

☙

VALENTINA LAY CURLED UP WITH JENS INSIDE HIS COAT. Dawn was not far away, a thin hairline crack of silver on the horizon. Beside them Lydia slept the sleep of the very young, wrapped in her cocoon of blanket. Valentina brushed her lips along her husband's smooth jaw. He had bathed and shaved in the river. She felt him smile in the darkness, eyes still closed, and she nestled her head in the crook of his neck. He smelled of pine needles.

"Jens?"

He kissed her hair.

"Jens, there's something I want to say." She spoke softly, but nevertheless she felt his limbs tense.

"There is no need to say anything." He lifted a hand and placed it over her mouth.

She let it lie there for a full minute, then shifted her head. "Jens, the journey we're on is dangerous. At any time we may get"—*killed, we may get killed*—"we may get separated."

He tightened his grip on her. "No. That won't happen."

"But if it does, promise me you'll take good care of our daughter."

He released a breath. "I do not need to promise."

"But promise me all the same. Please."

"Very well, my love, if it makes you happy. I promise I will take good care of Lydia." He turned his head, a black shadow in the darkness, his lips on her skin. "And you must promise me the same."

"I promise. I will care for her with my life."

"Satisfied?"

"No." Her lips found his and she felt the familiar and unquenchable ache for him. They made love under a clear night sky, beneath the stars. And though there was no sleigh and no fur rug like on the night of the Anichkov ball, there was no cart to interrupt them, no Arkin with his rifle to tear their world apart.

❧

I T'S COMING!" LYDIA CALLED. Smoke belched up into the blue sky, and the noise of the engine echoed through the crisp air. The river and the railway line ran in parallel tracks, and ice sparkled like new-cut diamonds between them. Fields and forest stretched as far as the eye could see, the perfect day for train hopping.

"Get ready," Jens said.

Valentina nodded but her heart was pounding. Lydia was on Jens's back, arms tight around his neck. His hand was gripping Valentina's. She gave her husband and daughter a tense smile. "I'm ready." Her breath curled between them like an icy curtain, and she clutched his fingers.

The train came. Only three freight wagons behind the engine. As it reached the bend in the river it slowed, just as the man in the tunnel had promised it would. The wagons bucked and rattled, lurching to one side, and Jens began to run alongside the track. Valentina matched him stride for stride, but his legs were longer and she had to struggle. The engine growled at their shoulders. Valentina glanced across at the driver and saw that he was shaking a stick at them, as if he would beat them off the train. At the front of the first wagon a metal ladder was fixed on its outside wall, and Jens reached out with his free hand as it passed him, seizing it effortlessly. Instantly he was whisked off his feet. For one split second he hung by one hand, with Lydia on his back and his pack, as well as Valentina's, slung over his shoulder. His other hand still held tight to his wife.

"Jump!" he screamed.

But her legs were at full stretch. She jumped. Stumbled, lost her footing. Felt her arm almost wrench from its socket. She was being dragged at full speed along the ground. Ripping, tearing, battering.

She let go. She felt her fingers slide out of his, felt her life slide from her grasp. She lay on the ice-covered ground and watched everything she loved in this life surge away from her. As the track straightened the engine gathered speed, pistons pumping, and bellowed its annoyance. The figures of Jens and Lydia disappeared.

She pulled herself to her feet to watch the train until the last possible moment, before it vanished from sight, unaware that she was trembling or that the skin of her legs was torn to shreds.

"Jens!" she screamed. "Lydia!"

She tried to breathe. Couldn't begin to. She'd lost everything. After all it had cost her to get this far, now when her life was ready to start again, she had lost it all. Automatically, she began to run. She would damn well run all the way to China if she had to. Her feet pounding on the ground, she stumbled again, but she caught herself and this time kept going. Thoughts rushed through her head. They had each other. Jens and Lydia. They'd be together. Together forever. Safe.

Her lungs began to hurt and she became aware of where she was, alone in the middle of nowhere. She had nothing except the certain knowledge: that Jens and Lydia were together, that they would take care of each other. It held her on her feet.

But the pain of being without them was killing her. Still she ran and ran and ran, and just when a ragged black shadow began to slide in around the edges of her vision, she saw in the distance the end of the train again. She blinked. It was still there, not moving on the line, gray smoke belching once more into the sky.

She ran. It came closer, closer, her heart thundering in her chest. She reached the end wagon, but still it didn't move, shuddering impatiently on the track. She reached the second wagon, lungs bursting, the first. Then the ladder. She grasped it tight. Nothing happened; the train remained still. Tentatively, she slid herself farther along until she made a sudden dash to the engine itself.

Standing there, with a gun to the head of the driver, was Jens. He smiled at her. "You took your time getting here," he said.

TURN THE PAGE FOR AN EXCERPT FROM
KATE FURNIVALL'S NOVEL

## *The Russian Concubine*

THE STORY OF LYDIA IVANOVA'S EARLY YEARS IN CHINA
AVAILABLE IN PAPERBACK NOW
FROM BERKLEY BOOKS

THE TRAIN GROWLED TO A HALT. GRAY STEAM BELCHED from its heaving engine into the white sky, and the twenty-four freight carriages behind bucked and rattled as they lurched shrieking to a standstill. The sound of horses and of shouted commands echoed across the stillness of the empty frozen landscape.

"Why have we stopped?" Valentina Friis whispered to her husband.

Her breath curled between them like an icy curtain. It seemed to her despairing mind to be the only part of her that still had any strength to move. She clutched his hand. Not for warmth this time, but because she needed to know he was still there at her side. He shook his head, his face blue with cold because his coat was wrapped tightly around the sleeping child in his arms.

"This is not the end," he said.

"Promise me," she breathed.

He gave his wife a smile and together they clung to the rough timbered wall of the cattle wagon that enclosed them, pressing their eyes to the slender gaps between the planks. All around them others did the same. Desperate eyes. Eyes that had already seen too much.

"They mean to kill us," the bearded man on Valentina's right stated in a flat voice. He spoke with a heavy Georgian accent and wore his astrakhan hat well down over his ears. "Why else would we stop in the middle of nowhere?"

"Oh sweet Mary, mother of God, protect us."

It was the wail of an old woman still huddled on the filthy floor and wrapped in so many shawls she looked like a fat little Buddha. But underneath the stinking rags was little more than skin and bone.

"No, babushka," another male voice insisted. It came from the rear end of the carriage where the ice-ridden wind tore relentlessly through the slats, bringing the breath of Siberia into their lungs. "No, it'll be General Korilov. He knows we're on this godforsaken cattle train starving to death. He won't let us die. He's a great commander."

A murmur of approval ran around the clutch of gaunt faces, bringing a spark of belief to the dull eyes, and a young boy with dirty blond hair who had been lying listlessly in one corner leapt to his feet and started to cry with relief. It had been a long time since anyone had wasted energy on tears.

"Dear God, I pray you are right," said a hollow-eyed man with a stained bandage on the stump of his arm. At night he groaned endlessly in his sleep, but by day he was silent and tense. "We're at war," he said curtly. "General Lavr Kornilov cannot be everywhere."

"But I tell you he's here. You'll see."

"Is he right, Jens?" Valentina tilted her face up to her husband.

She was only twenty-four, small and fragile, but possessed sensuous dark eyes that could, with a glance, for a brief moment, make a man forget the cold and the hunger that gnawed at his insides or the weight of a child in his arms. Jens Friis was ten years older than his wife and fearful for her safety if the roving Bolshevik soldiers took one look at her beautiful face. He bent his head and brushed a kiss on her forehead.

"We shall soon know," he said.

The red beard on his unshaven cheek was rough against Valentina's cracked lips, but she welcomed the feel of it and the smell of his unwashed body. They reminded her that she had not died and gone to hell. Because hell was exactly what this felt like. The thought that this nightmare journey across thousands of miles of snow and ice might go on forever, through the whole of eternity, that this was her cruel damnation for defying her parents, was one that haunted her, awake and asleep.

Suddenly the great sliding door of the wagon was thrust open and fierce voices shouted, *"Vse is vagona, bistro."* Out of the wagons.

❧

THE LIGHT BLINDED VALENTINA. THERE WAS SO MUCH OF it. After the perpetually twilit world inside the wagon, it rushed at her from the huge arc of sky, skidded off the snow, and robbed her of vision. She blinked hard and forced the scene around her into focus.

What she saw chilled her heart.

A row of rifles. All aimed directly at the ragged passengers as they scrambled off the train and huddled in anxious groups, their coats pulled tight to keep out the cold and the fear. Jens reached up to help the old woman down from their wagon, but before he could take her hand she was pushed from behind and landed facedown in the snow. She made no sound, no cry. But she was quickly yanked onto her feet by the soldier who had thrown open the wagon door and shaken as carelessly as a dog shakes a bone.

Valentina exchanged a look with her husband. Without a word they slid their child from Jens's shoulder and stood her between them, hiding her in the folds of their long coats as they moved forward together.

"Mama?" It was a whisper. Though only five years old, the girl had already learned the need for silence. For stillness.

"Hush, Lydia," Valentina murmured but could not resist a glance down at her daughter. All she saw was a pair of wide tawny eyes in a heart-shaped bone-white face and little booted feet swallowed up by the snow. She pressed closer against her husband and the face no longer existed. Only the small hand clutching her own told her otherwise.

❧

THE MAN FROM GEORGIA IN THE WAGON WAS RIGHT. This was truly the middle of nowhere. A godforsaken landscape of nothing but snow and ice and the occasional windswept rock face glistening black. In the far distance a bank of skeletal trees stood like a reminder that life could exist here. But this was no place to live.

No place to die.

The men on horseback didn't look much like an army. Nothing

remotely like the smart officers Valentina was used to seeing in the ballrooms and *troikas* of St. Petersburg or ice skating on the Neva, showing off their crisp uniforms and impeccable manners. These men were diff erent. Alien to that elegant world she had left behind. These men were hostile. Dangerous. About fifty of them had spread out along the length of the train, alert and hungry as wolves. They wore an assortment of greatcoats against the cold, some gray, others black, and one a deep muddy green. But all cradled the same long-nosed rifle in their arms and had the same fanatical look of hatred in their eyes.

"Bolsheviks," Jens murmured to Valentina, as they were herded into a group where the fragile sound of prayers trickled like tears. "Pull your hood over your head and hide your hands."

"My hands?"

"Yes."

"Why my hands?"

"Comrade Lenin likes to see them scarred and roughened by years of what he calls honest labor." He touched her arm protectively. "I don't think piano playing counts, my love."

Valentina nodded, slipped her hood over her head and her one free hand into her pocket. Her gloves, her once beautiful sable gloves, had been torn to shreds during the months in the forest, that time of traveling on foot by night, eating worms and lichen by day. It had taken its toll on more than just her gloves.

"Jens," she said softly, "I don't want to die."

He shook his head vehemently and his free hand jabbed toward the tall soldier on horseback who was clearly in command. The one in the green greatcoat.

"He's the one who should die—for leading the peasants into this mass insanity that is tearing Russia apart. Men like him open up the floodgates of brutality and call it justice."

At that moment the officer called out an order and more of his troops dismounted. Rifle barrels were thrust into faces, thudded against backs. As the train breathed heavily in the silent wilderness, the soldiers pushed and jostled its cargo of hundreds of displaced people into a tight circle fifty yards away from the rail track and then proceeded to strip the wagons of possessions.

"No, please, don't," shouted a man at Valentina's elbow as an armful of tattered blankets and a tiny cooking stove were hurled out of one of the front wagons. Tears were running down his cheeks.

She put out a hand. Held his shoulder. No words could help. All around her, desperate faces were gray and taut.

In front of each wagon the meager pile of possessions grew as the carefully hoarded objects were tossed into the snow and set on fire. Flames, fired by coal from the steam engine and a splash of vodka, devoured the last scraps of their self-respect. Their clothes, the blankets, photographs, a dozen treasured icons of the Virgin Mary and even a miniature painting of Tsar Nicholas II. All blackened, burned, and turned to ash.

"You are traitors. All of you. Traitors to your country."

The accusation came from the tall officer in the green greatcoat. Though he wore no insignia except a badge of crossed sabers on his peaked cap, there was no mistaking his position of authority. He sat upright on a large heavy-muscled horse, which he controlled effortlessly with an occasional flick of his heel. His eyes were dark and impatient, as if this cargo of White Russians presented him with a task he found distasteful.

"None of you deserve to live," he said coldly.

A deep moan rose from the crowd. It seemed to sway with shock.

He raised his voice. "You exploited us. You maltreated us. You believed the time would never come when you would have to answer to *us*, the people of Russia. But you were wrong. You were blind. Where is all your wealth now? Where are your great houses and your fine horses now? The tsar is finished and I swear to you that—"

A single voice rose up from somewhere in the middle of the crowd. "God bless the tsar. God protect the Romanovs."

A shot rang out. The officer's rifle had bucked in his hands. A figure in the front row fell to the ground, a dark stain on the snow.

"That man paid for *your* treachery." His hostile gaze swept over the stunned crowd with contempt. "You and your kind were parasites on the backs of the starving workers. You created a world of cruelty and tyranny where rich men turned their backs on the cries of the poor. And now you desert your country, like rats fleeing from a burning ship. And you dare to take the youth of Russia with you." He swung his horse to one side and moved away from the throng of gaunt faces. "Now you will hand over your valuables."

At a nod of his head, the soldiers started to move among the prisoners. Systematically they seized all jewelry, all watches, all silver cigar cases, anything that had any worth, including all forms of money. Insolent hands searched clothing, under arms, inside mouths, and even between breasts, seeking out the carefully hidden items that meant survival to their owners. Valentina lost the emerald ring secreted in the hem of her dress, while Jens was stripped of his last gold coin in his boot. When it was over, the crowd stood silent except for a dull sobbing. Robbed of hope, they had no voice.

But the officer was pleased. The look of distaste left his face. He turned and issued a sharp command to the man on horseback behind him. Instantly a handful of mounted soldiers began to weave through the crowd, dividing it, churning it into confusion. Valentina clung to the small hand hidden in hers and knew that Jens would die before he released the other one. A faint cry escaped from the child when a big bay horse swung into them and its iron-shod hooves trod dangerously close, but otherwise she hung on fiercely and made no sound.

"What are they doing?" Valentina whispered.

"Taking the men. And the children."

"Oh God, no."

But he was right. Only the old men and the women were ignored. The others were being separated out and herded away. Cries of anguish tore through the frozen wasteland and somewhere on the far side of the train a wolf crept forward on its belly, drawn by the scent of blood.

"Jens, no, don't let them take you. Or her," Valentina begged.

"Papa?" A small face emerged between them.

"Hush, my love."

A rifle butt thumped into Jens's shoulder just as he flicked his coat back over his daughter's head. He staggered but kept his feet.

"You. Get over there." The soldier on horseback looked as if he were just longing for an excuse to pull the trigger. He was very young. Very nervous.

Jens stood his ground. "I am not Russian." He reached into his inside pocket, moving his hand slowly so as not to unsettle the soldier, and drew out his passport.

"See," Valentina pointed out urgently. "My husband is Danish."

The soldier frowned, uncertain what to do. But his commander had sharp eyes. He instantly spotted the hesitation. He kicked his horse forward into the panicking crowd and came up alongside the young private.

"Grodensky, why are you wasting time here?" he demanded.

But his attention was not on the soldier. It was on Valentina. Her face had tilted up to speak to the mounted *soldat* and her hood had fallen back, revealing a sweep of long dark hair and a high forehead with pale flawless skin. Months of starvation had heightened her cheekbones and made her eyes huge in her face.

The officer dismounted. Up close, they could see he was younger than he had appeared on horseback, probably still in his thirties, but with the eyes of a much older man. He took the passport and studied it briefly, his gaze flicking from Valentina to Jens and back again.

"But you," he said roughly to Valentina, "you are Russian?"

Behind them shots were beginning to sound.

"By birth, yes," she answered without turning her head to the noise. "But now I am Danish. By marriage." She wanted to edge closer to her husband, to hide the child more securely between them, but did not dare move. Only her fingers tightened on the tiny cold hand in hers.

Without warning, the officer's rifle slammed into Jens's stomach and he doubled over with a grunt of pain, but immediately another blow to the back of his head sent him sprawling onto the snow. Blood spattered its icy surface.

Valentina screamed.

Instantly she felt the little hand pull free of her own and saw her daughter throw herself at the officer's legs with the ferocity of a spitting wildcat, biting and scratching in a frenzy of rage. As if in slow motion, she watched the rifle butt start to descend toward the little head.

"No," she shouted and snatched the child up into her arms before the blow could fall. But stronger hands tore the young body from her grasp.

"No, no, no!" she screamed. "She is a Danish child. She is not a Russian."

"She *is* Russian," the officer insisted and drew his revolver. "She fights like a Russian." Casually he placed the gun barrel at the center of the child's forehead.

The child froze. Only her eyes betrayed her fear. Her little mouth was clamped shut.

"Don't kill her, I beg you," Valentina pleaded. "Please don't kill her. I'll do . . . anything . . . anything. If you let her live."

A deep groan issued from the crumpled figure of her husband at her feet.

"Please," she begged softly. She undid the top button of her coat, not taking her eyes from the officer's face. "Anything."

The Bolshevik commander reached out a hand and touched her hair, her cheek, her mouth. She held her breath. Willing him to want her. And for a fleeting moment she knew she had him. But when he glanced around at his watching men, all of them lusting for her, hoping their turn would be next, he shook his head.

"No. You are not worth it. Not even for soft kisses from your beautiful lips. No. It would cause too much trouble among my troops." He shrugged. "A shame." His finger tightened on the trigger.

"Let me buy her," Valentina said quickly.

When he turned his head to stare at her with a frown that brought his heavy eyebrows together, she said again, "Let me buy her. And my husband."

He laughed. The soldiers echoed the harsh sound of it. "With what?"

"With these." Valentina thrust two fingers down her throat and bent over as a gush of warm bile swept up from her empty stomach. In the center of the yellow smear of liquid that spread out on the snow's crust lay two tiny cotton packages, each no bigger than a hazelnut. At a gesture from the officer, a bearded soldier scooped them up and handed them to him. They sat, dirty and damp, in the middle of his black glove.

Valentina stepped closer. "Diamonds," she said proudly.

He scraped off the cotton wraps, eagerness in every movement, until what looked like two nuggets of sparkling ice gleamed up at him.

Valentina saw the greed in his face. "One to buy my daughter. The other for my husband."

"I can take them anyway. You have already lost them."

"I know."

Suddenly he smiled. "Very well. We shall deal. Because I have the diamonds and because you are beautiful, you shall keep the brat." Lydia was thrust into Valentina's arms and clung to her as if she would climb right inside her body.

"And my husband," Valentina insisted.

"Your husband we keep."

"No, no. Please God, I . . ."

But the horses came in force then. A solid wall of them that drove the women and old men back to the train.

Lydia screamed in Valentina's arms, "Papa, Papa . . . ," and tears flowed down her thin cheeks as she watched his body being dragged away.

❧

V ALENTINA COULD FIND NO TEARS. ONLY THE FROZEN emptiness within her, as bleak and lifeless as the wilderness that swept past outside. She sat on the foul-smelling floor of the cattle truck with her back against the slatted wall. Night was seeping in and the air was so cold it hurt to breathe, but she didn't notice. Her head hung low and her eyes saw nothing. Around her the sound of grief filled the vacant spaces. The boy with dirty blond hair was gone, as well as the man who had been so certain the White Russian army had arrived to feed them. Women wept for the loss of their husbands and the theft of their sons and daughters, and stared with naked envy at the one child on the train.

Valentina had wrapped her coat tightly around Lydia and herself, but could feel her daughter shivering.

"Mama," the girl whispered, "is Papa coming back?"

"No."

It was the twentieth time she had asked the same question, as if by continually repeating it she could make the answer change. In the gloom Valentina felt the little body shudder.

So she took her daughter's cold face between her hands and said fiercely, "But we will survive, you and I. Survival is everything."